THE DEATH & LIFE OF LUCY WESTENRA

ROSIE FIORE

OAKHAMPTON
PRESS

DEDICATION

For Rebecca and Naomi, who made me look at Lucy and Mina with fresh eyes, and for all of the cast of Dracula *2019.*

I saw a woman sleeping. In her sleep she dreamt Life stood before her, and held in each hand a gift—in the one Love, in the other Freedom. And she said to the woman, "Choose!"

And the woman waited long: and she said, "Freedom!"

And Life said, "Thou hast well chosen. If thou hadst said, 'Love,' I would have given thee that thou didst ask for; and I would have gone from thee, and returned to thee no more. Now, the day will come when I shall return. In that day I shall bear both gifts in one hand."

I heard the woman laugh in her sleep.

Life's Gifts, Olive Schreiner

How these papers have been placed in sequence will be made manifest in the reading of them. All needless matters have been eliminated, so that a history almost at variance with the possibilities of later-day belief may stand forth as simple fact. There is throughout no statement of past things wherein memory may err, for all the records chosen are exactly contemporary, given from the standpoints and within the range of knowledge of those who made them.

Dracula, Bram Stoker

PROLOGUE

LETTER FROM L.W. TO MINA HARKER

14 SEPTEMBER 1894

Hillingham

Dear Mina,

I am so weak; I think I may not recover. Can you come to me? I know Jonathan needs you, but I am in terror for my life.

Oh Mina, I have never felt so alone. Mother is weak and frail and can offer me no aid. I pleaded with the Professor, but he scorned me and dismissed my words as the delirious ravings of a child.

I watch my window every night, waiting for that ominous shadow. I feel certain that he will return soon. Every time I try to sleep, I sense his dark eyes on me, slicing my skin like hot blades. He is relentless and I know that should he gain entry here once more, he will have no mercy.

I think if you came and came soon, there is a chance we

could plan my escape. Although he knows of our friendship, I believe I might be safe if I came to Exeter to be with you. I have considered fleeing to Whitby, but of course he would know to follow me there.

Please come if you can, but do not write of your intentions. If you do, he will be certain to intercept the letter and try to prevent you.

With all of my love, as you know,

L.W.

LETTER FROM NONI ROSEN TO JACOB BALCOMBE

10 FEBRUARY 1982

Hillingham Court

My beloved Jacob,

I'm writing this sitting up in bed, resting my notepad on the hot water bottle you gave me. Every now and then I have to stop and warm my hand. It's cold up here under the eaves. It was much cosier when you were lying in this bed beside me.

I've been experimenting with a new work – it's to do with different qualities of light. The light in the studio at the Slade is sharp and like steel. The light out on the Heath is thick and grey. But right now, the shaft slanting in through my dormer window is unexpectedly warm and rich – like melted butter. It feels denser, because of all the dust (I know, my love, I'm no good at housework!).

I raise my hand and the light rolls over my fingers. I want to squeeze out a tube of yellow cadmium, and then cut it with the smallest dab of cobalt so I can capture its essence. I know I'd have moments before it transmutes and changes again, as light does....

Oh Jacob. I wish you loved these small rooms as I do. You

say that it's an artist's garret, but it feels like home – unlike anywhere else I've ever lived. I lie here at night and imagine who slept in this room before me – the maids and manservants, maybe young, maybe homesick... and the people who moved through the rooms downstairs. What secrets does this house keep? I imagine you smiling at me, laughing at my fancy. But there are whispers in these walls and I'm learning to listen to them.

The light has changed again, even as I wrote those few words. It's filtering through the leaves of the ivy now... an almost indecent emerald green has crept in. My cold, cold fingers itch to paint it.

I cannot wait to see you again.

Your darling

Noni

x

CHAPTER 1

*T*he house loomed out of the darkness, creepers smothering its brick walls. I dragged my cases up the crescent-shaped gravel drive which was crowded with residents' cars. A few steps led up to polished, double wooden doors. I craned my head back and looked up. Light twinkled from dormer windows, high under the eaves.

I stopped to pull the keys from my pocket. Once I'd struggled through the door, I found myself in a circular, high-ceilinged hallway with a marble floor. A wide, curved staircase swept upwards and an institutional bank of mailboxes filled the wall beneath the stairs. This must once have been a Georgian family home, with big, elegant rooms, but someone had chopped it up into apartments with scant regard for its symmetrical proportions. These common areas looked dusty and unloved.

I grabbed a case in each hand and climbed up one flight of the wide, curved stairs, and then another. The third flight was suddenly narrow and straight. I must have passed beyond the main part of the house and into the servant's quarters. Each step had a noticeable dip in the centre, as if thousands of feet had trodden them down. That seemed right, given the description in Mum's letter. I turned left at the top of the stairs. A door directly ahead of me bore a brass number eight. I glanced up at the ceiling and saw how the door cruelly bisected the moulding. The partitioning work had been done by Philistines.

I wrestled my suitcases through the door. The still air smelled of disinfectant and the faint, wet-dog scent of recently shampooed carpet. I flicked on an overhead light. So this was it. The fabled apartment, owned by my family for all of my life-time, which until now, I had never seen.

Four small, square rooms branched off a single narrow corridor. A tiny living room contained a tired IKEA sofa and a melamine coffee table. There was a compact galley kitchen and a plain, serviceable bathroom. Everything was clean, but well-used, impersonal and sad.

The last room on the right was the bedroom, barely wide enough to accommodate the three-quarter bed. The walls were a dingy magnolia and the nylon carpet crackled with static. There was a narrow wardrobe and a chest of drawers. The grimy window was one of the square dormers I'd seen from outside and was overgrown with ivy. Depressing, but I'd stayed in worse over the years, in cities from Lisbon to Adelaide. At least there'd be no snakes.

I was floored with a sudden weariness. Toeing off my shoes, I sat down on the edge of the bare mattress, tipped sideways and turned my face to the wall. I imagined having to get up, open my bags and find space for my paltry possessions. I imagined morning after morning, waking up alone in this dreary little cell. There was a pressure in my lungs, as if someone were kneeling on my chest – a simultaneous feeling of breathless panic and bone-crushing inertia.

My phone began to ring in my inside pocket, buzzing against my chest. I wanted to ignore it, but I pulled it out anyway. Rafaella.

'Ciao, Kate... are you in?' Rafaella didn't bother with niceties.

'I've literally just come through the door.'

'What's it like?'

'Small. A bit... I don't know. Depressing.'

'Show me.'

I swapped to video call and gave her a quick guided tour.

'Not so bad,' she pronounced. 'If you paint the walls and tear up the terrible carpet...'

'It still won't be...'

'Of course not,' she said.

I knew she was thinking about the airy, high-ceilinged apartment in Milan with its wrought-iron balconies, the trams rattling past in the street below, the view of the Castello Sforzesco.

'It is yours though,' she said. 'Your very own space.'

'Technically, it's my dad's. He inherited it when Mum died.'

'It was hers?'

'Mum bought it when she was an art student – money inherited from her grandparents.' I laughed. 'Back in the early eighties you could buy a flat on the edge of Hampstead Heath for less than a zillion pounds. She loved living here ... I found a letter from her to my dad when I was home for Christmas. But he persuaded her to rent it out and go and live with him in Hertfordshire. Now I've seen it, I understand why. It wouldn't have been suitable for a family.'

'And after she died?'

'Dad got an agency to keep letting it out. But the last tenants left last week. It seemed a good solution for me... for now.'

'A very good solution. You can make it your own. A new start.'

I smiled at her lovely face on my screen. She was sitting on the sofa in her mamma's kitchen. I'd spent many hours curled up beside her right there.

'How was Christmas?' I asked.

'As you would expect. Too many people. Too much food. Everybody shouting. How about yours?'

'It was… well. Rain for ten solid days. My grandmother. A fake tree. Long, awkward silences. My father almost combusted from all the things he didn't say about what a disappointment I am.'

Rafaella laughed with rueful sympathy. She glanced past me.

'Clear the ivy from that window,' she said, 'and wash it. You will need more light.'

'I will. Not that I'll be here much in the daylight hours. I've got teaching work booked for all of January.'

'That's good?'

'Yeah.'

I couldn't think of anything else to say. Too late, I sensed a dangerous lull in the conversation.

'She giggles.' Rafaella said.

'Where did you see them?'

'Gianluca's New Year's party. She giggles and twirls her hair between her fingers and she hangs on Alex's arm. Tiresome.'

'She's welcome to him.'

'He asked after you. I said you were doing well.'

'Thanks.'

'And you are. I will come to see you for proof. In May, maybe? I've never been to London.'

'Yeah. That'd be good.'

'Now make your bed, and make some tea. Isn't that what you English people do to make a house a home? Send me pictures when the terrible carpet is gone.'

Moving slowly, I unpacked, stowing my clothes in the wardrobe and chest of drawers and arranging the few books I'd brought along the windowsill. I thought of the sagging shelves in the Milan apartment, crammed with volumes I'd lugged from country to country over fifteen years of travelling. I simply hadn't been able to bear the wrangling with Alex over what was whose. I took the bare minimum and told myself I was escaping with my dignity intact. Now, in this shoebox of a room, I was going to be living like a penniless student and I didn't even have my books. What use was dignity now?

LUCY WESTENRA'S JOURNAL

2 MAY 1888

My name is Lucy Rose Westenra. I was born upon the 28th day of September in the Year of our Lord 1874. I live at Hillingham, North End, in Hampstead. I am fourteen years and seven months old and this is my Journal.

Pa and I have been reading the diary of Mr. Samuel Pepys. He died more than One Hundred-And-Eighty years ago and yet people are still interested in what he did every day and even want to know about the Cheese which he buried to save it from the Great Fire of London.

Pa tells me that I am a person of considerable intellect and that I will be a pioneer of thought. It is never too early to start recording one's thoughts if they are important, and so I am beginning now. I do not want Mother to see this record because she may not approve of some of the things I will write. And even though Pa is the best person in the world, I do not think I want him to see it either, so I will hide it in my secret place in the library.

I found the hidey-hole many years ago, when I was eleven.

Between each of the library windows, there are square wooden panels. I think they are about twelve inches across. I was playing alone by one window when I noticed a strange mark on the wood. I pressed my finger against it, and the whole panel opened like a door. Inside was a hole like a tiny secret cave. It was empty. I used to hide my dolls in there, and sometimes treasures I found on the Heath – flowers or beautiful leaves. Like the hole where Mr. Pepys put his precious cheese, I will now hide my journal in this secret place.

CHAPTER 2

I was woken early the next morning by rain drumming on the skylight. I lay gazing up at the dim grey square overhead. I knew I needed to move. Stillness was a mistake. It always was.

A Sunday morning alone in bed drew inescapable comparisons with the hundreds of Sunday mornings that came before. Alex's comforting bulk in the bed beside me, his back turned, his hand reaching back to draw me close. I'd press myself against his warmth and the rise and fall of his breathing would soothe me back into a soft doze. Or we'd get up and go for breakfast, enjoying the quiet of the streets. Where was he now? In Fabrizio's bar on the square? Or still in bed, tangled naked in the sheets, reaching for Stacey…

I was up, standing in the middle of the room, my breath quickening. In the dismal January light, the bedroom looked even worse than it had the night before – the paintwork chipped and stained with the greasy marks left by old Sellotape.

I made coffee and showered, and then wandered through the rooms. So many people had lived here in the years since Mum. So many cheap sofas, framed prints and shaded lamps. Somehow, I had thought the space would be full of meaning – be full of her. But it was a dingy, boxy flat with the sad patina of a space long rented. If I stripped it back to its bare bones, would these rooms speak to me? Would I hear my mum's voice? I imagined bare white walls, scrubbed floors, everything clean and plain. As soon as the hardware store opened, I'd go down to get paint. But before that, the hideous bedroom carpet had to go.

It came up surprisingly easily. I worked methodically, moving bits of furniture, rolling as I went. I lugged the roll down and crammed it into the big dumpster down the side of the house. As I climbed the stairs again, the door of Number 4 cracked open, and I saw one narrowed, pale-blue eye peer out. I smiled and waved. The door clicked closed.

* * *

CLEANING AND PREPARING the floor was the perfect task – physically strenuous but mindless. It consumed all my attention. I hoovered up ancient dust and examined each floorboard, knocking in the odd protruding nail and filling cracks with wood filler. Here and there, a section was lighter than the rest – a more recent addition. But for the most part, the boards were thick, smooth and golden. Oak probably, and hidden under that awful beige carpet for years. I would scrub and sand them and apply a couple of layers of varnish.

Was this what the floor was like when Mum lived here? In her letter, she talked about a small bed, and said the flat was cold, but she didn't mention the floor. She said it was an artist's garret though, so I imagined bare boards.

I worked my way over to the wall furthest from the door and

felt my way along the last plank. In the middle, a section about two feet long wobbled. I rocked it experimentally with my left hand, preparing to hammer in a few nails and stabilise it. It creaked and flipped loosely under my palm, turning sideways and dropping into the cavity below. I peered into the hole. There was a section carved out of the joist. It looked as if it had been deliberately cut in this way, perhaps to make a hiding place.

I reached into the gap to draw the board out again. The hole was deep and I had to kneel on the floor and stretch in, my fingernails scrabbling in a thick layer of dust. My fingers grazed on something dry and unexpected. It wasn't the floorboard, but something lighter and smoother. Paper. I hooked a nail under a corner and flipped it up into my hand, a small, thick wad of pages.

The bundle was yellowed and brittle. I turned it over cautiously. A page had been wrapped around what felt like several others, and there was faded handwriting on one side of it.

> B,
>
> Please post this. I implore you, do not show this to my mother or to any other.
>
> L.

The handwriting was rounded and clear – even though the ink was faded, I had no trouble reading it. It was not my mother's handwriting though – hers was slanted and angular.

The outer page had been folded into a rough envelope shape. I carefully lifted the edge, feeling the paper crack. Inside, I found a sealed, stamped letter, addressed in the same curved, neat script:

Mrs. M. Harker
  Hawkins House
  Magdalen Road
  Exeter

THE STAMP SHOWED a woodcut profile of Queen Victoria. There was no postmark. Whoever B was, he or she never posted the letter as requested. I was desperate to open the letter, but it seemed an invasion of privacy. That said, the letter was so old... surely 'B' and 'L', as well as Mrs Harker, who never received this letter, must be dead by now? I turned the envelope over. There was a faded seal at the point where the flap joined the envelope. I slid one fingernail along the join, and with the slightest pressure, the flap lifted free. There were three small pages inside, closely covered in writing. I unfolded them with slow patience, terrified they'd disintegrate in my hands.

But once I spread them out, I couldn't read a word. Even though the handwriting was the same as that on the envelope, the pages were covered in line after line of unrecognisable symbols. I lifted the pages one by one, hoping to spot a word I recognised. I didn't think it was a different language – it wasn't an alphabet I'd ever seen before. Perhaps it was a code? With infinite care, I refolded the pages and slid them back into the envelope.

LUCY WESTENRA'S JOURNAL

14 JUNE 1889

I am furious today, but also in disgrace. Yesterday, I was in the parlour, immersed in the intrigues of Mr Dickens's *Bleak House*. Mother kept looking at me and frowning. She hates it when I read. She tells me that it will spoil my eyes and my skin. After ten minutes or so, she interrupted me to pass her a skein of embroidery silk, then a few minutes later to fetch her a handkerchief. Then she called me over to remind her of the name of Mrs Hunter's third daughter, and then she asked me to address an envelope for her. Well, I lost my temper then.

I exploded and said, 'I hope reading will make me ugly, so that I might be left quite alone!'

Now Mother has suffered a collapse and the doctor had to be summoned.

15 JUNE 1889

This morning at breakfast, Mother was absent. She is still in bed feeling weak. It is my fault. Mother has always been poorly –

she had scarlet fever when she was a child and it damaged her health. Then my birth was, Mrs Staines has whispered to me, "difficult". So Mother's weakness is also my fault, and I am supposed to treat her as if she is made of china.

I should feel bad that she is ill, but it was wonderful to have Pa all to myself today. He seems to feel the same. I must say, I have never understood how Pa and Mother came to marry. They do not share a single interest. Most of the time Pa ignores Mother, and when they are in the same room, he speaks over her as if she is invisible or he cannot hear her.

She in turn seems to hate everything about him. She winces at his clothes, his voice and his laugh. Mother comes from an aristocratic family – Yorkshire landowners – and she never misses a chance to remind us of her high birth and his common roots. Still, she does not seem to mind the beautiful house and fine clothes that she receives for being Pa's wife.

I cannot believe he was ever allowed close enough to her to touch her, to propose marriage, or to get her with child. To be sure, that part must only have happened once.

At breakfast. I buttered myself a most impressive stack of toast and began to eat my way through it. Mother is always telling me to curb my appetite, so while she is absent, I must take a full advantage. Pa sat watching me.

Then he said, 'Now, my dear. Be honest with me. What did you do that so upset your mother yesterday afternoon?'

I told him and he listened, turning his gold cigarette case over in his hand. When I had finished, he nodded calmly and did not offer any censure.

'Well, my Clio,' he said, 'you wish to read and learn. I wish you to read and learn. Your Mother wishes you not to. It seems we will need to find a way to get around her.'

I am Clio today, which means he has been reading history. He grants me the nickname of whichever of the Muses is appropriate to his current study. He ruffled my hair. Then he drew a cigarette from the case and lit it.

'I have loved instructing you, but now you outstrip my ability to teach, and you need a more rigorous curriculum. I have considered getting you another governess, a more highly qualified one, but your Mother would plague her as she plagues you. She will insist on controlling the syllabus, so that it only contained "ladylike" topics.'

'I would not stand for that,' I said.

Under Pa's guidance I have read the work of major philosophers, the writings of Mr Darwin and Mrs Wollstonecraft's *A Vindication of the Rights of Women*. There can be no going back to violin lessons and needlepoint.

'We need to remove you from the sphere of your Mother's influence,' said Pa, 'and while I will miss you every moment that you are away from me, I have decided that you will attend a boarding school.'

This is quite a shock. I am in equal measures excited and afraid. I am delighted at the thought of the teaching I will receive, and the adventure of living elsewhere, but I will miss Pa most fiercely. I wonder what kind of school he will find for me?

21 JUNE 1889

Pa has selected The Underhill, a girls' school in Exeter. It has, he tells me, a long history of rigorous and academic education for young ladies.

'Exeter?' Mother cried when he told her. 'Devonshire? Why so far away? I shall not manage without her!'

'You will manage perfectly well and she will return at half terms and holidays. That will be quite enough,' Pa said and then he turned away from her.

Mother began to sob. He is not always kind to her.

Pa has examined the curriculum of the school and he says that that while their teaching in religion, philosophy, art and history is exemplary, the sciences do not receive proper attention. He plans to make a substantial donation to the school, with the provision that they offer classes to the older girls in physics, chemistry and the natural sciences. I cannot wait to go there and begin my studies.

17 OCTOBER 1889

I am crouched on a box under the stairs as I write this journal entry. It is fortunate that I am not afraid of spiders, for many of them have chosen this quiet nook as their home.

There is no privacy here at school. I learned this lesson quickly – in my first week here, I met a girl named Hannah Beaumont. She too is new to the school. Her nose is perpetually pink and damp. Yesterday she received a letter from her mother. She is homesick, and the letter made her cry over breakfast. Last night in our dormitory, one of the other girls, a round-faced, spiteful minx called Elizabeth, snatched the letter from Hannah. She read it out loud in a high whine, affecting tears and fluttering. The other girls laughed as Hannah wept and pleaded, trying to claim her letter back from Elizabeth. Hannah has barely spoken a word since that incident. I suspect she may ask her parents to allow her to return home.

From Hannah's misfortune, I learn that it is vital to guard anything that is personal or precious to me. I sleep with my journal beneath my pillow and carry it with me all day.

I have been very lonely in these first few weeks at school. I have not made friends. While Elizabeth and her ilk are haughty and unkind, most other girls are merely serious and quiet. The majority hail from Exeter, or other nearby towns and have been at the school for several years. There is no room for newcomers – they have formed close knots of friendship, and cling to one another in studied conformity.

It is not only my newness they object to. It seems my character is also quite the shock to them, and they find me rude and abrasive. I do not know how else to be. I spent my formative years in vocal debate with Pa and his friends. As a result, I see nothing wrong with standing up and raising my voice to contend with my point, or to press home my argument. This is not considered polite, and my classmates shy away from me.

Now it has emerged that Pa has donated money for the new science laboratories. The building has been completed and crates of new equipment have arrived. A Mrs Crossley has been appointed as a science mistress. A young woman who had recently completed her studies at The Underhill will be her assistant schoolmistress in this new department.

The other day, as we passed the new building, a workman was engaged in mounting a brass plaque on the door. "The Westenra Laboratories", it proclaimed. I saw glances exchanged, eyes lifted heavenward. Pa intended his gesture to be generous, but I fear these quiet girls see it as brash and ostentatious.

I hear footsteps on the steps above my head. I fear discovery.

20 OCTOBER 1889

I am once more in my under-stairs hiding place. The last few days have seen a dramatic change in my fortunes here at The Underhill. I can now set down the wonderful events of yesterday, being Friday.

It did not begin well. We girls had been given a half-holiday and a pass to walk down to the high street in town. We were in the cloakroom when I noticed one of my classmates glancing at my hat. It is a straw boater like her own, but mine has been shaped by Mother's milliner, and the ribbon is silk. She sneered and leaned across to her friend. The other girl's disgusted glance told me all. It was not the first time I had been mocked, and it took the light out of the day. I unpinned my hat and

replaced it on the hook. I decided instead to go to the laboratory to complete the notes I had begun on that morning's
experiment.

The afternoon light was slanting in through the windows,
and I saw Miss Murray, the assistant schoolmistress. She was
standing at the window, looking out across the fields.

We all know her story. Miss Murray is an orphan, who was
cared for in her infancy by an elderly great aunt. She sat the
scholarship examination and entered the Underhill aged eleven.
Shortly after that, her aunt died, and so the Underhill became
her only home. She was a model student, and when she
completed her studies, she was offered this post, which guaran-
teed her lodgings and a modest income. She is tall, with a great
cloud of curly chestnut hair and bright brown eyes which seem
to snap with understanding as she observes everything around
her. I had often seen her in the corridors, but we had never
spoken... until yesterday.

I coughed to let her know I was there. She turned and smiled
at me, as if she had been waiting for me.

'You're Lucy Westenra,' she said.

'Yes.'

'I'm Mina ... er ... Miss Murray.' I was delighted by the broad
openness of her smile. 'I cannot get used to *Miss* Murray. It
makes me sound a hundred and fifty! How may I help you? Are
you not supposed to be on the half-holiday trip to town?'

'No, I ... chose to stay and work instead.'

There was a long moment, and then she said, 'I see.'

And I saw that she did see. As a scholarship girl, top of her
class, perhaps she too had been snubbed by the other girls.

'What work do you need to complete?'

I opened my notebook and paged to the exercise we had
done that day.

'We were working with copper sulphate. A fascinating

experiment. I recorded the results, but did not complete my conclusion.'

'I too have some work to do. Shall I bring my notes and sit beside you?'

And so Mina (for that is what she asked me to call her) and I sat elbow to elbow as the sun sank lower.

When we finished our work, we began to talk. When I had seen her in the corridors before, I had thought her a rather ordinary-looking young woman – neither beautiful nor plain. But speaking to her, I saw her features were mobile and lively and her eyes so bright that I found myself captivated. I could look at her face forever.

I have never met someone with whom I have such communion of mind and spirit. We shared our life stories and laughed. We spoke about our hopes and dreams. Mina wants to make a scientific discovery. I want to write a book. We daydream of travel, freedom and adventure – and money of our own. I pray this will be the first of many happy afternoons that we will spend together.

CHAPTER 3

12 JANUARY 2024 – KATE

'*M*y Kate!'

Gran kissed me on both cheeks, then led me into the dining room. She sat down at the table, straight-backed and expectant. The flat was warm, the air dense with the smell of books and furniture polish. Even though I'd not been here for several years, I knew every inch of it. Nothing had changed.

I spent every weekday afternoon in this flat, between the ages of six and eleven. Gran would meet me after school and walk me back here. She'd give me a sandwich, a glass of squash and a piece of fruit, and then I'd sit at this table and do my homework. When I was finished, we'd sit side by side on the sofa and watch TV, eating biscuits and drinking weak tea, until Dad arrived to collect me.

I sat opposite her now. I ran my finger across the polished surface of the table and felt the minute indentations in the varnish I'd made by pressing my pencil too hard as I wrote and drew.

'Well?' Gran held out her hand. 'Pass it over then.'

I opened my bag and drew out the letter, which I'd wrapped in a soft silk scarf and placed in a flat cardboard sleeve to protect it. Gran took it and unfolded it gently. She placed her reading glasses on the end of her nose and scrutinised the first page.

'Shorthand,' she said. 'You were right.'

She drew a notepad towards her and picked up a sharpened pencil. Then she opened a slim volume – an old, plastic-covered copy of *Pitman's Shorthand Manual*. She waved a distracted hand at me.

'I'll let you know when I'm finished. Turn on the big light. Now shoo out of here and let me get on.'

I went into the kitchen and brewed a pot of tea. I opened the old Quality Street tin, which was full of biscuits, as it always had been. I put some on a plate and took a tray into the living room. Through the open door, I could see Gran's head, still bent low over the papers. I wandered over to the fireplace. Above the mantle, one of my mother's paintings hung, illuminated by a down-light. It was a stark, fierce work, abstract in style, all straight lines and slashes in thick oil paint. The shadows were a dense, angry purple gathered at the foot of an imposingly brutal shape, which I assumed was meant to be a building. A shaft of rich yellow light bisected the picture diagonally, catching a wraithlike shape in one corner which seemed to be caught in motion – cowering away from the beam.

Along the mantelpiece below the painting, Gran had placed a row of photographs, showing Noni, my mum, at every stage of her life. There she was as a serious baby, chewing on one fist, her eyes already wide and dark. As a skinny five-year-old, peering out from behind her signature mane of black ringlets. As a sulky teenager, bent over a sketch. Here she was, hanging on my father's arm, wearing a high-necked Victorian wedding gown, her eyes fixed adoringly on his face. Standing on a beach with a chubby toddler – me – sitting on her hip. And the final picture – a close up of her beautiful face, pared back to the bone, her eyes huge and already gazing into the distance, towards a place where none of us would be able to reach her.

Dad didn't keep pictures of her on display. Once, I asked Gran why she did.

'Doesn't it hurt you to look at them?' I asked. 'Doesn't it hurt to remember?'

'I think it would hurt more not to remember,' Gran had said simply, 'I think of her every minute of every day. The pictures remind me she was real.'

'Right,' Gran called out behind me, making me jump. 'I think I've done it.'

I sat back down at the table and she handed over her notepad with a flourish. I read.

'Are you sure?' I looked up from the neatly written transcript.

'Completely.'

'So this L.W. was in danger, or believed herself to be in danger from someone – a man – and she wrote to her friend in Exeter asking for help?'

'But the letter never got there. Do you think it's real?'

'I googled the postage stamp. It's authentic for the time. And the paper and ink do look old. It seems a lot of work to forge something like this on the off-chance that someone would take up the carpet in that room.'

'Well then – you've found a real-life mystery. And it's lain under those floorboards all this time. Tea?'

We went to sit on the sofa.

'So how's the flat?' she said, passing me a bourbon biscuit.

'It's... well... a bit depressing right now. Unloved. But I'm fixing it up.'

'I haven't been there since she moved out when she married your father.'

'You're welcome anytime. You know that. Come and visit.'

'I will. She loved that flat. That house. She was fascinated by its history.'

'I wish she'd found this letter then. She'd have loved it.'

'She would have.'

'Maybe she knew who L.W. was.'

'Who knows what Noni knew? But you can find out who L.W. was,' Gran said. 'There's the internet, isn't there?'

'Well...'

'You're always telling me everything is on the internet. There'll be a record somewhere. A news article or something. 'If you want to find out, you can. You just need to work out where to look.'

LUCY WESTENRA'S JOURNAL

28 DECEMBER 1891

Now I am in my final year at school, with Mina as my friend, the future looks bright and full of possibility. Pa is delighted to see me flourish – Mother less so.

The rows this Christmas have been fierce. Mother has grudgingly agreed to Pa's wish that I attend university. But she will under no circumstances condone my leaving London, nor will she allow me to attend anywhere where there are male students. Cambridge is thus out of the question. After extensive wrangling, we have all finally agreed that I might undertake a Bachelor's degree at Bedford College for Women, if I can pass the entrance test.

14 FEBRUARY 1892

Pa took me to the College today so that I could sit my examination. We stood outside, among the clatter of traffic in Baker Street, and looked up at the imposing facade.

'What wonders you will learn, Lucy, my dear,' Pa said.

We pushed open the heavy wooden door and went into the reception area. We almost collided with a young woman walking swiftly, her arms full of books. Her flyaway hair was escaping its pins, and she wore metal sleeve garters over her plain white blouse. I could see her fingers were stained with something. It could have been ink or paint, or perhaps silver nitrate, from printing photographs. She glanced at us abstractedly, and then bounded off up a flight of stairs, intent on her next task. Mother would be horrified at her appearance, but to me she looked beautiful.

A teacher led us along the halls, and through every door, I glimpsed further wonders – an art class with a life model, the long benches of a proper chemistry laboratory, the ordered shelves of the library. I visualised myself painting in the art class, conducting experiments in the laboratory, gathering books in the library.

I concentrated fiercely in the exam, and when I put my pen down, I was confident I had done well. I hope I am right.

20 MARCH 1892

Such joy! This morning there was a heavy white envelope beside my plate at breakfast.

Dear Miss Westenra,
    We are pleased to offer you a place at Bedford College for Women. Classes will begin on the tenth of October 1892.

There are instructions regarding payment, equipment and dress. I gasped with joy and passed the letter to Pa. He read it swiftly and then leapt up from the table. He hugged me, delighted. Mother read the letter too. She frowned, touched her pale brow and sighed.

'Oh, this sounds dreadful. An establishment full of thick-waisted, bespectacled bluestockings. Must she go...?'

'I must!' I said passionately, 'I absolutely must! If I do not go, I shall die!'

She looked as if she might object further, but Pa stepped in.

'She will be going, Rose. It is decided.'

She turned her cold, blue eyes on him. 'I feared you might say as much. Well then, I insist that she travel there and back by carriage each day. And there is to be no loitering or fraternising with the other girls. I am certain they will not be our sort.'

'Of course, Mother,' I said. I am too happy to argue. Once I begin my studies, the smaller battles can be fought.

CHAPTER 4

14 JANUARY 2024 – KATE

'*C*ensus records,' yelled Suzanne over the chatter and music.

We were in a sleek wine bar in Canary Wharf. I'd vacillated about coming to this reunion, but for better or worse, here I was. Someone from my uni crowd had reserved a table and our group of ten sat on stools, wedged elbow to elbow.

When we finished our undergraduate English degrees at Sussex, these friends thought my bold plan to travel was daring and cool. They all stared in admiration when I told them I'd bought an open-ended ticket and was heading off with no set date to return and no fixed plan for the future. But a decade and a half later, they've all moved on. I'm the one who's stuck.

I'd come to the gathering straight from a day of supply teaching in a rowdy school in Lewisham. I hadn't had time to change, but even if I had, I didn't have anything to match the easy chic of my old classmates. I felt like an interloper in my ancient, calf-length denim skirt and roll-neck jumper.

The noise level was too high to talk to anyone other than the person directly beside you, so I'd been thrown together with sleek, pretty Suzanne for the evening.

Suzanne was an acquaintance rather than a friend when we were at university, so I needed to cast about for topics of conversation. I lit upon the letter, yelling the basics of the story into Suzanne's ear. I was taken aback by her instant and certain response.

'I'm really into genealogy,' she said. 'I've been working on our family tree for years. There are amazing web resources if you know where to look.'

'Like where?'

Suzanne tried to answer, but a gale of braying laughter from nearby drowned out her reply. Luke, who was sitting opposite her, caught her expression. He stood and leaned over the table.

'We were saying it's way too loud in here. Shall we go and get a bite to eat?'

We found a small Thai place close by, mercifully quiet and empty. A few people dropped out, so there were six of us around a round table. Once we'd ordered drinks, I leaned across and asked Suzanne to name the websites she'd mentioned. Suzanne took out her phone.

'Let's take a quick look,' she said. 'We can search census records by address and see who was living in the house at a particular time.'

'Can we? That's incredible. Well, the letter was dated 1894.'

'There was a census in 1891 and another in 1901,' said Suzanne, typing into the search bar. 'Let's check them both.'

I told her the address, and Suzanne tapped it into her phone. It took her seconds to bring up the 1891 Census.

'Westenra,' she said triumphantly and turned her phone around for me to see. 'The house belonged to a family called Westenra. Your L.W. is probably Lucy, the daughter of the house.'

I stared at the screen. A table entitled "Household Members" listed the inhabitants of the house on census day in 1891.

Charles Westenra; Married; Male; Age 59; Birth Year 1832; Occupation: Landowner.

Rose Westenra; Married (wife); Female; Age 41; Birth Year 1850; Occupation: –

Lucy Westenra; Unmarried (daughter); Female; Age 16; Birth Year 1874; Occupation: Scholar.

Isabella Staines; Widowed (servant); Female; Age 53; Birth Year 1838; Occupation: Housekeeper.

Eliza Dunne; Single (servant) Female; Age 19; Birth Year 1872; Occupation: Domestic Servant.

Beatrice Marks; Single (servant) Female; Age 16; Birth Year 1874; Occupation: Domestic Servant.

Micah Watkins; Single (servant) Male; Age 58; Birth Year 1833; Occupation: Gardener.

'Lucy,' I said, 'Lucy Westenra.' I looked at the list again. 'The letter was wrapped in a note, asking someone called "B" to post the letter. Might that have been Beatrice Marks, the maid? Maybe she lived in a room in my flat?'

Suzanne took her phone back. 'Let's check 1901 – see if anything had changed.'

She began typing and reading. A small frown creased her brow. She clicked back, typed again and then looked up at me.

'It's gone.'

'What is?'

'The house. It doesn't show up in the 1901 census listings.'

'It can't have gone. It's still there today.'

'Let me try something else,' said Suzanne, and clicked through a few more screens. A look of triumph crossed her face. 'Hillingham?'

'Hillingham Court, yes.'

'I searched "Hillingham" and it came up. Maybe back then, the house was just called Hillingham. Anyway, here it is on the handwritten census list. It's not in the typed record because it was uninhabited in 1901.'

'Uninhabited?'

'There could be many reasons for that. They might have had another house, in the country perhaps, and they were there on Census Night. Still, you'd think the servants would have been there...'

'I know the house was converted into flats around 1900. But what happened to the family?'

'Oy! You two!' Luke bellowed across the table. 'Stop looking at Instagram! Talk to the rest of us! What do you want to eat?'

Suzanne smiled and put her phone away. I opened my mouth to ask another question, but she had turned to talk to the man on her other side. The tide of conversation swept on, and I sat becalmed and alone.

Much later and still fuzzy from wine and noise, I got ready for bed. As I lay in the dark, watching the clouds drift by, I thought about Beatrice, the sixteen-year-old maid who had, in all likelihood, lain in her own narrow bed in this room, her treasures and secrets in the hidey-hole under the floor. Lucy had given her the letter to post and begged her not to show it to anyone – especially not her mother. But Beatrice hadn't done it. She had hidden the letter like a guilty secret and Lucy Westenra's impassioned cry for help had never reached her friend. There was a man Lucy feared, who was watching her – someone with terrifying power. But if her heartfelt cry was never heard, what had happened to her?

Gran had said Mum was interested in the history of the house. I wondered if she had somehow learned about Lucy and her family. What would she have thought about the mysterious letter? I could hear the wind whispering through the trees outside, and distantly, the roar of traffic on the North Circular. I wished for a purer quiet, a silence so profound that I could hear the voices of the dead. I wished Mum and Lucy's voices could come to me, through the years, and tell their stories.

LUCY WESTENRA'S JOURNAL

2 SEPTEMBER 1892

I have neglected this journal, of late! After I finished my last term at The Underhill, top of my class, Pa took me to Europe, and we saw the wonders of Paris, Rome and Barcelona. I have of course, recorded all the details of that trip in a separate scrapbook.

Briefly though, I will note that we travelled east and visited some of the magnificent Gothic castles in the Balkans. I was most struck by the extraordinary Bran Castle, on the very edge of a terrible precipice. A stone falling from the window would fall a thousand feet without touching anything. It was both beautiful and terrible, and as we toured its stone halls and corridors, I felt a cold finger of apprehension touch the back of my neck. Pa tells me that at one point, the evil Vlad Tepes, known as Vlad the Impaler, was imprisoned there, so perhaps it was his malevolence I felt around me.

14 SEPTEMBER 1892

Writing this entry is the hardest thing I have ever done. Some days ago, I travelled down to Exeter to spend a few days with Mina. We spent happy hours in her little apartment in the deserted school building, toasting bread over the fire and sharing stories of our summer adventures.

But this morning, we were walking in the grounds arm in arm when Mina glanced up.

'Look, Lucy,' she said, and pointed. The headmistress's formidable silhouette stood on the crest of the hill. She beckoned to us. As we drew nearer, I saw her face was set and grim.

'Miss Westenra,' she said gravely.

I believe I knew at that moment that my life was about to change forever.

* * *

Pa is dead. His heart stopped as he sat at his desk in his office in Chatham Street. His bright light is snuffed out. He was 60 years old.

Mina and I left immediately to travel to London. We reached Hillingham and discovered a house in mourning, with the mirrors draped in black crepe. Mrs Staines met us at the door, her eyes red and puffy.

Mother's bedroom was dim. She sat in a chair by the fire, which blazed, even though it is a warm autumn day. Her mourning dress was both opulent and severe, made of a luxurious, dull silk and edged with jet beads.

She turned to look at me as I came in. Her face was bone-pale and smooth.

'Lucy,' she said, 'I am so glad to have you back.'

She looked stronger and more upright than I have ever seen her. I thought – she is happy he is dead.

'Mr Marquand,' Mother said, with a little sneer – she has little time for Pa's solicitor – 'has charge of the funeral arrangements. The service is to be held Tuesday next. You and your friend will require mourning gowns. Jay's of Regent Street will do for that. Mrs Staines is insisting that she can manage the preparation of refreshments, although I hardly think she knows how many important people will be attending.'

She stressed the word 'important' and gave a thin smile.

'I must go and rest, Mother. Such a long journey from Exeter.'

She waved her long hand at me, like a pale silk ribbon. I turned and fled back to my room and wept in Mina's arms. I realise now that Mother did not mention Pa once.

* * *

After we ate a sparse, sad dinner, Mina came with me to see Pa. His room was lit with many candles, and he was laid out with a square of lawn placed over his face. Missy, his cat, was curled at the bottom of the bed. I have never before beheld a dead body, and I hesitated at the door, but Mina took my hand and led me forward.

She gently lifted the lawn, and I beheld the waxen, still face. I did not recognise it.

'His spirit has departed,' she said calmly, 'but it is still your dear old Pa.'

'My Pa would never have lain so neatly arranged,' I said. 'He mangled his pillows and coverlet most dreadfully. He always made a bear's nest of his bedclothes.'

To my horror, a laugh escaped me. For I remembered that when I was a little girl, Pa would hide under his covers when I came into the room. I would creep close to the bed, thinking him asleep, and he would leap out and roar, catching me in a big hug.

'Papa Bear!' I would gasp, and he would pretend to eat me all up.

The laugh turned instantly to tears. I was horrified at myself for giggling in the death chamber. I felt my knees give way and I slid to the floor, covering my face with my hands. My sobs were raw and loud. I felt Mina's arms encircling me. But Pa – Pa was silent.

For the first time I truly understood that he was gone, and he would never roar again.

20 SEPTEMBER 1892

Today is the day of Pa's funeral. The sky is a bright, clear blue. It should be raining, however. The sky should weep. In Pa's room, down the corridor, the undertakers are making their preparations. I can hear furniture being dragged across the floor and an ominous thump, as if something has been struck with a mallet. It made me flinch and I have begged Mina to take me away from here.

Later

By the time we came downstairs, the house was in a state of chaos. It was clear Mina and I would only be in the way. We gathered up our cloaks and bonnets, slipped out of the side gate and went for a walk on the Heath. Even though it was only September, the wind bit fiercely. Clouds scudded across the bright blue sky as we panted our way to the top of the hill.

'You are so lucky to have all this beauty on your doorstep,' Mina said.

'It has always been my playground. I walked with Pa every day. There is not an inch of these fields and forests I do not know. I do believe I could live here, if I had to.'

Mina laughed. 'Like a wild woman? Or a witch?'

When we returned the house reeked of lilies. Guests began to arrive, and as Mina and I stood in the hall, now dressed in our funeral gowns, Mother descended the stairs. Her pale, beautiful face was partially obscured by a fine black veil. Her posture was as upright and strong as I had ever seen it. She paused halfway down and the assembled company held its breath. She looked like a vengeful fairy queen from the tales of the Brothers Grimm. She was born to be a widow.

'Rose, my dear!' Mr Marquand said. Mother floated gracefully down the last few stairs, and as Mr Marquand reached her side, she sighed and curved against him, resting her hand on his arm. He guided her into the dining room and I followed behind.

After the service, we went through to the drawing room. Mother and I sat side by side, and the guests processed through in single file, passing close to the coffin to see Pa, then coming to pay their respects to us. There was a blur of faces, damp hands and scratchy gloves, red eyes and endless exclamations about how proud Pa would have been of my beauty. I wanted to tell them he would not have given two figs for my face or figure. He had been proud of my ability to debate, my quick wit and my knowledge. I felt myself disappearing under their kind gazes and platitudes.

First in the queue was an elderly woman, stooped and lined, wearing a rusty shawl. She clasped my hand in both of hers and her eyes filled with tears.

'Oh, I see dear Charles in your lovely eyes,' she said.

'Thank you.'

She could see from my uncertain expression that I did not know who she was.

'Why, I'm your dear father's cousin! Matilda Fallon. And this is my much-beloved grandson, Gabriel.'

She indicated the young man who hovered at her elbow. He was a little older than me, a drooping boy with a moist, red nose. He looked mortified. His eyes slid off my face and his cheek contracted in a momentary rictus of acknowledgement.

Mrs Fallon continued, undeterred. 'I'm his sole guardian,

poor mite. Since my son died, we have been all on our own, eking a living. We're not far away, you know, just over in Finchley...'

'Excuse me,' Mother said, her voice steely, 'If you wouldn't mind moving along. The line is beginning to build behind you...'

Mrs Fallon muttered a platitude and squeezed my fingers before she and Gabriel were swept rapidly past Mother and then out with the tide. Mother gave me a quick, disgusted look.

'Really Lucy, you should know better than to give them the time of day.'

'Who are they?'

'Irish peasants. Distantly related on your father's side. Forever plucking at his sleeve with a begging bowl. And now here they are, panting to know if there is anything for them in his Will. Vultures.'

I felt my cheeks flush, and I looked up to greet the next well-wisher.

I remember eyes of a deep and fathomless brown; so dark they were almost black, all the more remarkable because his hair was so blond. My own hair is light in colour – flaxen, I am told, and I am pale-skinned. While this man's hair was also fair, it had a metallic sheen, somewhere between gold and copper. His skin had a similarly rich glow. Perhaps he was moulded and cast, rather than merely born? I offered my hand and was irrationally surprised that he was made of warm flesh, rather than cold metal. Most gentlemen barely touch a lady's fingertips, but this man engulfed my hand in his and held it firmly. I felt he was trying to attract my attention through his handclasp.

'Miss Westenra,' he said, and his voice was deep and resonant, 'I am so sorry for your sadness. I was a business associate of your father's, and I found him a most agreeable man.'

'Thank you,' I said. 'What business did you undertake with him?'

He seemed surprised by the question. 'I – er – sold him a parcel of land, near my home in...'

I sensed Mother stiffen and turn to glare at yet another upstart, slowing down the line. She inhaled as if to reprimand, but when her gaze fell on the man, her eyes widened.

'Arthur Holmwood, Mrs Westenra,' he said smoothly, bowing and taking her hand in his. 'My sincere condolences.'

I sensed the hint of a smile behind Mother's veil, 'Mr Holmwood? You are Lord Godalming's son, are you not? So very kind of you to come today.'

'Not at all, Mrs Westenra. I wished to pay my respects. I was so glad to be able to come – my time in London has been brief. Later this week, I set sail once more.'

'Where are you going?' I asked.

'South America,' he said, 'Bolivia, Peru ... perhaps other, more uncharted lands.'

'I had heard that you are widely travelled,' Mother said. 'I am sure you have many fascinating stories to tell.'

He nodded. 'I have been fortunate to see and experience so much.'

I glanced to my left and saw that, once again, the reception line had concertinaed. Mother seemed less concerned than she had been when I spoke to Mrs Fallon.

'Perhaps when you return from your great adventure and our time of mourning is past,' she said. 'you might come and call upon us. Share some of your exciting tales and brighten our sad home.'

'I should be delighted to do so.' He bowed. 'Mrs Westenra,' he said, and then he turned to look at me. 'And Miss Westenra...'

He was still bent over Mother's hand, so our faces were close together. I saw my own face reflected in his dark eyes.

CHAPTER 5

19 JANUARY 2024 – KATE

*W*hen I woke up on Saturday morning, the day stretched before me emptily. Of course I could do more decorating, but I felt an odd urge for company.

I'd spent years living like a nomad, teaching English on three continents. I owned next to nothing – no home, no furniture, no car. And somehow, I'd also kept very few people. Travelling alone and then with Alex, I made some connections, but left them behind when I moved on. There were people like Rafaella all over the world – dear friends – but no one within a hundred-mile radius that I could ask for a coffee.

Gran, I knew, was out for the day with friends. I thought about hopping on a train to Hertfordshire to see Dad, but his weekend routine is as set and immovable as his work week. Saturdays are for housework and he wouldn't welcome the interruption.

I thought of Rafaella's parents' home in Milan where not just the children and grandchildren, but nephews, nieces, friends and hangers-on wandered uninvited into the kitchen and court-yard, eating and drinking, helping with the cooking or clearing up.

When I left Alex, stepping precipitously out into a chilly November night lugging two hastily packed bags, I hadn't known what to do. I had walked over to Rafaella's house. Her mother Alessa opened the door, took one look at me and drew me in. Over the blank, aching days that followed, Alessa occu-pied my hands with repetitive tasks, like shaping gnocchi or folding laundry. The blanket of noise and chatter and coming and going in the house held me together and stopped me shat-tering. I would give anything to be back in that warm, fragrant kitchen now.

Rather than wallow in self-pity in the flat, I walked briskly on the Heath extension for half an hour and then took myself down the hill to a coffee shop.

I commandeered a sofa and sipped my coffee, trying to warm up. I thought about Lucy and Beatrice and the mystery of the undelivered letter. With scant hope, I googled "Westenra." A wide range of hits came back – a singer in New Zealand, a hotel in Cornwall called the Westenra Arms. I tried "Lucy Westenra", but there were no results that related to Hampstead or the late nineteenth century. Then I typed in "Charles Westenra", Lucy's father's name, and struck gold.

A Wikipedia entry was the first result:

Charles Theodore Westenra, born 12 January 1832 (Hendon) died 14 September 1892 (Hampstead), a self-made property magnate and developer. Westenra bought land on the outskirts of London and used it to build improved accommodation for the working poor. His homes ameliorated overcrowding, as well as the moral and sanitary problems resulting from it. West-enra and Co. was successful in developing properties in areas such as Hendon, Cricklewood and Brent. Westenra was a long-term resident of Hampstead, although he never forgot his roots in the village of Hendon. He had a mausoleum constructed at his family parish church in Hendon, where he is buried with his mother, wife and daughter.

His daughter. Lucy.

I had found her, and her final resting place was a bus ride away. I looked further down the search results. There were still Westenra and Co. buildings and housing developments in London, and most of the results concerned these. As I clicked onto the second page, I felt a thrill down my spine. There was a profile on Westenra on a historical blog about property developers in Victorian London, and the writer had located a photograph. I clicked on the image and expanded it.

Charles Westenra was a short man, broad and jolly. He was standing, feet apart, thumbs hooked into his waistcoat pockets, at the top of a short flight of stone stairs. Behind him were heavy wooden double doors. I recognised Hillingham Court, or Hillingham, as it would have been then. A woman stood to his left, slightly apart. She was slender and pale, but beautiful. His wife, Rose? She had her head angled away, as if she was wishing herself out of the picture. And to Charles's right, a gangly teenage girl with thick, curling blonde hair tumbling over her shoulders. She was smiling at her father in unmistakable adoration. Lucy.

I glanced at my watch. It was past midday. Impulsively I stood, threw on my coat and headed to the bus stop.

I'd never been to Hendon before. It was now an ordinary suburb of London, but in Lucy's day, it would have been a small village surrounded by farmlands. As the bus trundled past chicken takeaways and betting shops, I imagined rolling fields and picturesque cottages.

The church was on the summit of a hill, opposite a university campus. The gate to the churchyard was open, and I entered cautiously. Graves were arranged in higgledy-piggledy chaos, pressing in on the path, in flowerbeds and between the great yew and cedar trees. At first glance I saw a few above-ground tombs, but nothing big enough to merit the description of a mausoleum.

I followed the path deeper into the churchyard and caught a glimpse of something with walls and a roof at the northeast corner of the church. As I walked closer, I saw the name etched into the stone. Westenra. The mausoleum was an imposing Grecian-style structure, built of Portland stone, decorated with stone rosettes and topped with a shallow, pyramid-shaped roof. There must once have been a door, but it had been bricked up, but there was an engraved plaque beside the sealed doorway:

Sacred to the memory of:
Niamh Westenra (nee Fallon)
Adored mother and grandmother
14 February 1814 – 28 June 1879
Also her son
Charles Theodore Westenra
12 January 1832 – 14 September 1892
His wife
Rose Eleanor Westenra (nee Barraclough)
9 November 1850 – 17 September 1894
And their beloved daughter
Lucy Rose Westenra
28 September 1874 – 19 September 1894
Vade retro satana

I knew enough Latin to translate these last three words – "*Vade retro satana* – Get thee back, Satan." The phrase, so portentous and Catholic, was out of place in this genteel Church of England churchyard.

More shocking was the story told by the dates. The

letter from Lucy was dated 14 September 1894. Three days later, Lucy's mother had died, aged forty-three. Two days after that, Lucy was dead – nine days before her twentieth birthday. What had happened in those few, appalling days? If Lucy's letter was true, the person she feared may well have succeeded in his intention to kill her.

As I stepped back to take a picture of the mausoleum, I noticed something in the long grass in front of the sealed doors – a bunch of white roses, bound with a simple ribbon. They were scarcely wilted, as if they'd been placed there within the last few days. I snapped a picture of the flowers with my phone, but then frowned. Surely graves were tended and visited by the living who knew the deceased? There could be no one living who knew Lucy Westenra or her family. Who had laid these flowers here?

* * *

I WAS SCRUBBING down the walls in the bedroom with sugar soap the next day when my phone rang. I wedged it between my shoulder and my ear.

'Hi Gran.'

'Darling girl, are you home?'

'I am, but it's a bit of a mess...'

'I have something for you. I'll see you in an hour.'

I'd managed to run down the road to get milk and biscuits and get the heating on to warm up the living room when the buzzer went. I went downstairs to meet her. She paused in the atrium, resting a hand on my arm. She looked around her, and I could see she was assailed with memories. Then we climbed the stairs. She pushed on, but I could see the three flights were a strain for her. She was always been so strong and elegant, but now she was in her eighties, there were hints of frailty. I guided her through the door and let her catch her breath. She gazed about her, then turned to me.

'Come my dear, give me the grand tour.'

Holding my arm, she walked through the rooms. I felt a twinge of embarrassment at the dusty chaos of the flat.

'I know it doesn't look like much yet, but...'

'My dearest, you have to go backwards before you can go forwards, I know that.'

I settled her in the living room and brought her tea and a digestive. She smiled up at me.

'Besides, it looked like this when Noni was here. She didn't have much furniture. I tried to offer her carpet and curtains and so on, but she liked it bare and empty.'

'I love that you came here when she lived here. I wish I knew more about what it looked like then. But people didn't take so many photos in the eighties.'

'Noni didn't take photographs anyway. She recorded anything that was important by drawing.'

I thought of the notebooks that filled a shelf in my father's study – pencil and charcoal sketches of my baby face, my father's elegant hands, the rowan tree in our back garden. I had the faintest childhood memory of her hand flying across a page making sure lines and strokes. Gran interrupted my thoughts.

'That's why I'm here.'

She drew something from her handbag – a pale cardboard folder, tied closed with a ribbon. She passed it over to me. I loosened the ribbon and opened the folder. There was a stack of pages of various sizes – sketches in pencil, charcoal and oil pastels.

'Seeing the name of the house on that letter – Hillingham – well, it reminded me of something. It took me a few days to find this – it was in a suitcase in Noni's old room. She left some stuff with me before she went to America.'

'She went to America? I didn't know that.'

'Between moving out of the flat and moving in with Jacob. She took a solo trip to the States. I thought you knew.'

I shook my head. There was so much I didn't know about Noni. I turned back to the drawings.

The topmost picture showed the facade of Hillingham Court, perfectly captured. But either side of the entranceway, Noni had drawn great tangled hedges of thorns, obscuring the windows. The wicked plants interlocked their branches, barring the door, stopping anyone from entering – or were they preventing someone inside from leaving? The thorns looked as if they might choke or crush the house. A fairy-tale nightmare.

The next picture showed a girl's hand – slim and elegant, but with a softness to it that suggested she was very young. Her ring finger was weighed down with a heavy, teardrop-shaped stone. While the sketch was in pencil, Noni had added a smear of thick carmine pastel to the gem so it looked like a drop of blood.

The next showed a walled garden. She had drawn the view as if seen through high, wrought iron gates, the metal twisted into whorls and tendrils. It took me a moment to see that within the complex ironwork, a word was visible: "Proserpine".

When I lifted out the next page, I gasped. I recognised the subject instantly. The wall of a church loomed behind a small building with a pitched roof and Grecian columns. I looked up at Gran, my mouth open in shock.

'The girl who wrote the letter... Lucy. Lucy Westenra. This is a sketch of her tomb! It's in a churchyard in Hendon. So Mum knew! She knew about her.'

Gran folded her hands in her lap and grinned.

'Well, I hoped there was a connection. How exciting!'

With mounting excitement, I leafed through the remaining drawings. There were faces – male and female – but whether they were related to Lucy's story I couldn't say. There was a detailed sketch of a building – a wide, neoclassical structure at the top of a hill. She had used a soft wash of watercolour to give the walls a warm, golden glow. There was an image of a table littered with bottles and a tangle of tubes – some kind of archaic medical equipment, I guessed. There was a page filled with a pattern of more plants and flowers – in the centre, glossy black berries nestled among oval leaves. She had rendered a cluster of bell-shaped flowers using a soft purple pencil. The page was bordered with the shiny leaves and the white, star-shaped flowers of wild garlic.

I put this page aside and revealed the last drawing. Two women were depicted in profile, their faces tipped towards one another, almost touching. They were gazing into one another's eyes. One was dark-haired and strong-featured. The other had a rope of plaited flaxen hair draped over her shoulder. Who were they? Was the blonde one supposed to be Lucy? She looked too old – I knew from Lucy's date of death that she had not yet turned twenty when she died, and this woman looked to be some years older than that, though still beautiful and youthful. It was unlikely that Noni would have seen the photo that I had found online, so maybe this was an imagined picture of the house's mysterious resident. And if so, who was the other woman? Lucy didn't have a sister. Could it be a cousin? A friend?

I looked up and caught Gran's eye.

'I wish I knew what all these drawings meant. I don't know what Mum knew about Lucy but she knew something. A lot more than I know, that's for sure.'

'But she didn't have the resources you have.' Gran reached over and gripped my hand. 'Find out. Find out who this girl was. Let Noni's drawings tell their story again.'

LUCY WESTENRA'S JOURNAL

28 SEPTEMBER 1892

My eighteenth birthday. Mother has given me a new silver-backed mirror and hairbrush. We have not marked the day in any other way. Even if we were not in mourning, I would not wish to. The rain never ceases.

10 OCTOBER 1892

Today, I should have attended my first classes at Bedford College. There was no way I could ask to go. We have fallen into a twilight, sitting in Mother's room with the curtains closed. The rain continues to fall. The loss of Pa is monstrous – too catastrophic to contemplate – and it is impossible to imagine a future without him.

20 OCTOBER 1892

Mr Marquand came to see us to discuss Pa's last Will and Testament. He took Mother and me into the library, and began to read in measured tones. Mother soon became impatient with the arcane legal language.

'Come, Mr Marquand,' she sighed. 'Give me the meaning, not the obfuscation. I am very tired.'

Mr Marquand looked up from the pages, discomfited.

'Mrs Westenra, by and large, the Will is as you would expect. In the main, your husband's estate passes to you. The house, properties and investments. You are, as I am sure you are not surprised to hear, a very rich woman.'

Mother glared at him, '"By and large"? "In the main?"'

'There are a few small bequests to relatives, colleagues and friends. And Mr Westenra has stipulated that the library–' he looked around him at the high shelves crammed with books, the piles of journals on the floor and the teetering stacks of newspapers on the desk. '– and all its contents should belong to Miss Westenra.'

'But it is a room within my house!'

'I have, in fact, never drawn up such a clause in a Will before. Nevertheless, it is so. He has declared the library to be a separate apartment within the property of Hillingham. I have drawn up a deed, and it now belongs to Miss Lucy.' Mr Marquand turned to me. 'The Will includes the right to ingress and egress – so you and your heirs will evermore have the right to pass through the house to reach the library.'

Mother stared at him, then at me. I looked back, my eyes wide with shock. I had had no inkling. She sighed, as if we had done her a great disservice, then rose and glided from the room.

26 OCTOBER 1892

Now that the library is my domain, I spend my days in here, Missy the cat by my side. It was a mess when I first took occupancy – the maids had never been allowed to enter and clean it.

At first, it was inexpressibly comforting to be surrounded by Pa's happy chaos, but I know I need to bring order, for my own sanity. So far, I have separated books from journals, and arranged everything by subject and chronology. The work will take weeks and is strenuous and dusty. I have unearthed so many hidden treasures, and by the time I complete my work, I will be proud to say I can put a hand on any volume in minutes.

I imagine sitting at the leather-topped desk in my library to write my university essays. I am impatient to begin my studies at Bedford College. I feel sure that I can catch up with my class-mates if I am able to join them in January. I had been reading and annotating the prescribed texts we had been recommended. Mother develops a 'headache' every time I mention it, but I remained determined.

LETTER FROM MINA MURRAY TO LUCY WESTENRA

27 October 1892

My dear Lucy,

Today has been rather out of the ordinary. As you know, since you went to London, my Saturdays and Sundays have been lonely and quiet. However, the other day, I received a letter from Mr Peter Hawkins, who was a friend of my late father's. Mr Hawkins, a solicitor, is a widower. He said that he remembered me with great affection and invited me to visit him for tea at his house in Magdalen Road on Saturday.

I was delighted to oblige, and arrived at the house promptly at three o'clock. Mr Hawkins had also invited his solicitor's clerk, Jonathan Harker, a very pleasant young man. He is studying the law and will soon be taking his examinations to enter the legal profession.

Mr Harker is some inches taller than me – and as you know, I am no little flower! He has quite the kindest face, and cornflower blue eyes, which twinkle behind his spectacles. The young men I have met before often chatter on volubly about themselves, but as soon as you respond with some anecdote of your own, their eyes acquire a faraway aspect and they look over your shoulder. It is as if they must endure the time that you are speaking so they can continue to tell their own, more fascinating story.

Mr Harker is different. He asked about my work at the school, and listened with such grave attention that I felt that he regarded me as an equal. We spoke without pause for some hours, and our topics ranged from science to history, to advances in technology. He is particularly interested in photography and has his own camera.

The afternoon flew by, and before I knew it, Mr Hawkins' housekeeper was lighting the lamps. When I stood to go, Mr Harker stood too, and quietly asked if I might perhaps like to accompany him on a walk beside the river one afternoon. I am a solid and sensible girl, as you know, my darling Lucy, but I do believe I blushed with pleasure at his request. When I looked over at Mr Hawkins, he was sitting forward in his armchair, resting both hands on the top of his walking cane. He smiled quite smugly, as if his plan had unfolded exactly as he intended.

Other than you, my dear Lucy, I have never before met someone with whom I experienced such an instant communion of spirit and mind. Will Mr Harker become a friend? I find myself hoping that he will. When you return to visit at The Underhill, it will be my great pleasure to introduce him to you. I think you will like him very much.

With all my affection,
Mina.

31 OCTOBER 1892 – LUCY WESTENRA'S JOURNAL

I read Mina's letter a second time. I pulled on my winter cloak and some sturdy boots and, without telling anyone where I was going, slipped out onto the Heath. There was barely an hour of daylight left.

How selfish I am. Why am I unable to feel unalloyed joy for Mina? There is no doubt about the real subject of her letter. She has met her future husband.

It may seem absurd, but it has never occurred to me that Mina would marry. Marriage has no place in my own future – I have no interest in sharing my life with a man who would become my guardian. But now I realise I am childish and naïve. I had a hazy dream – a future where Mina and I shared a cottage, reading, learning and writing together. It is no more than fantasy. Not only would Mother block these plans, this is also not Mina's aspiration.

I reached the brow of the hill. Twilight was falling fast, and mist swirled in the dip below me. I glimpsed the lake in the grounds of nearby Kenwood House. I could see no one else on the Heath and without realising I was about to do so, I let out a great howl of frustration. I heard it echo off the opposite hill and roll around the valley. I howled again, and louder. I imagined Berserker, the great wolf in the Zoological Gardens in Regent's Park raising his grey, shaggy head when he heard my call on the wind. Would he howl back? I listened hard, but I could hear nothing, except the rain pattering on the fallen leaves. I gathered my skirts and began to run down the hill, faster and faster, as I had when I was a child. The cold air filled my lungs and tears stung my cheeks. I felt as if I might take off, as if my feet might leave the ground and my arms spread into wings, carrying me into the clouds above the Heath.

However, imagination cannot defeat gravity. I caught the toe of my boot on a stubborn tussock of grass, and pitched headlong, landing flat and then rolling down the slope. I came to rest in a muddy ditch a few yards further on.

I lay there for some moments, staring up at the dark sky. I was winded, but not injured. After a minute or so, I stood and attempted to brush the worst of the mud from my dress, but it was soon clear that there was no way to fix the damage. I limped back up the hill and made my way home, every now and then pausing to extract a twig from the tangled mess of my hair.

The front door was open, and I could see Mrs Staines standing silhouetted in the doorway, lights blazing behind her.

'Oh for heaven's sake, Miss Lucy,' she said when she saw me. She made me stand on the step while she unlaced my boots. I stepped out of them and into the hallway in my stockinged feet. If I was lucky, Mother would still be resting and I could slip up to my room.

I was not. Mother was sitting in a chair in the hallway, her hands in her lap. Above her head hung a burnished silver shield, a relic from one of her noble ancestors. I glimpsed a distorted version of my reflection in it – hair in a mad cloud, my dress caked in mud, a dark streak down one of my cheeks. Mother looked me up and down, her pale eyes expressionless. I could hear drops of muddy water falling from my skirts onto the floor.

'You are not to go out unaccompanied again, Lucy. I forbid it.'

Her benign indifference to my walks since Pa's death had been my greatest boon. But now she had directly forbidden me. I sensed doors slamming, walls closing in. With a nauseous sense that I was standing on the edge of a precipice, I knew I had to ask the question directly, even though I dreaded the answer.

'When can I go to university?' I blurted.

She looked at me with pity, almost. And then she smiled. 'Oh Lucy. You know the answer to that, surely. Never. You will never go.'

CHAPTER 6

21 JANUARY 2024 – KATE

*H*e made excuse after excuse, but eventually, Dad accepted my invitation to dinner. I was in the kitchen stirring a sofrito when the doorbell buzzed. He was at the door within a minute of my buzzing him in – he clearly hadn't lingered in the hallway or on the stairs.

He brushed my cheek with a dry kiss as he stepped in. He's very tall and lean, and the narrow hallway made him seem even taller, as if he would need to stoop to pass through these small rooms. He handed me a bottle of wine and took off his coat.

'I'm making a risotto,' I said. 'I hope that's okay.'

'Well, it smells very good,' he said carefully. 'I'm sure you learned a lot about cooking in Italy.'

I found myself babbling about finely chopped carrots and celery and the importance of bay leaves, but as I spoke, I saw his eyes slide to the left. I had bought plain, cheap black frames and hung all of Mum's sketches on the wall in the hallway, opposite the kitchen door. I expected him to cross over and examine them more closely but he looked at them warily from a distance, then carefully folded his coat and went to place it on the arm of a chair in the living room.

'I can hang that up for you.'

'Don't trouble yourself.'

He sat awkwardly on the edge of the sofa, as though he'd come for a job interview. I hovered in the doorway for a moment, and then went into the kitchen to open the wine. I took a glass through to him. He was still sitting upright, and I saw him steal another glance at Mum's drawings. There was an odd tension in his jaw.

'I'll need to keep stirring the risotto once I start. Would you like to come through and keep me company?'

He nodded, uncertain, then rose and followed me into the narrow kitchen. I had left a heap of mushrooms on a board. I thought of Rafaella's mamma, occupying my hands and freeing my mind.

'Why don't you chop those?' I said, pointing to the mushrooms. Dad picked up a knife, and started to slice them precisely and thinly. I tipped the rice into the pan.

'How was the drive?' I asked, stirring and watching as the grains began to turn glossy and transparent.

'A little traffic coming off the M1, but quite manageable,' he said.

I looked over at him. His shoulders relaxed a little.

'And work?'

'Fine.'

He's not rude or unkind. He's a scientist and words are for imparting facts. He's no good at small talk. When I was growing up – after Mum died – our house was as quiet as a library. I learned not to chatter on then, even though the urge to fill the sad silence with noise was strong.

Now, he chopped. I stirred. I leaned over and clicked on the radio and classical music flowed out like a calm ribbon.

When the food was ready, we carried our bowls through to the living room. I had set up a small table and two chairs and we sat opposite one another to eat. He cast a quick glance around the room as he sat.

'I see you've repainted.'

'And taken up the carpet. The place wasn't in bad nick... just a little tired.'

'Well it looks... fresher.' He ate a mouthful of the risotto. 'This is very good, Kate. Thank you.'

'When were you last here?'

'Probably... ten years ago? I've inspected it occasionally between tenancies, but mostly I left all that to the agents.'

'But you must have spent time here when Mum lived here.'

'Yes.'

'What was it like?'

'Colder. No central heating then, of course. I think we had the radiators fitted in the mid-nineties.'

I smiled into my bowl. I should have known better than to ask an open-ended question. Dad only dealt in specifics.

'I meant ... how did it look? How did Mum have it decorated? Did she have lots of friends come here? Were there parties?'

He considered his answer.

'She wasn't a party person. She was quite shy... didn't like to talk much. She said she expressed what she wanted to say through her art. She loved to work here. She had her easel there, by the window. She liked the light.'

He pointed. I had left the curtains open and the window formed a navy square in the white wall. I imagined Mum in front of it, a shaft of rich sunlight touching her face, illuminating her canvas.

'Do you remember I told you about that letter I found under the floor?' I said suddenly. 'The one where Gran translated the shorthand? It was written by a previous inhabitant of the house.

A girl called Lucy Westenra who grew up here at the end of the nineteenth century. Anyway, I think Mum knew about her.' I pointed to the framed sketches on the wall. 'Gran gave me these... and this one ...' I indicated the image of the churchyard '... is Lucy's tomb in Hendon.'

He glanced up at the sketches, but his eyes did not linger.

'I haven't seen any of these before,' he said shortly.

'So she never mentioned Lucy? It seems clear she knew about her. And some of the others are really mysterious. Look at the one with all the medical paraphernalia... and the one of the outside of the house with the vines. It's a bit like Sleeping Beauty, don't you think?'

'I don't recall her mentioning anyone called Lucy.'

He turned his eyes back to his food and took another small mouthful, but I could see his appetite was spoiled. He placed his fork neatly on the edge of the plate.

'Thank you for a lovely meal, Kate. I should probably head off soon. Work tomorrow.'

Once he had gone, I checked the time. It was not yet nine pm... scarcely a late night. I rang Gran.

'Hello my sweet,' she said. 'I'm trying to do a jigsaw puzzle someone gave me for Christmas. How infuriating they are. You know all the pieces are there, but the one you need stubbornly refuses to make itself known.'

I laughed. 'I know exactly how you feel.'

'How are you?'

'Dad came for dinner.'

'Well. That's a surprise.'

'Is it? Why?'

'I think he's always found it difficult to go to that flat. It's full of memories of Noni... the beginning of their love. His heart is still so sore, you know.'

I sank down onto the sofa.

'I hadn't even thought about that. I thought he was being his usual, awkward, self.'

'It's a quarter of a century since she died. He hasn't remarried. Hasn't even been on a date. She was my daughter and I adored her, but even I would have liked to see him move on.'

'He saw the drawings you gave me. He said he'd never seen them before, and then he left.'

'Well, then.'

'Well then? What does that mean?'

'Even after all these years, she still had secrets from him. That must be hard to take.'

'But you don't know why she drew them either. She had secrets from you too.'

'It's the job of children to have secrets from their parents. I'm sure there are things about you that your father doesn't know.'

'That's true. Sometimes, I wonder if he knows me at all.'

'He does. In his own way. And what he doesn't understand, he loves anyway.'

I wasn't sure I agreed with her. But as I cleared the plates, I peered at the picture of Hillingham Court, its doors barred with tangled vines. So many questions – and the voices who knew the answers were lost forever.

LUCY WESTENRA'S JOURNAL

LETTER FROM LUCY WESTENRA TO THE PRINCIPAL, BEDFORD COLLEGE

1 NOVEMBER 1892

Dear Miss Bostock,

With regard to your letter of 18th March 1891, I was offered a place to study at Bedford College, in October this year, a place which I accepted. I was unable to attend my first classes as my father recently passed away. I would very much like to take up my place in January but find myself without financial support. Are there any scholarships for which I might be eligible to apply?

With best regards,

Miss Lucy Westenra.

LETTER FROM THE PRINCIPAL, BEDFORD COLLEGE TO LUCY WESTENRA

5 NOVEMBER 1892

Dear Miss Westenra,

We regret to inform you, that we have already received notice from your guardian, Mrs Charles Westenra that you would not be taking up your place. It has been allocated to another candidate.

Kind regards,

Miss Eliza Rostock

Principal.

19 MARCH 1893

Despite my fury, I have tried to fill my days these past months. If I cannot study formally, I will make use of what I have – the library. I am designing myself a course of study, choosing topics and undertaking research, as I might have done in my university classes. Mother might control where I go, but my mind and the shelves of my library are my own.

Now I have free rein in the library, I have read Pa's books on anatomy. I have discovered, too, that he had some other arcane and obscene volumes, which illustrate what might unfold between a man and a woman. I have looked at these drawings and photographs with avid curiosity. I have looked at my own naked form (Mother would be horrified at this, I know). I find myself wondering – how might it feel to fit my body together with someone else's?

At night, my sleep is plagued with intense, confusing dreams. Afterwards, I am unable to remember the details, but I recall that the dreams are full of sensations – heat, touch and breath. Last night, I awoke in the darkest hours and found myself standing on the landing outside my bedroom door. Mrs Staines was holding my arm and speaking my name quietly.

'Lucy. Come back to bed, my dear. You have been walking in your sleep.'

She guided me back into bed and drew the covers up to my chin. As sleep began to overwhelm me, I remembered the flavour of the dream that had brought me out of my bed – the confusing tastes and impressions, a sense of a nameless, faceless body pressed hotly against my own.

30 JUNE 1893

Mother and I are leaving for our annual trip to Whitby. Mother is proud of her Yorkshire roots, and every July, we travel to spend some weeks in the pretty seaside town, where she enjoyed summers when she was a girl. I wrote to Mina, begging her to join us. Her reply, which arrived this morning, dismayed me.

LETTER FROM MINA MURRAY TO LUCY WESTENRA

28 JUNE 1893

Dearest Lucy,

I am so grateful for your kind invitation. However I have already committed to visiting Lyme Regis in the company of some friends.

Dear Mr Harker will be joining us on this jaunt. He has given me a generous gift – an actual typewriter! I have been practising shorthand very assiduously. I hope that I shall be able to be useful to Jonathan, and if I can stenograph well enough, I can take down what he wants

to say in this way and write it out for him on the typewriter, at which also I am practising very hard. He and I
sometimes write letters in shorthand!

    With all my love,
    Mina

He and I, she writes. I have tried to quell my envy and loneliness. I have purchased a Pitman's shorthand manual from a
local bookshop, to train myself in the same skill.

15 JULY 1893

Today, Mina's first typewritten letter arrived at our lodgings in
Whitby, joyfully announcing that Jonathan (no longer Mr
Harker) had asked for her hand. I will do my best to feel unin-
hibited pleasure at her happiness. I have composed my reply to
her, offering my congratulations entirely in shorthand.

1 SEPTEMBER 1893

We are back at Hillingham. The leaves were already blowing
across the drive when we arrived. It is a matter of four weeks
until my nineteenth birthday. I am delighted to be back in my
library.

    This afternoon, we sat together in the drawing room, but I
could not keep still. I tried to read, but the restlessness was in
my legs, and I kept jumping up and pacing up and down.

    'For heaven's sake Lucy,' Mother said. 'Sit down. You are like
a puppet on a string.'

    'I'm bored. So bored. I want to go outside.'

    Mother glanced out of the window. A fine rain was falling
from an iron-grey sky.

    'Well, that is clearly out of the question.'

    I went up to my bedroom, which was over-warm and stuffy.

I crossed to the window and, struggling with the mechanism, opened it and raised the sash as high as I could. The rain had stopped. My room is at the side of the house, overlooking a gravel walkway. I sat on the windowsill, looking out at a sky rinsed clean by the afternoon's rainfall. If I leaned out a little, I could see along the side of the house and look out over the Heath stretched below us. The green hills glittered in the afternoon light. A small boy was flying a kite, and an excitable terrier raced across the grass.

I glanced down into the garden below and saw Missy the cat stalking a blade of grass. I called to her, and she looked up at me. I saw her little mouth open in a silent miaow, and then she trotted across the lawn. She passed out of view, and I heard rustling. In seconds, her pretty, triangular face appeared at the window, and she rubbed her cheek against my hand, before leaping down from the windowsill and going to curl up on my bed.

I knelt on the floor and looked out of my window, straight down the wall. The thick, winding branches of an ancient wisteria grew up a wrought iron trellis. The upper branches had been trained under the sill and climbed further up the wall to either side. The branches were bare of leaves or flowers. As they twined around the bars of the trellis, they resembled the snakes and ladders game I had played with Pa as a child. Missy had bounded up them easily. Could I slide down the snakes and find my way to the ground?

I went to peer out into the corridor. The house was shrouded in the quiet of the afternoon. I drew my door shut as quietly as I could and turned the key in the lock. Then I went to my wardrobe and replaced my afternoon attire with a heavy walking skirt and sturdy boots.

I sat on the sill, swinging my legs out. It was easy enough to grab a stem of the wisteria that grew up alongside the window, but it took courage to launch myself out onto the trellis, using the vine for additional handholds. The branches of the wisteria were thick and strong. I was lucky that it had been well maintained and the trellis was firmly attached to the wall. However, the rain had drenched the creeper and my skirts and sleeves were soon soaked. My boots slipped on the slick metal of the trellis and my arms ached as I carefully descended.

I stood on the path beneath my window, looking up. The ascent looked rather more daunting, but I had no choice. Tucking my skirt between my legs, I hauled myself back up. It took a prodigious effort to swing back into my window and I worried I had made too much noise, but no one came running. I slumped onto the floor, breathing hard. My hands were scratched and muddy, but I was exhilarated.

Now I have discovered my secret ladder, I have the means to escape, and, most usefully, a route back into the house where I will not be detected. As I write this, Missy regards me from her perch on the pillow, her golden eyes wide and blank.

CHAPTER 7

23 JANUARY 2024 – KATE

*A*nother rainy Tuesday lunchtime, another grimy staffroom. I ate my sandwich alone on a sagging sofa. Knots of fulltime teachers sat around me, chatting and eating. They didn't bother to try and include me, and I made no effort to join any of the groups. I checked my watch. Forty-five minutes until my next class. My phone buzzed with an incoming email.

Kate,
   I've done some research and thought this would work well
for you.
   Dad.

He'd appended a web link and I tapped it. It was a job ad – a permanent post, teaching in a further education college in Buckinghamshire. There was a swirl of green and a drone's-eye-view shot of the lavish grounds of the college. I flicked through the website and wondered, not for the first time, how Dad could know so very little about me.

When I rang him from Milan to say that Alex and I had split up and I was coming back to London, I had sensed him biting back words. I knew he was fighting the urge to say, 'I told you so'. I knew he wanted to tell me to clamber onto the path I should always have been on – steady career advancement and financial stability. I thought – he will only be truly happy when I have a mortgage, a brace of ISAs and kitchen cabinets from IKEA.

When I told him I wanted to live in Mum's flat and do supply teaching, he had had to leave the room. I was paying rent at the same rate as the previous tenant – I insisted – but I could see he was still disappointed.

He knew the battle needed to be fought by stealth rather than open confrontation, so he emailed me links. This one was far from his first salvo – he sent at least two or three job ads a week. I felt his disapproval like a chill wind on my skin. I swept the website from my screen, and typed a terse "Thanks" in response to his email.

As soon as I hit send, I felt a twinge of regret. Was I being a petulant child? He was trying to help, in his own way. Of course I didn't want to teach in some featureless college in the Home Counties, but my life did need to move on. I couldn't live in Mum's tiny flat forever and at some point, I would need to think further ahead in my work life than next week. But not yet.

To distract myself, I typed "Westenra" into the search bar for what felt like the hundredth time. I skimmed the first few pages of results. All the links showed that I'd clicked on them before. Not expecting much, I passed onto the fourth page of searches. Scanning down, my attention was caught by an image of two schoolgirls, holding up a trophy between them, dated 2015. It was an article from the *Exeter Daily News*. The two girls in the picture had won a national science competition. The caption read: "The winners, pictured at the Westenra Science Block at The Underhill."

I didn't expect much, but a quick search brought up the website of the Underhill, an exclusive girls' private school in Exeter. The gallery page showed rolling lawns and an elegant main building. Another shot showed a red-brick, double-storey block with a plaque identifying it as The Westenra Laboratories. I found the section on the school's history.

> The Westenra Laboratories were originally built in the early 1890s, thanks to a generous donation from Charles Westenra, a London property developer, whose daughter attended the school.

The lunch break was coming to an end, but something snagged in my thoughts. Exeter. Mina Harker, the woman to whom Lucy wrote her terrified plea, lived in Exeter. Lucy had talked about going there, if she escaped the man she feared would harm her. Maybe Lucy and Mina had met at school?

I checked the time. Ten minutes left of lunch. I opened the genealogy website. "Mina Harker" I typed, and added Exeter to her search, along with a range of birth dates – 1870-1880.

And there she was – listed in the 1901 Census – Wilhelmina Harker, living in Magdalen Road at the address to which Lucy had tried to send the letter. Her maiden name was Murray. She was listed as "Wife" and was married to a "Jonathan Harker, solicitor". The bell rang and I cursed inwardly. I saved Mina's search result and slipped my phone into my bag.

* * *

WHEN I GOT HOME, I decided to record everything I'd learned in a single document. I took pictures of the letter with my phone, and typed up Gran's typescript. Then I photographed and uploaded each of Mum's drawings. As succinctly as I could, I recorded everything I'd learned since finding the letter under the floor. I've always liked writing, but I was rusty. My sentences were clumsy and it took me a couple of hours to type up a few pages of text I was vaguely happy with.

I went back to digging on the genealogy website. I learned that Mina and Jonathan had been at the Magdalen House address in 1901 and were still there in 1911. By then, they had one child, a boy called Quincey. In 1921, Mina and Quincey were listed as living at the house, but not Jonathan, and in 1931, the house was under new ownership. At that point, the trail seemed to go cold. Had they moved away from Exeter? I sat back in my chair, frustrated and gazed at the screen. A small box on the right-hand side caught my attention.

"Make a Connection. Find others who are researching Wilhelmina Harker in Public Family Trees."

Below, there was a link to "The Harker Family Tree". I clicked into the tree and when it opened, I felt a thrill of excitement. It gave Mina's date of birth, along with those of her husband and son. There was even a picture – a grainy family portrait. Mina was tall and straight-backed, with thick, curly hair. She had her arm looped through that of her husband. He too was tall, stooped and bespectacled, with broad wings of white in his thinning hair. He looked much older than Mina, or perhaps he was ill. Quincey – it had to be him – stood in front of his parents, a freckled, open-faced boy of about eight, with his mother's hair.

The family tree recorded Quincey's marriage in 1928. He fathered a son, Luke, born in 1930, and a daughter, Annabel, in 1934. Annabel had no children, but Luke had one son called Matthew, who in turn had three children: two boys and a girl. One of these, James, was born in 1984, and when I glanced up at the top of the page, I saw it was James Harker who had compiled this family tree. There was a small thumbnail image on his profile and I opened it. He was smiling in the picture – a kind-faced man of about my age. Beneath, a green button proclaimed "Message". I sat with my hands hovering over the keyboard. Then I clicked and began to type.

LUCY WESTENRA'S JOURNAL

14 SEPTEMBER 1893 – LUCY WESTENRA'S JOURNAL

A year since Pa died. The loss of him is incalculable and I miss him every minute of every day.

14 OCTOBER 1893

Today Mother hosted our first 'At Home' since the official end of our mourning. A few of Mother's friends from Hampstead Parish Church came to take tea with us this afternoon. In the past, I would have found such an occasion insufferably dull. However, we had been starved of company for so long, I found myself looking forward to this event. Mother's friend, Mrs Howarth, came with her two daughters, Emmeline and Maude. There was also a Mrs Nash and her daughter Rosamond.

The Howarth girls were as giggly as I might have expected, but Rosamond, a tall girl with an eager, bony face, was lively and interesting. She had read the classics and had an interest in botany. The afternoon passed in happy communion.

When our guests got up to leave, Mrs Nash and Mrs

Howarth extracted a promise from both Mother and me that we would attend the concert of Lieder, to be held at the church next Wednesday evening.

Mother was delighted at our first attempt at entertaining as an all-female household. She was very tired, but insisted on hearing all about my conversation with Rosamond.

'I am so pleased you have found a companion here in Hampstead,' she said. 'I know you miss Mina very much.'

'I do,' I admitted, 'but with her engagement, she has moved into a different stage of her life. It is not just geography that separates us.'

'That is, I hope, a situation which will be temporary,' said Mother, and patted my hand.

For a moment, I did not understand her. Then I realised what she was saying. She imagined that I too would soon be engaged and then married. I laughed, despite myself.

Before I had time to think better of speaking my thoughts aloud, I said, 'I am not sure I want to marry at all.'

'I beg your pardon?' Mother said, her tone cold.

I knew that "I beg your pardon" of old. She was giving me the opportunity to pretend I had misspoken and change my remark. I was not, however, going to do so.

'We are on the verge of a new century,' I said. 'Many women attend university. They become doctors. The clamour to grant women the vote grows ever louder. At some point, I will be financially independent...'

'At some point? Do you mean when I die?'

'Oh Mother...' I said weakly. She was right. What I had said sounded unfeeling. 'I do not mean that. As an adult woman, I will have no need of a man to support me financially.'

'Marriage is about more than money. If – when – you marry,' she said, with steely emphasis, 'you will gain so much. Companionship. Love. Family. And a social status that matches our history.'

I resisted the urge to laugh. Her marriage to Pa had had no companionship, and no love that I had ever observed. But as she said the word 'family', she touched her throat lightly with one hand. She means a social status that matches her own family history. She wants me to marry up, to restore her social standing, and remove the whiff of industrial new money from our pedigree.

20 OCTOBER 1893

When we arrived at Hampstead Parish Church for the concert, it was already bustling. Rosamond rushed over to greet us and drew us down the centre aisle to seats she had reserved for us all.

We felt the ripple of excitement in the room before we saw anything. Fans were raised to cover faces and eyes darted towards the doors. Rosamond glanced over her shoulder and I heard her sharp intake of breath.

'Oh my,' she whispered.

I turned. A trio of young men walked abreast up the centre aisle of the church. They were all tall and broad-shouldered. The first was classically handsome and sharp-featured. He looked intense and serious, with jet-black hair and lowered brows, as if he was already weighted with heavy thoughts and responsibilities. The second loped rather than walked. He was lanky and loose-limbed and a fall of reddish hair tumbled over his bright eyes. His mouth was wide and generous, and he looked as if he might burst into laughter at any moment. The third had lustrous golden hair, and with a shock, I recognised him. It was Arthur Holmwood, he of the dark eyes and magnetic gaze, whom I had met at Pa's funeral.

The three men were stopped by many as they entered. From the snatches of conversation I overheard, it appeared they had recently returned from exotic adventures, travelling and hunting through South America. I recalled that when we had met a year before, Mr Holmwood had said he was leaving to visit Bolivia and Peru. Indeed, all three of them showed evidence of a strong foreign sun on their skins, and Mr Holmwood's hair was even brighter than I remembered from our first meeting.

Mrs Howarth bustled up the front, shooing people to their seats. The three young men sat across the aisle from us. Rosamond leaned forward and gawked at them, unashamedly curious.

'Who are they?' she whispered.

'I know only one of them,' I whispered. 'We have met once. The fair-headed one is Mr Arthur Holmwood.'

'The Honourable Arthur Holmwood,' Mother whispered to us both, without taking her eyes off Mrs Howarth, 'only son of Lord Godalming.'

Rosamond opened her eyes wide and formed her mouth into an 'O' of surprise.

'Well, well, well,' she whispered, 'one with a title, and the other two so handsome. I hope they are well-armed. The young women of Hampstead will fall upon them like a pack of beribboned wolves.'

My snort of laughter was loud and unladylike. Mother's glare should have turned us both to stone. Fortunately, for all of our sakes, Emmeline Howarth swept onto the dais, took her seat at the piano and began to play.

After the concert, refreshments were served in the adjoining hall. Rosamond and I took our glasses of punch and found an alcove under a window where we might sit and observe the crowd. Fans fluttered, and the atmosphere was oppressive. I experienced an almost uncontrollable urge to flee into the cool of the evening. I stood, and, to my surprise, found Mr Holmwood directly before me.

He bowed and offered his hand.

'Miss Westenra,' he said, 'I am not sure if you remember me...
I am Arthur...'

'Holmwood. Of course I remember you,' I said, and my tone
was more abrupt than I intended.

'You have been well this past year, I trust?'

'I have been in mourning, as you know, but tolerably well.' I
was conscious of Rosamond, who had stood too and was close
to my elbow.

'This is my friend, Miss Rosamond Nash.'

Mr Holmwood bowed to Rosamond and gave her the full
benefit of his smile.

Before she could respond, Mr Holmwood's companions
came towards our little group. He smoothly introduced them.

'Miss Westenra and Miss Nash, may I present my old friend
Dr John Seward,' he indicated the dark-haired, sharp-featured
young man, 'and Mr Quincey Morris, of Texas in the United
States of America.'

I offered my hand to Dr Seward, who bowed low, and then
turned to Rosamond. Mr Morris took my hand in his and bent
to kiss my fingers. This was not usual in our circle. I may have
jumped a little in surprise when his lips touched my glove. He
must have felt the movement, for he looked up and caught my
eye. A lock of his warm russet hair fell across his forehead. With
his face still bent over my hand, he gave me a slow and private
smile and pressed his thumb into the centre of my palm. There
was something both intimate and transgressive in that moment
– as if we had exchanged something secret. Time hovered and
bent, slowing down. Then he turned to greet Rosamond and
kissed her hand also.

The three young men launched into a lively account of their
hike to the Yucatán Peninsula and what they had experienced
there. From their boisterous, teasing conversation and easy
manner with one another, it was clear that they were good
friends and shared a long and intimate acquaintance.

Dr Seward told us that he had recently completed his medical studies, and that his primary interest was in the health of the brain. He hoped to make his career in working with those who suffered agonies of the mind.

'I believe by studying those people we class as "mad", I may unlock some of the secrets of the human consciousness,' he said earnestly.

'I am told the treatment of the insane has advanced very much in recent years,' I interjected. 'I read about the improvements at Hanwell Asylum, where patients were allowed to work and were not restrained. Harriet Martineau was much impressed by what she saw there.'

'You have read the work of Miss Martineau?' He looked surprised.

'Of course. She is one of the primary social theorists of our age.'

'Indeed.' He flushed, and I suspected I had wrong-footed him by knowing something of his area of expertise. He took a deep breath and regained his composure.

'I am hoping to open my own asylum soon. I believe I may be able to conduct more efficacious research when the patients whose cases I wish to study are resident and I can observe them on a regular basis.'

'What sort of conditions do you hope to study?'

He described various manias and delusions he had seen in the course of his studies – the patients who believed themselves to be a famous personage, or even to be God.

'So these patients will serve as subjects for your experiments? Like rats kept in a cage?'

'Not at all! I...' Dr Seward looked shocked at my forward remark.

'My understanding of an asylum is that it exists to keep the patients safe and to aid their recovery so they can return to freedom and normal life.'

'Indeed, and mine will operate in this way...'

'But you speak as if the patient would be there for you to study, rather than to be given treatment.'

'On the contrary! I hope I will develop new therapeutic techniques under these circumstances, and...' Dr Seward was becoming agitated, and his voice was rising.

I saw Mr Holmwood glance at me and realised that I had forgotten myself. I had imagined I could debate this man rigorously, as I used to do with Pa.

'I apologise, Dr Seward,' I said, 'I do not mean to be argumentative. I am sure that in your asylum, the patients will both thrive and recover.'

'Do you have a potential location for your asylum, Dr Seward?' Rosamond said smoothly.

'I have found a house in Purfleet in Essex, which I think will suit my purposes admirably. It is not far from London, but it is in a remote location and has extensive grounds. There are no close neighbours – the only other house nearby, a ruined abbey known as Carfax, has been uninhabited for many years.'

How extraordinary to have such an ambition and realise it. From his accent and bearing, I surmised that Dr Seward comes from a family of means. He has been able to undertake medical study and specialise in his area of interest, to travel with his friends and broaden his experience of the world, and now he has the financial means and support to open his own hospital. My curiosity and aptitude are as great as his, and the means of my family equal or greater, but I am not even permitted to walk alone on the Heath near my own home.

Then Mr Morris began to recount how the three friends had hunted on the plains of Argentina. His face was mobile and with his deep, resonant voice and slow American accent, he painted vivid pictures.

'We were at the foot of the Andes,' he said, 'and the grass stretched out before us like a golden sea. Those gauchos...' he angled his head toward Rosamond and me. 'That's the name for the horsemen of that region, well, they ride a horse like it's a part of their own body. I could see nothing, but one of the gauchos points and when I squint, I see the smallest movement and sure enough, there was a jaguar, standing still as a statue in the long grass.'

I sensed eyes on me and looked to my left. Mr Holmwood was watching me with that intense, dark gaze once more. I looked straight at him, to show I had seen. I was curious to see if he would look away, but he did not. To my frustration, I was the first to drop my gaze.

I turned back to look at Mr Morris. He is perhaps twenty-seven or eight, but outdoor life has weathered his face. I like the faint laugh lines around his eyes and his graceful, loose posture. He looks like a man for whom everything is easy. He raised a hand in a descriptive gesture, and I noticed how strong and well-shaped it was. His movement drew my attention again to his mobile, wide mouth. He, I think, would know how to kiss... and more.

21 OCTOBER 1893

O Journal, today has proved a most exceptional day. Last night, my dreams were vivid and my sleep fitful. I woke in the mid-morning, fuzzy-headed and thirsty. I tiptoed downstairs, still in my nightclothes, and made my way to the kitchen. Mrs Staines was taking a freshly baked loaf out of the oven, and I pleaded with her for a slice of the warm bread.

'A gentleman called this morning and left his card,' she said, pretending nonchalance.

'Oh yes?' I said, taking up a knife and digging it into the butter.

'Tall and very handsome.'

'Dark or fair?' I asked, taking a bite. 'Moustache or clean-shaven?'

Mrs Staines pretended shock at my questions. 'Do you know so many fine gentlemen, Miss Lucy, that you need to classify them?'

'Indeed. There are thousands. I alphabetise them and put them on the shelves of my library, with an index card tucked into their top pockets!'

This remark made her laugh loudly.

'He was a tall, dark-haired gentleman. Clean-shaven. A Dr Seward. He said he met you and your mother at the concert last evening. He hopes to return to pay a call soon.'

I thanked Mrs Staines, ran up the stairs to my bedroom and locked the door. I shed my nightgown and pulled on my old skirt and a blouse. It was a glorious autumn day, with a sky of brightest azure. I took a small bag, into which I slipped a sketchpad and some pencils and with now practised ease, swung out of the window and down the trellis.

The muggy stillness of the night before had cleared. Keeping to the winding, overgrown paths, I worked my way along the edge of the Heath until I was high on the hill, close to the Spaniard's Inn. I found a tree stump to sit on and took out my sketchbook. Trailing my pencil over the page aimlessly, I formed patterns as I thought through the events of the previous evening. Without meaning to, I began to sketch some of the people I had encountered. I tried to capture the smooth planes of Mr Holmwood's face, using my softest, blackest pencil to draw in his compelling dark eyes. With a sharpened point, I drew Dr Seward's hawk-like profile, and added a sketch of Rosamond, fascinated, beside him.

But what of Quincey Morris? Could I draw him? I had just turned the page and raised my pencil when I heard footsteps drawing near. I gathered up my things, clutching them to my chest and stood, ready to slip between the trees out of sight. But

I was too slow. Whoever it was, was moving too fast. I decided to brazen it out. The footsteps rounded the bend, and a man emerged down the slope from where I was standing.

It was as if I had conjured him out of thin air with the lifting of my pencil. Quincey Morris stopped on the path, looking up at me. He was bareheaded and in shirt sleeves. He had his jacket slung over one arm and his hat hanging from the other hand.

'Well now, Miss Lucy,' he said, strolling closer. 'What a pleasure it is to find you in this clearing. Like a fawn, startled.'

'I heard your tales of hunting last night, Mr Morris,' I said, 'I hope you have not brought your Winchester rifle with you, if you mistake me for a fawn.'

He raised his arms wide. 'I am as you see me. Entirely disarmed.'

'Disarmed or unarmed, Mr Morris?'

'Both, Miss Lucy, both,' he said and walked nearer.

He was standing so close to me now I could smell him. There was a fresh, clean tang to his sweat, a hint of tobacco and something spiced– not hair oil, as his hair was loose, long and untamed. Rum, perhaps? I was acutely conscious that we were alone in an isolated part of the Heath. That we were not talking. That we were standing closer together than decorum permitted. I raised my gaze to his face. He let his eyes—hazel, strangely light and bright, like cat's eyes—play over my face with delicious slowness, and then moved his gaze down the full length of me. I had never had anyone look at me in such a way. It was impossibly discourteous, and yet I did not object. I stood and let him look.

'Well, well, Miss Lucy,' he said, very quietly, 'Aren't you the prime article?'

And in a single fluid motion, he let his hat and coat fall to the ground, slipped an arm around my waist and lowered his mouth onto mine.

I was right – he knew how to kiss. He knew how to press his

lips onto mine, both softly and insistently, how to tease my lips apart, how to hold me against him with both strength and gentleness. My sketchpad and pencil dropped from my numb fingers. The universe was concentrated in the small, warm place where our mouths joined. It went on for a moment, or for hours. I had no sense of time passing. But when he finally released me and stepped back, the core of me felt molten and intensely hot. My breath came shallow and fast.

'This did not unfold quite as I had intended,' he said calmly. 'But if you're expecting a grovelling apology, Miss Lucy, I'm afraid I'm all out.'

'I'm not sure I understand.'

'I was on my way to call on you, in the correct and English way,' he said. He flicked a calling card from his shirt pocket and let it play between his fingers. 'But as I came up the hill toward your house, I saw you slip from the gate. You glanced around to check you hadn't been seen, and darted off across the road. I went to follow you, but by the time I made my way onto the Heath, you'd disappeared. I'll warrant you know these parts better than I do.'

I nodded. I did not trust myself to speak.

'I've been looking for you ever since. I promised myself if I made it to the top of this hill and couldn't find you, I'd give up and go and leave my card at your door, the way Art taught me to.'

Art. Arthur. Mr Holmwood.

'But it seems the angels kept a watch for me. Because here you were.' He took a step closer, and his voice was slow and deep. 'I'm sure it's not the done thing for a man who's just met a young lady such as yourself to kiss her. But when I saw you last night, well – I thought I would mightily like to do so. When the opportunity presented itself, it seemed like providence. I thought that if I did, and you didn't want me to, you'd tell me right enough, or push me away, or slap me. But you didn't.'

'I did not.'

'Should I take it then that you have no objection?'

I shook my head. He moved in even closer, but did not take me in his arms. He stood near enough for me to feel his heat, and the small motion of his breathing. Without meaning to, I matched my breathing with his. I imagined our hearts adopting the same rhythm. He inclined his head towards me, the smallest amount and waited for me to close the gap between our mouths. I did so with eagerness.

The sun was high in the sky when he walked me back to the garden gate. I stole one last, lingering kiss before darting in and running swiftly around the side of the house. In a matter of minutes, I had scrambled up the trellis and into my open bedroom window. I drew down the sash and, before I closed the curtains, dared to look out. Quincey stood by the gate and he raised a hand in nonchalant greeting before thrusting his hands into his pockets and strolling off down the hill.

I stripped off my crumpled clothing and thrust it into the bottom of the wardrobe. I pulled on the dress Beatrice had laid out for me and spent some minutes taming my hair. My face in the glass was flushed, my lips swollen and soft. Would Mother notice? I hardly cared. My body tingled and I could still feel the heat of his hands on my waist. That such sensations were possible, that people could make each other feel this way... why does everyone not spend every minute of every day doing so?

When I opened my door, I was surprised to hear bustle downstairs, and Mother's voice raised in sharp command. I walked down the stairs. She was standing in the hallway.

'Lucy!' she said, 'There you are. I knocked on your door earlier, but...'

'I was asleep,' I said quickly, 'I am so sorry. A headache.'

'I trust you are recovered. We have guests this afternoon.'

'Guests?'

'It is Thursday. Have you forgotten our "At Home"? Your dress will do. But your hair...'

'What about it?'

'You are a young woman now,' she said. 'No longer a gauche schoolgirl. You would do well to wear it up.'

A picture flashed in my mind of Quincey tangling his fingers in my tumbling hair as he kissed me. I had not been a gauche schoolgirl in that moment.

'I will ask Beatrice to fix it,' I said demurely.

I came downstairs at ten to four o'clock, as Maude and Emmeline swept into the drawing room on a gust of excited chatter. Then Rosamond arrived.

'I was quite exhausted this morning,' she said, 'I could scarcely bring myself to rise before noon. What has your day held so far, Lucy?'

I was afraid that colour would flush in my cheeks, as I thought about what had happened that morning on the Heath.

'A little drawing,' I said. 'But not enough reading or study. I need to refocus my efforts.'

'What are you currently reading?'

'I am interested in the folklore of the Balkan states,' I said, 'having travelled there. My father bought some fascinating books concerned with those wild lands. I have been reading about the Carpathian region, as well as a collection of folk tales of the Magyars.'

'Gracious! What are the Magyars?'

'Some of the indigenous peoples of Hungary are known as such.'

She grimaced. 'Why would you read such books?'

She seemed determined to argue with me. An awkward silence fell between us.

'Why, this morning, I think,' I heard my Mother say to Mrs Howarth, and then: 'Lucy? Is that not correct?'

'I beg your pardon, Mother?'

'Dr Seward. He called here this morning, did he not? But we were not yet ready to receive callers.' She laughed, 'Perhaps it is due his medical training that he thinks we should all be up with the dawn chorus!'

'Or perhaps,' said Mrs Howarth ponderously, 'his eagerness to see members of your household outweighed his good manners.'

Mother smiled serenely. 'Well, we shall see. He will be joining us shortly, I believe, along with Mr Holmwood.'

A buzz passed through the assembled group. How dull, I thought, how they all perk up at the thought of male company. They are like animals in cages, eagerly anticipating the approach of the zookeeper.

I turned to Rosamond to whisper a comment to that effect, but she was gone. I looked around the room and saw that she was standing by the window. I rose and walked to her.

'Are you all right?' I asked.

'Why did you not say?' she said, her voice low and harsh.

'Say what?' I was perplexed.

She looked at me, and I was shocked at the venom in her glance.

'That Dr Seward had called here this morning. Why did you not mention it?'

'I...' I was at a loss as to how to reply. 'I did not see him,' I said finally.

She took a long breath and then said quietly.

'Funnily enough, he did not call at our residence.'

At that moment, the gentlemen were admitted. Dr Seward hung back while Mr Holmwood swept in. He went straight to my mother and bowed low. While Mr Holmwood wore a coat of a rich burgundy red, Dr Seward's own attire was black and austerely cut. He looked more like a clergyman than a doctor. Despite this severity, his features were handsome, and he was tall and well formed. I could see why Rosamond might find him appealing.

Once tea had been served, Rosamond and I found ourselves seated with Mr Holmwood and Dr Seward. Mr Holmwood told us of the horse he had gone to buy that morning – a chestnut mare with, in his words, "an untameable nature."

'Another horse, Art?' Dr Seward said, 'What will the old man say?'

'He is up at Ring,' Holmwood replied. 'What he does not know will not concern him.'

'Ring?' asked Rosamond.

'Art's ancestral home,' said Dr Seward.

'Do you have any travel plans for the near future?' I asked Mr Holmwood.

'Sadly, my father is not terribly well. Our next adventure will have to wait. Although Jack here –' he gestured at Seward '– is all but ready to settle down, what with his little hospital.'

Seward laughed. 'Never mind. Quincey will always be ready to go with you.'

'I am sincerely envious,' I said, 'I had a little experience of travel with my late father and would love to see more of the world.'

'Lucy wishes to go and live among the wild gypsies of Hungary,' said Rosamond.

I detected a drop of acid in her tone. I decided to play up to her barb.

'I think I would look well in one of those embroidered gypsy aprons. I could learn to hunt on horseback with a sling or bow and arrow.'

Dr Seward looked at me seriously. 'I would not be surprised if you did, Miss Westenra. It seems to me likely that you will always achieve what you set out to do.'

Rosamond sniffed and Mr Holmwood turned to her. 'What

about you, Miss Nash? If you could travel anywhere, where would you go?'

'My ambitions are more modest, Mr Holmwood. I should like to visit Lake Windermere. I am a keen botanist, and I am told there are beautiful plants to be seen.'

'There are some rare flowers on the cliffs in that region,' Mr Holmwood said eagerly, 'They are usually seen only in the Alps or the Arctic regions. Not to mention the mosses, liverworts and lichens.'

I could not help myself, I laughed. 'Mr Holmwood! I would not have imagined you to have an interest in flora.'

'I spent much of my childhood hunting for obscure plants in boggy woods and on treacherous dunes with my mother. The gardens at Ring are something to behold. I very much hope that one day you will come to see them.'

'I am most interested in the restorative properties of plants,' Rosamond cut in.

'Plants can do many things,' Mr Holmwood said. 'My mother has created a special garden of plants with medicinal and other qualities.'

'Other qualities?' Dr Seward asked.

'Some plants are calming, while others can excite. Some can alter our perceptions of the world, causing hallucinations. Some others are extremely toxic. Mother collected them all and made a study of their various properties.'

'That sounds like a medieval poison garden,' observed Dr Seward.

'Not just poison, although some of the plants are very dangerous. The garden offers a cornucopia of experiences for the learned gardener!' Mr Holmwood smiled mischievously.

Out of the corner of my eye, I glimpsed a small shadow slipping into the room. Little Missy the cat. I was surprised. She had never been particularly enamoured of visitors and noise. Perhaps she hoped someone might give her a treat. She had always loved a drop of cooled, milky tea poured into a saucer – Pa gave it to her each evening, and I knew Beatrice gave this to her in the kitchen sometimes. Most people ignored her as she wound her way between the guests, making a slow circuit of the room, sniffing at skirts and shoes.

A moment later, I almost laughed out loud when I saw her small, cushioned shape curled neatly on Mr Holmwood's lap. That she had chosen him to bestow her attention upon was as good an endorsement as I could imagine. He looked up and saw my eyes on him. I glanced down at the cat on his lap and he smiled. He stroked her, and she purred contentedly.

CHAPTER 8

26 JANUARY 2024 – KATE

A black square appeared on my screen and I sat nervously, waiting. The square flickered into life and I saw a man with dark hair and a beard, very blue eyes and a bright smile.

'You didn't have a beard in your profile picture,' I blurted.

'Well, I'm glad to see you're not a disembodied grey egg.'

'I haven't got round to putting up a photo yet. I'm Kate Balcombe.'

'James Harker. Nice to meet you, Kate, if virtually.'

'Thanks for making time to speak to me.'

'Not at all. I'm a nerd about genealogy, so any chance to expand my knowledge... well, let's say I'm delighted to talk to you. So, you're interested in Mina? My great-great grandmother?'

'In her, and her connection to someone else. A woman – a girl really – called Lucy Westenra.' James's expression didn't change, and my heart sank. 'Does the name not mean anything to you?'

'I'm afraid not.'

'Lucy went to school in Exeter – she attended a place called The Underhill?'

'Well, there's your connection,' James said, 'Mina went there too. She was an orphan, but her aunt encouraged her to apply, and she got a scholarship. When she finished school, she became an assistant schoolmistress and lived on the premises until she married Jonathan Harker.'

'She was a few years older than Lucy, according to the dates on your family tree. Odd that they became friends. She must have been a teacher when Lucy was a pupil.'

'If she was only three years older, she would have been a very young teacher – scarcely out of her teens.'

I tried to imagine the two young women meeting more than a hundred before. Lucy – intelligent, home-educated, the only child of a rich man. Mina, orphaned scholarship girl and charity case.

'Were they two misfits who found each other?'

'To be honest, Mina's a bit of a mystery. Of all the people in my family tree, I have the least information about her. I've been able to find her date of birth only on census records – I've never been able to trace a birth certificate – nor a death certificate for that matter. That's less surprising, given that she left the country.'

'She left the country?'

'Her husband Jonathan died in 1911, and her son Quincey Harker, my great-grandfather, married in 1928. Shortly after that, she immigrated to the US. I have a record of the passenger manifest of the ship she sailed on. That was in 1930, so she would have been around sixty years old. The ship docked in New York, but I've never found any record of her after that. She could have gone on anywhere. She might have died, or remarried and changed her name... come back to the UK or gone somewhere else... but I can't find her. The trail goes cold.'

'I see.'

'Sorry,' James said, and grinned again, 'I've gone off on a tangent, it isn't Mina you're interested in, is it? It's this... Lucy?'

'Well, Mina could have played a significant part in what happened to Lucy.'

I told him about the letter, and about the correlation between the date of the letter and Lucy's and her mother's deaths. He stared at me, his eyes wide with shock.

'Wow,' he said, and leaned back in his chair. 'That's quite a story. Is there any chance I could see this letter?'

I'd expected this, and I pinged over an image of the letter and the transcript. I waited while he read it. Emotions chased across his features – shock, confusion, and, when he reached the end, sadness.

'So the letter was never sent?'

'It was under the floorboards in my room – what must have been the room of the maid – B I think stands for Beatrice. For whatever reason, Beatrice never posted it. In all likelihood, Mina received news of her friend's death and never had any idea of Lucy's cry for help.'

'That's awful. And the story has been hidden for all these years? Amazing.'

'Well...' I hesitated, but then leapt in. 'This flat actually belonged to my Mum, before she got married. She was an artist. She drew some sketches when she lived here, and from those, it looks like she knew something about Lucy and her story too.'

'Well, can't you ask her about it?'

'She died when I was six. Cancer.'

'I'm so sorry,' he said. His voice was deep and kind.

'There's more to the mystery than that,' I continued. 'I found out where the Westenra family is buried. And when I visited the churchyard, there were flowers.'

'Flowers?'

'Fresh flowers. White roses, left there a few days before I went there, I would guess. Someone else remembers Lucy, or her family, and visits the grave.'

'That's incredible!'

'I don't suppose...' I said tentatively. 'You have any letters that belonged to your great-great-grandmother? Or journals?'

'Nothing. It's odd, because Quincey was a prolific correspondent and diarist. But there are no papers from either his mother or father. Maybe Mina took them all with her when she went to America.'

'Maybe.' I felt my shoulders sag with disappointment.

James must have seen my expression, because he leaned in towards the camera.

'Listen, Kate, don't give up. Keep digging. There are lots of avenues you can try.'

'Like what?'

'Well, it sounds like Lucy's dad was a wealthy man. Follow the money. There's often information in Wills. Sometimes there's just a list of effects and money, but you might find a clue to a family feud, or a favoured friend or relative. See who's in the Will and who is left out, or who gets a small gift where they might expect more. You've got dates and places of death for the whole family. Start digging.'

He gave me a crash course on where to search for Wills and probate. I thanked him and was about to ring off when he held up a hand.

'I know I have no right to ask, but can we keep talking? I... well, anything you find might give me more clues about Mina, so I can fill in the blanks in my own story. Maybe we could help each other out? Share resources?'

I looked into his handsome, open face. I'd enjoyed our conversation, and I suspected he had too. He may be a few hours' away in Exeter, but my supply of friends was thin on the ground.

'Of course,' I grinned at him. 'Let's chat soon.'

LUCY WESTENRA'S JOURNAL

12 NOVEMBER 1893

While I was eating breakfast this morning, Mrs Staines came into the dining room.

'A gentleman is here, Miss,' she said. 'He says he knows it is early, but thought you might be awake. Shall I tell him to come in?'

'Of course,' I said, dabbing my mouth with my napkin. 'Although I do not have long. I am going to church.'

Soon, Mr Holmwood stood in the doorway of the dining room, his hat in his hand, his bright hair shining in the early morning sun.

'I am so glad to have found you still here, Miss Westenra,' he said, bowing. 'I know that you attend church in Hendon. I thought perhaps I might take you there in my carriage?'

'Oh,' I said, caught off guard. 'I, er... it is my habit to walk.'

'Would you prefer to do that?' he asked. 'Then if I may accompany you, we shall walk together.'

I was surprised. He did not strike me as a man who would undertake a walk across muddy fields.

'Are you sure?' I said, glancing at his highly polished boots and smart coat.

'Never more sure. It is such a beautiful morning.'

I fetched my cloak and hat, while Mr Holmwood gave instructions to his coachman. Then he offered me his arm, and we set off. The walk was new to him and he asked many questions as we strode along. He wanted to know about the ownership of the various farms, about the public houses, shops and taverns we passed, and the history of our church. Our conversation was easy and light. He was a good listener, and an observant companion. He pointed out some trees and plants along the way, again drawing on his encyclopaedic knowledge of botany.

As we passed into the valley between Golders Green and Hendon, I paused to look at the land alongside Dollis Brook. Cows grazed along the banks, and I could see that the ground was waterlogged.

'I see Mr Boyden has not yet decided what to do with this land,' I said, almost without thinking.

'Mr Boyden?' asked Mr Holmwood.

'My Father's manager,' I explained, 'Pa bought this land, but in summer, and when the winter rains came, it was clear he could not build on the banks of the brook. When he died, the issue of what to do with this land was as yet unresolved.'

'You are knowledgeable about your Father's business,' he observed.

'I know a little, but my information is no longer current. Pa kept a ledger of his affairs in the library at home, but of course that is more than a year out of date now. I would dearly love to visit the offices in Chatham Street and see what Mr Boyden is doing. Father trusted him implicitly, but I am still curious.'

'I do not think that would be a good idea,' he said, and I glanced at him surprised.

'Why not?'

'Mr Boyden would see your visit as interfering, I am certain. Feminine power is a mysterious thing, Lucy. I for one, have no doubt that it is women who run the world. It is, however, a power best exercised with stealth. Men like Mr Boyden will never acquiesce to a hectoring woman. But they will respond to gentle, pretty persuasion. A little flutter of the lashes, a tentative request, and the Mr Boydens of the world will be doing your bidding without even realising they have been led.'

'Perhaps if I was trying to influence the colour of the morning room curtains, that might work. But I scarcely think giggling and sighing will make Mr Boyden accountable to me in the management of Westenra and Co.'

'It is not your company, is it?'

'No, I...' I was taken aback.

'It is my understanding that your mother is the majority shareholder, and Mr Boyden is tasked with managing all business affairs, unless your mother decides otherwise?'

'Which she will never do.'

'Which she will never do,' Mr Holmwood agreed. 'But it is not your company to run.'

'It will be,' I said stubbornly, 'One day it will be. And then Mr Boyden would do well to listen...'

'To your husband? Surely the man you marry will manage the affairs of the business?'

He was not the first young man who had declared his opinions on the place of women to me thus, and I was sure he would not be the last. I could not help a faint feeling of disappointment however. I had hoped he might be more enlightened.

'Why look at that magpie!' Mr Holmwood said, pointing 'He is giving that poor cat a stern talking to.'

When we came to the gate of the church, his carriage waited outside, the coachman bundled in his coat. Mr Holmwood opened the gate for me and tipped his hat.

'Good morning, Miss Westenra.'

'Are you not coming in to the service?'

'I suspect were I to do so, it would only cause gossip. Alfred here...' he tipped his head towards his driver, '... will be happy to collect you after the service and take you home.'

'And you, Mr Holmwood?'

'I will pay my respects at your father's resting place and then I must be off. I wish you a lovely day, Miss Westenra.' He gave me his graceful bow, then briefly touched my fingertips before striding off through the churchyard.

What a surprising man he is. Charming and sociable, yet also thoughtful. Before I could think about what I was doing, I crept through the churchyard, and stopped at the corner of the church. Peering around, I saw him, standing beside our family mausoleum, hat pressed to his chest, praying.

* * *

After the service, the wind was keener, and a fine drizzle had begun to fall. I was relieved to ride home in Mr Holmwood's carriage, wrapped in a warm rug. When I got home, Mother had but lately returned from her own church service. She would be surprised to see me. With the walk, I was often not home from Hendon much before luncheon. As I walked into the drawing room, unpinning my hat, I found her standing by the window. She turned to me, raising one questioning eyebrow.

'Is that...?'

'Mr Holmwood's carriage. Yes.'

'Why did he not come in? He would have been most welcome to stay for luncheon.'

'He was not in the carriage,' I said. I told her briefly what had transpired that morning. She was horrified that I had made Mr Holmwood walk to Hendon.

'I did not make him walk!' I countered fiercely. 'He was well within his rights to go in his carriage, or to let me walk on my own as I had planned to do.'

She shook her head in disgust and went to sit in her chair by the fire.

'You are wilful, Lucy, perversely so. A gentleman like Mr Holmwood...'

'Will take me as he finds me,' I snapped.

Before she could answer, I swept from the room.

I spent the rest of this afternoon poring over a history of France. At four o'clock, I stretched my aching limbs. I looked out of the window and saw that once more, the sky had cleared. There were a couple of hours of daylight left and a warm golden light fell across the driveway of the house. I piled up my books and cautiously opened the library door. The corridors of the house were quiet, and Mother's door was firmly closed. Once in my room with the door locked, it was a few minutes' work to change my clothes and swing down the trellis.

The wind on the Heath was keen, and as I had suspected, the paths were muddy. I gathered up my skirts and walked quickly to reach the crest of the hill. Without planning to do so, I returned to the clearing where I had previously encountered Quincey Morris. I sat on my tree stump and looked out across the valley. It was too much to hope that he would choose this afternoon to come to the Heath. I was not even sure if I wanted him to. He had aroused such powerful sensations in me, but I knew next to nothing about him. He had not called on us in the conventional way. But had I not vowed to scorn the social rituals my Mother forced me to endure? Should I not embrace Quincey's free-spiritedness? Chance encounters, physical pleasure, no promises or false compliments... was this not the enlightened way?

Either way, no one was ascending the path to my secret hiding place. The wind had begun to whistle through my shawl, and the sun was sinking. I sighed and began to make my way back down to the house.

Quincey found me close to the gate. He whispered my name and then caught my hand. He drew me under the branches of a weeping beech tree and pulled me into his arms, kissing me hungrily. I tangled my fingers in his thick auburn hair. When he finally released me, I was panting, as if I had been running. His eyes glittered dangerously.

'Oh, Lucy.'

He took my hand and dropped a soft kiss in the centre of my palm, and I felt a sharp, pleasurable shock between my legs, so acute it was almost like pain. I closed my eyes for a second and concentrated only on the touch of his lips and tongue on my hand. I swayed, almost losing my balance, and he caught me around the waist. When I opened my eyes again, I was shocked to see that dusk had begun to fall. I shivered. It was properly cold now.

'I must... I have to go...'

'I know,' he said gently, releasing me. 'Come along. I'll see you home.'

We walked in silence for a few moments. I was shaking with the cold now, and he put an arm around my shoulders, warming me against his body. We kept to the shadows, but there was no risk of seeing anyone. The keen cold had driven everyone indoors.

'It isn't practical for us to meet like this. Out on the Heath, I mean,' he said as we opened the garden gate and slipped inside. 'Winter's coming in fast.'

I nodded, 'Although I can't imagine my Mother would consider our behaviour appropriate were we to meet in the drawing room.'

He grinned at this. 'You may have a point there, Miss Lucy. As to my own situation, it's not fixed up any better. I'm sharing rooms with Art at present, and even if I had my own quarters I can't see as how I could get you in there without a scandal.' He paused. 'There is, of course... the secret route into your own room.'

I looked at him quickly, 'The trellis?'

'You scramble up and down it quick enough, and I'm an agile fellow...'

'But what if someone were to come in?'

'You could lock your door.'

'I could...' I said dubiously.

'And if I came say, after midnight, when the servants and your mother were fast asleep, and we were mighty quiet...'

I imagined Quincey in my bed. I imagined what it would be like to have the leisure to touch him and be touched by him in a warm, dark room. I let out a ragged sigh.

'We would have to be very quiet indeed,' I said.

'Well, Miss Lucy, I can be stealthy as anything,' he said. 'It's your cries that might rouse the household. If you swear to be silent, so do I.'

We were now under my window. It was almost dark.

'Up you go,' he said, taking my hand and placing it on the lowest branch of the wisteria. 'I'll see you tonight, at midnight. Leave the sash unfastened.'

I felt almost sick with anticipation. I kissed him one more time, then I scrambled up the trellis and into my window. Now, as I write this by candlelight, I await his arrival...

13 NOVEMBER 1893

When I came down for breakfast, Mother was already in her chair. She glanced up as I came into the room.

'My goodness, Lucy!' she said sharply, 'Are you ill? Perhaps you have been sleepwalking again? You are uncommonly pale, and the shadows under your eyes ... my goodness! Perhaps you should spend the day in bed.'

Bed. Just the word brought back last night. My head filled with a flurry of images and remembered sensations.

'I think my sleep was disturbed.'

'Have a nap this afternoon,' Mother said. 'We are expected for an early dinner at the Howarths this evening. I would like to see you looking your best.'

She rose to leave the room. I shrank back as she passed. I imagine if she passed close enough, she might smell Quincey on me. I could certainly smell him on myself – the essence of him seems pressed into my skin. After breakfast, I would ask Beatrice to draw me a bath.

I fell on the food Eliza had placed on my plate. I was ravenous. As I buttered toast and devoured slice after slice, I let images from the night before play through my mind. I saw Quincey's dark shadow as he climbed in through the window. I remembered the feeling of his warm fingers as he drew my nightgown over my head. I recalled the firelight playing on our bare skin as we lay together. I remembered the extraordinary sensations he roused in me with his fingers and then his mouth. I had had to turn my face sideways into the pillow to stifle the sounds that escaped me as he lowered his face between my legs.

His touch built an unbearable pressure, which made me quiver and writhe until it burst, and shards of electricity seemed to shoot down every limb. After he wrought this gasping climax from me, he rested his cheek on my slick thigh and smiled up at me.

'Well, then,' he whispered. 'That was some time coming. I thought of doing that the very first time I laid eyes on you, Miss Lucy.'

Later he lay on his back, one arm raised behind his head, naked and magnificent, and encouraged me to sate my curiosity. I examined every inch of his strange male body, touching and cataloguing the differences between our forms. He showed me how to give him pleasure too, using my hands and mouth.

Feeling him arch at my touch brought the most extraordinary sense of power.

After some time, he eased away from me. He reached into his bag and produced a small tin. It was printed with Egyptian hieroglyphics and bore the trade name "Ramses". I thought he might be about to take snuff, but he opened the tin and produced a small circle of what looked like rubber.

'What is that?' I whispered.

'Well, Lucy, it's a sheath, or what we call a French letter,' he explained. 'It's a little trick so that we can enjoy ourselves without consequences, if you take my meaning.'

As he rolled the rubber casing over his length, I recalled reading of such measures in Pa's more frank literature. In days gone by, such items were made from sheep's gut, but this version looked most scientific and effective. Quincey eased me onto my back, and with slow concentration, he eased himself inside me. It was an extraordinary sensation, both thrilling and disturbing. As he began to move, I watched his eyes lose focus. He seemed to move both closer and further away, absorbed in his pleasure, but fused into my body in the most intimate and all-encompassing way. I liked it, but not as much as the touch of his mouth and fingers.

We spent the night lying together and finding new ways to give and receive pleasure. The effort was silent and intense – we were too afraid to speak above a whisper and risk being over-heard. Finally, he lifted his head from where it rested on my breasts.

'I'd better be going, Lucy, my dear,' he said. 'The light's creeping over the horizon out there.'

After he had brought me to gasping pleasure one final time, he slipped from the bed and dressed. We spoke no more, and he disappeared through the window. He has made no promise to return.

After my bath, I dressed and went to the library. Unsurprisingly, my thoughts turned to the notion of sin, and I went looking for religious and moral texts on the subject of carnal pleasure. Their views are unequivocal. I am damned and fallen. The pleasures Quincey and I experienced together have a place only in the marital bed. Outside of it, they are evil. This distinction seems arbitrary. How could the wearing of a ring change the moral aspect of an act?

The books also suggest that our pleasures should be 'moderate.' Our nakedness and frank explorations are contrary to everything I had ever been taught about modesty. And yet I had consented enthusiastically to everything he asked of me. There was, perversely, an innocence to what we did. We played like Adam and Eve in the garden before they knew the meaning of shame. I have questioned my conscience, and after some deliberation, I conclude that I feel no disgrace, only pleasure at the experience, and a desire to repeat it.

14 NOVEMBER 1893

Mr Holmwood visited the house again today, and was, as always, friendly and easy company.

20 NOVEMBER 1893

Mr Holmwood visited again. He and Mother seem to get on very well.

22 NOVEMBER 1893

Quincey came to my bedroom window last night. Bliss.

30 NOVEMBER 1893

I entered the drawing room to find Mr Holmwood deep in discussion with Mother. They seem to have become close confidantes, and spend many hours by the fire in quiet conversation.

15 DECEMBER 1893

No Quincey at my window for two weeks. Last week, we saw him at an event in town. He was courtly and charming and behaved just as a friendly acquaintance might. Then last night, he knocked on the glass. His behaviour was not courtly, but he pleasured me until I gasped for mercy and then grinned at me in the dark, before disappearing once more through the window, as if he had never been there.

25 DECEMBER 1893

Mother and I were invited to join the Howarths for dinner on Christmas Day, and a very pleasant day it was.

27 DECEMBER 1893

Today, Mother and I hosted our largest ever 'At Home,' with a table groaning with festive treats. The drawing room was full of chattering friends, and the fire blazed warmly. I went to the door to say goodbye to a departing guest, and I stood alone for a moment admiring the Christmas tree in the hallway. It was a large fir, festooned with cornucopiae, each filled with sweetmeats. We had made colourful paper chains to drape round the tree, and the effect was arresting. Fancy cakes hung from ribbons on the branches. How Pa would have loved it.

Grief is always a stealthy thief, and it came to me then, tiptoeing up and robbing me of joy. How have I moved on so quickly? It is not yet eighteen months since his passing, and I am living as if he had never existed. I felt the pain almost as a physical blow and it doubled me over. I caught at the newel post and breathed deeply, unable to stop the tears that sprang to my eyes. At just that moment, Dr Seward emerged from the drawing room and caught sight of me.

'Miss Westenra?' he said, 'Are you all right?'

He was too close for me to dissemble. There was no time to dash the tears from my cheeks or to adopt a bright smile. I could only be honest.

'Oh Dr Seward,' I said. 'This time of year is notorious for ghosts, is it not? The Christmas tree has reminded me of my father. I miss him most dreadfully.'

Dr Seward spoke in a quiet voice. 'You have my deepest sympathy, Miss Westenra. I lost both of my own parents before I reached adulthood.'

'I am sorry to hear that.'

'My father died in a riding accident when I was ten years old. My mother never recovered from his death. She fell into a most profound melancholy and would not rise from her bed. She would not wash or eat properly. The doctors seemed unable to help her, so they gave her laudanum and she spent several years in a torpor. She was emaciated – and when she took ill with a chill, she could not fight it. It turned to pneumonia, and she died. She was not yet forty.'

'I am so sorry,' I said. 'You must have felt quite alone.'

'I did. I was cared for by a succession of tutors, and was nominally under the guardianship of relatives, but they did not bother with me much.'

'Do you suppose your mother's mental torment is what brought you to your current profession?'

'Exactly. I could not believe that nothing could have been done for her. Surely, with all the wonders of medicine at our disposal, we can do better for those in mental turmoil than drug them and chain them?'

'And so you undertook medical studies?'

'I did a great deal of research to find training that suited my purposes. I knew I did not merely wish to learn surgery at a London hospital. Eventually, I resolved to study under a Professor Van Helsing, who is a resident of Amsterdam. He takes on a small class of pupils each year. He considers himself a philosopher and a metaphysician as well as a doctor.'

Dr Seward laughed at a memory, and I looked at him in wonder. He was more animated than I had ever seen him.

'There was a time,' he said eagerly, 'when we were engaged in an amputation. A bargeman had badly broken a leg, and the limb had turned necrotic. Removing it was the only possible way to save his life. One of my classmates, a Jan Boerma, a nervous fellow, was tasked with severing the limb. Professor Van Helsing stood by to help him, grasping the patient's thigh to steady it. But Boerma was so nervous. The hand holding the scalpel shook. It skidded from the diseased skin and pierced the Professor's thumb, where he held the leg!'

I tried not to look shocked. No gentleman would consider this an appropriate story to tell a lady.

He continued: 'I realised immediately that the scalpel likely carried the poison of gangrene, and that should it enter the Professor's bloodstream, it could prove fatal. I did not pause to think of decorum. I grabbed the Professor's hand and sucked hard on the wound, drawing out the blood. I spat it out upon the floor and then did so again until his blood flowed freely. He thanked me most profusely, and I do believe that was the moment when our lifelong friendship was born.'

I noted the high colour in Dr Seward's cheeks, and wondered if he was not perhaps drunk. That would account for his uncharacteristic candour and volubility. He swayed back on his heels, and then corrected his alignment. I saw that my diagnosis was correct. I liked drunken Dr Seward a great deal more than the sober version. I had learned more about him in this brief conversation than I had in months of polite social discourse.

'What else did you cover in your studies?' I prompted.

'Well,' he began, 'The Professor is a profoundly religious man, and all his teaching is rooted in his Christian faith. There was one time...'

'Jack, you old devil!' Mr Holmwood came strolling out of the drawing room. 'Are you stealing away our Miss Westenra and keeping her all to yourself? That won't do at all.'

Dr Seward flushed even redder than he had before, and I saw the reality of our situation dawn on him. He had spoken with shocking inappropriateness to a young lady. I saw him recall his tale of gangrene and surgery and blood, and I saw the colour leach from his face.

'Dr Seward has been excellent company,' I said. 'I was overcome with sadness, remembering my dear old Pa, and he has comforted me and distracted me with fascinating stories of his training.' I turned to face Dr Seward and made sure he was looking into my eyes. 'I am so very grateful for his kindness.'

Mr Holmwood looked from one of us to the other. Then he smiled his easy smile and offered me his arm.

'Well, my dear, you must come back into the drawing room at once. There is a most fierce argument brewing about the words of a song in one of Mr Gilbert's comic operas, and the Misses Howarth are threatening to sing. It is a quite desperate situation, and only you can bring us all back from the brink.'

I laughed, 'Well, as long as it is the Misses Howarth that wish to sing, and not Colonel Donnelly, all may be well. He has a voice akin to the foghorn on HMS Pinafore!'

CHAPTER 9

2 FEBRUARY 2024 – KATE

J practically bounced in my chair with excitement, waiting for the video call to connect. I'd texted James as soon as I made my discovery, and to my surprise, he replied immediately.

"Give me five minutes to make a cup of tea and then let's chat! x" his text read. I couldn't help but notice the "x".

Soon, his smiling face popped up on my screen and he held up his tea in a salute. It was a battered white mug with the words "Archaeologists Rock!" in faded writing on the side.

'Are you an archaeologist?'

He frowned, confused for a second, and then turned the mug to face him. 'Nothing so glamorous. I'm a web developer. This was left by an old housemate. It's just the perfect size and shape. You know how there's only ever one mug that's just right?'

In answer, I held up my own floral china mug.

'I've carried this with me all over the world. Wherever I've lived, it's brought me comfort. I think this mug is the closest thing to home for me.'

'Have you lived in a lot of places?'

I filled him in on my travels, and he raised an eyebrow in surprise.

'Very exotic. I'm appallingly poorly travelled.'

'It's not too late.'

'Maybe you're right. I am footloose and fancy-free, as my mum likes to say – although she doesn't always say it in a good way. I've disappointed her by not presenting her with the requisite wife and two-and-a-half kids.'

'Well...' I said, 'No one likes half a kid.'

James laughed. 'Well? I got your message. What have you found? Spill!'

'Charles Westenra's Last Will and Testament! You were right... it's quite a shocker.'

James's bright blue eyes were fixed on my face and I felt myself colour. I looked down at the notes and printouts I'd spread on my desk.

'He was loaded. I mean, properly rich. It's not surprising, given the size of his house, but his property empire was significant. Anyway, almost all of it went to his wife – except he had the library at Hillingham declared as a separate property – both the room and its contents – and he left it to Lucy!' James's gasp of surprise was gratifying. 'I'm not quite sure how that would have worked, but I suppose it was only temporary... when Lucy's mother died, the rest of it would have come to her, anyway.'

'Probably,' James agreed.

'But the gift of the library... interesting, isn't it? Not jewellery or money, or gowns... Books. Obviously, Charles had ambitions for his daughter. Unusual for the time, don't you think?'

'Yeah.'

'What blows my mind is that all of this – the intrigue, the

Will, the library itself – all happened right here. Under my feet. In this house.'

'You say the house is divided into flats now?'

'Yes, has been for years.'

'So you have no idea which was Lucy's room? Or where the library might have been?'

'Not a clue. Not that there'd be anything to be found. This all happened more than a hundred years ago.'

'Still... James said wistfully, 'still. It'd be so great to know.'

After we'd rung off, I drummed my fingers on the edge of the desk. Then, on impulse, I grabbed my keys and let myself out of the flat. I looked across at the door of Flat 7. It must be the mirror image of mine... a number of small rooms off a central corridor.

I descended the narrow staircase and found myself on the landing outside flats 5 and 6. On this floor, the ceilings were much higher and the corridor wider. This must have been where the family had had their bedrooms. At the turn of the stairs, there was a tall window through which light flooded, looking out over the wintry garden.

Diagonally opposite the window, next to the door of Flat 6, there was a narrow door. It looked old, part of the fabric of the original house. I hesitated, then turned the doorknob, expecting it to be locked. But to my surprise, the door opened inwards. The room within was long, narrow and bare, with a window at the far end. The walls were crowded with metal racks of gas pipes and electrical cables – the room was obviously a point through which the building's services passed. It wouldn't always have been so – the house was built well before piped gas or electricity. What had the room been originally? A room for a nanny? Or maybe when guests came to stay, their maid or valet might have slept there.

I walked down the next flight of stairs to the first floor and paused between Numbers 3 and 4. There was another floor-to-ceiling window, but no corresponding narrow door here. The rooms on this floor were probably bedrooms too. I pressed close to the window, looking down into the garden. The sun was setting and it looked desolate – the grass was patchy and lumpy and the flower beds bare. I tried to imagine how it might have looked in Lucy's day. There might have been a smooth expanse of lawn, with neat rose beds. Maybe there was a kitchen garden where they grew their own food.

I sensed rather than heard something to my left, and turned my head. The door of Flat 4 had opened a crack, and a shaft of light spilled out. Where it fell on the carpet, the light was distorted by a twisted shadow. Someone was standing behind the door, watching me. I felt the unseen person's gaze like a cold touch on my cheek. I waited for them to speak but there was only silence. Gathering my courage, I turned towards them. The door eased closed with a quiet but emphatic click.

LUCY WESTENRA'S JOURNAL

21 FEBRUARY 1894 – LUCY WESTENRA'S JOURNAL

In an attempt to escape the dismal weather, Mina and I have united to enjoy a short holiday in Lyme Regis. When I initially received Mina's invitation my heart sank. I did not imagine Mother would permit me to go, but to my surprise, she acquiesced easily.

How can I describe my delight at seeing Mina again? When I stepped off the train at Axminster, she was standing on the platform, a pretty straw hat pinned jauntily atop her chestnut curls, her dear, dear face bright with happiness and anticipation. We embraced and I did not want to let her go, but she drew back to look at me.

'Why, Lucy Westenra,' she said, 'you are a woman! And a beautiful one at that.'

I laughed and clasped her to me once more. 'Oh Mina,' I said, 'I am truly delighted to see you. We have been apart for far too long.'

It is more than a year and a half since we were last together in the heart-breaking days after Pa's death. Yet within minutes it was as if we had never been apart. We spoke without ceasing in the carriage. We took a brief pause when we arrived at the rooms in Lyme Regis, while Mrs White made us comfortable and brought us tea, and then we talked and talked again until the sun set.

How have I managed all these months without her? She is so intelligent, so calmly practical and insightful. We spoke about the books we had been reading. We discussed religion, the political situation, the impact of history, and we talked about the place of women in the modern world. Mina tells me that Jonathan's employer, Mr Hawkins, had been tasked with finding a property for a foreign nobleman who had most specific requirements. Mr Hawkins is not well enough to undertake the task, so Jonathan will be doing a great deal of travelling to fulfil this obligation. Thus, in the summer, Mina will be alone. We decided that when Mother and I visit Whitby, she will join us.

Mrs White served us a simple supper and once we had eaten, we went upstairs. There were two small beds in the cosy room, but we pushed them together so we might lie side by side. I knew I should sleep – it was late and I was tired from the journey. We lay in silence in the dark, listening to the waves crash on the beach beyond the window. I felt ready to share confidences with Mina in the darkness of the room.

'Mina,' I whispered. She responded by reaching for my hand in the darkness. I squeezed her warm fingers. 'Do you...' I began, but could not find the words to continue.

'Do I what?' she said, and her voice was gently encouraging. 'Come, Lucy, I have seen a thoughtful look in your eyes all day. There is something you wish to ask me. Or is it something you need to tell? You know how I love you. There is nothing you cannot share. I will never judge you, and I will always keep your secrets.'

'Do you and Jonathan...' I stopped. I did not know how to put what I wanted to know into words without sounding vulgar. 'Do you experience physical closeness?'

She was silent for a long time. 'I trust you are speaking of a closeness more... intimate than the joining of hands or kissing?'

'I am,' I said.

'We are in an... unusual position,' she said hesitantly, 'in that neither of us has parents or guardians. And we are, of course, engaged to be married. Nevertheless, Jonathan is committed to preserving my virtue, and his own until our wedding night.'

'Jonathan is committed? And what about you?'

'For myself, I know that I have found my life's companion. We are as one in our minds. I see no reason why we should not...'

'... Be as one in your bodies?' I finished for her. 'But what about God's censure? The wages of sin?' I was probing to see what her response would be. Mina had always been more religious than I.

'I have always wondered whether it is God's censure we fear, or man's,' she said. 'I feel our love is pure and whole, and blessed by God, whether we are married or not. As I say, there is nothing to prevent our closeness. There are few limits on our relationship other than the bounds of decency.' I snorted, and I could see the gleam of her smile in the darkness. 'I know too well your views on the "bounds of decency", Lucy.'

'We shame people for human frailty,' I said hotly, 'and we know well enough that many people – many men – commit acts in private for which they condemn others publicly.'

Mina laughed softly, as she so often did at my heated pronouncements. She reached over and stroked my hair away from my forehead.

'But why are you asking me this, Lucy? Is it a concern for you? Is there someone with whom you wish to experience physical closeness?'

I got out of bed then, and sat on the windowsill. The moon

spilled her light extravagantly across the sea. Now I had to put this into words, it seemed impossibly difficult. What if Mina was horrified, and rejected me? What if she told my mother? She was sitting up now, her hair in its neat plait draped over one shoulder. I looked into her kind eyes.

'There is someone with whom I have experienced it already,' I said quietly. I watched her face and it did not alter. She nodded.

'Do you want to tell me?' she said.

And hesitantly, slowly, I did. I told her of my first encounter with Quincey on the Heath and his subsequent visits to my bedroom. I told her of the pleasure. I told her I did not love him, and, I was certain, that he did not love me. She did not interrupt, and waited until I had finished my tale.

'I do not judge you,' she said quietly, 'but it seems likely that these activities must at some point result in him getting you with child. And then what will happen?'

'Quincey takes steps to make sure I will not be made pregnant.'

Mina frowned at me. She was of course, relatively innocent where these matters were concerned. She had not had access to the frank and unambiguous books to be found in my father's library. I explained what would be required for me to conceive, and Quincey's careful use of the rubber sheaths he ordered from Germany.

'But what if, at some point he loses control and...?'

'He will not. If he did, and it resulted in a pregnancy, he would have to marry me, and Quincey is unambiguous on this point. He is not the marrying kind.'

'And this does not bother you?'

'Not in the slightest. He is not a serious person. I could not imagine spending my life with him in any case. Besides, I will do anything to avoid the prison of marriage.' She gave a small frown. 'Oh Mina, my darling, it is not a prison for everyone. But for me... the thought of a man who would own my property, who would dictate what I did with my home, my money, my body...' I shook my head vehemently. 'And yet, I enjoy the closeness I experience with Quincey. I enjoy the friendly company of other men too – Mr Holmwood is most congenial. Even Dr Seward is amusing. Why can I not have them in my life without having them own me like a pet dog?'

'Because ...' Mina, paused and thought. 'Because society will not permit it.'

'On the contrary. Society may disapprove, but they cannot force me. I am my mother's only heir. I will be a woman of means and I can make my own choices. It is a rare privilege and I mean to make the most of it.'

Mina exhaled. 'Lucy Westenra, you are a most exceptional woman. I wish more had your courage and originality.'

Soon after, Mina slipped into sleep. I lay close to her, watching the dark curve of lashes lying against her dear cheek, holding her hand pressed between my own. When I read some of the writings of the New Women, they proposed that men and women should be allowed to see each other asleep before proposing or accepting. Oh, if Jonathan could glimpse Mina thus, how he would yearn to press a kiss on the soft ruby of her plump lower lip. How he might love to stroke the smooth curve of her neck and shoulder. Perhaps his scruples with regard to her virtue might then fall away...

LETTER FROM LUCY WESTENRA TO MINA MURRAY

11 MARCH 1894

My dearest Mina,

Given the confidences we shared in Lyme Regis, it occurs to me that we should be careful in what we write to one another in letters that might be intercepted by others. I propose that we write any confidences we wish to share in shorthand. I cannot wait to be with you in Whitby so we can speak freely.

All my love,

Lucy.

12 MARCH 1894

I kept the letter under my pillow overnight, and the next morning walked to post it. But once I had sent it, I wondered if I had chosen the best course of action. If someone intercepted our letters and read them, might they not be suspicious that we were corresponding in something resembling a cypher or code? I pondered this problem, pacing in the library. Unable to find a solution, I took up Mina's letter and went to slip it into its envelope and take it back up to my room. At that moment inspiration came to me. The envelope! Mother has always insisted we shun shop-bought envelopes and fold our own, using the best quality, creamy paper. She said that the quality of the envelope and the penmanship were an indication of our social standing.

I took up a sheet of paper and folded it into the shape of an envelope. Empty and with the flap folded open, there was a visible expanse of paper, which would need to be left unmarked. When I opened the paper out, however, there was a large portion of the surface upon which I could write, which, once the envelope was folded, would be invisible. I could use this secret surface for private letters to my friend.

I will also begin a new journal. I will write only in shorthand. This first of my journals will stay concealed in the hidey hole in the library, for it contains many inflammatory secrets.

4 APRIL 1894 – LUCY WESTENRA'S SECOND JOURNAL

This evening, as I sat on my windowsill looking out towards the Heath, I was startled by a low whistle and looked down the path to see Quincey standing by the gate. He waved, and beckoned me. I signalled him to wait and swung my way down the vine as quietly as I could.

I met him by the gate and he kissed me sweetly and deeply.

'You are returned from Italy.'

'Arrived this morning. It's a beautiful night,' he whispered. 'I figured we might as well be abroad to enjoy it.'

He picked up the canvas bag at his feet, took my hand and led me across the road and onto the deserted Heath. We found a secluded clearing, where the grass was soft and thick. Quincey opened his bag and drew out a tartan rug, which he spread on the grass. We sat on it, and he produced a bottle of wine and two tin mugs. The moonlight dappled the grass, and the silence was profound, broken only by the rustling of small animals and the hoot of a distant owl. We sipped wine for a few minutes, then Quincey took the mug from my hand and placed it on the grass. He drew me down onto the rug and pressed himself against me, unbuttoning my blouse. I do not know how long we lay there, laughing, talking softly, kissing and touching one another. It was delightfully exciting to lie under the stars, my skin bared, and to gasp and sigh without worrying we might be overheard.

When we were sated, I lay with my head pillowed on his chest and we looked up at the stars through the leaves above our heads. He twisted his fingers absently through the curls in my hair.

'Well, this will do,' he said quietly.

I sighed, 'I do believe the Heath is my favourite place in all the world.'

'It's a grand place, I can't argue with that,' he said, 'But Lucy, the world is full of great places. I sincerely hope you'll get to see a great many of them.'

'I hope so too.'

'Now there's one place I'd like you to see. My ranch in Swisher County.'

'You have a ranch?'

'That's where I was born. My Pa claimed the land, just south of Happy. It's beautiful.'

'Just south of Happy?'

He laughed softly. 'I forget, the name sounds peculiar to outsiders. Happy is a town in Texas... just a few hours from Amarillo.'

'Why is it called Happy?'

'Some cowboys came upon a stream there. They were grateful for it, so they named it Happy Draw, and the town sprung up around it.'

'And you're "happy" there?'

'Well, it's my place now. Pa and Ma are both dead...'

'I'm sorry to hear that.'

'Oh, it's been a while now. I miss them, but I'm at peace being a man alone. I love to travel, but sometimes, I just want to be back on my porch, a cup of coffee in my hand, watching the sun come up over the plains. The house faces the river. We planted a grove of trees to protect it from the wind. If you didn't know it was there, you'd never find it. I like to sit there and listen to the wind. Feels like it's a breeze that's travelled a right long way. I imagine it's bringing me news from all across the world. I think you'd like it.'

At length, we became aware that the moon had moved behind a hill and the cold was creeping up through the ground and chilling our bones. Somehow the shadows between the trees looked sinister now, where before they had been merely beautiful. We dressed hurriedly, shivering. He walked me back to the house in silence, then kissed me softly one last time. I saw him turn to walk down the hill.

I crept along the side of the house and climbed up the trellis. Once I was in my room, I knelt on the floor and looked out of the window. In the velvety darkness down by the gate, I saw a tiny flare of red light, and then another. It took me a moment to work out that I was seeing a match being struck and the glow of a cigarette. The two lights appeared for a split second, like two bright eyes in the night. I smiled. Quincey must have returned to stand at the gate after all, to see that I was safely in my room. I waved and then drew down the sash and crept into my bed.

I am still wide awake, so have recorded all that happened this evening in this new journal. But now that I write it, it strikes me that I have never before seen Quincey smoke a cigarette. Odd.

CHAPTER 10

18 FEBRUARY 2024 – KATE

'Happy birthday, my dear' Dad said, opening the door and dropping a kiss on my cheek. 'Your grandmother has requested you come in and work the gravy miracle.'

'It's scarcely a miracle,' I said, taking off my coat.

I went into the living room and hugged Gran. She squeezed my hand and waved me into the kitchen. Dad brought me a gin and tonic as I deglazed the roasting tin with red wine. I took a grateful gulp.

'Busy week?' Dad asked.

'Oh, you know. A teacher had a burst appendix, so I've been in the same school in Enfield for a few weeks now. I'd kind of settled in. Friday was my last day, so on I go. New school, new rules, new kids whose names I'll never learn.'

He let the silence grow, but I could feel him wrestling with himself. I stirred slowly. Eventually, it burst out of him.

'Is it time to take a permanent job?'

I countered swiftly. 'How are things at the lab?'

'Don't change the subject,' he said testily. 'It is possible to live like you're not on the verge of doing a midnight flit.'

'I'm not,' I cursed myself for the note of petulant teenager I could hear in my own voice. I was thirty-six years old, and he could still make me react like that within minutes of walking through the door.

I looked around for a whisk and Dad wordlessly passed me one. I waited for his next salvo. But to my surprise, he walked out of the kitchen and returned a few moments later with a cardboard box in his arms.

'This came for you, yesterday,' he said, placing it on the kitchen table.

'What is it?'

'It's from Milan.'

I turned my attention back to the gravy, draining it through a sieve into the gravy boat, putting the pan in the sink to soak and wiping my hands. I handed the gravy boat to Dad, who left the room with it. Then I sat at the table and drew the box towards me.

My name and Dad's address had been scribbled on the top of the box in Alex's familiar spiky handwriting. I used a sharp knife to split the tape on the top and cautiously lifted the lid. The box held a jumble of objects – scarves, gloves and ornaments. A note lay on top and I unfolded it.

Hey K,

Stacey asked me to make sure you got the last of your things from the flat.

Hope you're well.

Ax

Weasel, making this brutal gesture Stacey's fault. And this was scarcely *all* my stuff – just what they'd deemed 'personal'.

I lifted a few of the objects from the box. There was a tangle of cheap jewellery and a framed etching of the Charles Bridge in Prague. A brightly coloured wool scarf released a whiff of scent – my perfume, the smell of our flat, a trace of wood smoke. It struck me like a blow to the solar plexus.

There was something heavy and flat at the bottom of the box, and I reached in to lift it out. It was a big, square photo album and as familiar to me as my own face. I'd made it as a gift for Alex on the anniversary of our first year together. I was besotted with him, despite his studiedly casual attitude to our relationship. The album had been a sort of manifesto: a record of all we'd done together, what we meant to each other. I'd filled the first ten pages with photographs, ticket stubs, restaurant receipts and funny love notes. He loved it, or said he did, and for a few years after, we'd both added to it, making a book of memories. Unsurprisingly, we'd got out of the habit more recently, and the last third of the album was empty.

I opened it to the first page, to a photo of the two of us on the banks of the Seine, eight years before. Alex's hair was shaggy, mine short and spiky, and we were laughing into each other's eyes. There was a youthful roundness to our faces. I slammed the album shut, feeling a hot fury. How could he? He was forcing me to be the sole guardian of our shared past. If he had timed it to arrive on my birthday, it was unimaginably cruel. If he hadn't, that meant he'd forgotten my birthday. I couldn't decide which was worse.

At lunch, I picked at my food, nauseous and miserable.

'So how's the flat?' asked Gran.

'Good.'

'And how's work?'

'Fine.'

'Kate doesn't want to discuss her life circumstances,' Dad said.

'There's nothing to discuss.'

I heard the catch in my voice and it made me furious. I wanted to tell Gran about the box and its contents, but I couldn't bear to do it front of Dad. I couldn't bear what he would say, or what he wouldn't say. What he would be thinking.

Gran tried again. 'Are you doing anything interesting? What about that letter you found?'

'What letter?' said Dad.

Gran gave him the frown signal and Dad bent his head over his plate. I ground my teeth. I knew I was being managed. That said, it was easier to go with this conversation than to resist it.

'I've done some research,' I said. 'I've learned who the family was who lived in the house at the time. The girl who wrote the letter died just a few days after she wrote it, and her mother did too.'

Gran's raised eyebrow of surprise encouraged me, and I began to speak more freely, telling them about visiting the churchyard, and about Charles's unusual Will.

'There's so much I don't know, but I've made a friend who's into genealogy, and I plan to keep digging.'

'Why?' Dad cut in.

'I beg your pardon?'

'Why? To what end?'

'Well... I...' I felt cornered. He had lowered his brows and was giving me that steady look that I was sure skewered his lab assistants. 'I've started writing about it.'

'A book?'

'No. it's a... I don't know what it is yet. Just notes so far.'

'So you don't know what form it's going to take?'

'A blog maybe?'

'And what will that lead to?'

'Oh my god, Dad... I don't know! I've got, like, ten pages of notes and downloaded documents. I don't know what it'll be. It might not be anything.'

Dad pressed his lips together and nodded. The silence

spread across the table between us, and then he gave the tiniest derisive snort.

'What was that?'

'What?'

'That snort.'

'I don't know what you're talking about.'

'You do. You snorted like... "Oh look at Kate, being useless again."'

'I did nothing of the kind.'

'Why can't I just write? And investigate? Be interested in something? Everything doesn't have to be a clinical study or double-blinded trial. Why does my research have to be *for* something?'

His jaw clenched hard and I knew it was taking all his willpower to hold words back. I leaned back and folded my arms. I knew he wouldn't be able to resist.

'It would be good if one thing in your life was *for* something. If there was some sense of direction. Planning. Commitment.'

I thought about the photo album in the box. There was my commitment. What good had it done? To my horror, I felt tears threatening. Gran reached across the table and grasped my hand.

'I think it sounds fascinating. So you say this Lucy's father left her the library in his Will? What do you think that was about?' She squeezed my hand tighter, transmitting strength. I drew a deep breath.

'Well, I suppose it's the gift of knowledge. What educational opportunities would a girl of that time have had?'

'Some women did go to university then,' Dad said brusquely. He had dropped his eyes, and I could see he regretted his snipe.

'Not many, though.'

'At least she came from money,' said Gran. 'She'd have got some schooling. My grandmother worked on a butcher's stall in Smithfield Market from the age of ten. She could only just read and write. A bit like the maid in your attic room. Even if they were the cleverest girls in all of England, they wouldn't have been able to work their way out of their situation. The path was set, and the options were menial work, marriage and mother-hood. Or prostitution, I suppose.'

'There's an argument,' Dad said, 'that there's such a thing as too much choice.'

I endured the rest of the meal and the apple crumble that followed. At last, at four, I felt I could leave without being rude. I stood to go, and Dad followed me to the door.

'For you, my dear,' he said, producing an envelope from his pocket. 'I hope...' he paused. 'Well, I hope it's of use. And that you'll see it as...' he stopped himself. 'Well. Happy birthday.'

On the train back to London, I slit open the envelope. It was a birthday card, signed in Dad's neat capitals. Inside, there was a cheque for two thousand pounds. I stared at it and picked up my phone and dialled him.

'Dad. Are you crazy?'

'You opened the card.'

'I can't take this.'

'You can. I want you to.'

I knew he could afford it. He earned well. He lived alone and frugally and was prudent with money.

'Well, I...' I could feel my pulse pounding in her temples. 'Thank you, Dad. It was... a big surprise. I really didn't expect it. I have to go.'

'It's a pleasure,' he said. I could hear the hurt surprise in his voice at my brusque tone but I couldn't back-pedal now. I had to get off the phone.

'I have to go,' I said.

'Er, Kate, you should know...' Dad began but I was already ending the call.

LUCY WESTENRA'S SECOND JOURNAL

18 MAY 1894

The day after I made my last entry, Mother took ill. Our family doctor, Dr Oliver, had to be called. Over the last weeks, she has not stirred from her bed. Her feet and ankles are swollen, and unless she is propped up on many pillows, she struggles to breathe easily. I have moved a small desk into the corner of her darkened room so that I can continue reading and studying but be on hand should she need anything. She sleeps a great deal and does not want to talk, but seems to take comfort from the fact that I am there.

19 MAY 1894

Dr Oliver has been coming every day, and today, he found me in the sun parlour.

'She seems brighter today,' he said cautiously. 'If we can persuade her to rise and sit in a chair by the window, so she will benefit from the fresh air and light, it would restore her to herself, I am certain.'

Mother seemed pleased to do this, and with Beatrice on one side and me on the other, we managed to help her to the large wing-backed chair in her room. She is not yet forty-five years old, yet she looks so frail. I sat at her side and drew her hand into my lap, holding it tightly, trying to rub some warmth into it. She has always been pale and cool, but now the flame of life flickers very low in her. Impulsively, I reached out and touched her soft cheek. She turned, startled, and looked at me.

'What is wrong, Lucy?'

'Nothing, Mother. I am just happy to see you sitting up and looking well.'

'I do feel a little better.'

'What can I get Mrs Staines to make for you? There must be something that will tempt your appetite.'

'Perhaps some soup? And fruit?'

When I brought her the tray, however, her hand shook so much she could not bring the spoon to her mouth. I took it from her hand, and gently and slowly fed her every mouthful. We did not speak.

After she had eaten, she looked brighter.

'Would you read to me, Lucy dear?' she said.

'Of course. What would you like...?'

'Nothing too strenuous. Not a novel. I do not think I could concentrate. Perhaps something from that magazine?'

'Of course.'

When I reached the end of the article, she said, 'You do read prettily Lucy. Your husband will so enjoy hearing you reading to him in the evenings once you are married.'

I could not help myself. I laughed at this. Mother's brow lowered in a frown.

'Your father did spoil you most dreadfully. You have never had an appropriate sense of your place in the order of things. You are a young woman, Lucy, of limited education...' It took all my self-control not to scream – she alone was the reason my education was curtailed. '... and as such, can have no real understanding of the world.'

'Pa would have wanted me to have control of my own future,' I said stubbornly. 'It was his wish, and it is mine.'

'But it is not mine,' said Mother, and her eyes seemed as flat and pale as ice. 'I am so glad that I...' she stopped suddenly, and turned toward the darkening window, folding her hands tightly in her lap. 'I am tired now. You may go now. I wish to rest.'

'You are so glad that you what, Mother?' I said. I had tightened my hands into fists and buried them in my skirts. Blood hummed in my ears. I sensed we were on the edge of a dreadful precipice. She did not reply. 'What have you done, Mother?'

'I cannot speak to you when you are like this,' she said. 'Your temper is out of control. You harangue a sick woman. Have you no mercy?' She allowed a single tear to roll down her pale cheek. 'Please call Eliza for me,' she said faintly, 'I need her to help me back to bed.'

'I can help you,' I said, relenting.

She waved me away and rested her head against the wing of the chair.

20 MAY 1894

This morning, Dr Oliver came to find me in the sun parlour once again. He led me over to the window and sat down opposite me. His face was drawn and serious.

'I know you are very young, Lucy, but in the absence of other family, I must speak to you frankly. Understand that I do this without the permission of your mother, but in my professional capacity, it seems to me imperative that you should know how thing stand.'

Having begun so firmly, he seemed reluctant to continue. I prompted him.

'Is she very ill?'

He nodded. 'She is, my dear.'

'Is it her heart?'

Again a nod.

'Is she likely to recover?'

Slowly Dr Oliver shook his head.

'I have seen many cases like this, when the heart has been weakened by childhood illness. The prognosis is, inevitably, poor.'

'Is there nothing you can do?'

'I'm afraid not.'

'And so... what are we to expect?'

'At best, I would expect her to live some few months,' Dr Oliver said gravely. 'I am so sorry, Miss Westenra.'

Months. My own heart beat fiercely in my chest. I do not know what to feel. Mother was demanding, often cold, always critical. But she was my mother. I think of myself as an adult, but in the face of losing my second parent before I was yet twenty years old, I realise I am just a child.

'Thank you, Doctor,' I said. 'I appreciate your kindness in helping me to understand.'

EXTRACT FROM LETTER, MINA MURRAY TO LUCY WESTENRA

20 MAY 1894

Dear Lucy,

Jonathan left for the Carpathian Mountains at the end of April. He wrote to me as he travelled through Europe, describing the peoples he saw and the food he ate (he does love to send me recipes!), but since he arrived at the Count's castle near the Borgo Pass, I have had just one brief, formal note, informing me that he was safe and well. I am sure he will write more fully soon, but I miss hearing from him. I am desperate for details of the wild country and the Count himself, who sounds like a most mysterious figure!

23 MAY 1894

I was busy replying to Mina when Beatrice came to the library door.

'Miss Lucy? There's a gentleman to see you.'

'If it is Mr Holmwood...'

'It's not, Miss. It's that Doctor Seward.'

Surprised, I smoothed my skirts and went down to the drawing room. I found Dr Seward standing before the fireplace. He had placed his elegant silk hat on the chair behind him and was dressed with some care. He stared at his reflection in the glass above the fireplace and turned an object between his fingers. As I drew closer, I saw it was an oddly shaped, bone-handled knife – a medical lancet of the sort used to draw a sample of blood. While his demeanour seemed composed, it was belied by the agitated way he manipulated the sharp instrument. I feared he might cut himself at any moment.

'Dr Seward,' I said, and he jerked in surprise. He must not have heard me coming.

'Miss Westenra,' he said, and bowed low.

'What a pleasant surprise. I do hope you will stay for lunch.'

'Well, I...' he said carefully. 'It rather depends.'

'On what, Dr Seward? Shall we sit?'

Once I was seated, he dropped into the nearest seat as if his legs would no longer support him. Unfortunately, it was the chair where he had placed his hat, and he had to perform an awkward sideways manoeuvre to extricate it before he crushed it. With anyone else, I might have made light of the moment, but

Dr Seward is so solemn. I waited until he had composed himself.

'Miss Westenra,' he said, with quiet seriousness. 'I do not know how to dissemble, nor to use flowery words, so I ask you to let me speak frankly to you.' I nodded. 'You are... very dear to me,' he began, and my heart sank. 'Very dear indeed,' he continued, 'although we have had little time together and we do not know each other well. I admire your intelligence and your spirit, and your...' he gestured with a hand at my person, 'your beauty,' he finished uncomfortably.

I moved uneasily in my seat.

'Dr Seward,' I began gently, but he held up a hand.

'Please Lucy, let me finish.'

I was so surprised by his urgent tone that it took a moment to realise he had used my first name. He was sweating now, beads of moisture standing out on his brow, and his hands worked the lancet between his fingers with great agitation.

'I cannot offer you an exciting life, Lucy, nor a glamorous one. I could only offer you the rooms I have in the hospital, my modest means, my honour, and my protection. And, well, I have imagined how my life might be with you to help me and cheer me. So Lucy...'

It was my turn to hold up my hand to silence him. I could not countenance the thought of marriage to John Seward. Where would my dreams be then? He may be kind, but he was conservative. He would never let me live the life I dreamed. And besides, I could not see Mother giving her consent to my marrying a doctor and going to live in a lunatic asylum.

'Thank you so much for your kind words, Dr Seward,' I said, as firmly as I could. 'However I must refuse your proposal.'

He nodded and looked down at his shoes. There was a long silence, and I feared that he might be angry, or worse, that he might weep. Finally, he spoke.

'Whatever you choose to do, Lucy, I hope you will be

happy. And know that if you ever want a friend, you must count me as one of your best.' He stood then, and bowed, bending to pick up his hat. 'I will bid you good day, Miss Westenra,' he said, all formality again. 'And know that if you need help... any help, at any time... you may turn to me. Good afternoon.'

As he turned to go, I saw that with all his agitated fiddling, he had indeed cut himself on the lancet. A drop of blood stained the grey silk of his hat.

I sat where I was, trying to still the trembling of my hands. To my surprise, I heard the rumble of male voices outside the door, followed by an easy peel of laughter. I crept to the drawing room door and eased it open. Dr Seward stood, hat in hand, talking to Mr Holmwood, who was leaning, arms folded against the newel post at the bottom of the stairs.

'.... with two Winchesters and a satchel full of gold!' Mr Holmwood said. He turned when he saw me standing in the doorway. 'Ah, there she is,' he said, and smiled. 'Dear Lucy. I was just telling Jack here how Quincey is off on one of his madcap exploits somewhere in Spain. He left this morning. He asked me to pass on his regards to you.'

I caught Dr Seward's eye – he looked back at me, miserable and furious. He seemed to be pleading with me with his eyes.

'Well,' I said, with false brightness, 'I wish Mr Morris a great adventure. No doubt he will regale us with tales upon his return.'

'Jack was just on his way,' Mr Holmwood said. The lunatics will not care for themselves. You must tell Lucy about the one who eats flies, Jack, if it isn't too shocking for her. Not now, though. For today I want the lovely Lucy all to myself.'

He pushed himself away from the newel post and advanced toward me, turning his back on Dr Seward. I saw Seward sag then, as if he had been struck. He noticed the spot of blood on his hat and brushed at it ineffectually. He nodded once, twice, and then without meeting my gaze or Holmwood's, bade us goodbye, and left.

Mother came down the stairs then, wearing an attractive peach gown I had not seen before. She leant on the banister and advanced slowly, and was quite breathless by the time she took her seat in the drawing room. There was a brightness to her manner, despite her weakness.

Most unusually, it seemed that we were expecting other guests for luncheon. The doorbell rang and Eliza admitted Mrs Nash, Mrs Howarth and their respective daughters. It seemed Art would not be getting me all to himself, as he had said to Seward.

We all took our places at the table – Mr Holmwood to Mother's right, me to her left. The meal was simple – clear soup, cold fowl and salad, but Mrs Staines had put out the good china and silverware.

After the dishes were cleared, Beatrice entered and placed champagne coupes before us all. I tried to catch Mother's eye, but she was engaged in animated conversation with Mr Holmwood. Dread began to rise in me.

Mrs Staines herself came in to fill the champagne glasses. There was no escape now, and I stayed in my seat, immobilised in horrified fascination. Mr Holmwood cleared his throat and stood, raising his glass.

'Ladies,' he said, and gave his brilliant smile, making eye contact with everyone at the table, 'I hope you will forgive my impetuous actions. I brought a bottle or two of champagne and prevailed upon Mrs Westenra to serve it. Today is, you see, a very special occasion, and I am unable to contain my happiness.'

I glanced down the table. Every face was rapt. They knew what was coming. He reached into his waistcoat pocket and withdrew a small object. I glimpsed the glint of gold and a heavy red stone.

'My dearest Lucy,' he said, and his eyes fell on me. 'My lovely

Lucy Westenra, will you do me the honour of becoming my wife?'

I heard the whole room draw in its breath. The air around me shimmered, as if I were trapped in a bubble. Desperately, I looked across at Mother. She had her hands resting either side of her plate and was looking down at her nails. I looked at them too. They were a peculiar slate blue. I glanced up at her face. The colour I had observed before had drained. She met my gaze. I saw her fear, her anger, her weakness. I saw she was terrified of her own mortality, desperate to have me safely married off, hungry for the grandeur conferred by Mr Holmwood's title and ancient family. I saw her tremble at the thought that I might cause a scene by publicly refusing him, and I imagined what that might do to her precarious health. Months to live, Dr Oliver had said. Months. An engagement could easily last months. A betrothal was not a marriage. It could be ended when...

I turned back to Mr Holmwood. I smiled shyly, dipped my eyes and whispered.

'Yes.'

So, dear journal, I record the events of today and find I am a changed woman. A betrothed woman – the fiancée of the Hon. Arthur Holmwood. I feel panic rising every now and again, but I must reassure myself that this is a temporary state, a brief interlude in my life. I have no wish to hurt him… Art, as I suppose I may now call him. He is as good a man as I have encountered. However, as soon as Mother – no. I cannot write it. So for now, the great, ugly Godalming ruby weighs down my left hand. But as soon as is politely possible, I will return it and my hand will be light and free once more, along with its owner.

11 JUNE 1894

Art comes for luncheon once or twice a week and sits with Mother in the drawing room afterwards. He is sweet with me and always polite and pleasant, although it transpires that he and I are almost never alone together.

He told me that he had written to Quincey of our engagement. Quincey had replied and Art showed me the letter, in which he paid me exactly the light and pretty compliments I would have expected. There was no hint of envy. Art said he, Quincey and Jack Seward would be gathering to toast his engagement as soon as Quincey returns from Spain.

30 JUNE 1894

I have prevaricated and delayed as much as I could, citing Mother's ill-health, but I have finally run out of excuses. Today Art came to collect me and take up to Ring to meet his parents.

It is a journey of some fifteen miles into the countryside of Hertfordshire. It was a grey, close day and we sat side by side in the carriage, speaking little. Art seemed agitated, and his right knee jigged up and down. Every now and then he pressed his palm to it, as if to remind it to be still, but soon enough the knee would begin to vibrate once more.

'Are you all right?' I asked.

'Quite well,' his reply came quickly. 'It is only that this journey takes so very long by carriage. On a fast horse, I can accomplish it in just a few hours.'

He stared out of the window of the carriage and his knee began to move again, convulsively.

It has been one thing to accept Art's proposal and to maintain the pretence of our engagement in my own household. But to meet his parents, to dissemble to them, to pretend to be an obedient, loving fiancée, when I had no intention whatsoever of becoming their daughter-in-law... well, that is altogether a different matter. I resolved to say as little as possible. Let them think I was mute and characterless. The fewer of my words that could stand in evidence against me, the better.

The trees began to press in closer to the road and every now and then, a branch would scrape along the side of the carriage like a fingernail. Art wedged himself still further into the corner of the seat and began to chew on his thumbnail.

Abruptly, the carriage pulled up. I heard Alfred, the coachman, step down and after a few moments, the screeching grate of metal on metal. Peering out of the window, I saw Alfred wrestling open gigantic, blackened gates. They were between two great pillars, which in turn punctuated a high stone wall.

We jolted past a tumbledown gatehouse, then down the long driveway, which was pitted with potholes. The grounds were wild and untended, but as we drew near the house, I noticed a cultivated garden beside the path, surrounded by a stone wall. The plants within were planted in neat rows and concentric circles. The garden was secured behind elaborate gates, formed of wrought iron stems and leaves. The word "Proserpine" was formed by vines of twisted metal.

'What a lovely garden,' I said, pointing.

'Ah yes,' Art said, glancing. 'My mother's pride and joy.'

'You mentioned that she grows medicinal plants,' I said, but he did not reply.

We were rounding the last bend, and Ring, in all its crumbling glory, was before us.

Alfred drew up finally in a weed-filled courtyard. We alighted from the carriage and climbed up the worn stone steps. Before us there was a great door, old and studded with large iron nails. Someone must have observed our approach, because immediately, there was the sound of rattling chains and the clanking of massive bolts drawn back. A key was turned with the loud grating noise of long disuse, and the great door swung back.

An old servant in a rusty black coat greeted us with a grunt and guided us through an echoing hallway and down a freezing, dark corridor. I glanced left and right as we walked, and saw that the rooms we passed were empty, or the furniture within was shrouded in dust sheets.

At length, the servant eased open yet another heavy wooden door and we passed into what must once have been the Great Hall. Dusty tapestries covered the walls. There was a long wooden banqueting table, and, at the far end, a high fireplace. The only light in the room came from the blazing fire. Large though it was, it was not enough to warm the cavernous space and I shivered.

Two tall wingback chairs were drawn close to the fire. As we walked the length of the room, our footsteps echoed on the flag-stones. A woman rose from one of the chairs and walked towards us. There was no doubt she was Art's mother – she had his strong features and the same rich olive skin, although her hair was black, with wings of grey at the temples.

'My dearest Arthur,' she whispered and I heard the hint of an accent.

She must be of foreign extraction – Spanish or Italian. She took his face between her hands and kissed him on the lips with passionate fondness. She smoothed his hair away from his fore-head and gazed into his eyes with patent adoration.

'How was your journey? It has been too long, my darling. Too long.'

'Oh Mother,' he said, 'how you fuss. I was here just a few weeks ago to fetch the ring. And you know how it is.'

'I know my love, I know,' she murmured. She continued to stroke his head and shoulders, as if he were a beloved pet. I could see him flinch, as if he would push her away. I had thought his comment about the ring offered a segue to allow him to introduce me, but his mother's eyes did not stray from his. I was loath to interrupt, so for a long moment, we were trapped in an awkward tableau.

Suddenly, there was a long, rumbling cough from the other

chair, followed by a deep groan. Art's mother released him and, turning swiftly, bent to pick up a silver basin which sat on the floor. She held it before the inhabitant of the chair who coughed again, hawked and spat. After another long fit of wheezing and groaning, followed by more spitting, the paroxysm finally passed. She replaced the basin on the floor and covered it with a cloth, and motioned for us to step in front of the chair.

Lord Godalming was shrunken, hunched over in his seat. He appeared small, although the breadth of his shoulders suggested he had once been a big man, as his son was. His face was a strong – a very strong – aquiline, with high bridge of the thin nose and peculiarly arched nostrils; with lofty domed forehead, and hair growing scantily round the temples but profusely elsewhere. The mouth, so far as I could see it under the heavy moustache, was fixed and rather cruel-looking, with peculiarly sharp white teeth.

'Boy,' he rasped.

'Father,' Art said, and his voice was barely above a whisper.

He leaned over and kissed his father on the cheek. Lord Godalming brushed him away as if he was a fly. His eyes raked over me as if I were horseflesh.

'This is my fiancée, Lucy Westenra, Father,' said Art. 'Daughter of Charles Westenra, and Rose Westenra, born Barraclough, of the Yorkshire Barracloughs.'

The old peer shrugged, uninterested. 'I have never heard of them.'

'My mother can trace her lineage back to 1315,' I said, hating myself.

'Lucy's father built a prosperous property empire in London before his death,' said Art, and I could hear the wheedling note in his voice. Lord Godalming turned his face away and called for the servant.

'Bring me wine,' he barked peremptorily, 'and the ledger.'

We stood awkwardly before his chair. There was nowhere

for us to sit. My heart ached for Art. The charming, affable man I knew in London had vanished. The oppressive darkness here at Ring dimmed his light, and his father's dripping disdain shrunk him even further. The old servant brought a carafe and a single glass, as well as a leather-bound book which Lord Godalming opened on his lap with shaking hands.

'I have had an account from your club,' he began. 'Why did you order so much claret?'

'I was entertaining a friend...' Art stammered, but Lord Godalming cut him down. 'He jabbed at entry after entry in the ledger, barking out questions about shirts, horses, carriages, and not waiting for answers. I could feel Art shaking beside me.

Before he could complete his interrogation, the old servant gestured that the meal was ready, set on the end of the long banqueting table. Lord Godalming threw off his heavy rug and struggled to his feet. He was bent and gnarled, and his legs and arms were stick thin. However his belly was swollen and distended. Leaning on his wife's arm, he shuffled across to the table where a mean repast had been laid. We followed them and sat.

Lord Godalming glanced down at the food and pushed his plate away. He watched the rest of us as we ate – the sound of our knives and forks echoing in the cavernous hall. Art's mother did her best to keep the conversation going, telling Art of her work in the garden.

Determined to make a good impression for Art's sake, I turned to Lord Godalming.

'I have been admiring these tapestries,' I gestured to the moth-ravaged hanging opposite. 'They seem to represent the four seasons. If so, is that Ceres, the goddess of agriculture, who represents the summer?'

He did not reply. He did not even glance my way. Art caught my eye and shook his head. There was no point.

Halfway through the second course, Lord Godalming

gestured to the servant who came to his elbow. He struggled to his feet and leaning heavily on the servant's shoulder, shuffled from the room.

'My husband is tired,' Lady Godalming said. 'He must rest.'

* * *

Later, in the carriage on the way home, Art was effusive in his apologies.

'He is very ill,' he explained, 'and in constant pain.'

'He dismissed me,' I said wonderingly, 'as if I were a beggar, or vermin. He heard my lineage and decided I was a non-person – of no interest to him.'

'Oh Lucy, it is hard for you to understand. He cares only for Ring, for the estate. You saw it. It is an insatiable beast that must always be fed. The house is in dire need of repairs, much of the farmland has fallen into disuse. It cannot pay for itself. He is drowning in debt and consumed with worry. All that matters is that Ring should survive and the line should continue.'

He fell silent then and I looked across at him. The trembling knee that had plagued him on the journey to Ring was still. Instead a muscle at his jaw worked. His handsome face was hardened and grim with determination. For the first time, I could see his father's features in him.

CHAPTER 11

*I*t was fully dark when I got back to Golders Green from Dad's and began the trek up the hill. The box from Alex was heavy and my arms ached. The cardboard was soft and it felt as though it might split at any moment, spilling my paltry memories onto the pavement.

Several times, I was tempted just to dump the whole thing into a bin. Just as I reached the corner of my road, my phone rang. In relief, I balanced the box on a low wall and scrabbled in my bag.

'*Tanti auguri!*' Rafaella sang out. 'Happy birthday!'

'Thanks,' I sank down onto the wall beside the box.

'You're out of breath. And you sound upset.'

I explained about Alex's ill-timed birthday gift.

'What a bastard,' Rafaella spat.

'Yeah, well. We knew that. And then my dad ...'

To my surprise, I began to cry. The tears that had threatened since I opened the box spilled over.

'Your dad?'

'He gave me a cheque for my birthday. A big cheque.'

'And this is bad?'

'No. Yes. I mean... everything is loaded coming from him.'

'Loaded how?'

'He thinks I should be getting a permanent job. Probably buying my own property. Settling down.'

'*Dio mio*, I wish someone would give me a cheque for that.'

'He had a huge go at me at lunch about making choices, about committing to something.'

'Committing to what?'

'He didn't say.'

'So he did not specify what the money was for?'

'No, but...'

'I do not know your papa, Kate, but it seems to me he has tried to give you a gift of freedom. And what a gift that is.'

'Yeah, well... you don't know him. Look, I'd better go. I'm not actually home yet and it looks like rain. I'll call soon.'

I scooped up the box and struggled the last few hundred yards to the front door. I scrabbled in my bag for my keys and elbowed the front door open. Despite the wintry chill, I was sweating. I dumped the box at my feet, unbuttoned my coat and paused to catch my breath.

The house may have been hacked into flats, but the hallway had at least retained its elegant proportions. The staircase made a graceful circular sweep down to the marble floor. The space in the curve of the staircase was often cluttered with bicycles and pushchairs, but I could still imagine how it had once looked. I imagined Lucy scampering down those stairs as a child. She might have swept down them, beautifully dressed as a young woman. It was quite possible she had even danced here on this marble floor.

And Mum? I was so small when she got ill, so I have no memories of how she moved before she became the narrow, empty shape in the bed. Did she bound down these stairs on her way to art school? Drift dreamily? Was she also thinking about Lucy when she stood in this hallway?

There was a scuffed magnolia wall to the right of the stairs. In Lucy's time, this wall was probably covered in flocked wallpaper and hung with family portraits. Now, half of it was taken up by wooden pigeonhole letter boxes. Next to these, there was a row of mass-produced artworks – prints of watercolours of buildings – and a cork notice board covered in leaflets for rubbish collection and French conversation lessons.

As I bent over to pick up the box, my eye rested on one of the framed pieces of art. I stopped short. It was different from the others. How had I never noticed that? This wasn't a reproduction graphic stuck in a frame to fill a stretch of wall space. Along the bottom of the image, the words: "Hillingham, 1830" were written in elaborate script. Above this, there was a hand-drawn plan of the house, with its two large wings and the central, circular staircase. The image was not an original – the paper looked newish. Someone must have copied the architect's drawings. It was a floor plan of the four levels of the original house when it was built. Each floor was shown in outline and each room labelled. I'd passed this picture dozens of times on my way in and out of the building, and had never once paused to look at it.

I stared, transfixed. On the diagram of the top floor, I could see the tiny, boxy rooms which were allocated to the servants of the house and which now formed my flat. The second floor had several large bedrooms on either side of the corridor. Each was just labelled "bedchamber", so it was impossible to guess which might have been Lucy's. The utility room I'd seen was, as I'd guessed, a valet's room.

On the ground floor, what was now flat Number 1 off to my left, had once been the drawing room. The dining room (Number 2) was towards the back of the house, overlooking the garden, and incorporated what had once been a sun parlour. The original kitchen, as far as I could see, no longer existed.

My heart quickened when I looked at the plan of the first floor. To the left of the stairs, there was a large, rectangular room, which ran the length of half the house. It was labelled "Library". I stepped back and gazed up the staircase. I knew which flat now inhabited that space.

Number 4.

I didn't pause to think what I might say. Leaving the box and my coat and bag in the hallway, I ran up the first flight of stairs and knocked on the heavy wooden door. At first, I heard nothing. Was the elderly woman out? It seemed unlikely at eight on a Sunday evening. After a full minute, I heard faint footsteps. A key grated in the lock, the door opened a crack, and I heard the rattle of a chain. A narrow sliver of light spilled out. The slight figure of the woman was silhouetted. She held the edge of the door in one small hand and stared out at me silently.

'Hi,' I said, suddenly uncertain. 'Um, I'm Kate. I live upstairs, in Number 8.'

The woman didn't reply.

'I'm so sorry to bother you, I, er ... I just happened to see the plans of the house on the wall downstairs. I'm interested in the history of the house, and...' I faltered. With the light behind the woman, I couldn't read any expression on her face, and she wasn't saying anything. I drew a deep breath and forged on.

'I can see from the plans that this room – your flat – was the library in the original house?'

The woman's hand gripped the edge of the door, and then she withdrew it.

'I don't know anything about that,' she said. Her voice was surprisingly strong and deep. 'Now please excuse me. It's late.'

I opened my mouth to apologise, but the door slammed shut and I heard the key rotate in the lock with a determined click.

Disappointed, I went back downstairs to collect my things. I took one last look at the plans, peering closely at the fine penmanship. And there, in the bottom right-hand corner I saw it. Two tiny initials and a date. "NR, 1982." I'd seen that signature a thousand times: the spiky points of the N, the elegant swoop of the R. Noni Rosen. Mum.

LUCY WESTENRA'S SECOND JOURNAL

4 JULY 1894

This morning, to my surprise, I came down to breakfast to find Mother already at her place, a notebook beside her plate.

'Ah, Lucy,' she said briskly, 'I will be writing to the dressmakers. Is there anything you need? A new summer frock perhaps? I will contact the milliner as well. Your old bonnet will not do.'

'My bonnet is perfectly serviceable, Mother.'

'Nonsense. It is much too heavy for the seaside. You need something lighter, in straw, with some bright flowers.' She made a quick note in her notebook.

'For the... seaside?'

'Yes. It is just a matter of weeks before we depart for Whitby.'

'Whitby, Mother? Are you sure? Will the journey not strain you unduly?' I chose my words carefully.

'I shall sit in a carriage, and then on a train. That cannot be much of a strain, can it?'

'But you have not been... strong. Would it not be better to be close to London and the care of Dr Oliver?'

'Dr Robinson in Whitby brought me into the world. He is not young, but he is a very fine physician. If I need medical care, although I cannot imagine that I will, I would be as well-tended in Yorkshire as in London, if not better.'

I opened my mouth to discourage her, but my tongue was stayed. If Mother had a limited time yet to live, why should she not spend some of her remaining days in the place she loved best? I would take every precaution on our journey to Whitby, and once there, I could install her by the window in our rooms on The Crescent, where she might enjoy views of the harbour and the Abbey up on the cliffs. Mina had promised to join us in Whitby, and her presence would cheer Mother.

'I would love a new bonnet,' I said. 'Perhaps with some peonies upon it? Or roses? Something cheery to welcome the summer. Let me go directly and write to Mina, so she can plan her journey.'

24 JULY 1894

The days and the minutes passed maddeningly slowly, but today, I stood on the platform at Whitby Station as the train pulled in. I waited for the smoke and steam to clear, and when I saw Mina's neat, purposeful form, it was as if no time at all had passed since we were last together in Lyme Regis. My fierce embrace almost knocked her off her feet.

I took a step back and held her at arm's length. My own worries fled at the sight of the deep crease between her pretty brows. I linked my arm through hers and walked with her to the little trap that would take us to our rooms. She talked brightly, noting all the features of the town as we went. But her chatter did not deceive me. Disquiet sat heavy on her.

'Have you heard from Jonathan?' I asked quietly as we wound our way up the cobbled street to our lodgings.

'For some time, we have had only the briefest and most

formal of communications,' she said, 'The letters he sends come to Mr Hawkins, and Jonathan asks him to pass them on to me. They are short and impersonal – so unlike him.' she paused and looked across at the Abbey looming on the hill above us. 'I cannot help but wonder. Has some red-lipped Roumanian maiden bewitched him? Have I lost his love?'

'Mina!' I cried, taking her hand. 'You know that cannot be true. You have told me about Jonathan's steadfastness, and I do not doubt the sincerity of his affections – he would not have his head turned so easily. Perhaps the Count keeps him so occupied he is unable to write. When is he due to return?'

'I do not know,' she sighed, 'I never imagined he would be gone so long. He went merely to show the Count some photographs and the plans of the property he has found for him, and to get his signature on some documents. I imagined he might be gone for a few weeks – a month at most. But now almost three months have passed.'

I squeezed her hand. I could not imagine her suffering, for I had never loved a man in the way that she did Jonathan.

Mina broke off then and took my left hand in hers.

'So this is the Godalming ruby?'

I looked down at the ring. The stone was large and pear-shaped and the setting old-fashioned. I was forever snagging threads on the great clumsy claws that gripped the stone.

'It is hideous, is it not?'

'I cannot lie, dearest Lucy. It is not the handsomest ring I have ever seen.'

'It resembles a drop of blood, or a great clot.' I said flatly.

This made Mina giggle and her brow smoothed, which delighted me.

'What a turn of phrase you have, Lucy, my love. A clot!'

'Perhaps some ancient Lord Godalming squeezed it out of a stone in days of yore,' I said, and she smiled all the more.

We arrived at our rooms, and Mina regained some of her

habitual effervescence. She hopped down from the little trap and thanked the driver sweetly. Her loving greeting to Mother put colour in the poor sick woman's cheeks, the like of which I had not seen for weeks.

After lunch, Mina elected to go for a walk, and she set off to explore the town. She returned a few hours later, her cheeks flushed, full of stories. We all shared a pleasant supper and went to bed. It is a joy to hear Mina's quiet breathing across the room from me, as I write these words.

25 JULY 1894

I awoke early and restless and went downstairs, leaving Mina sleeping. As I sat at the kitchen table, there was a sharp rapping on the door. The letter carrier doffed his cap to me and wished me a cheery good morning. I took the letters inside to sort them. There was a brief note to me in Art's untidy scrawl, telling me that he hoped to come to Whitby to see us. I saw that Mother had also received a letter from Art. Most of the other letters were addressed to her too.

The last letter caused my heart to leap. It was a heavy envelope, addressed to Mina in a courtly, old-fashioned script. The return address was given as Magdalen Road in Exeter. This must come from Jonathan's employer, Mr Hawkins. I ran up the stairs and shook Mina awake, and she sat up befuddled. I placed the envelope in her lap and watched comprehension dawn. She gasped and turned the envelope over, ripping open Mr Hawkins's seal.

There were two sheets inside – one was the same heavy stationery as the envelope. The other was the tissue-thin paper of international correspondence.

She scanned Mr Hawkins's note and tossed it aside, unfolding the other letter with trembling fingers. It took her seconds to read it, and as soon as she finished, her eyes filled with tears and she let it fall to the coverlet.

'Oh Mina,' I said, drawing her into my arms. 'Is it bad news? Has something happened to Jonathan?'

'It is worse than bad news,' she sobbed into my shoulder, 'it is no news. Another impersonal note. See.'

She handed me the letter.

LETTER FROM JONATHAN HARKER TO MINA MURRAY

29 JUNE 1894

Dearest Mina,

My work with the Count is concluded. I have left the castle and arrived at Bistritz. I look forward to returning home.

Yours ever,
Jonathan

I looked up at her and frowned.

'Surely this is good? He is on his way. This letter was written almost a month ago. He will be home any day now.'

She shook her head. 'Firstly, if all was well, he would have been home weeks ago. The journey should not take more than a few days. But more than this, the strangeness of the letter disturbs me.'

'I grant you, it is brief.'

She flung back the bedclothes and walked barefoot to her luggage. From a pocket in her travelling bag, she drew some papers and brought them back to the bed. She spread them out in front of me. There were two other letters from Jonathan, written on the same thin, blue paper. One was dated the 12th of June and said that Jonathan's work at the castle was nearly done, and that he should start for home within a few days. The second, dated the 19th, said that he was leaving on the next morning from the time of the letter. I looked up at Mina and frowned.

'These letters seem to bear out the theory that he is on his way.'

'Look at them more closely,' she said. She placed the letter she had received that morning alongside the others.

'What am I looking for?' I asked. 'They are all in Jonathan's hand. Indeed, they are all very much the same.'

'That is it exactly!' her eyes blazed with excitement. 'The hand is identical. The ink has a strangely rusty cast. And see here, on every curved letter, there is an odd blot, as if there was something amiss with his pen.'

I shook my head in silence. I could not see the path of her argument.

'If I write three letters on three different days,' she continued, 'I might use a different sort of paper. I might refresh my ink bottle. If I had a pen that blotted, I would certainly change it – and believe me, Jonathan is never without a wide selection of pens. He is quite the collector.'

'And so...' Understanding was beginning to dawn.

'I believe these letters were all written on the same day. That Jonathan penned them one after the other and they have been posted at intervals ever since.'

'By Jonathan?'

'Or by another. I do not know. All I know is that if my theory is correct, Jonathan's whereabouts are unaccounted for, and there has been no real word from him since before the twelfth of June.'

Her eyes were wide, and the skin beneath them looked bruised. There was nothing to say. I could only hold her in my arms as she wept.

Later, we took another walk up to the churchyard near the Abbey. When we returned to the rooms, I greeted Mother and went up to our attic bedroom to read and study in peace. After just a few minutes, I heard Mina call up to me, a note of urgency in her voice.

'Lucy! Come quickly! Your mother is not well!'

I ran down the stairs, and found Mother slumped in her chair, her lips turning blue. She was short of breath and her hands shook.

'Shall I send for Dr Robinson, Mother?' I asked.

'It is nothing, nothing,' she said, waving us away. 'Do not bother the doctor. I have merely overtaxed myself. If you help me to my bedroom, I will rest for an hour.'

Mina looked alarmed, but I reassured her that Mother's attacks were not infrequent, and she merely needed to go to bed, and be propped up on pillows, to rest. Between us, we helped her to her room and settled her. She closed her eyes immediately. Mina hovered, nervously.

'Perhaps you could see to it that dinner is prepared?' I said gently. 'I will sit here with her.'

Mother soon dozed off. In her sleep, she drew the coverlet up towards her chin and I heard an odd rustle. Curious, I peered closer and saw she had a piece of paper clutched in one of her hands. I uncurled her fingers and removed it. I smoothed it out and was about to fold it and place it on the bedside table when I recognised Art's distinctive handwriting.

LETTER FROM ARTHUR HOLMWOOD TO ROSE WESTENRA

23 JULY 1894

My dearest Rose,

I hope this finds you well, and that your journey to Whitby was not too onerous. I hope to join you and Lucy for a few days, my father's health permitting. I have missed you both, and I look forward to seeing Lucy's pretty smile when I arrive in Yorkshire.

I recall your late husband speaking of Lucy. We were discussing my investing in Westenra and Co., and he laughingly told me how Lucy would come to his office, sit on a high stool, and check the columns of figures in the ledgers. 'She can add faster than any of my clerks,' he said. She is a clever girl, and her bright mind makes her all the more adorable.

That said, despite her intelligence, we must agree she is impetuous and hot-headed, with notions well beyond her capabilities. The precautions you have suggested seem all too appropriate. I hope, once we are married and our own children come along, Lucy will emulate you and show the calm and ladylike nature which I am sure is hidden within her.

Yours ever,

Arthur Holmwood

25 JULY 1894

It took all my willpower not to shred the letter into fragments and fling them into the fire. How dare he condescend to my pretty smile and my 'adorable' intelligence, as if I were a tame parakeet kept in a cage and taught to sing? How could he dismiss me as impetuous and hot-headed? And what were the "precautions" to which he referred?

For the first time, it came to me that perhaps Art was not the harmless, pleasant man I had imagined. It was increasingly apparent that he turned different faces to different people. There was something slippery about him – a poreless self-interest that made me uncomfortable. I had imagined the inevitable end of our engagement as something amicable, polite and straightforward. But now I wondered if I might not have underestimated him. Did I really know him at all? With one last glance at Mother's sleeping face, I stole out of the room.

Later

I wrote all of the above before Mina and I got ready for bed. I was exhausted and overwrought. The words of Art's letter kept running through my head. Every time I was about to fall asleep, some new memory of what he wrote would jerk me awake. It was not just the insulting tone – there was something I had read that had unsettled me. Some words in that letter had rung false, and for the life of me I could not remember what they were. I considered creeping from my bed to go and read it again, but it would mean taking a candle or lantern into Mother's room, and she would be sure to wake then.

Eventually sleep came. Deep in the night hours, I dreamed Art was holding me tightly, looking down at me with those fathomless dark eyes. In the dream, his mouth opened, and I saw his white teeth. I wrested myself from his grasp and turned to run, but I was caught in another strong pair of arms and I looked up to see Quincey's face. I could feel the burning hardness of him pressed against me. As we kissed, Art pushed against my back, and I was trapped between them, encircled in their arms, their breath hot and loud in my ears.

I jerked awake, and to my shock, found myself standing in the middle of our bedroom. Mina was beside me, her hand on my arm.

'Oh Lucy, my dear,' she whispered, 'I awoke to find you trying the door. You were sleepwalking.'

She led me to my bed and sat me on the edge. She lifted my legs and tucked them under the covers. She drew up a chair and sat beside the bed, holding my cold hand in her own.

'I will stay right here until you fall asleep again, and tomorrow, you can tell me what has distressed you so.'

I nodded obediently and closed my eyes. I recognised the hot, insistent pulse of arousal, deep in my belly, a residue from my disconcerting dream. I pushed the dream from my thoughts, and, to distract myself, thought once again of Art's letter.

Suddenly, I remembered the sentence that had troubled me so. "I recall your late husband speaking of Lucy," he had written, "We were discussing my investing in Westenra and Co."

When I first met Art at Pa's funeral, he had said he knew Pa because Pa had bought some land from him. He had said nothing about investment, nor had Pa ever mentioned it. In point of fact, Pa had always been resistant to the idea of outside investors – he did not want to be beholden to anyone else, nor be told how to conduct his business.

One way or the other, Art was not telling the truth about how he had met Pa. Either what he had told me or what he had written to Mother in the letter was untrue. But why? Why would he need to lie?

26 JULY 1894

This morning, I had just finished writing about my sleep-walking episode when I heard a rapping on the door. Mina was already dressed and she flew downstairs to answer it. By the time she came back upstairs, I was up, tidying my hair before the glass.

'A telegram for you,' she said, holding it out.

I opened it and saw the brief message:

TELEGRAM, HOLMWOOD, RING, TO LUCY WESTENRA, WHITBY. 25 JULY_

Lucy, Father unfortunately much worse. Cannot leave him at present. My apologies. All my affection, Art.

25 JULY 1894

I let out a long breath and sat down on the edge of the bed.

'Why Lucy,' said Mina, 'that can only be good news. The colour has quite come back into your cheeks.'

'Good news indeed, or at least a temporary reprieve,' I handed her the telegram. 'Art will not be coming to Whitby just yet.'

We gathered fruit and bread and wrapped them in a cloth, then set off to cross the bridge and climb the stairs to the churchyard. There was a bench near the gate which gave the best view of the harbour and the town below us.

Hesitantly, I confessed to Mina that I had read Art's letter to Mother the night before.

'I know that to read another's correspondence is an unforgivable breach of trust,' I said. 'But I am glad I did, for there was something in that letter that disturbed me. I believe he has lied to us – to Mother and me. It is a small matter. Perhaps it is nothing, but it makes me uneasy.'

'Perhaps you are right,' she said, 'Perhaps it is nothing. You may have misunderstood what he said at your Father's funeral.'

'I cannot ask Art,' I said, 'I would have to admit I had read his letter to Mother.'

'No, but you could always write to your Father's manager – Mr Boyden, was it? You could ask him to clarify the matter. You have told me he is very fond of you, I am sure he would keep your confidence and answer discreetly.'

29 JULY 1894

Mina has said that my sleepwalking continues night after night, although I am never aware of it. I recognise now that the sleep-walking is related to my fevered dreams of sexual pleasure, but there is no relief to be had. With Mina sleeping beside me, I dare not even touch myself, to gain some measure of release.

On her advice, I wrote to Mr Boyden. I began with a pretty description of Whitby and some news of our holiday. Then, in as gushing a way as I could manage, I wrote about my excitement at my engagement. I ensured the letter was in the post before Mina and I set off for our daily walk.

EXTRACT FROM LETTER, LUCY WESTENRA TO MR SILAS BOYDEN

29 JULY 1894

... I believe you first met my fiancé some years ago. When he came to do business with my late Father. I am always hungry for stories of him – so please, do tell me how he and Pa came to meet? I would be delighted to hear the tale of their meeting from you. It would give me a memory of my darling Pa, and a new one of my dear love. What could be sweeter?

LETTER FROM MR SILAS BOYDEN TO LUCY
WESTENRA

1 AUGUST 1894

17 Chatham Street
London

My dear Miss Westenra,

How lovely to receive a letter from you, and may I
offer sincerest congratulations on your engagement, both
personally and from all at Westenra and Co.

Indeed, I remember my first encounter with The Hon.
Mr Holmwood. He made an appointment with your
Father, having heard of his reputation as a developer of
land. They were not previously acquainted, as far as I
know. Mr Holmwood came to see us at Westenra and Co,
acting as his Father's representative, because Lord
Godalming wished to sell a parcel of land on the border
of the Ring estate. Your father, as you know, deals mainly
with property closer to London, but Mr Westenra agreed
to go and see it. Lord Godalming was in fact away from
the estate when he visited.

Some weeks later, Mr Westenra told me he had
decided to conclude the deal with Mr Holmwood. I was a
little surprised at the decision, but your father, as you
know, was always a man to make his own rules. The land
remains in the possession of Westenra and Co., although
we have yet to find a use for it.

There were some concerns with the paperwork on
the land, as I recall – Lord Godalming's solicitor was
indisposed at the time, so Mr Holmwood engaged
another solicitor to conclude the deal – a Mr Bevington.

So, all in all, it was a slightly unusual business relationship. I can only surmise that your father undertook it because he saw something special in Mr Holmwood. I am sure he would be only too delighted to know that Mr Holmwood has formed a lasting attachment to your family.

Wishing you a most salubrious summer, and all good wishes to your dear mother,

C. M. Boyden.

2 AUGUST 1894

There was much to consider in this letter. Why had Pa bought the land at Ring? He had never told me, of it, nor could he have had any use for it that I could see. If it was because he had developed a personal affinity for Art, why had he never mentioned him to me or invited him to the house? The story about the 'indisposed' family solicitor also sounded odd. I sat at the table in the kitchen, staring out of the window. Mina came downstairs and saw me with the letter before me.

'Has the post arrived?' she asked eagerly.

'Yes, although I am afraid there was nothing for you.' I saw her shoulders sag. 'This came from Mr Boyden, however,' I pushed the letter over to her and she read it.

'What will you do?'

'I will have to wait until I am back in London, but I fancy the mysterious solicitor, Mr Bevington, might shed some light on the issue.'

Mina nodded, but her own brow remained creased with worry. I know that all she could think of in this moment was that there had been no word from Jonathan. I reached over and patted her hand.

'I am certain there will be news soon.'

CHAPTER 12

❦

2 MARCH 2024 – KATE

With no weekend plans, I spent Friday evening doing housework. I cranked up the music as I cleaned and polished. I was about to lug the hoover back to the hallway cupboard when my phone rang. It was James Harker, video calling. I felt a shock of pleasure to see his name.

'Hi,' he said, 'I'm not interrupting anything am I?'

'Well, you know, it's all glamour, glamour, glamour on a Friday night in North London. I was just on my way to a Ball.'

'I'm not up on Ball etiquette, and obviously you're much more modern up there in the big city. Is it fashionable to go to a Ball in dungarees with a smear of dirt on your nose?'

'It's an *avant garde* Ball,' I laughed, rubbing at the smudge on my face. 'Is it gone yet?'

'I have to say, I like the bandanna in your hair. Very Rosie the Riveter.'

I flexed my bicep in the famous World War 2 poster girl's pose.

'I'm trying to grow my hair,' I said, 'I've worn it short for years, and it's at that really annoying stage right now. I have to do something to keep it out of my eyes or I'm going to go at it with clippers.'

'Oh, don't do that,' said James, then hastily added, 'I mean, do what you want, and I'm sure it looks cool short, but it's really nice, all curly like that.'

'So what's keeping you at home on a Friday night, Mr Harker? Isn't your town full of funky student pubs?'

'Probably. I prefer to party in my own way... by shunning human company and staying home with a good glass of red, while ferreting out the history of the long dead on my laptop.'

'That does sound like a good party.'

'Why don't you get a drink too?' James said, and then blushed.

He's shy, I realised. It made me smile.

'Excellent idea.' I went to the kitchen to pour a glass of wine.

'So, what's up?' he said, once I'd settled myself on the sofa.

'Well, I did make an amazing discovery... right in my own building! After walking past it who knows how many times, I found a reproduction of the floorplan of the house in the foyer downstairs!'

I'd snapped a picture of the plan on my phone and I shared it with him.

'Oh wow...' he breathed.

I watched his handsome face as he peered at each room and asked questions. His eyes were the most intense blue, and I liked his methodical, careful attention to detail. Something deep in my body flickered.

'What a house it must have been,' he said, 'Can you imagine the parties they would have held? The intrigues... births... deaths... do you suppose it's haunted?'

I laughed. 'Does Lucy's ghost wander the halls holding a candle aloft? You don't strike me as the woo-woo type.'

'I'm not, promise.'

He smiled and I felt that little internal tug again. I'd like him to smile at me like that in person.

'Still…' he said wistfully. 'All those lives lived. You'd think there'd be some... echoes.'

'Speaking of echoes, I haven't shown you the best part. Can you zoom in on the pic? Look at the bottom right hand corner.'

'NR? The artist's signature?'

'Noni Rosen. My mum.'

'Your mum? Kate, that's amazing! Have you asked your family about it?'

'Of course I have. Both Dad and Gran had no idea it existed. Neither of them have ever seen it before, and they have no idea when or why she would have done it.'

I told him about my frustratingly brief conversation with the woman who lived in what had once been the library. 'She's called Mrs R. Baylis, or at least that's the name on her post-box.'

Well, if she doesn't want to talk, there's not much you can do,' said James. 'I suppose there's no reason to think she'd know anything.'

'I know. I just, well... I would love to go into her flat. To see what was once Lucy's library. Even just for a moment. There's probably nothing left. I'm sure the shelves and fittings were all ripped out decades ago. It's most likely magnolia walls and beige carpets, like this one was.'

A silence fell and we sipped our wine. We'd been chatting for some time, but James had given no reason for this call. Had we moved from acquaintances that shared research to... friends? I saw him shift, uncomfortable with the pause. He squared his shoulders and took a deep breath.

'Listen,' he said, 'I wondered if you maybe wanted to... Maybe see where Mina lived? And the school?'

I saw the small, anxious wrinkle between his eyebrows. I felt the vertiginous swoop of being poised at the top of the roller-coaster. He babbled on nervously.

'It would be so nice to meet you... in person.' He dropped his eyes.

I couldn't help smiling. 'That would be great. I'd love to. I've never been to Exeter.'

'I thought, maybe,' he said, talking quickly now, flustered, 'next weekend? I have a spare room in my house, if you'd be happy staying, or I could find you a hotel...'

'That's really generous of you,' I felt a blush rising. 'I'd love to stay with you, if I may.'

Relief lightened his expression, and he smiled broadly. He gave me his address.

'Great! Well, look into trains, and I'll pick you up from the station.'

We rang off, and I grinned at the darkened screen for some time. Then I did a little dance and went off to have a shower.

LUCY WESTENRA'S SECOND JOURNAL

5 AUGUST 1894

Last night, the weather turned. It had been still and hot all day, and by evening the air was thick and oppressive. We slept with our window open, but even this did nothing to cool the room. In the morning, as we walked along Whitby's harbour wall, one of the fishermen told Mina that we were in for a storm. It was a grey day, and the sun was obscured by heavy clouds. A thick mist rolled in from the sea, and it somehow magnified the sound of the waves so that they boomed with a threatening echo. The fisherman's prediction seemed accurate, because we could see the fishing-boats racing for home.

As we walked further along the wall, Mina was waylaid by an old gentlemen.

'There's something in that wind,' I heard him say portentously, 'that sounds, and looks, and tastes, and smells like death.'

'Oh dear,' I giggled when Mina returned to me, 'Who knew there could be so much information in the wind?'

As we stood talking, the coastguard came up to us with his spyglass under his arm. He stopped to talk with us. His attention was divided, however. He kept looking out to sea at a strange ship.

'I can't make her out,' he said, peering through his glass; 'she's a Russian, by the look of her; but she's knocking about in the queerest way. She's steered mighty strangely, for she doesn't mind the hand on the wheel; changes about with every puff of wind.'

Something shifted in me, looking at the black hulk of that ugly Russian schooner, far out to sea. I cannot say what it was. A leaping within – a sense of something unexpected beginning.

6 AUGUST 1894

The storm struck at midnight. We were awoken by the ferocity of the gale and the crashing waves. Mina and I both arose from our beds and went to the window. The noise was immense – the wind roared like thunder – but a thick fog hung everywhere. I crept along to Mother's room to check on her, but she seemed undisturbed. We could hear the shouts of men echoing faintly up from the harbour. Mina was disconcerted by the buffeting wind, so I crossed to her bed and climbed in beside her. She turned on her side and I curved myself around her back, wrapping my arm around her waist and burying my face in her fragrant hair. Her breathing quietened as I held her, and I matched my own breath to hers, drawing comfort from her soft sleeping form in my arms.

In the early hours, there was a crashing, grating sound, the like of which I had never heard before. I crept from Mina's bed and looked out of the window, but could see nothing through the thick grey mist. Perhaps what I had heard was merely thunder.

The grinding sound seemed somehow to signal the end of the storm, for the wind abated almost immediately and the mist began to lift. The street below me was revealed, and within minutes, it was as if the storm had never happened. I looked across at Mina, deeply asleep now, with her head pillowed on her hand. I knew I would sleep no more, so I wrapped myself in a blanket and sat in a chair by the window.

An unnatural russet light filtered through the streets, for the clouds were still heavy and low. A movement caught my eye. Someone was coming up from the quayside. Was it a fisherman, returning from securing his boat against the storm? As the figure drew closer, I saw it was not a man but a dog, a great black beast, like an Irish wolfhound. It loped silently, keeping to the shadows. It must have sensed me watching, for it stopped dead across the road, in line with our house. Our eyes met. The rising sun gave its eyes a strange red glow. Would it growl or bark or skulk away? It did none of these things, but stood still and held my gaze with calm attention. I fumbled with the window catch and raised it, leaning out. Still, the dog watched me. Then, without warning, it turned away and loped further up the hill and out of sight. Tiredness overwhelmed me then, and I crept into bed and slept deeply without dreaming.

When we finally arose it was to discover that the noise I heard in the early hours had been a shipwreck. A vessel had been blown into Whitby Harbour in the height of the storm and had run aground on Tate Sands. Mina shivered to hear this, for we had often walked on this beach.

We walked down to the harbour to see what had occurred. It was a shocking sight, for this was no small fishing boat, but a full-sized schooner. Her sails flapped uselessly in the breeze and she lay canted to one side on the beach. We could see men moving around on the deck of the ship. A lanky longshoreman saw us looking and sidled over to talk to us.

'Quite the nightmare, this, young Misses,' he said. I think he meant to sound regretful, but his feverishly bright eyes showed his excitement.

'Is that not the Russian schooner we saw out to sea last afternoon?' I asked.

'It is indeed. The Dmitry. She's come from Varna.'

I felt Mina start beside me.

'Varna!' she murmured. 'So close to where Jonathan was.'

The longshoreman continued, 'She is almost entirely in ballast of silver sand, with only a small amount of cargo. But that isn't the strangest thing about the ship. Not by far.' He leaned in then, and I could smell his hot, sour breath. He whispered hoarsely, 'There was not a living soul on board.'

'What do you mean? There must have been a crew.'

'Not a one miss. The captain, or we think it was the captain, was lashed to the wheel. By all accounts, he had been dead for some days. His neck were broke.'

'But where is the crew?' Mina asked, 'He could not have sailed this great ship from Varna alone. Perhaps they jumped off as soon as it ran aground.'

'There was hundreds of us watching from the harbour and up on the cliffs, Miss,' he said. 'And no one saw any person.' The way he leaned on the word "person" made me look at him curiously. He was clearly waiting for this response. 'A great dog shot up on deck as the ship hit the sand. A big black one. And it jumped off the ship and disappeared.'

'A dog?' Mina said, 'Are you sure?

'Sure as anything, Miss. I seen it with my own eyes. A hellhound.'

I took Mina's arm and bade him farewell. I told her about the dog as we walked into town to do our shopping.

'That is intriguing,' she said. 'For I assumed everything about his story was based on lies and superstition. But perhaps there is a dog. If it is so, it will be found sooner rather than later. It will be hungry and will no doubt seek human companionship.'

'Or perhaps it will find its way out onto the moors and

survive by hunting. It did not look like a domesticated animal to me.'

'As to the rest of the story,' Mina said, 'Seafaring folk are notoriously superstitious and fond of ghost tales. I take everything that longshoreman said with a great pinch of salt.'

Her simple pragmatism was comforting, and we soon forgot the wreck as we wandered the pretty lanes of the old town. We discovered a bookshop in a hidden courtyard and spent a happy half an hour looking at the volumes arranged on tables in the sun outside the shop.

As I paged through a book of sonnets, a shadow fell across the table before me. I glanced to my left and caught a glimpse of a tall gentleman in a black suit, with a top hat and cane. He reached close to me to pick up a volume and I was struck by the pale skin on the back of his elegant hands. He wore his nails rather longer than most gentlemen might, but they were scrupulously clean and well-shaped. Curiosity got the better of me and I turned to look at him more fully.

The stranger was looking directly at me and our eyes locked together with an intense shock I can only describe as recognition. I had never seen him before, and yet I knew him, and felt he knew me. His bone structure was so fine that his face appeared to be carved from marble. His eyes were as dark as Art's, but where Art's were blue black, these eyes glowed with a heat deep within, like fire. His skin was smooth and unblemished, with no hint of the shadow of a beard, even though his hair was as dark as his eyes. He was, quite simply, beautiful.

Confused, I lowered my head, and saw that his hand rested on a copy of *Whitaker's Almanack* for the year 1880. He picked it up, and with a rush of fear, I realised that he might turn to go and I would never see him again.

'A fascinating volume,' I said hastily, 'If what you require is lists of weights and measures, or the names of insurance companies.'

He turned to look at me. I saw a twitch of amusement at the corner of his beautiful mouth.

'Perhaps in your experience, the Almanack is dull, but for me, finding it here is like meeting an old friend.' I heard a hint of a foreign accent in his carefully rounded vowels. His voice was husky – deep but not harshly masculine. I found it most compelling. I wanted him to speak again.

'How so?' I prompted.

He gave off the faintest odour of something exotic and oriental: sandalwood or ambergris.

'I have this very edition in my library at home, along with many other books in English – shelves full of them, and bound volumes of magazines and newspapers.'

A library. Someone who valued books, as I did. I could not hide my delighted smile. 'Indeed? I too have an eclectic library. What is the focus of your collection?'

I liked the surprise in his eyes. He let the Almanack drop back onto the table and turned to face me fully. I had his attention.

'My books are of the most varied kind – history, geography, politics, political economy, botany, geology, law – all relating to England and English life and customs and manners.'

'Even though you are not English?'

'I am not. I note you hear my accent, even though I speak so carefully.'

'Your English is impeccable,' I smiled. 'I am pleased to meet an Anglophile, and another book lover.'

'I am a book lover indeed,' he said. He spoke softly, so I had to lean in closer to hear him. 'My books – these companions – have been good friends to me, and for some years past, ever since I had the idea of coming here to England, have given me many, many hours of pleasure.'

I was about to make a witty reply, but there was something in the way he said the word "pleasure" that stopped my tongue. I dropped my eyes, confused. When I raised my gaze to his face, I was again transfixed by his beauty. I knew it was impolite to stare, but his face was so changeable – one moment sunny with laughter, the next dark with intensity. As I watched, his eyes shifted from deep black to rich brown, to an almost cat-like hazel. It must have been a trick of the light, but it was arresting.

He looked back at me with frank silent appraisal. The silence between us grew longer than was polite or comfortable, but I could not bear to move or look away. He was the first to speak.

'And what of your library? You say you too have one of your own?'

'Yes. It is rather catholic, I must confess – I inherited it from my father, but I have catalogued and expanded it.' He nodded, as if fascinated. I raised a hand to my throat, where I could feel my pulse beating rapidly, and then tucked a lock of hair away behind my ear. 'As a young woman, my access to travel and education is curtailed. However, I can experience much of the world between the covers of my books.'

He leaned in close now. Again his woody scent reached me. He spoke into my ear. 'You cannot experience everything through reading,' he said, and there was a huskiness to his tone. 'Some things in life must be – sensated.'

'Sensated?'

'Is this not a word? Perhaps it is a new one I have made. Some things must be felt. Experienced with all the senses.'

'Sensated. A good word. I will adopt it.'

'Well then. We have only just met, and I have given you a word. Who knows what else I may...?' he stopped and allowed a small smile to play across his lips.

He raised a hand and touched his hat, turned and disappeared through the archway leading out of the courtyard.

I stared at the empty space where he had been and then turned to find Mina. Had she seen him? But she was immersed in a volume. I realised he had not introduced himself, and I knew nothing about him, other than that he had a library and was not English, was tall and slim and his clothes were expensive. I could not guess his age – his skin was flawless, but he did not look young. In fact, there was a wisdom in his gaze that suggested he was older than he appeared. I knew beyond doubt that I had to see him again.

What was I thinking? Yes, I had met a handsome, erudite man. There were not many such in this sleepy Yorkshire seaside town. I was merely inventing some drama for my own amusement. I chided myself for this romantic delusion, went to Mina and chivvied her to complete her selection so we could move on.

We spent the rest of the day in town, and there were several moments where I felt sure I was being watched. As we selected some roses from a flower stall, I sensed something and spun around. The stranger stood across the road, arms folded, watching me with a cool smile. He nodded when our eyes met but did not approach. Instead, he turned to look in the window of a jewellery shop. I glanced across at Mina. She was engrossed in conversation with the flower seller. I crossed the road and stood beside him. We both gazed into the jewellers' window. There was a display of jet necklaces, rings and earrings.

'These black jewels,' he said. 'Most unusual.'

'Jet. I believe it is mined in the area.'

He pointed at a bracelet of glittering, square-cut stones.

'Those would look well encircling your wrist.'

I did not reply, and we both continued to gaze at the display. Calmly, he removed his glove and reached over. He touched one cool finger to the inside of my wrist, stroking lightly. I felt the hairs rise at the back of my neck. The skin all over my body prickled and my pulse thundered in my ears. It seemed the most intimate touch I had ever experienced. I wanted him to caress my wrist like this forever. I wanted him to slide my sleeve up and... I was excited almost beyond endurance. But any moment now, Mina would turn from the flower stall and look for me. She would see me standing too close to the stranger. Any moment...

'Lucy?'

The enquiring tone of her call meant she had not immediately seen me. I jerked my arm away as if his touch burned me.

I spun around and called, 'I am here, Mina.'

Her brow cleared when she saw me, and she crossed the road, smiling. When I dared to glance back, the stranger was gone.

Later, as we took tea in our favourite tearoom, I saw a tall dark form pass by, distorted by the dimpled glass of the window. I stood, letting my napkin tumble unheeded from my lap and ran to the open doorway, but there was no one in the street that matched the shape I had seen. Mina frowned when I returned to the table, and I felt compelled to explain.

'I met... a stranger when we were looking at the books earlier,' I said. 'He was ... I have never encountered anyone like that. Not here in Whitby. Not ever.'

'In what way was he extraordinary?' Mina asked.

But I was unable to find the words. Tall. Beautiful. Fascinating, changeable eyes. A gentleness and a focus I had never experienced in any man. He had spoken to me like an equal. All of these sounded like clichés from a romantic novel. Mina listened to my halting attempts to describe him.

'Do you think that you are responding to this person as you once did to Quincey Morris?' she asked carefully.

I thought about this. 'My liaison with Quincey was born of attraction, that is true. But that was where it ended. Quincey was amusing company, and I very much enjoyed the physical aspect of our interaction. But that was the limit of it.'

'Are you sure?'

'I miss the physical pleasure Quincey gave me. But I do not miss him as a person. I think of him with vague nostalgia and friendly warmth. But this person.... I felt something instant and profound. A... connection.'

Later

I recorded the events of the day in my journal and fell asleep, but in the night, the mysterious stranger filled my dreams. I imagined that I rose and sat by the window, as I had the night before, during the storm. As the sun rose, I dreamed that he appeared below the window and beckoned to me. What was his name? I had no idea. If he had a name, I did not wish to know it. In my mind, he was only the Stranger. I went to him. In the vision, his face blurred and merged with Mina's dear features and the form in my arms was both strong and male and soft and female – all the sensations at once. I felt the strength of an arm about me and I rested a hand on a waist as slender as my own. Where Quincey's lips had been seeking and gentle, the lips that pressed on mine were hard and demanding, pressing my mouth open and seeking for something. I felt desire rise in me and crash, sudden as a wave.

I awoke with a gasp. I was standing naked in the middle of the room with Mina beside me, murmuring words of reassurance. She coaxed me to put on my nightgown, which lay discarded on the floor and then folded me back into my bed. I could not look at her, for in my moment of desire, it had been her lips, her tongue I had imagined against mine. I know dreams are not truth, but my mind had created this image and it disturbed me.

Mina sat with me and I pretended to fall asleep, so she would creep back to her own bed. The images of the dream were still vivid in my mind's eye, and the powerful sense of physical arousal I had felt had not abated. I was restless and there was a pressure deep in my belly so intense it was almost painful.

9 AUGUST 1894

Wherever we have been in Whitby over the last couple of days, I have looked for the mysterious Stranger's tall frame. Mina reports that my sleepwalking has become even worse – she finds me pacing the room or trying to open the door every night. Poor dear, considering how disturbed her sleep must be, she remains resolutely cheerful, although I can see that worry about Jonathan clouds her thoughts at every turn.

In true Mina style, however, she puts her worries to one side and busies herself in taking an interest in the wreck of the Dmitry. She has cut out the report from the local newspaper, the *Dailygraph*, about the wreck of the ship. It was written in such a high dramatic style that we quite giggled to read it. The 'Correspondent' seemed determined to drum up the maximum intrigue about the ship running aground. He speculated wildly about what might have happened to the captain – the dead man lashed to the wheel – and to the missing crew. He even appended a "transcription" of the log of the ship. The Correspondent gave himself a disclaimer in that what he wrote was "translated" by a clerk at the Russian consul. It was full of speculations about an evil spirit on board and detailed the crew disappearing one by one. Mina has dismissed it as an elaborate fiction.

CUTTING FROM "THE DAILYGRAPH," 10 AUGUST

Yesterday two residents of Sandsend, Mr and Mrs William Cawse, took advantage of yesterday's fine weather to undertake a fossil-hunting exhibition upon the fine sandy beach of their town.

Rounding a corner, they were shocked to discover a group of eight or so men of rough appearance, camping on the beach. The men had built a fire and had drawn up a lifeboat beside them, suggesting they had arrived at that locale from the sea. When Mr Cawse attempted to speak to them, they shrugged and professed to speak no English. Upon hearing them in conversation with one another, Mr Cawse thought that they were speaking Russian or some other language of the Eastern states.

Mrs Cawse was distressed by the appearance of the men, who looked most threatening. The couple retired from the beach and informed the coastguard of what they had seen.

The only ship to have arrived lately at Whitby from the East of Europe is the Dmitry, so lately run aground upon Tate Sands at Whitby. It is therefore possible that these ruffians were the crew of the Dmitry who may have mounted a mutiny and killed their captain. They may have escaped the ship in the chaos of the storm before it ran aground.

However when the guard visited the beach, the men had disappeared, leaving only the detritus of their camp behind. The mystery of the wreck of the Dmitry remains, therefore, unsolved.

10 AUGUST 1894

Today was the day of the captain's funeral. We walked up the stairs toward the churchyard and Mina pointed down into the harbour. A cortege of boats went up the river to the Viaduct and came down again. Then the coffin was carried by captains all the way from Tate Hill Pier up to the churchyard. We stood back and paid our respects from a distance.

Later, Mina took me on a frankly exhausting hike along the cliffs as she puzzled out the story of the Dmitry and the death of the captain.

'It seems to me,' she said as she scrambled up a steep path strewn with rocks, 'that the power rests with the person who tells the story. The anonymous Correspondent does not risk his own reputation because his name is not printed in the newspaper. He has spun a version of the tale that most satisfies the salacious tastes of his reading public and his editor, and it merits the widest coverage on the front page. The second version of the story, the tale of the mutinous crew, merited just one small column on an inner page of the paper days later. It is less sensational, even if it is true.'

'But what is the truth?' I hurried to catch up with her. 'Do you believe that the Russian men on the beach were the crew of the Dmitry? Is that not an equally convenient version?'

'Perhaps it is. My point,' said Mina reaching the highest point of the cliff walk and stopping to look back over Whitby Harbour, 'Is that the person who writes the story decides which version is the truth. Thus, the story on the front page of the *Dailygraph* becomes the received version.'

We walked as far as Robin Hood's Bay and stopped at a tearoom. I found the tea that was served particularly delightful – the flavour was strong and dark, so unlike the pallid Lady Grey Mother insists we drink at home. I asked the landlady of the tearoom for the name of the leaves they served, and she most obligingly gave it to me. She brought plates piled with cakes and sandwiches to our table. Mina and I were both ravenous and ate with gusto.

I noted then that Mina kept glancing left and right to see if other patrons were concerned by our enthusiastic enjoyment of our meal.

'Why do you suppose we as young women are encouraged to eat little and to eat blandly?' I asked her.

'I don't know,' said Mina.

'I have long suspected that society believes if we as women have too hearty an enjoyment of food, it might lead us to a dangerously enthusiastic attitude towards other bodily pleasures.'

Mina almost choked on her sandwich. 'Do you truly believe that?'

'I am not alone in thinking so,' I told her of an article I had read by Sarah Grand, quoting from memory: "'Women were awaking from their long apathy, and, as they awoke, like healthy hungry children unable to articulate, they began to whimper for they knew not what." Women are beginning to speak up,' I said, 'saying out loud that there are things we want. Work, freedom. Physical pleasure. Why not cake too?'

'So to enjoy my meal is a political act?' she said mischievously. 'That said, whenever I have been judged for eating greedily, it has been by other women, rather than by men. My aunt was forever requiring me to eat more daintily, and girls at school frowned upon the enjoyment of meals and treats. Jonathan, on the other hand, always laughs with pleasure when I relish my food.'

'My mother sees slimness and abstinence as a virtue,' I said, helping myself to a further sandwich, 'but I am revelling in this too much to care whether I am shocking anyone.'

By the time we had walked all the way back to Whitby, we were exhausted. Our own little churchyard was a welcome sight when we rounded the last bend. We began to descend the stairs to the town, eager to get home and get to bed.

The shadows were lengthening and formed deep pools of obscuring shade at every bend of the staircase, so we were almost upon the Stranger before we realised. The tall, slender figure was standing still and calm on one of the landings, as if waiting for someone. Mina did not pause, nodding a polite greeting in passing. I was a few steps behind her and I slowed, my heart thudding in my chest. Our eyes met and again I felt the powerful shock of recognition and attraction.

I revelled in the opportunity to examine this compelling face again. There was something extraordinary about the features – the curved nose, the eyes widely spaced and tipped up at the outer corners, the soft, full lower lip, the small, neatly formed chin. It was face that Mother might have dismissed as effeminate, but it was not. It was – if I were to impose a description – not quite human. It had the same beauty as a mountain or the sea – timeless and impassive, an otherworldly being. I wondered what I would have to do to make emotion break across those perfect features.

'Lucy?'

I jumped when I heard Mina call my name, and scurried to catch up with her. She did not comment on the Stranger we had passed on the stairs.

She simply said, 'Come on. I am exhausted and cannot wait to unlace my boots.'

True to her word, Mina fell asleep almost as soon as we reached home. As I write in my journal, she sighs and frowns, no doubt dreaming of Jonathan. For myself, I cannot shake my feeling of trepidation and excitement. Perhaps I might encounter the Stranger once more?

CHAPTER 13

10 MARCH 2024 – KATE

*J*ames was waiting on the platform when I got off the train. I saw him before he saw me, so I had a few seconds to observe him. He was tall – probably at least six foot four, wearing clean jeans and an ironed shirt. He looked... nice. Nothing at all like the scruffy, edgy men who had peppered my dating history. Nothing like Alex. If we'd met at a bar or a dinner party, I wouldn't have given him a second glance.

He was scanning the people getting off the train, looking up and down the platform. He turned then and caught my eye, frowning uncertainly, and when I waved, his face lit up. Hs smile was so wide and genuine, I couldn't help smiling back. He strode up the platform towards me.

'Kate!' he dropped a quick, unselfconscious kiss on my cheek. 'May I?' he took my suitcase from my hand. 'My car's this way.'

James drove a newish hatchback car. It was clean and free

from litter. His maisonette flat was tidy and furnished with items that looked like he had chosen them himself.

He showed me to his spare room, where a single bed was made up with fresh linen. There was a towel folded on the pillow. I paused there alone for a moment, oddly reluctant to go back out to the kitchen. James hadn't done anything exceptional, but most of my friends are itinerant travellers who pride themselves on their ability to fit their whole lives into a backpack. This was the home of an adult – someone established and settled. I ran a hand over the surface of the neat bedside table. It held a reading lamp, a clock radio, and a box of tissues. He'd chosen all these things and arranged them. I went to the bathroom, tidied my hair and put on some bright lipstick, then fetched the bottle of wine and chocolates from my bag.

James was in the kitchen brewing coffee. Soft music spilled out of the radio on the windowsill. I paused in the doorway and watched him. He moved around his small kitchen with practised economy. He was really very tall, with a slight stoop. He'd put on glasses to drive, and he was still wearing them. He had recently trimmed his beard. Despite everything I thought I knew about myself, I found him heart-thumpingly attractive.

I knew from our video chats that he was handsome, but seeing him in person made this theoretical knowledge painfully real. He had greeted me at the station with a warm smile and that light kiss. I'd felt my face flush as I drew away from him. I'd been aware of his warmth beside me every minute we were in the car. And now, standing just a few feet from him, I had to quell the urge to step closer and lay a hand on his forearm. I had no idea what he thought about me – whether he found me attractive. But next to him I felt scattered, messy, unmade.

He noticed me now, standing in the doorway, and smiled.

'I've got Hobnobs – chocolate or not chocolate, or ginger nuts. Or all three.' He held out a biscuit tin.

'Thanks,' I said. 'And here.' I held out the gifts I'd brought.

'Well, you can keep the biscuits. I'm having chocolate.'

He opened the box of chocolates and took great care to read the leaflet and identify each one before making his choice. I perched on a barstool and sipped my coffee.

'So, I thought we'd go out for lunch, if that's okay. There's a nice Italian place... Oh,' his face fell. 'You lived in Italy.'

I laughed. 'I'm not a food snob, honest. I promise not to be sniffy about whether the pasta is al dente. Although I do draw the line at pineapple on pizza.'

'I think that's a reasonable line. Anyway, after lunch, I'll take you on the deluxe, air-conditioned tour of my family history. I can guarantee a rollercoaster of emotions, even if one of those emotions is boredom.'

The Italian restaurant was indeed excellent, and James seemed delighted that I approved of the bruschetta and melanzane alla parmigiana we shared. As we chatted, the ease of our online conversations began to return. When we finished, I insisted on paying.

'The Harker hotel is so well appointed. Please let me treat you.'

'Well, if you insist,' he said. He reached across the table and squeezed my hand in thanks, and I felt my breath catch.

'Come on then,' I said, pulling my hand back and standing, 'where's the air-conditioned bus?'

'Well, it's just a Ford Focus, but if you're good, I'll let you sit on the top deck.'

The first stop on James's tour was around the corner from the restaurant. He stopped the car and pointed across the road. There was a Tesco Express, sandwiched between a barbershop and a dry cleaner.

'What am I looking at?'

'Er... nothing,' said James. 'Sorry, this part of the tour is a bit rubbish. There was a rooming house here, back in the day.

Jonathan had a couple of rooms here. It was demolished in the sixties and this building replaced it.'

'Just a couple of rooms?'

'He was a trainee solicitor and an orphan. I suppose he was quite poor.'

He started the car again and drove down towards the river.

'I like to think of Jonathan walking along this road, briefcase in hand, on his way to work.' He smiled at this mental image.

'You look a little like him,' I said, 'I mean ... from the photo you sent me.'

'Well, we're both tall and blue-eyed, I suppose,' James said, but I could see he was pleased.

Next, James showed me the imposing red-brick building where Hawkins and Harker had had their offices.

'Quincey, my great-grandfather, studied law too, and took over as the managing partner at Hawkins and Harker. Jonathan died fairly young, so I don't think they worked there at the same time. But Quincey lived to a ripe old age. None of his children followed him into the firm, so it closed down in the seventies when he retired.'

'Quincey?' I said, 'I've been meaning to say... it seems an unusual name for an English solicitor, especially in a family of Jameses, Matthews and Jonathans.'

'I know. Named after an old family friend, apparently. Quincey says so in his journals.'

'Who was Hawkins?'

'Peter Hawkins – Jonathan's mentor. Jonathan was his solicitor's clerk, and when he qualified, Hawkins made him a partner. He introduced Mina and Jonathan, according to a letter my grandfather had. He had no children of his own, so they inherited everything – the firm and a beautiful old house in Magdalen Road.'

'Quite a benefactor.'

'Indeed. Come on. I'll show you the house.'

We parked across the road. The house was old, ivy-covered and set back from the street.

'It's beautiful.'

'I know,' James said, looking up at it, his arms folded. 'I really, really wish it hadn't been sold. No member of my family could afford to buy it now.'

'Quite a jump in circumstances for Mina and Jonathan,' I observed. 'From two rooms in a rooming house to this.'

'Well, yes. They could put down real roots.'

I glanced up at him. I fancied he looked wistful. He turned and caught my look.

'Come on,' he said, 'it's getting late. We can go out to The Underhill tomorrow. It's on the outskirts of town. Let's go home and make dinner.'

He held out his hand. I looked into his eyes and felt the air shift between us. I put my hand in his and we walked back to the car.

LUCY WESTENRA'S SECOND
JOURNAL

11 AUGUST 1894

I recount the events of this night after the fact. But first, I must assert that while Mina is convinced that I sleepwalked, I did not. I was fully awake and remember every detail.

After I completed my previous journal entry, I slept deeply for perhaps two hours and then woke suddenly, as if someone had shaken me. I sat up and looked around, expecting to see Mina or Mother by my bedside. But the door was shut and Mina slept on peacefully. Had there been a knock on the door? I listened, but the house and the street outside were silent. The moon was bright and its light pooled on the rug as I crossed to the window.

The Stranger was outside, standing on the pavement opposite, looking up at my window. We watched each other for a long moment, and then I stepped back and went to the door. Mina usually locks it in case I walk in my sleep, but in her exhaustion, she had merely latched it. I crept down the stairs and out of the front door.

I thought the Stranger would be waiting for me, but when I emerged, I saw the loping strides of a figure disappearing away, down the street towards the harbour. There was no backward glance – only the certain knowledge that I would follow. It was not until I reached the rough cobbles of the quayside that I noticed that I had neither dressed nor put on shoes. I wore only my white nightgown and was barefoot. I hesitated, but the tall, slim form was still moving away. It was too late to go back.

I passed over the bridge. A fish leapt as I went by, and I leaned over to look at it. I heard a lot of dogs howling – the whole town seemed as if it must be full of dogs – as I went up the steps. The Stranger was ahead of me, never looking back, but never moving so fast that I could not keep those slender shoulders in sight. My feet were cold and sore, but I did not stop.

The Stranger was waiting for me, as I had expected, on the bench in the churchyard. I stepped into open arms and every-thing – everything changed forever. The taste of that mouth – bitter and sweet. The caresses – hovering at a point where pain meets pleasure.

I knew I should be cold, but as the Stranger gathered my nightgown up around my waist, baring my flesh to the night air, I felt only the heat of touch. I lay back along the bench. As the Stranger loomed over me, I arched my back and gave myself up utterly.

I expected some of the physical sensations I had experienced with Quincey, but this was different. Yes, there was pressure, lips and tongues, pleasure. But this as something other – a merging of bodies and spirits. This was not man and woman – this was a transforming, a union, I could not tell where my self ended and the Stranger's began. The body above mine did not seem to have physical form – there were moments when I laid my hand on hot skin, and times when I seemed to be enveloped in a swirl of cold mist. But all of this seemed distant and unimportant in the intensity of the pleasure I felt.

It seemed to me that I left my body then. I felt myself floating above the harbour, looking down on the lights reflecting on the water. I could see the great beams of the lighthouses, swinging ceaselessly below me and hear the creaking of boats at rest along the quay. In my incorporeal form, I turned back towards the cliffs and observed my insignificant body, like a wisp of white, spread beneath the dense, moving blackness of the Stranger. How could I be in my body, acutely feeling every sensation as we merged together, and yet also be here, so far above, watching it happen? I could feel something building between us, dark, inexorable and irresistible.

With vague curiosity, from my position high above the harbour, I spied a small figure climbing the stairs and approaching the place where the Stranger and I were joined on the bench.

Time stretched and then snapped, cruelly and suddenly. I felt the Stranger draw from me, leaving me cold and bereft, and then I was dragged fully back into my singular body with an agonising wrench. With a great effort, I opened my eyes, and saw Mina leaning over me, her face shining with concern.

I sat up, breathing hard, and looked around. Where was the Stranger? How could I be left in that surpassing moment of...? But Mina was shaking me, trying to rouse me, and talking.

'Lucy,' she said breathlessly, 'Lucy my dear. You have been sleepwalking again. My poor dear love. Let me get you home.'

I hated her in that instant. Really, purely hated her. She seemed not to notice my distress. She drew the shoes from her feet and put them on mine and wrapped me in her shawl. She led me down the stairs and back through the silent town. At one point, a drunken man crossed our path and she dragged me into a doorway until he had lurched by. I could feel her trembling beside me.

We made it back to the house without further incident, although Mina was hobbling by the time we reached the door. Once inside, she bathed her feet and mine, and sank to her knees to pray a fervent prayer. She asked no questions – she clearly assumed I had experienced a more extreme version of one of my sleepwalking episodes. If she had seen the Stranger, or what had passed between us, she made no mention of it.

Once she was sure I was safe and tucked beneath the covers, she slipped into her own bed and fell almost instantly into a deep, still sleep. I lay on my back, feeling warmth creep back into my limbs. The darkest part of the night had passed, and light had begun to glow over the horizon. I ran my hands gingerly over my own face, neck, limbs and body, looking for tenderness or pain, for signs that I was forever changed. As the first limpid rays fell into the room, I raised my fingers above my face to see what I had sensed in my tentative exploration.

A single ruby drop of blood.

12 AUGUST 1894

We awoke at noon. I lay in my bed for some time, trying to order my confused memories from the night before. I felt a powerful, languorous pleasure through my body, and within in it, an ache of hunger, I wanted more. I did not know this Stranger – I did not even have a name. We had not exchanged a single word on the previous evening, and yet I had willingly – ravenously – granted access to my whole self. Should I regret it? Perhaps I should, but I did not. While the memories were still fresh, I rose and recorded them above. When Mina awoke, I reassured her that I was well, and suggested we go out and enjoy the fine weather.

Mother was surprisingly strong – as strong as I had seen her in months, so we urged her to leave the house for a picnic. We sent her by carriage to Mulgrave Woods and walked there ourselves. We spent happy hours there in the bright sunshine.

This evening, we all strolled a few streets along from our rooms to attend a chamber concert, where local musicians were playing a nonet by Spohr, among others. The hall was small and close, and the heat of the summer evening pressed in on us. The rustle of ladies' fans made an accompaniment to the music. I glanced around at the assembled crowd, who looked as though they too would rather be elsewhere. I too was restless and could not concentrate. I moved in my seat and sighed.

I sensed the Stranger before I saw the shadow standing at the back of the hall. Our eyes met, and with a single, almost imperceptible nod, that slight figure turned and left through the open door. I was on my feet without realising I had moved. Mina grasped my wrist.

'I feel a little faint,' I whispered. 'Stay with Mother, please. I just need a breath of air.'

The Stranger was waiting in the alleyway along the side of the concert hall. Even though the sun had not fully set, the shadows were deep black. I was drawn into a doorway, which concealed us completely from view.

'I have looked everywhere for you...' I gasped, but a hand was pressed over my mouth.

This time, the touch was peremptory, rough and demanding. I was excited beyond endurance as the Stranger gathered up my skirts and pressed my back into the rough brick wall. As the music rose to a crescendo in the hall behind us, we claimed our pleasure with fierce, fast concentration. And as the applause pattered politely, I was set back on my feet, and with a light kiss, the Stranger disappeared into the lowering night. On trembling legs, I found my way back into the hall and sank down next to Mina and Mother. I felt I had travelled to another planet in the few minutes I had been absent.

Mina was clearly fearful that my 'sleepwalking' episode might repeat itself, so that night, she locked our bedroom door and placed the key on a ribbon around her wrist.

TELEGRAM, HOLMWOOD, RING, TO LUCY WESTENRA, WHITBY. 15 AUGUST _

Father is much improved. He would like us to marry as soon as possible.

16 AUGUST 1984

I stared at the telegram and handed it to Mina. It might as well have been written in a foreign tongue, for the words did not reach me at all. Art seems a distant shadow.

Mina tells me my sleepwalking persists. I have no recollection of these episodes. I do not mind that she keeps me locked in, for the Stranger has not come for me in the night again.

Mina's worries about Jonathan make her distracted, and it is all too easy to make an excuse to go for a walk on my own, to say I want to visit the bookshop alone, or to make a sketch from a particular beauty spot. Wherever I walk, I am found. That irresistible form moves through crowds toward me, and I cannot understand why everyone does not turn to stare. The Stranger seems to know every corner and cranny of Whitby, and draws me into hidden rooms, concealed doorways and deserted cellars. Our encounters are brief, intense and always silent. Not a word passes between us. Each time, I am pushed to an explosive and aching climax, which is closely followed by the Stranger's own silent, shuddering pleasure. My body vibrates constantly with the memory of it.

This afternoon, I saw Mother and Mina, their heads close together. Mother held Mina's hand and whispered to her urgently. This evening, Mina confided that Mother had spoken about her health concerns. She spoke at length to Mina , saying she feels happier now she knows I will be in Art's care when she dies. She is particularly afraid of receiving a sudden shock, which Dr Oliver has said could cause her heart to stop entirely.

'We must protect her,' I said. 'She must be kept calm at all costs.'

'I have not mentioned your sleepwalking,' Mina said carefully. 'It would help nothing, and to make her worry would place her in unnecessary danger. And besides, since I have been keeping the key on my wrist, you have not been able to leave the bedroom.'

I should feel a pang about deceiving Mina.

17 AUGUST 1894

The house was quiet today. Neither Mina nor Mother could bring themselves to stir abroad. They sat in the drawing room and occupied themselves with sewing and desultory conversation. I contrived to go out, using the excuse that I wished to purchase some of the tea Mina and I had enjoyed in the teashop in Robin Hood's Bay. I went from shop to shop looking for it. Eventually, I was able to purchase several packages, but this did not curtail my wandering. I was not looking for tea – I was looking for the Stranger. I walked the town from end to end, but there was no sign.

Mina and I retired early. She, as usual, fell asleep quickly, while I lay staring at the ceiling, fidgeting with restless energy. I must have fallen asleep or at least closed my eyes, for in the darkest hour, they snapped open as if someone had pressed a hand to my shoulder. The night was silent, but I knew what had woken me. I rose and went straight to the window. A dense sea mist swirled and there, in the street below, those beautiful black eyes gazed up at me. I had been woken by proximity alone.

I glanced back at Mina. She had buried herself under the covers so that only the top of her head showed above the counterpane. There was no way to loosen the key from her wrist without waking her. I opened the window and leaned out. The Stranger stood, neither beckoning nor speaking. I reached out a yearning hand, but the distance was too great. Our fingers could not touch.

I knew why the Stranger had come. I felt a deep wrench. I could not bear this loss, and yet I knew I must. We stayed like this, me reaching longingly, the figure standing straight and still in the road below. Then with a single, swift bow of the head, the Stranger turned and moved off up the hill with long strides. Passing into the shadows, it seemed to me that the Stranger dropped onto all fours and began to lope, like a wolf, and as the mist became denser, that wings spread and a creature seemed to fly. It must have been a trick of the pre-dawn light, but as I strained to gaze along the now-empty street, it was obvious that that dear figure had disappeared, and I knew we would never meet again.

The tears came unbidden and thickened my throat, almost choking me. The loss felt physical, as if something had been wrenched out of me. I did not hear Mina getting out of bed, but sensed her once she was beside me. She knelt on the floor in her nightgown and wound her arms around me.

'Lucy, darling girl,' she whispered, 'what is wrong? Oh Lucy, are you ill?'

How could I begin to explain the strange events of the past few days to Mina, the truest love of my heart, my confidante?

'You are distressed, Lucy,' she said gently, 'Your Mother's health, Art, fear for your future – all of these things press on your mind. Try to rest now. In the morning all, will seem clear.'

She urged me into bed then, and climbed into her own. She was soon asleep, but I lay awake, tormented. My dark lover was gone and would not return. This strange liaison showed that I was, and had always been set apart. I was not like other women. Whatever pressures Mother and Art applied to me, I could not marry obediently and take my place in normal society.

I climbed quietly out of bed and fetched my journal. Mina sleeps on as I record this. I must try to sleep now. I must.

19 AUGUST 1894

I was awoken by a tremendous cacophony from downstairs. I flung a shawl around my shoulders and ran down. Mina stood in the kitchen, wearing only her nightgown, with tears flowing freely down her cheeks. She saw me, and her face broke into the widest smile. She rushed to me and hugged me, and I heard the crackle of paper clutched in her fist.

'He is alive! Alive and safe, although he has been very ill.'

She handed me the letter, crumpled and damp with her tears. It came from a Sister Agatha, at the Hospital of St. Joseph and Ste. Mary in Buda-Pesth. Jonathan had been in her care for some six weeks, suffering from a "brain fever". He had been brought in to the hospital after he arrived by train from Klausenburg. He was insensible when he arrived, and they were thus unable to trace friends or family, but now they had managed to find out who he was, they were writing to Mina, care of Mr Hawkins.

'I will go to him at once,' Mina said, 'I will bring him safely home.'

Her powers of organisation are truly formidable. She went upstairs and dressed, and departed immediately for the train station and the telegraph office. By lunchtime, she had booked all the necessary travel and packed a small bag with a single change of dress. She asked me to arrange for her trunk to be conveyed to London. She will send for it upon her return to England.

She was booked on the evening train to Hull, where she

would board a boat to Hamburg. I accompanied her to the station to say goodbye. I felt shaken. Her departure was so precipitous. I felt there was so much unsaid – secrets between us and confidences unshared. I had imagined we would have more time.

'Do not look so sad, Lucy,' Mina said, stroking my cheek. 'This is not goodbye. We will be together in London before long, and you will come to visit us in Exeter.'

'Do you think you will marry in Buda-Pesth?'

'I do not know whether Jonathan will be well enough, or even if he will still want to...' her face clouded.

'How could he not? He loves you so, and there is no finer woman. None in the world.'

I embraced her as tightly as I could – it was almost impossible to will myself to let go. I knew she was right; that our parting was temporary and we would see one another again soon, but it did not seem so.

I stayed on the platform after her train had gone, feeling very alone. Then I trudged home in the lowering evening light, to Mother and our silent little rooms. I felt a low ache in my belly, and when I reached the rooms, realised my menses had begun.

20 AUGUST 1894

Just one day has passed since Mina's departure and I could scream to the heavens with frustration. Mother is querulous, petulant and demanding, and cannot be persuaded to leave the house. When I do manage to escape and go out alone, I find the town to be no comfort. Every place I visit is full of memories.

I climbed the stairs to the churchyard and walked the cliff paths until I exhausted myself. Now the heat of our encounters has passed, I find myself trying to understand what happened between me and the mysterious Stranger who laid claim to my body. How had I allowed the transgressions that had taken place? Who was this person with whom I had joined so freely? The Stranger had come, taken and given, and gone.

Eventually, I concluded that my unions with the Stranger were not the same as those I experienced with Quincey. Our bodies had joined in ways I had not imagined possible. I did not have the words to name the ways desire had risen and flowed between us – and I knew I could not brush off this relationship I had the one with Quincey. Not because I loved the Stranger – how can you love someone you do not know? But because the pleasures I had experienced offered new possibilities – new ways to love and be loved.

Putting these troubling musings aside, I turned my thoughts to the puzzling letter I had from with Mr Boyden. It had posed more questions than answers about Art's relationship with Pa. I found it and read it again. Perhaps I did not have to wait until my return to London to investigate?

On a whim, I made my way down to the Whitby Library, which stood at the Coffee House end of the quay. I enquired of the librarian whether they kept the trade and business directories for London, and he was proud to say that they did. Within minutes, I had found an address for a solicitor named Mr Bevington, the only one of such a name in London. His place of business was in Jamaica Lane, Bermondsey. This was not an area I had visited, although I knew it was not a salubrious part of the city. It was in the Docklands, a place of wharves and warehouses. Why would Art engage a solicitor in such a place? He was concerned with appearances and liked to show his breeding and wealth. Surely he would be more likely to retain a man with elegant offices in Lincoln's Inn or Mayfair?

This evening I have written to Mr Bevington. I considered asking him directly what work he had done for Art with regard to his dealings with Westenra and Co., but I knew he would not be bound to answer. For all I knew, he and Art were the best of friends, and his first act would be to show Art my note. I decided to approach Mr Bevington with a fictitious case and use this to learn about him and the nature of his business. It took several drafts to pen a letter with a tone that I thought would excite no suspicion.

LETTER FROM NORAH SWANSON TO JEREMIAH BEVINGTON

20 AUGUST 1894

Dear Mr Bevington,

I hope this letter finds you well. Your services come very highly recommended as a conveyancer of property, and I wondered if you might help me in a matter of business. I am at present resident in Robin Hood's Bay in Yorkshire, but hope to return to London soon. An aunt of mine has recently died. She lived alone in a small house in Ilford in Essex. She promised me when she was still living that this property would come into my possession, but unfortunately she has passed away without leaving a Will. Would you be able to aid me in resolving this delicate matter? I look forward to your prompt reply. Please reply care of the Post Office in Robin Hood's Bay, as I will be changing my lodgings soon.

Yours respectfully,
Norah Swanson (Miss)

21 AUGUST 1894

Today dawned bright and blustery. I put on my sturdiest walking boots and made the long hike to Robin Hood's Bay. I posted the letter, ensuring that the postmark would show a location other than Whitby, and arranged for the postmaster to hold any return correspondence for me.

LETTER FROM JEREMIAH BEVINGTON TO NORAH SWANSON

22 AUGUST 1894

Dear Miss Swanson,

Thank you for your letter of the 20th inst. I am sure I will be able to help you in this matter. I have a few questions, so that I may better establish how we might proceed.

Are there any other relatives who might lay claim to the property in question? Was your aunt the sole owner? Lastly, do you have any letters written in her own hand?

With answers to these questions, I may well be able to resolve this for you, both simply and effectively."

Yours respectfully
Jeremiah Bevington

23 AUGUST 1894

I embarked on the long walk from Robin Hood's Bay to Whitby, puzzling over this odd letter. What exactly was Mr Bevington suggesting? Why would he require letters from my fictional aunt? One thing was for certain. I needed to investigate further.

I had been gone for most of the day, and was wracked with guilt for my long absence, so I burst into the house in Whitby and ran up the stairs, eager to see Mother. She was in her customary seat by the window, and when she turned to greet me, I saw her cheeks were flushed with excitement.

'You look well, Mother,' I said, going over and bending to kiss her cheek. 'You are quite brightened up.'

'I hope I can take some credit for that,' a voice said behind me.

I spun round and saw Art lounging in the easy chair by the fireplace, one ankle crossed over his other knee. He stood slowly. I had forgotten how tall and broad he was. He seemed to fill the small room. He reached his arms out to me.

'Come here, my dear,' he said. 'You must be shocked to see me. You have not closed your mouth for fully ten seconds.'

Obediently I walked over to him, and he held me firmly by the arms and bent to kiss my cheek. I stood as still as I could, afraid that if I moved, he would hear the rustle of Mr Bevington's letter or feel the hard corners of my journal in the pocket of my skirt. He stepped back and gave me his most brilliant smile.

'You look quite wind-blown, Lucy. Why not run along and tidy yourself up? I thought we could dine out. The hotel where I am lodging this evening is a little shabby, but I am assured the dining room will be able to supply us with a decent repast.'

I nodded and backed away, then rushed upstairs. I could see as soon as I stepped into the room that someone had searched through my things. My letters and papers had been replaced on my desk in a different order. I felt faint with relief that I had been so careful – the only record of my encounters with the Stranger was in this journal, which I always keep with me. I took the letter from Jeremiah Bevington from my pocket now, and wrapping it in a scarf, concealed it amongst my undergarments. Before Art could come looking for me, I changed my blouse and tidied my hair. I took a deep breath, smoothed my skirt and walked back down to the parlour.

Dinner was an odd, stilted affair in the dining room of Art's hotel. I suspect the outing was rather more than Mother could manage. However, she insisted on putting on a brave face, even though I could see she was tired and her lips had a blue cast. When we got home, I helped her up to bed and she collapsed against the pillows, breathing heavily.

'Arthur has decided it is best if we return to London tomorrow,' she said, patting my hand, 'So be sure to pack up your things this evening.'

'Tomorrow?' I said, shocked, 'But we were not meant to return for several weeks yet.'

'Nevertheless,' Mother said.

It seemed that if Art willed that something should happen, it would inevitably be so. I wanted to argue further, but her eyelids closed inexorably and she fell into an exhausted sleep.

I went back to the parlour, ready to argue with Art and insist that I wished to stay in Yorkshire, but to my surprise, he had already departed. I went over to the window and looked out. The evening was still light, and I could see both up and down the road.

I was surprised to see him a short distance away, walking toward the quayside. His hotel was in the opposite direction. Perhaps he was taking an evening stroll? His pace slowed, and he stopped, looking off to his left, down one of the many narrow alleys that ran off every road in Whitby. He beckoned to someone and after a moment, a young woman stepped out of the alleyway. Her gown was cut low and her hair messily tumbled about her shoulders, I had seen her and her like before, talking to the sailors who arrived in the port. She lifted her chin enquiringly, and she and Art exchanged a few words. He dug in his pocket and gave her a handful of coins, and, glancing left and right, followed her into the alleyway.

Who exactly is the Hon Arthur Holmwood? He is undoubtedly not the blandly pleasant, well-born man I have imagined him to be – he uses prostitutes, consorts with solicitors of dubious morals and undertakes business deals that verge on the suspicious. I am even more certain of my resolution not to marry him. Moreover, if there is a way to wrest Mother free from his influence, I will need to manage that too.

Now that I have recorded the events of the past week in this journal, I will make sure it is concealed about my person until we are back in London. Then I can replace it in the secret cubbyhole in the library where it will be safe.

CHAPTER 14

⁂

10 MARCH 2024 – KATE

*N*ow we'd made our intentions clear, there seemed to be no hurry. Neither of us was hungry, so we made do with toast and pâté for dinner. We settled on the sofa in James's small living room with the bottle of wine and quiet jazz.

'So, genealogy. How did you get into that?' I asked.

He smiled. 'Well, I've done some extensive self-psychologising, and I've got a really glib answer to that question. Do you want to hear it?'

'I'm a big fan of self-psychologising, and I love glib, so off you go.'

'It all began when I was born...' he proclaimed theatrically and I laughed. 'No seriously. I was born into a really close-knit, happy family. Grew up around here – less than a mile from here, in fact. Dad was a local lad. He met Mum when she came here for uni from Scotland. We had a great childhood – lots of lovely holidays, Christmas traditions, Labrador in the garden, the full works. Then my Grandad died.'

'Quincey's son?'

'Grandad Luke, yes. He was well off after the sale of Hawkins and Harker and the house, so we all inherited a nice bit of money.'

'Um, good?'

'Well, you'd think so. But these things can be a mixed blessing. In my Dad's case, it seemed to spark a mid-life crisis. Such a cliché. He started an affair with someone from work – someone much younger – and before we knew what was happening, he buggered off to live with her in France.'

'I'm sorry.'

'We kids were all grown up by then. My sister had already moved to London, and shortly after that, my brother took a job in the States – Dallas. So Mum decided to move back to Glasgow. That's where she's from.'

'Wow, so you went from happy, close family to...'

'All on my own, yeah. With my family scattered across the world.'

I reached across and rested my hand on his. He turned his palm up and clasped my hand.

'My reaction was to put down roots. I used my part of Grandad's inheritance to buy this place and start my own company. I was determined to show that I could make a good life in Exeter. That it wasn't the right thing to flee, just because you could. And I got into the family tree stuff because I wanted to dig those roots a bit deeper. Show that the Harkers do belong here. And of course, as you know, once you start researching, you get addicted. You find one clue, then another, then you get obsessed with the unsolved mysteries. I guess not knowing what happened to Mina has always frustrated me. There's a gap in our family story.'

'You must miss them – your family.'

'I do, but they're all happy where they are. Mum remarried – some guy she went to school with – my sister is a rich City type and my brother has two lovely kids. That old family life – well, it's never going to come back, is it? No use crying over it. None of us are the same people anymore.'

'And a future family?' the words were out before I knew I was going to say them. What was I thinking? Yes, I was a bit drunk, but... James didn't seem disconcerted by the question though.

'Do you mean, do I want one?'

I nodded. It seemed safer than speaking.

'Yes, definitely. With the right person. But so far...'

'So far?'

'Is this the "previous relationship" conversation? I'm a serial monogamist, I guess. Three long-term relationships since my early twenties – none of them made it over the wire, all for different reasons.'

I felt very warm, all of a sudden. Standing and wobbling slightly, I went into the kitchen to get a glass of water. I got one for James too. When I was settled back on the sofa, he angled himself towards me and took my hand again.

'So you've had my whole history – family, relationships, warts and all... how about you?'

'I'm an only child. As I told you, my mum died when I was small – cancer. Dad's a research scientist. He works on what they call solid state chemistry – something to do with developing better energy sources. So his work is very worthy, but not something I understand, even though he's tried to explain it to me countless times. I spent a lot of my childhood either alone or with my Gran – Mum's mum – because he was always working. Dad is very impressive. Certain. He always knew what he wanted to do – he had a vocation from birth, practically. He thinks I'm woolly and unfocused. Maybe he's right. I do find it difficult to pick a path and stick with it. Well, I have until now.'

James was watching me intently and his hand felt warm and smooth. I laughed nervously.

'Seems I'm doing my own glib self-analysis. Anyway, I did a degree in English, and then went travelling, mainly to stop Dad asking what I was going to do with my life. And I liked it. I liked the unpredictability, and teaching English meant I could go pretty much anywhere and find work. I met Alex...' his name sounded odd here in this quiet room so far from Milan. '... teaching in Paris in 2010. At first, it was all meant to be casual – mates who were lovers, working and travelling together. I think I was always more invested than he was. And after we'd been together eight years, I genuinely believed we were in a real relationship. We had an apartment together, and years of shared experiences.' I took a deep breath. 'I was trying to find the courage to say I might be ready to – you know – think about a more permanent home, maybe kids, maybe even marriage? Then I came home early from work one day and found a naked girl in my living room. With naked Alex.' I tried a laugh. 'Such a cliché. Anyway, that was when he told me he was actually in love with her. She's called Stacey. She's a twenty-two-year-old Welsh exchange student with a pierced bellybutton.'

'Ouch.'

'Ouch indeed. It all got pretty ugly. Anyway, Stacey's moved into our beautiful apartment in Milan, and I'm living in Beatrice the maid's room and doing crowd control in the schools of North London.'

'I'm sorry.'

'I'm not. I was devastated at the time, but now I realise that he was never going to settle down. Or not with me. I just wish I'd seen it earlier.'

I took in a deep breath, surprised at myself. I'd articulated this without having thought it through, but it was true. Deep down, Alex and I had been doomed from the start. He'd been so careful about never making any promises or talking about the future. He never even introduced me to his parents. He'd said it was because he rejected conventional expectations. But it was more likely because he had always hoped to trade up, so there was no point in integrating me into his family.

James gently took my water glass out of my hand. In that instant, our faces were close together. He leaned in and kissed me softly – just a peck on my lower lip. Then he drew back and looked into my eyes, his eyebrows raised enquiringly. I leaned in and kissed him, sliding an arm around his neck. The kiss deepened. It had been close to a decade since I'd kissed anyone but Alex. It should be strange, but it was just very, very...

James drew back and sat up.

'I'm sorry,' he said.

'Why?'

'I don't want you to think I'm some creepy Internet dude who chats up women and then lures them to my house...'

'I contacted you, remember?'

'I just...' he moved even further away on the sofa and folded his arms. 'I really like you Kate. I think you're interesting and funny, and you've lived a brave life. I don't want to... muck this up.'

I felt a smile creeping across my face.

'Muck what up?'

'Well, the possibility of us having something... real. A real relationship. I would like that.'

Extraordinary. In one day, James had made a clearer declaration of his feelings than Alex had in eight years. Was this how adults began things? No bragging, flirting, lying or pretending? I felt a swell of calm happiness. After years of trying to second-guess Alex's slippery, shifting affections, this felt remarkably simple.

'I like you too,' I said, and he let out a sigh of relief. 'And you're probably right. A drunken shag the first day we actually meet isn't the best way to start.'

'Start?'

'Yes. I would like to start something. With you. Mr James Harker.'

He leaned in and affected a wicked grin, 'Technically, we've had coffee and lunch and dinner, which makes this the third date...'

I laughed and picked up my water glass again.

'Good try.'

* * *

I SLEPT in James's neat spare room that night – deeply and well. I woke when the sun rose and went to use the bathroom. When I emerged, his bedroom door was open and when I looked in, he was lying awake in his bed, arms behind his head. I hesitated for a moment, then walked across the carpet. He folded back the duvet, and I climbed in beside him. It felt like coming home.

LUCY WESTENRA'S SECOND JOURNAL

24 AUGUST 1894

Art booked us onto the earliest possible train. It was a struggle to get Mother and all our luggage to the station in time. We arrived back at King's Cross this afternoon, and Art's carriage awaited us. When we got back to the house, Mrs Staines was waiting on the steps to greet us, harried and red-faced. Art had sent a telegram to say we were coming home earlier than expected, but she had had scarcely twelve hours' notice to re-open the house and ready it for our arrival. Once we were through the door, Art took his leave immediately.

Mother took to her bed and fell into an exhausted sleep. I ate in the kitchen with Mrs Staines, Eliza and Beatrice. Mrs Staines served a hearty stew followed by rice pudding, and we laughed and chattered and had a jolly time. Missy was delighted to see me, and wound herself around my ankles purring, before settling down to sleep on the edge of my skirt where it pooled on the floor. It was just like the nursery suppers I had enjoyed as a child, and it warmed me and gave me strength and courage to plan what I had to do. I have spent the last few hours in my library consulting various almanacs, maps and timetables. It is now ten in the evening, and I feel I am ready.

25 AUGUST 1894

I woke early and dressed carefully in a nondescript grey skirt and white blouse, with a close-fitting jacket. I packed everything I needed into a carpetbag and went down to breakfast.

In as calm a voice as I could muster, I said, 'Mrs Staines, I am sure Mother will be remaining in her room today. When she wakes, could you tell her I decided to do some sketching? I have asked Watkins to drive me to the Royal Academy. I have my drawing materials here.' I patted the bag. 'I plan to return in the early evening.'

'What shall I say if Mr Holmwood comes to call?'

'Just what I have told you. I missed the galleries of London so much when I was in Yorkshire...' I forced myself to stop. I was babbling.

I itched with impatience as Mrs Staines packed a small meal for me. Then I waved goodbye and went to the kitchen door. On my way out, I snatched Mrs Staines's large brown bonnet from its peg and slipped it into my bag. Heart pounding, I walked quickly around the house and met Watkins, who was waiting for me beside Mother's carriage.

London was quiet so we made excellent time on our journey. Watkins dropped me off at the gates of the Academy, and I instructed him to return at four o'clock. I walked purposefully in through the doors and went to the ladies' cloakroom. Once in there, I pulled out the ragged lawn overskirt I had brought, and drew it on over the one I was wearing. Next, I put on a rough wool shawl to cover my tailored jacket and pinned up my distinctive flaxen hair, which I concealed under Mrs Staines' large bonnet. I drew Art's heavy engagement ring from my finger and tucked it into the pocket at my waist. I checked my reflection in a glass. A smart young woman had entered the cloakroom, and a down-at-heel girl – perhaps a governess, or maid on her day off – emerged. As I left the gallery, the disdainful glances I received from the staff and other visitors told me my disguise was effective.

I boarded an omnibus, disembarking near Waterloo Station and began to walk, following the map I had drawn the previous evening. The noise on the streets was cacophonous. Smells assailed me from all quarters, and the footing was treacherous and uneven. I kept my eyes on my feet, but that did not stop the lewd yells and cat calls from workmen and fruit sellers. Some drunken wag even snatched at my skirts, but I managed to dart away, splashing in a puddle of muddy water as I fled.

As I passed into Bermondsey, the streets became narrower and dirtier, and the glances from passers-by appeared more menacing. I was trembling by the time I finally turned into Jamaica Lane. The grim, fishy smell of the river was strong here. I found the house at number 18, a mean, narrow building that leaned drunkenly against its neighbours. The topmost bell had a grubby square of card affixed beside it, which read: "J. Bevington, Solicitor". I hesitated, then pressed it firmly.

I waited so long that I was almost ready to turn away. Mr Bevington must not be at his place of work. I pressed the bell one more time, and heard it ring high above me. Moments later, the street door was wrenched open, and a man stood before me. He was corpulent and sweaty, and his collar had escaped its fastenings on one side and flapped below his left ear. He looked to be about fifty years old. His shirt was none too clean and even though it was not yet lunchtime, I could smell wine on his breath. I could not imagine a less likely acquaintance for Art. I positively stared. He gawked at me in return.

'Did you ring the wrong bell?' he wheezed. 'Are you here for the washerwomen?'

I frowned, confused, but then a gust of steam from behind

him and the scent of boiling washing made all clear. There was clearly a laundry within the premises. I allowed myself a smile. My disguise had done its job. I did not look like a prosperous daughter of Hampstead.

'Mr Bevington?' I said, taking care to flatten my vowels. 'Am I speaking to Jeremiah Bevington?' He stared at me, confusion and guilt chasing one another across his features. Perhaps visitors frequently brought trouble to his door. I hastened to put him out of his misery. 'I'm Norah Swanson? I wrote to you about my aunt's house?'

His jowly face sagged in relief, 'Ah yes, Miss Swanson, I recall your letter very well. A missing Will, was that it?'

'It was indeed,' I said, and smiled guilelessly. He beamed and ushered me in with obsequious ceremony.

We climbed a great many stairs to his "premises" which were at the very top of the house. On the way up, I gained an impression of the building through the mediums of smell and sound. Babies wailed, and scents of refuse and cooking filtered into the hallways. When we reached Mr Bevington's rooms, he hesitated before he opened the door.

'Perhaps you might wait in the anteroom for a moment, Miss?' he said pompously. 'Your visit was a little unexpected...'

'Of course.'

He opened the door, and I had to stifle a laugh. The "anteroom" was an entrance hall so small I could have touched all four walls without moving my feet. He squeezed his considerable bulk through the next door and closed it behind him. I heard feverish sounds of tidying. I untied the ribbons of Mrs Staines' bonnet, but then thought better of it, He might note my unusually light-coloured hair and I did not want to be memorable.

At length, he wrenched open the inner door and ushered me in. His 'premises' consisted of this single room, and formed both his place of business and his home. A bed was pushed against a wall. He had pulled the covers roughly straight, and piled it with files and folders. A desk by the window similarly overflowed with papers. A box in the corner was filled with soiled dishes. I assumed he had his meals brought to him. The air in the room was fetid and close. This was not the lawyer's office I had envisaged.

He swept a further pile of pages off a rickety chair and motioned for me to sit down. He settled himself at the desk, folded his arms over his belly and gave me an oily smile.

'Now, Miss Swanson, if I recall the story, your dearly beloved aunt has died, God rest her soul.' I nodded and tried to look suitably grief-stricken. 'And you are certain that before her death, she made it clear that her house in... Essex, was it, was to pass to you?'

'But she never wrote anything down...'

'Ah yes, but you are sure that that was her intention? Because of course, all we want to do here,' he smiled again, 'is to serve the dying wishes of a dear old lady. And to find the best possible outcome for you, her much-loved niece.' I nodded again. The less I said, the better. 'Now, I am something of a specialist in cases of this sort. Very often when a legal document has been – mislaid – it can serve all parties if a reasonable facsimile can be procured. So, if for example, the title deed to a property was missing, or a Will that had been promised had never been committed to writing, I am able to... how shall we put it... fill the void.'

I looked more closely at the papers piled on his desk. Instead of legal documents, I saw now that they were largely blank – parchments and pages of varying weights and ages. Some of them looked very old. There were also multiple pots of ink and an enormous jar with many pens of different types. Another box was piled with sticks of sealing wax.

He was a common forger. Perhaps he had legal qualifications, or perhaps he did not – he clearly knew enough to write the documents in the correct legal language.

He saw my scrutiny of the desk and shifted in his seat.

'I think I mentioned in my letter that a sample of your aunt's handwriting – especially her signature – would be particularly useful?'

I nodded and drew from my carpetbag a letter I had composed the night before, ostensibly from my fictional aunt Agnes Swanson, written in a shaky hand. He looked at it carefully and then nodded, satisfied.

'Capital, capital. That will do very nicely. Now, as to my fee...' He named a modest sum. I nodded and drew the required banknotes from my bag. 'Now, my dear, if you would be so kind as to grant me an hour or so, I will have the document you need all prepared...'

I looked nervously out of his grimy window into the street below. 'There is nowhere for me to go...'

He looked discomfited, but conceded the point. A young woman alone could scarcely go and sit in the alehouse on the corner, as his other customers might have done. He went out and I heard him knock on the other door on his landing. Some minutes later, he returned with a cup of strong tea on a scratched wooden tray, which he balanced on a pile of papers at my elbow. Then he sat down to work.

For a large man, he had surprisingly fine-boned and delicate hands. His left hand was weighed down with a gold signet ring. Working with smooth efficiency, he selected a piece of paper – not too elegant, but not too rough – and a beautiful, gold-tipped pen. He began by inscribing the words, 'This is the Last Will and Testament...' across the top of the paper in effortless calligraphy. Then he began to write. Every now and then he would turn to me to check a fact. He wrote:

'... Of Miss Agnes Swanson, spinster, of Dalkeith Road, Ilford Essex. I give, devise and bequeath all my real and personal property, including my house at Dalkeith Road, which I own at my death not otherwise effectively disposed of, to my niece...?'

At this point, he inclined his head toward me.

'Norah Wilhelmina Swanson,' I gabbled.

He added the name and concluded the Will in the correctly florid legal language. Then he held out his hand for the letter I had brought, and with breath-taking ease, copied the fictional Miss Agnes Swanson's signature in a single flourish. It was a perfect facsimile in every detail. He invented two witnesses, named them, and witnessed the Will with two different signatures. Once the ink was dry, he folded the Will, applied sealing wax and used his distinctive signet ring to seal it. It bore an image of a rearing unicorn. I allowed myself a little smile that he used an image of this fantastical creature to legitimise his fictional documents. The entire process had taken him less than ten minutes to complete.

He handed me the completed Will, bade me a polite goodbye and saw me out to the street. When the door closed behind me, I stood looking at the document in my hands. I am no legal expert, but to my untrained eye, it looked entirely authentic.

What had I learned? That Jeremiah Bevington was an accomplished forger of legal documents? This did not conclusively solve the mystery of why Art had hired him. Slipping the Will into my bag, I began to walk purposefully back towards Southwark.

Once I was near to Chatham Street, I slipped into a secluded doorway and removed my ragged overskirt and shawl. I tidied my hair as best as I could and replaced Mrs Staines' bonnet with my own elegant hat. I replaced the Godalming ruby on my ring finger, then I squared my shoulders, walked to the door of 17 Chatham Street and rang the bell of Westenra and Co.

I swept into Mr Boyden's office with as much confidence as I could muster. His eyes bulged with surprise when he saw me, and he leapt to his feet.

'Miss Westenra! What a lovely surprise!'

'I am so sorry to barge in unannounced,' I said, smiling sweetly, 'I hope you can forgive me. I was drawing at the Royal Academy, and I had a whim to come and visit the offices. I hope I am not inconveniencing you.'

'Not at all! Not at all!' he rubbed his hands nervously. 'Let me send for some tea.'

He seated me in his office and went to look for a clerk. As soon as he left the room, I leapt from my seat and looked feverishly around the room. Every wall was lined with high filing cabinets. Each drawer was labelled alphabetically and was locked with a heavy brass bar and a large padlock. There was no way I would be able to access the files related to Art's transaction, even if I knew where to look.

Mr Boyden returned, followed by a clerk who set down a tray of tea and backed out of the room. The fine bone china and silver sugar bowl served as a stark contrast to the chipped cup I had been given in Jeremiah Bevington's dingy room. I made small talk and blushed prettily every time Art's name was mentioned. Mr Boyden gradually relaxed and became more expansive.

'Marriage is the greatest gift, Miss Westenra. Mrs Boyden has made me a very happy man. Mr Holmwood will be so lucky to have you as a help and comfort. Will you be making your home at Ring?'

'Well, Arthur does prefer London. But as you probably know, Lord Godalming's health is poor...'

'Indeed. How very lucky he is that his son already has such an interest in the management of the estate.'

My pulse quickened. He had opened the conversational door I had hoped for.

'So he does. He is quite the businessman, my fiancé. I find it so touching that a commercial arrangement between my own father and Arthur brought him into my life. Indeed, in a strange sense, it is almost as if Arthur was Pa's parting gift to me.'

'Who knows how life will unfold, Miss Westenra?' Mr Boyden regarded me with fondness.

'Indeed, Mr Boyden. And I cannot wait until our lives are intertwined, as they should be. Our hearts will be joined, our families mingled, and our estates made as one.'

'A lovely sentiment.'

'With that in mind, I was thinking about the portion of the Ring estate which has passed into the possession of Westenra and Co.' I smiled as innocently as I was able. 'In your letter some weeks ago, you mentioned that it had not been developed. Is that still the case?'

'Indeed,' said Mr Boyden uncomfortably. 'It has not ... been a priority. I will at some point send an agent to visit the property and then we can see how we might best...'

'Oh Mr Boyden,' I said breathily, clasping my hands in an approximation of girlish excitement, 'Imagine if we could do something wonderful with it? Something full of heart. Then I might tell my husband of our actions once we are married. It could be... a wedding present?'

'Oh, I...' he looked confused.

I pushed on while he was wrong-footed. 'You may not know this about my future husband, but he is a soft-hearted man. Some time ago, we visited an orphanage in the East End, and he wept to see the plight of those poor mites.'

My heart pounded at this lie. I prayed that Mr Boyden would not repeat this conversation back to Art.

'I had a thought, while I was sketching at the Academy. What if we took the undeveloped land at Ring and made it into a holiday retreat for unfortunate children? A place where they could escape the hostile air of the city and scamper around in the countryside?'

Mr Boyden stared at me incredulously. To be fair, it was a

preposterous notion. I lowered my eyes. Perhaps tender emotion would move him. I made a show of twisting my engagement ring on my finger. I gazed hard at my lap and then looked at him. My eyes glistened with tears. Sir Henry Irving himself would have been in awe at my performance.

'Oh Mr Boyden,' I whispered, 'I know the land is not in my gift. It is my mother's to give. But she is so very ill... perhaps you might help me to develop my idea, so when I take it to her, it is easy for her to understand? I would so love to do something to make Art happy upon the occasion of our marriage.'

He went very pink indeed. Like many men, he was disarmed by female tears. He blustered, and then, to my surpassing relief, he rose and went to a nearby cabinet. He drew an enormous bunch of keys from his pocket and unlocked the topmost drawer, the one marked with the letter G (for Godalming, I supposed). He withdrew a manila folder and brought it to the desk, opening it between us.

There was a folded map, which Mr Boyden opened and spread on the desk. It showed the dimensions of the estate at Ring. A red line delineated the portion of land purchased by Westenra and Co. I had seen many such plans of land purchased, but I had never seen one such as this. The area with the red perimeter was a tiny part of the estate on its Southern border. I could see no reason why this piece of land, no more than a few acres, had been carved off. It was far from the river that ran along the North edge of the estate, and so had no easy access to water. It was not large enough for cultivation or animal husbandry. I could not see how it would be of use to anyone.

I turned to the other documents – there was a standard Westenra and Co. contract detailing the terms of the purchase of the land. Again, I had seen many such, and I scanned through the text automatically, looking for the amount Pa had paid. I had to stop myself from gasping. It was an enormous sum of money – many times what he would have paid for a similar piece of land in London. I fought to keep my features composed and turned to the next page. There was the deed for the land. It looked like an impressive and credible legal document – a great sheet of parchment, closely covered in elegant copperplate writing and signed by Lord Godalming himself. Even Mr Boyden would have found little to argue with in this weighty artefact. I too would have believed it to be genuine, were it not for the seal – a great blob of red wax, marked with the imprint of a rearing unicorn.

I had seen all I needed to. I made more small talk with Mr Boyden, and we agreed we might build two or three small cottages on the land that could serve as a holiday home for the children of the East End. When I returned home, I would write to him and say I had thought better of the scheme. Hopefully that would put it out of his mind and he would never mention it to Mother or Art. I glanced up at the clock and realised it was past three o'clock. I had less than an hour to make it back to the Academy where Watkins would be waiting to take me home. I bade a hasty farewell to Mr Boyden, and he sent a clerk to hail me a hansom cab.

Now I have written all this down, I realise I came away from Westenra and Co. with more questions than answers. I have learned that Art paid Jeremiah Bevington to draw up fraudulent deeds for the land he sold to Pa. It is likely he sold it without the knowledge or permission of his father. Why? And why had Pa bought it, and for such an inflated price? He was a shrewder businessman than that. The answer will not be found in a folder in Westenra and Co.'s filing cabinets. But where will I discover it? Pa is dead, and his motives have gone with him to the grave.

CHAPTER 15

11 MARCH 2024 – KATE

*J*ames and I didn't get out of bed until nearly noon. I would quite happily have stayed right where we were. It didn't feel like we were new lovers – our bodies fitted together with an ease I'd never experienced. But eventually, hunger eventually drove us from the crumpled sheets and into the kitchen. James scrambled eggs and I buttered toast. The radio played softly and we grinned at each other like idiots.

'What time is your train?' James passed me a mug of coffee.

'Trying to get rid of me?'

'Definitely, definitely not. But I did promise to take you to Mina and Lucy's school.'

'It's at three.'

He checked his watch. 'If you eat your breakfast in ten minutes and we each take fifteen minutes to shower, the Under-hill is twenty minutes away. We'll probably want an hour there...'

I saw the glint in his eye.

'Probably just half an hour...' I suggested.

'Well, the school is close to the station. That leaves us with a free half an hour...'

'Whatever will we do?'

* * *

It was close to 2pm when James drove up the winding country road that led towards the main building of The Underhill. I stared at the rolling lawns and velvety hockey pitches that surrounded the school – the grounds couldn't have been more different from the modern comprehensive I'd attended in Hertfordshire. We'd had one tarmacked basketball court and a scrappy patch of lawn. James swung around a bend and then pulled over into a roadside picnic spot. He pointed up the hill.

'There it is. It's Sunday so the gates will be locked, so I can't get any closer.'

I got out of the car and stood on the verge looking up at the main building. It was built of a warm, golden stone and was elegantly symmetrical, in the neoclassical style.

'I'd love to get closer and see the Westenra Laboratories... maybe there's an archive about previous pupils.'

'I've written to them about Mina, and they weren't able to tell me much – just the dates she studied and worked there.'

I stared up at the school. Something about the building niggled.

'I know this sounds crazy,' I said, 'but it seems familiar – more than it would be from the pictures I've seen online.'

'Could you have come here at some point in the past?'

'I don't think so. As far as I know, I've never been to Exeter before.'

'Maybe you came here as a child. Or in a past life.'

. . .

SOMETHING about his words tipped my memory into action. I scrabbled in my bag for my phone. Feverishly, I started scrolling through my camera roll until I came to the shots I'd taken of Mum's drawings. There was her sketch of the honey-coloured building on a hill. I held my phone screen up so James could compare.

'That's...' he stared open-mouthed. 'That's incredible!'

'I'm not going crazy, am I? It's the same building. Drawn from pretty much exactly this spot.'

James looked closely, comparing details.

'That's definitely the portico, and those columns look identical.' He counted windows. 'Yup. Unless we're both crazy, that's definitely The Underhill.'

I gazed up at him, my heart pounding in my chest. 'So... she came here. Mum... when she was learning about Lucy. She came to the school. And she stood right here, and she drew it.'

LUCY WESTENRA'S SECOND JOURNAL

BUDA-PESTH, 24 AUGUST

Dearest Lucy,

I found my dear one, oh, so thin and pale and weak-looking. All the resolution has gone out of his dear eyes, and that quiet dignity which I told you was in his face has vanished. He is only a wreck of himself, and he does not remember anything that has happened to him for a long time past. At least, he wants me to believe so, and I shall never ask. He has had some terrible shock, and I fear it might tax his poor brain if he were to try to recall it. Sister Agatha, who is a good creature and a born nurse, tells me that he raved of dreadful things whilst he was off his head. I wanted her to tell me what they were; but she would only cross herself, and say she would never tell.

26 AUGUST 1894

So Mina is married. In her letter, she describes their wedding, which took place as soon as Jonathan was able to sit up and participate. I wanted to feel unalloyed joy at this news but I could not help but be concerned. Mina was tying herself to a man whose last four months were a blank. He could have done anything or had anything done to him. For one with such an analytical brain, she is allowing herself to be ruled by the heart over the head.

Jonathan kept a journal during his travels, although he remembered nothing of what he wrote within the pages. He has given it to Mina and said he did not want to know what is within. She wrapped the journal in paper and sealed it up. She has promised not to read it unless it is necessary for his own safety.

There is an odd formality to this letter– as if she is constrained. It feels as if I have lost her. And in a sense, I have. Mina is married. She will never again be free to be with me in the way we have been.

With a sigh, I refolded the letter and prepared to slip it back into the envelope. As I did so, I glimpsed a mark on the inside of the envelope and my heart leapt. With great care, I unfolded the envelope, and there, sure enough, was a second letter, written in Mina's precise shorthand. I raced to the library and sat down with my shorthand manual to decode it.

LETTER, MINA HARKER TO LUCY WESTENRA

BUDA-PESTH, 24 AUGUST

Dearest Lucy,
     This letter contains confidences I would not want

Jonathan to see, so I have taken the precaution of using our secret method.

He is not the man to whom I bade farewell in early May. He is profoundly changed. He stoops like an old man, his hands shake and he cannot maintain eye contact. He stumbles over his words, where before he was smoothly articulate in his speech. Although I swore I would not, while he slept, I read some pages of his journal. Lucy, I fear he is truly mad. His thinking is disordered, and he suffers from delusions about the Count he went to visit. He believes him to be an evil, supernatural being. Jonathan also maintains that the castle was inhabited by malevolent "voluptuous" women who wished to devour him in some way. I know little about the science of the mind, but it seems to me that my beloved is very ill indeed.

You may then wonder why I acquiesced to our precipitous wedding. All I can say is this. I love him. The priest asked us to swear our loyalty to one another in sickness and in health, and I did so with a glad heart. Will he ever be well again? I do not know. But I will be by his side and will do my best for him. If it is in my power to nurse him back to health, I will do so. If not, I will care for him and make him feel as safe as I can.

I hope you will keep us both in your thoughts as we prepare to travel back to England.

With all love,

Mina

I heard footsteps on the stairs, and I went to the door of the library, expecting to see Mother. To my surprise, Mr Marquand, Pa's lawyer, came down the corridor, a folder of papers under his arm.

'Lucy!' he said. 'How good to see you.'

I went to take his hand. 'I am glad to see you.' And indeed I was. He was a good friend to my father and has always been kind to me.

'I... er... have been engaged in some business with your mother,' he said and squeezed my hand. I could not help but notice that even while he smiled warmly, his eyes slid off my face, as if he could not bear to hold my gaze.

'Will you stay for tea?' I asked.

'No, no... thank you very much, my dear, but I must decline. Mrs Marquand will be wondering where I am.' Eliza emerged and handed him his hat and coat. He hesitated for a moment, then turned to me. 'Your mother has rather overdone it today, I fear. She felt faint, and I had to call Mrs Staines to help her to bed. Perhaps you might go and sit with her?'

'Of course'

He patted my shoulder lightly and managed a wan smile.

'You are a lovely girl, Lucy. I wish you every happiness in the future.'

It seemed an odd farewell, but I acknowledged his kind words and waved to him as he set off.

Mother was fast asleep. She lay propped up on a high stack of pillows and her breathing was slow and laboured. Her lips had that odd blue cast once more. I dimmed the lamp beside the bed and settled in a chair near the window. I took up a book of poetry from the table beside my chair and tried to read, but I was unable to concentrate on the words.

Now I had a moment to consider it, it struck me as odd that Mother had called Mr Marquand to the house. What had she wanted to discuss with him? She had not mentioned he was coming. Was it a longstanding arrangement, or had she summoned him at short notice? I glanced over at Mother's desk in the corner of her room. I knew what I was doing was wrong, but I was unable to stop myself. I glanced over at Mother. Her mouth was slightly open, her jaw slack. She was deeply asleep. I cleared my throat to see if she jerked awake, but she did not stir.

I crossed to the desk. I saw a handwritten document on heavy, creamy paper. Beneath the Wholeman, Sons, Marquand & Lidderdale nameplate, the words "Last Will & Testament" were inscribed in heavy gothic script. These facts I absorbed almost unconsciously, because it was a name further down the page that had caught my eye. With trembling disbelief, I read the lines:

First, I revoke and make void all former and other Wills and Testaments by me at any Time heretofore made and of this my last Will and Testament do appoint The Honourable Arthur Holmwood sole Executor. I give and bequeath all and every part of my present estate and effects whatsoever and wheresoever unto The Honourable Arthur Holmwood.

Some further legal language followed, but unlike most Wills I had seen, it was remarkably brief. She had made provision for some small bequests – to the servants and the church. Nothing for me. Not even a piece of jewellery. The whole estate, real and personal, was to be left to Art.

I felt my knees weaken and begin to shake. I sank into the chair beside the desk and read the words again. The document was signed and witnessed. This was not a draft – it was a final copy, left by Mr Marquand for Mother's records. A legally binding document. I felt a small, hysterical laugh bubble up in my throat, and, unable to quell it, I rushed from the room and out of the house.

Once on the Heath, I burst forth with an ugly cacophony of hysteria and sobs. I began to walk fast, with little thought as to where I might go. Evening had fallen completely and an icy wind blew. I was chilled, but I gave the cold no heed.

I had imagined that if I held steady in my resolve not to marry for as long as she was alive, the rest of my life would be mine to live as I wished. But she had outplayed me. Mother would argue that she had done nothing wrong. She had undertaken a housekeeping task, and nothing more. Art and I were engaged. Upon our marriage, ownership of all my property would pass to him anyway. She had merely pre-empted this. How was she to know that I had no intention of marrying him?

But as I began to stride up the hill, a chill thought crashed over me. What if she did suspect my plan? I knew she wanted me to make a high-born match more than anything in the world. Would she knowingly trap me into this marriage, even if it was against my will? My breath came short and fast, because of course, she would. She would and she had.

Could I beg her to change her Will again? If I did, it would mean admitting that I had read it. It would lead to vicious arguments and great upset, and I knew from Dr Oliver's confidences how frail her health was. What if defying her brought about her final collapse? No. There was no way to admit what I knew, and no way to reverse her catastrophic action. Father's legacy, which would have given me the freedom to live as I chose, had been snatched from my grasp.

I found myself at the crest of Parliament Hill. Clouds swirled across the darkening sky and I looked up, up, up into the wide heavens, searching for an answer. And then everything seemed passing away from me; my soul seemed to go out from my body and float on the air, just as it had on that memorable night in Whitby with the Stranger. For glorious, endless seconds, I felt myself soar free, released from the cage of my body, freed from earthly concerns and agonies. I floated high as the clouds, gazing down on a vista across all of London. After a few long breaths, I returned to myself, and bracing my hand against the rough trunk of a tree, blinked reality back into being.

In that brief, breath-taking departure from my body, an

inescapable truth came to me. Art and Mother would not chain me with the bonds of money and duty.

'I will not marry him.' I said this out loud into the silence.

But as I said this, the truth hit me like a stone. If I did not marry Art, I would be both penniless and homeless when Mother died. Could Art be persuaded to reverse Mother's wishes? To give me back what was mine, if I broke our engagement? Not willingly, I guessed. If I were to wage this battle, I would need ammunition and be willing to fight.

Velvet night fell. If I did not know every inch of the Heath, I would have been afraid, but I made my sure-footed way across the dark grass towards Hillingham.

27 AUGUST 1894

I was in my library the next day, writing to Mina. I had scarcely begun when I was disturbed by a firm rapping on the door. I took a moment to slip my letter into the desk drawer before I went to open the door.

Art stood outside, beaming. There was a glow to him, as if he had won a prize. He wished me good morning and swept past me and into the room.

'What a day, Lucy,' he said. 'What a very lovely day. Have you seen the sky? It is the brightest blue. I am surprised to find you locked away in this stuffy room.'

'I was just completing some correspondence.'

I felt uncomfortable to see him in my private space. I made my way back to the desk and sat down.

'You love your sanctuary, don't you, Lucy?'

'Very much.'

He made a circuit of the room, running a cursory finger along the shelves. He did not speak for some time. I was about to ask what it was that he wanted when he turned to face me with a wide smile.

'My father, in a rare moment of lucidity, has asked me to set a wedding date. It is fixed. We are to be married on the 28th of September. On your birthday.'

I stared at him incredulously. 'September? That is just a month away.'

'Indeed. It seems to me you had better engage the services of a dressmaker, Lucy. You will want to look your best on the day.'

My breath came fast and shallow. Art's sudden appearance on the day after Mother completed her new Will made me suspicious. If I did not resist, I would be swept into a maelstrom of wedding plans. I blurted the words even before I had thought them.

'I cannot marry you, Art.'

He turned to face me. He was across the room, but I could feel his dark eyes searching my face. Oddly, he did not seem surprised. My pulse pounded in my ears. He waited for me to blush, or demur, or explain, but I stood as still as he did. He let out a short, sharp laugh.

'I know that the wedding date is soon, and that there will be much to do, but with the help of my mother and yours, I feel sure we can arrange everything...'

'I will not marry you in September, nor on any future date, Art.' I was surprised at how calm and strong my voice was. 'I was taken by surprise by your public proposal, and conscious that it was my mother's wish that I accept. I had imagined we would have a long engagement, and that at some point in the future, after your father and my mother... well. That we could end our engagement amicably and quietly. I do not wish to marry you, nor to marry anyone. On this point I am immovable. I am sorry.'

He crossed to the window and gazed out. He had his hands clasped behind his back and he was very still. I resisted the urge to further explain myself. I waited.

'You wish to marry no one?' he said quietly.

'No one.'

'You eschew the company of men?'

I remained silent. He turned to face me.

'Like marble,' he said conversationally.

'I beg your pardon?'

'Your thighs. Your beautiful thighs, parted in the moonlight looked as if they were carved from marble. So slender and pale. I was interested to learn that you mew like a kitten when your climax is upon you.'

His handsome face was smooth and his expression remained bland. Then he smiled.

'Quite the fellow, our friend Quincey, is he not? A nomadic man. Were he challenged, or if someone were to mention to your mother or to any other what he has been doing, he would be on the next steamer out of Southampton quicker than – what is his charming expression – a raccoon up a drainpipe?'

I began to shake uncontrollably, and folded my arms across my chest. I remembered the twin lights of the cigarette and match at the gate, the last night I had been with Quincey. Art must have followed us and watched us in the clearing as we made love. What he would have seen.

'He does not love you, Lucy, I am sorry to say.'

'I know he does not, nor I him. And know that our association has not continued during the time I have been engaged to you.' I wanted to sound defiant, but my voice cracked. 'For the duration of our brief liaison, we were both content with the situation. But it is long over. Quincey has no bearing on my decision.'

He caught my wrist then, and his grip was not gentle.

'Let me go!' I hissed, 'I will scream.'

'Scream if you will, but if you do, I will get the servants to rouse your mother, and I will tell her exactly what I witnessed on the Heath that night – her precious daughter, whoring for an itinerant American, her body shamelessly bared. I would not have to lie. And once I have told her, I will make sure the news travels around your social circle. You will be ruined, your family name irreparably tarnished, your mother's heart broken. Who knows what that would do to her already precarious state of health?'

'If I am a whore,' I bit back at him, 'why would you marry me?'

'Oh Lucy,' he grinned unpleasantly, and his teeth were sharp and white. 'I will marry you because I want to.'

We were close together now. I could feel the heat of his breath on my cheek. Were someone to walk into the room, they might mistake our pose for a lovers' embrace. His determination to marry me could only mean one thing. He wanted the Westenra fortune above all else. But did he know it was his already? He had only to wait for my mother to die, and he would have it all. There was no provision in her Will that the estate would not pass to him if he were not wed to me.

My mind raced. I had to provoke him – to frighten or anger him to the point that he admitted his deception. Only then might I have a chance of getting Mother to change her Will. I wrenched my arm free from his grip.

'You are a fraud, Arthur. A fraud, a hypocrite, and a blackmailer. Not only have you coerced me into this situation, you extorted my Father too, and I have proof. And when Mother reads it, she will see you for the repulsive individual you are, and she will send you packing.'

'Don't talk nonsense,' he said, but I saw the tiny, panicked sideways slide of his gaze.

'You see, I met your good friend Jeremiah Bevington.' Now his eyes flashed with real alarm. 'I went to see him and I know what he is. At Westenra and Co., I saw the counterfeit deeds that he so admirably created, ostensibly for the portion of the Ring Estate you sold. But it was never yours to sell, was it? While your father lies in his sickbed, you are carving up the estate and selling it off for your own ends. I am sure he and his solicitors would be interested to see the title deed which Mr Boyden has in his possession...'

As fast as a snake, Art grabbed me by the throat and pushed me backward until my head struck the bookshelves. I gasped. His face was a rictus of fury and fear.

'You will say nothing,' he spat in my face. 'Nothing, do you hear? You are a dangerous little viper, Lucy Westenra. You slither in where you are not wanted, and you meddle in things you know nothing about.'

His fingernails were long and sharp, and I could feel them digging into the delicate skin of my neck. I tried to draw a wheezy, constricted breath. He gripped tighter. He leaned in and pressed his hot mouth against my ear.

He whispered, 'Ask yourself, why saintly Charles Westenra gave me so much money for those pitiful few acres? What exactly was he paying for?'

I could not breathe. My body sagged limply until I was hanging by my throat in Art's grip. My vision began to blur, and I could feel darkness closing in. He came back to himself and released me, and I slid to the floor at his feet, drawing grateful gulps of air into my lungs. Art walked away from me, breathing heavily. He went to look at his reflection in the mirror above the fireplace. Locks of his bright hair had tumbled over his sweating forehead and he swept them back into place.

'Since you fancy yourself an amateur detective, may I recommend you take a trip to Shepherd Market, near Mayfair? That is where I first met your Father. Near the Market, at Number 17 Clarges Mews, there is a house you should visit. Go Lucy. Go this afternoon. Take my carriage. I will tell your Mother you have gone to the dressmaker. And when you return, we can discuss whether we want to begin the business of disclosing secrets.'

He brushed an invisible speck of dust from his waistcoat and strode from the library.

I got shakily to my feet and crossed to the mirror where Art had so lately stood. I tentatively touched the skin of my neck where he had held me. His nails had broken the skin, leaving a pair of tiny incisions on one side of my pale throat, like teeth marks.

CHAPTER 16

23 MARCH 2024 – KATE

When I turned into the gates of Hillingham Court, panting and harried, James's car was already parked in one of the visitors' bays. He was leaning against the boot, arms folded, smiling. I rushed over and kissed him.

'I'm so sorry. A perfect storm of an administrator who wasn't around to sign my timesheet and delays on the Tube.'

'No worries,' he said, pulling me close. 'I've only been here a few minutes, and you are totally worth the wait.'

'I had such plans. I wanted to be all fragrant and elegant when you arrived, with a cordon bleu dinner on the table. Not smelling of public transport, with a supermarket carrier bag.'

'You look good to me,' James said. 'And besides, it's given me time to wander round the outside of the house. Do you know, there's a beautiful wisteria down the side?'

'Wisteria?'

'It's a climbing plant. Come and look.'

He took my hand and led me around to the side of the building. A gnarled creeper climbed up the side of the building.

'In the summer, it'll sprout beautiful hanging purple flowers,' James said. This plant is pretty mature – maybe fifty years or so, but I suspect there's always been one here. Look at this.' He parted the leaves and showed her a rusted and pitted metal framework, 'There's a wrought iron trellis here. It's really old. This would certainly have been here in Lucy's day.'

'I imagine this was a lovely gravel path then,' I said, looking at the uneven clumps of soil at my feet. 'It's been too muddy to explore the gardens until now.'

Hand in hand we followed the path to the back of the house. We stood in the desolate garden, and I looked back up at the building. I pointed out the tall windows on the first floor which must belong to Flat 4, the apartment which had once been the library. They were obscured with heavy drapes, through which no light escaped. But as we stood there, the drapes at one window parted and a figure appeared in silhouette. The woman didn't seem to see us in the garden below. She pressed her palm against the window pane and paused, looking out into the darkness. Then she turned away. In the instant before the drapes fell back into place, I saw the ghost of a handprint on the glass.

Arm in arm, we returned to the hallway. James stood in the middle of the marble atrium and turned full circle, gazing up at the sweep of the staircase.

'Look at those double doors!' he said, admiringly, pointing at Number 1.

'That would have been the drawing room,' I showed him Mum's plan of the house.

'I can just imagine sweeping in there in my top hat, swishing my cane,' said James.

'I hope you'd take your hat off, Mr Harker.'

'Do you think Mina and Jonathan ever came here?'

'Mina, possibly, Jonathan less likely. They were married in

the same year Lucy died, so it's quite possible he never met his wife's friend.'

I guided him upstairs, pausing to point out the heavy door of Flat 4. Once we were inside the flat, James put down his overnight bag, lifted all my bags and books from my arms and set them aside.

'First things first,' he said, and pulled me close.

Later, we sat side by side on the sofa devouring bowls of pasta by candlelight. I grinned at James, who smiled back.

'So it was a bit of a day?' he asked.

'Oh, no worse than usual. I spend my life battling the admin of different schools, and then just holding space for the kids. They don't expect to learn anything from me, and there's no point in our getting to know one another. I want to be able to teach them stuff, but sometimes it just feels like being a prison warden.'

'Sounds like you don't love it.'

'I don't love it, but it's a job. I needed something I could get straight into when I got back from Milan. It's quick money.'

'Do you like teaching?'

It was a perceptive question and I thought about it carefully.

'Actually I do. I've taught English all over the world in so many different countries. I've taught tiny children, housewives, businessmen... all sorts. I like teaching teenagers best of all. And I like longer-term courses, where there's a chance to see some progress. I suppose...' I formed the thought almost as I spoke it – 'I'm interested in how different people in the world learn differently. I could write a book about that.' I laughed.

James didn't laugh. He looked at me seriously.

'So do.'

'Oh no, I don't know enough to...' I stopped myself. I thought of Dad's cheque, still lying uncashed in my desk drawer. 'You know, maybe that's an idea. Not a book... not yet... but further study?'

'That sounds brilliant.' James looked at me seriously, as if he genuinely thought this was something I might be able to do. Then he slapped a hand to his forehead. 'Oh! I forgot. I have something for you – a surprise.'

He jumped up and left the room. A moment later, he returned with a brown envelope.

'What's this?'

'It's so good. I could have emailed it, but I wanted you to see it. And I wanted to see your face when you saw it.'

I slipped a finger under the flap of the envelope and opened it carefully. There was a single sheet of paper inside, and I drew it out. It was a scan of an old document.

'"Last Will & Testament",' I read, and then squinted at the words below. I gasped and looked up at James. 'Oh my God!'

'I know!' he said, 'Rose Westenra's Will!'

I read through the brief document and then looked up, frowning. 'But who's The Hon. Arthur Holmwood?'

'Well, that's the question, isn't it?' James looked extremely pleased with himself.

'And what's the answer? I'm assuming once you found this, you did some digging?'

'I did. The most likely candidate I could find was an Arthur Hale Holmwood, born in 1865 – only son of Lord Godalming – who had an ancient estate somewhere in Hertfordshire.'

'But why would Rose leave everything to him, and not to Lucy? She didn't leave Lucy anything at all.'

'I thought about that, and the only reason I can think of is that he and Lucy were due to be married.'

'Was that usual?'

'For the future son-in-law to inherit? I don't know. There are no aristocrats or rich people in my family, so I have no experience with this sort of thing. I mean, had Lucy married this Holmwood – or any man really – the house, the company and all the property would automatically have become his, anyway.'

'Well, that stinks.'

'Agreed. But that was the law at the time.'

I sat back, staring at the Will. 'This is dated 26 August 1894. That's less than a month before Rose and Lucy both died.'

'There could be any number of reasons for that,' said James, 'and it might actually explain why she did it. Maybe Lucy was already ill, and so was she.'

'But what about Lucy's letter? She was convinced someone was trying to kill her.'

'I had a look and there doesn't seem to have been an inquest into either death.'

'What does that mean?'

'There's an inquest if there's any suggestion that the death was unexpected.'

'How could the death of a nineteen-year-old girl be expected?'

'Maybe she'd been ill for a while.'

I sighed in frustration, 'I just wish we knew for sure.'

'Well,' James hesitated, 'I did do something else. I hope it's okay.'

'What?'

'I've ordered copies of Rose and Lucy's death certificates. They may list their causes of death. That might help us to understand what happened.'

'Brilliant! Why didn't I think of that?'

* * *

THE NEXT MORNING AFTER BREAKFAST, James drove us to Hendon. We parked outside a nearby pub and I led him through the churchyard. Spring flowers were sprouting everywhere, and the sky was bright and clear. It felt different from my last visit in bleak January. A man with a strimmer cleared a path between the higgledy-piggledy gravestones, and a woman with a saw cut back a bush with brisk efficiency.

We stood outside Lucy's tomb. James took a snapshot of the names and dates, and rested his hand on the bricked-up door. Then with a gasp, he pointed down. Resting up against the door was a bunch of flowers – fresh white roses.

'Again! Who puts them here?' I said.

'We could ask that woman,' James indicated the gardener, who was now putting the branches she had pruned into a green bin.

We walked over and she greeted us warmly. James gave his most charming smile.

'We've been doing some historical research into the West-enra family,' he began.

'Ah yes, the mausoleum,' the woman said.

'We just noticed the flowers by the door,' I cut in, 'I was here earlier this year, and there were flowers then too.'

'Well yes,' the woman said, 'there are always flowers. They arrive once a week.'

'How do they arrive?'

'No idea. Delivered by a florist, I think. But they've been put there every week for as long as I can remember. And I've been coming to the church for forty years.'

As they walked back to the car, James sighed, frustrated.

'A florist.'

'I checked, there's no card. So we can't even tell which florist.'

'Well, unless you're prepared to spend a week sitting in the churchyard, hoping to apprehend the mysterious flower leaver, it's another dead end.'

LUCY WESTENRA'S SECOND JOURNAL

Alfred, Art's driver, was waiting for me in the driveway when I emerged an hour later. I had tied a narrow black ribbon around my throat to cover the marks Art's nails had left. I did not want to answer any awkward questions.

It was a grey, hazy afternoon, and I watched the city go about its business through the window of the carriage. Art's venom and fury had shaken me, but made me no less certain of my resolve. I was not going to spend the rest of my life tied to that man.

I had not visited Shepherd Market before, but I knew it was close to Mayfair. I had heard the name of the Market spoken in polite society with a certain raised eyebrow, but I did not know why. Alfred slowed at the entrance to the Market on Curzon Street and I alighted from the carriage.

'Mr Holmwood said that you would be going on to Clarges Mews,' Alfred said, and I was interested to note he would not meet my eye. 'It's just around the corner from the Market. I'll be waiting for you here when your business is concluded.'

I passed down a narrow passageway into the Market. I could not imagine what I might see, but to my surprise, there was a pretty piazza surrounding a duck pond. The market itself was two storeys high, and bills posted outside told me there was a theatre at the top of the building. The people around me looked no different from those in Curzon Street – a mixture of working people on the move, and well-heeled ladies and gentlemen out shopping. There was a large public house. Was that where Pa met Art for the first time? I was still unsure what I might be here to see.

Just then, a door opened in the building opposite – a narrow entrance, leading to apartments situated above the emporia. I caught a glimpse of rich, red wallpaper in the stairwell, and then two young women stepped out, linked arms, and walked toward me. They passed a lady who sneered and pressed herself against the wall to avoid them. I could not imagine why – from a distance, they looked like two pretty girls. They might have been friends of the Howarth sisters.

They wore attractive summery gowns and had their hair neatly arranged. But as they drew closer, I realised that the one on the left, a plump brunette, wore her dress cut lower than was proper for daytime wear. The tops of her creamy breasts were visible. The other laughed lightly, and I saw that half an inch at the roots of her spun-gold hair was as black as coal. It had been artificially coloured. As they drew close to me, I was enveloped in a cloud of their scent – expensive and elegant, but heavily applied. They both wore powder on their faces and had darkened their lips and eyes. But these were not the garish, painted faces of the streetwalkers I had seen on the docks at Whitby. These two young women were works of art. However, there was no doubt as to what they were. As they passed, the dark-haired girl looked up and saw me and then let her gaze slip off, clearly finding me of no interest. With her dark eyes outlined in sooty kohl, her luscious bosom and soft, red, inviting mouth, she was the image of delectable femininity. I felt bloodless and invisible in comparison.

Was this what Art had sent me to see? Did he expect me to be scandalised that my beloved Pa had visited high-class courtesans? I considered this for a moment. I was neither shocked nor repelled. I was in fact, delighted. Mother was cold and had treated him with such disdain. If he was able to find pleasure and comfort in the arms of women such as these, I could only applaud him. I assumed that the address Art had given me in Clarges Mews would be a bordello – the actual location of their meeting. I would go, only so that I could tell him I had done so.

The streets in that part of Mayfair were winding and confusing, so it took me some time to find my way to the Mews. It was a pretty little street, close to the bustle of Piccadilly but far enough away to be peaceful. The house at number 17 was modest but attractive, with window boxes filled with violas, pansies and primroses. It did not look like a brothel, but I supposed that such establishments did not advertise their purpose to the wider public.

I strode up to the door and knocked. As soon as I had done so, I regretted my impetuous action. What would I do when someone came to the door? Ask for a tour of the premises? Ask if there was someone who knew my Pa?

Before I had time to think, the door opened and I beheld the smallest maid I had ever seen. She had a bright, mousy face and looked barely twelve years old. She was swamped by her uniform, although it was clean and neatly pressed.

'Are you here to see Mrs Hammond, Miss?' she said, before I could speak. 'Come in. She's just upstairs at present.'

I thought it best to remain silent and followed her into the house. The miniature maid took my hat and wrap and settled me in the parlour, then went off to call the mysterious Mrs Hammond. I looked around the room. It was small but beautifully appointed, with flocked wallpaper and cosy, elegant furnishings. It looked like a respectable family home. I sat on the edge of the sofa. It was placed opposite a large brown leather armchair with wide arms and a high back.

Unlike the other furniture, this chair was old and cracked. It was also profoundly familiar. It had stood in Pa's library for years until he replaced it with a newer, red velvet one a few years before he died. On the occasional table beside the chair, there was a pipe in an ashtray. The pipe too, was well known to me. So too was the well-thumbed volume of Homer bristling with many paper bookmarks. A cold trickle made its way down my spine. Pa had been here. In fact, it felt as if he had been there until moments before, and had just left the room.

Mrs Hammond came in then. She was about thirty years old – pretty in a muted way, with coppery hair and pale, smooth skin. She wore a dove-grey, high-necked dress and on her left hand, I saw the dull gleam of a gold ring. I stood abruptly and faced her. She opened her mouth to offer a polite greeting, but the words died on her lips. I saw her eyes scan my face and recognition dawn.

'Lucy,' she whispered.

'How do you know me?'

'I have seen photographic portraits of you.'

'I have seen none of you.' My voice was louder than I had intended, and bitter.

'No, you would not have.'

I gestured wordlessly to the chair. She glanced at it.

'I could not bring myself to move anything. It is just as he left it.'

'How long?' I asked.

'We have lived here for more than five years.'

I nodded. I felt suddenly dizzy, and sank back onto the sofa. It took me a moment to register what she had said.

'We?'

For the first time I realised that there was someone behind her, concealed by her skirts. Mrs Hammond drew her out.

The little girl looked to be about six. With a dizzying sense of recognition I saw her face was my own, exactly as I had been at that age. She had the same bright, pale, curly hair and wide blue eyes. She stood silently, pressed close to her mother.

'This is Violet,' said Mrs Hammond.

My sister.

* * *

Somehow, I found my way back to Half Moon Street and Alfred drove me home. In the carriage, my thoughts were a dizzying whirl of confusion. Another family? Another home? I had been content to imagine Pa seeking comfort in the arms of other women, but I had never imagined he had a permanent arrangement. Suddenly, all the late nights away from home, the weekends he told us were spent in the office made sense. The betrayal pierced me deeply. I had thought I was the person closest to him in the world, and yet he had kept this monumental secret from me. And, most agonisingly, I now knew that I was not his only beloved daughter.

Art was waiting for me on the front steps when the carriage drew in. I followed him mutely into the drawing room. He shut the door, and went to stand by the window, as I sank into a chair.

'I had her, you know,' he said calmly, 'When she was still a whore.' I made no reply, so he continued. 'She was such a delicate little thing, very demure. She commanded a very high price. Perfect for the nervous teenager I was in those days. I went away travelling, but I always remembered her. When I returned to London, I sought her out again, but she was gone. Moved on, the other girls said. It took some detective work, but I found her. She was in rooms in South Audley Street, and already with child. She told me that she was no longer working and tried to send me away. She said she was under the care and protection of a kind gentleman.' Art crossed to the cabinet to pour himself a drink. 'I waited in a coffeehouse across the road until the gentleman came to call and then waited again until he left. I followed him back to his offices in Chatham Street. From there, it just took a trip to Companies House to find out who he was.'

'So you blackmailed him? That was sheer spite.'

'Really Lucy, how vulgar. It isn't spite. At first I just wanted to show him up for the hypocrite he was. Respected business-man, devoted husband and father, nouveau riche parvenu, all the while with his little strumpet tucked away in Mayfair. So I set up a meeting with him and told him what I knew.'

'And then?'

'Well, he was very rich, wasn't he? He could certainly afford to buy that little corner of the Ring estate and give me the ready cash I needed at the time.'

Slowly, awfully, comprehension began to dawn.

'But you didn't stop there, did you? You pressed him for more. You threatened him. Did that lead to his heart attack?'

'Really Lucy, you border on hysteria. That is conjecture, and potentially libellous. That is not a course of enquiry you wish to pursue. Imagine the publicity.'

'You're disgusting,' I spat at him. 'I despise you. You're a filthy, grubbing parasite, with nothing to offer the world. You will not win. I will fight you to my last breath.'

'That's quite a claim, Lucy,' he said. 'Your last breath. I hope it will not come to that. Now, I must take my leave. I look forward to seeing you tomorrow. We will discuss wedding flowers.'

Then he swept from the room.

I sat down, trembling. Despite my bravado, I knew Art was right. Could I challenge him and risk Father's secrets being disclosed? It seemed Mrs Hammond and her daughter were well provided for. I had no wish to change that. But if the story of Charles Westenra's second family came to light, Pa's name would be sullied. Not to mention what the revelation would do to Mother. And what she in turn might do to Mrs Hammond and Violet.

I went to my library, taking care to lock the door behind me and pocket the key. I took down the ledger Pa kept in the library, so that he would have a record of his business at home. I paged back. Sure enough, since January 1887, there had been regular payments to a company called Hammond and Co. In 1889, there was a record of the purchase of the house in Clarges Mews and subsequently of its transfer to the ownership of Hammond and Co. I had to admire how elegantly he had concealed his subterfuge. An annual payment was made to Mrs Hammond in the name of this spurious company. The house was in her name. Yet the transactions looked like so many others in his ledger. If you did not know what to look for, you would never know. Pa had arranged everything so that even if he died, his secret would not come to light. Did Mr Boyden know about Mrs Hammond? It was entirely possible. But he would never tell.

To my surprise, as I reached up to put the ledger away, I heard the rattle of carriage wheels and the sound of hooves. I stepped out of the library onto the stairs and looked through the window onto the drive. Art's carriage was only just leaving. What had kept him occupied in the house this past hour?

28 AUGUST 1894

In the darkest hour of the night I awoke in the library, freezing and shivering. When I stood, every part of me ached. I opened the door, and the house was silent and dark. I made my way slowly to my bedroom. The fire burned low, but the room was warm.

I discarded my clothes and drew on a fresh flannel night-gown. I was just about to get into bed when there was a light knock and the door opened. I turned, instantly apprehensive, but Beatrice's narrow face appeared.

'I thought you might be chilled, Miss, coming to bed so late, so I brought you some tea. It's the one you like– the tealeaves you brought from Yorkshire. Good and strong.'

She crept into the room, carrying the steaming cup.

'Thank you, Beatrice, this is most welcome,' I said. I took a sip of the hot brew. It warmed me. Beatrice fetched a comforter from the cupboard and spread it on my bed. I finished my tea and thanked her before climbing in. Gradually, the uncontrollable shaking left my limbs and I could feel sleep drawing near.

1 SEPTEMBER 1894

I do not know whether it was the shock of the previous day's events, or the cold in the library, but I fell ill that night. I remember little of the next few days – bouts of nausea, a dreadful headache and aches in my bones. I could not bear the bright light from the windows and begged Beatrice to close the curtains and keep them closed.

Whenever I awoke, Beatrice was by my side, lifting my head and helping me to drink sips of tea. I was also vaguely aware that Art was frequently in the room. I would often open my eyes, my vision blurred, to find him leaning over my bed, peering closely at me. I tried to tell him to go away, but my mouth was dry, so very dry, and my throat gave me great pain. I could bring forth no more than a hoarse whisper.

I knew I was ill, but more than that, I was afraid. I felt a looming danger hanging over me. I remember trying to weep, but my eyes were dry, and I recall calling for my mother. In my delirium, I felt sure if I could go to her room and creep into her bed, she could keep me safe. In a rare moment of lucidity, I begged Beatrice.

'Please,' I croaked, 'ask her if I may sleep in her bed beside her.'

Beatrice nodded and stepped away. She went out into the hallway. My bedroom door was ajar and I heard her speaking in a low voice.

'I don't know what to do,' she was saying. 'She's so drained of colour, Mrs Staines. I've never seen pallor like it. And she plucks at the covers so and cries out in her sleep. She's asking for her mother now. What shall I say to Mrs Westenra?'

I raised my head off the pillow and saw Mrs Staines peer in and look at me. When she saw I was awake, she grasped Beatrice by her elbow and drew her away. I dozed then, and when I awoke, Beatrice gently told me Mother had refused my request.

'She said that having you in her bed would disturb her sleep.'

I turned my face into the pillow and sobbed, but my eyes remained dry. Tears would not flow. I felt as if someone had drained me of all moisture. My breath rattled and rasped in my aching throat.

Some time later, there was a soft knock on the door. I assumed it was Beatrice returning, so I called, 'Come in!' but did not turn my head.

I smelled him before I saw him. Art's lemon verbena cologne reached me and I scrambled to sit up. He placed a glass of water on the table beside my bed. Then he fastidiously twitched the creases of his trousers and sat down.

'Now then,' he said, with a facsimile of tenderness, 'you are not well, are you, Lucy, my dear?' I drew the covers up to my neck and looked at him in silence. He continued: 'I think it is time for some medical intervention.'

I felt a small pulse of relief. Dr Oliver would know what to do.

'I do not want to alarm your mother. We have kept the seriousness of your condition from her.'

'We?'

'Why, Mrs Staines and Beatrice and me. Now, I have written to Jack Seward, and he will be here to see you tomorrow. I am sure that by then, you will be strong enough to rise and eat lunch with Jack and your mother and me. Then we will find some pretext for you and Jack to be alone so he can examine you.'

'Dr Seward is coming here? Why?'

'At my request.'

'Why can I not see Dr Oliver? He has cared for me since the day I was born.'

'I only want the best for you, Lucy,' said Art, taking my hand, 'And Dr Seward is such a talented physician...'

You know what happened between him and me,' I said, snatching my hand away. 'You know I refused his proposal of marriage and it will be profoundly uncomfortable for both Dr Seward and me to be placed in this situation. Why are you doing this? I have a doctor who has my confidence. Let me see my own doctor!'

'Really, Lucy,' he said, making his voice silky, 'can you not trust me? Put your faith in me, that I will make the best possible choices for my future wife.'

I stared at him. His face moved, as if the bones shifted under the skin. As I watched in horror, his brow drew down, broadened and wrinkled. His eyes transformed from their usual black to a glittering gold and moved to the sides of his head. His mouth opened and his lower jaw detached, like a gigantic serpent about to devour its prey. His front teeth elongated into fangs and his skin was at once covered in glistening scales. I screamed loudly and scrambled from the bed. In my haste, I sent the glass of water flying. I crawled away desperately and crouched in the corner by the window.

'Get away! Get away!' I croaked.

The monstrous snake that had been Art rose from the chair and slithered towards me.

'Lucy...' he hissed, and venom dripped from his fangs.

I could feel unbearable pressure in my bladder, and I felt sure that I would wet myself, so great was my terror. But nothing came. Instead, my vision darkened, and I collapsed to the floor. My limbs shook and trembled, and in the last moments of lucidity I saw the snake loom above me.

* * *

When I next came to consciousness, I was back in my bed. Beatrice sat beside me, her face pale with worry. I jerked into a sitting position and looked wildly around the room.

'Where is he? Where is it?'

'Mr Holmwood went home,' said Beatrice soothingly. She guided me to lie down again. 'He said you were delirious. Seeing things.'

'He... he...'

'He said you told him he was a serpent, and that he was going to eat you. He was terrible upset, Miss Lucy. He wept. He ran out in the corridor to call us, and we found you on the floor, unconscious.'

Was that it? Delirium? Had I suffered an hallucination? But why? I was not, as far as I could tell, feverish. Perhaps I was more ill than I had imagined.

'What time is it?'

'It's morning, Miss Lucy. Just past eight o'clock. How are you feeling?'

I drew a deep, experimental breath and took a careful mental inventory of my body. Yes, my limbs ached a little, but the pain in my throat had subsided. I had a powerful need to urinate. I recalled that I had felt like this the night before, but had been unable to pass water. Now, however, the urge was very strong, and I carefully swung my legs over the edge of the bed. Beatrice rushed to my side and helped me to stand. She put a hand under my elbow as I made my way to the water closet, but to my astonishment, I was able to walk alone. The relief in emptying my bladder was indescribable, and afterwards, I felt weak, but otherwise well.

I spent the morning in bed, updating this journal, but felt so much better that I rose around eleven and dressed. When I made my way downstairs, I found Mother sitting by the window in the drawing room. She looked up when I entered.

'You look quite restored to yourself, Lucy. Mr Holmwood did say you were poorly, but that once Beatrice had got you into bed, you drank a few drops of tea, and you seemed to settle down and sleep quite well.'

So Art had not told her about my hallucinations.

She said: 'it is a great pity he has been called away. He sent a telegram this morning saying his father is suddenly worse.'

'I am sad to hear so.'

'However, I believe Dr Seward is going to be joining us for lunch.'

I frowned, confused, and then remembered that Art had said the night before, just as my delirium began, that he had asked Dr Seward to come and see me. I still felt awkward at the thought of seeing him, but this was swept away by my profound relief at Art's absence.

Dr Seward arrived promptly at two pm. I felt a rush of affection when I saw his earnest, handsome face. I was still very weak and my appetite was poor, so it took a great deal of energy to be vivacious and engaging at the lunch table. When Mother excused herself after lunch to go and rest, I could have wept. I sank into an armchair in the sun parlour. I could see Dr Seward watching me closely. Then he spoke, in a formal, doctorly tone I had never heard him use before.

'Perhaps we might go upstairs to your boudoir, Miss West-enra, where I can conduct a consultation, to see what has been ailing you?'

I saw that he needed to adopt this professional demeanour to protect himself, so I fixed my face in a serious expression and spoke in similarly proper tones.

'Of course, Dr Seward, come this way.'

Once we were in my room, he took a notebook from his bag, and listened attentively as I described the symptoms I had suffered in the previous few days. He made careful notes, then looked at my eyes, pronouncing my pupils to be dilated, and examined my throat, which, to my surprise, he said was not inflamed. He took my pulse, noting it to be normal. His concentration was absolute and his manner methodical. He was, I thought, a very capable doctor.

'You are pale,' he noted, leaning so close to me that I could see the golden flecks in his brown eyes and smell the sweet, clean scent of his breath. It put us in an oddly intimate position – the two of us alone in my bedroom. I felt suddenly hot, and I stood, crossing to the window to open it.

To my frustration, the window mechanism jammed. I jerked it hard and the sash cord snapped. The window came down hard in the frame and one of the small panes of glass shattered. A shard of the glass struck the back of my hand. I watched as a drop of blood welled up. Dr Seward leapt to his feet and rushed to my side. He drew me away from the window and sat me back in the chair. He held my hand in his and examined the cut.

'It is superficial, but it could be helpful to us. If you will permit me, I will capture a drop of your blood to test for anaemia. Your pallor suggests to me that you may be deficient of iron, and a simple test will allow me to see if that is the case.'

I was happy to allow him to do so, and he decanted the drops of blood into a small vial with great care, before bandaging my hand.

Once this operation was complete, he packed away his medical paraphernalia and sat back in his chair.

'Now Lucy,' he said with quiet seriousness, 'are you able to tell me how you are? In yourself?'

How to begin? I had been drawn in by his manner – indeed, when he bandaged my hand, I could have wept with gratitude for his kindly, capable touch. But I knew I must not let my guard down. He was Art's spy.

'I have been... tired,' I said. 'For some months, my sleep has been very poor. I sleepwalk and suffer from disturbing dreams.'

He nodded and made some notes. He asked many more questions about my health, my appetite, and my habits. I answered as truthfully as I dared. As our conversation progressed, he frowned. I think he had hoped for an easy answer to my malady.

'Lucy, if I may call you that, I ask that I may speak to you frankly. This situation,' he made a vague gesture, '... This situation is both awkward and strange. The spectre of my... proposal ... sits between us. When you refused me, I said that I would always be a good friend to you, and I truly meant it. I know that I am here at Art's request, but you are my patient. You alone have my loyalty and expertise. So if there is anything you wish to tell me, or anything that concerns you, rest assured that your confidences will not pass beyond these walls.'

'I have a great deal on my mind,' I said, smoothly. 'The impending wedding. My mother, as you probably know, is not well, and Art's father too. I am sure all of this has had an impact on my health.'

He nodded. I think he was disappointed. Then he said, more formally, 'With your permission, I would like to contact my old friend and teacher, Dr Abraham Van Helsing.'

I frowned. I had heard the name before. Then I recalled Dr Seward, drunk at Christmastime, telling me about the man who had been his teacher in Amsterdam.

He continued: 'I will ask him to come to London to see you.'

'What will this Dr Van Helsing offer that another doctor could not?'

'He is a philosopher and a metaphysician, and one of the most advanced scientists of his day; and he has, I believe, an absolutely open mind,' he said. 'He is kind, if a little bombastic. He sees each case from many angles – the philosophical and spiritual, as well as the medical. I also believe...' he paused, as if choosing his words carefully, '... that his age and many qualifications make him impressive. A man such as Art is likely to listen to both his diagnosis and treatment plan.'

I looked at Dr Seward sharply. Why would he choose the words, "A man such as Art?" I wondered about his relationship with Art – did he believe in the charming facade, or did he know more than he was acknowledging? Dr Seward was a quiet man – a watcher and listener. Had he seen through Art's veneer? They had travelled together and seen and done so much. But yet, I knew well the loyalty men had to one another – they kept one another's secrets.

CHAPTER 17

8 APRIL 2024 – KATE

I sighed and snuggled deeper into the sofa. My feet rested on James's lap and he wrapped a warm hand around one of them, gently massaging the arch. He was engrossed in his book, and he pushed his glasses up his nose before turning the page. I admired his profile in the pool of light from the lamp.

We had had an idyllic week together. I'd come down for the Easter break, and we'd been tourists in Devon. We strolled along the beach at Burgh Island and mooched around Torquay and Paignton. We spent a day in Dartmouth, which I loved, and James booked us on a horse-riding trek across the moors, which I liked less, but he enjoyed immensely.

I had no memory of relaxing in silence like this with Alex. He was always restless – he seldom read and even struggled to watch television. He'd sit for twenty minutes or so, jiggling a knee, then would jump up to look out of the window or fetch another drink. He seemed always to be moving away from me.

James's hand slid up the leg of my jeans. He encircled my ankle with his fingers. I looked at him, and a half-smile curved the corner of his mouth. He raised an eyebrow. His eyes did not leave the page of his book. I climbed into his lap. His book slid to the floor and he held me close and kissed me.

* * *

ON OUR LAST DAY, he drove us down to the Jurassic coast where we looked for fossils on the beach. We ended up walking along the parade in Lyme Regis, eating ice creams.

'So that's the Cobb,' I said, pointing.

'The Cobb?'

'The harbour wall.'

'I thought you'd never been here. How did you know that?'

'Every self-respecting Jane Austen nerd knows about the Cobb! Can we walk along it?'

'Of course,' he said, offering his arm.

The wind buffeted us, and we had to lean into it to keep walking.

'I won't be all impetuous, like Louisa Musgrove.' I said.

'Who now?'

'In Austen's *Persuasion*, Louisa jumps off a step on the Cobb, expecting Captain Wentworth to catch her. He misses, and she gets concussed.'

James flung an arm across my shoulders and pulled me to him. 'I wouldn't miss,' he said, 'I'd catch you. I'll always catch you.'

He kissed me then, and I leaned into him, because I knew I should. After all, he was kind. So kind. Why then did I feel the tiniest impulse to pull away?

'Right, I definitely have no cobwebs left in my brain,' said James. 'Can we go and sit in a pub now? Have we been sufficiently literary?'

* * *

LATER, as I sat on the train, I sent a quick text to thank James again. He responded immediately.

'No ... thank YOU. I had the best time. You're amazing.'

I smiled at the memories of the last week – coffee in bed, slow, pleasurable lovemaking, laughing until we wept at a silly rom-com, breathless walks along the cliffs. I liked him, and I liked Exeter. But then I remembered my moment of unease when we were on the Cobb in Lyme Regis. What was that about? He'd just said that if I jumped, he'd catch me. It was sweet.

If Alex had ever said something similarly lovely, he would immediately diffuse it with a joking insult. It was a reflex. I'd got so used to that pattern, I expected it. James's open, direct affection was a source of confusion. I just wasn't used to someone freely admitting he liked me. He was perfect. This relationship was perfect. Was it too perfect?

I imagined telling Rafaella. How would she respond? 'Relax and enjoy it,' she would say. So I would. James was steady, committed and stable. In months or years, I'd come to trust that. Wouldn't I?

I shook my head at my own foolishness. If anyone should know better than to imagine a future... Before I gave into impulse and texted something soppy to James, I put my phone down on the tray table. It buzzed with an incoming email.

Hey K,

I've been thinking about you this week. A lot. Remember last Easter when we went to Volterra and walked the city walls? Those amazing views. And that hotel with the four-poster bed? Anyway, I just wondered if we could maybe talk? Just, you know... a catch up. I miss you. I really do.

Alex x

LUCY WESTENRA'S SECOND JOURNAL

Dr Van Helsing is a physically impressive man: barrel-chested and vigorous-looking even though he is not young – in his fifties, I would estimate. He has an abundant head of greying hair and heavy eyebrows. I know from Dr Seward that he is widowed and has no living children.

When he arrived at Hillingham, he swept straight into the drawing room without removing his coat. He scooped up my hand and kissed it with continental charm. He showered me with compliments about my prettiness, and was extravagant in his admiration of the house, the gardens and our leafy corner of London. He spoke at length and did not pause for reply. Then he shrugged off his overcoat and thrust it at Mrs Staines without acknowledging her, as if she were a convenient hat stand.

He has the confidence that certain men have – I believe it comes from a lack of opposition. You can see that in every situation, he knows he is right and no one will ever be able to tell him otherwise. As a doctor and a teacher, he is used to others deferring to him, and thus he expects it in every situation. Men such as he have condescended to me at hundreds of dinner tables. His views on women are written in his every action. He sees me as a pretty pet, or a tiny child. He would never see me as any kind of equal.

I was sweet and biddable, as he would expect me to be. We spoke easily of anything and everything except my illness. After some time, Dr Van Helsing leaned over and took my hand.

'My dear young miss, I have the so great pleasure because you are so much beloved. They told me you were down in the spirit, and that you were of a ghastly pale. To them I say: "Pouf" But you and I shall show them how wrong they are.'

With the same peremptory manner with which he had handed his coat to Mrs Staines, he dismissed Dr Seward to smoke a cigarette in the garden. He performed much the same physical examination Dr Seward had undertaken the day before, looking inside the lids of my eyes and at my gums, listening to my heart and taking my pulse. He asked me to summon my maid and stepped out into the corridor to speak to Beatrice. I knew he must be asking her about my menses and wondered why he did not just ask me directly, as Dr Seward had done. He clearly considered me too delicate for such a frank conversation.

After some time, he called Dr Seward, and they held a whispered conversation. Then Dr Van Helsing bade me farewell, and told me that he had to return to Amsterdam but would come to see me again. The two doctors then took their leave.

4 SEPTEMBER 1894

I have kept to myself as much as possible for the last few days. My appetite is poor, so I eat little and drink only water. I have written again to Mina, telling her of Dr Van Helsing's visit, even though she has not replied to my previous letter. As much as I can, I remain alone and walk in the garden.

I have thought much about my future. If Mother dies, and Art retains the estate, what might I do? I will be alone in the world and penniless. There is no point in railing against this – it will be a fact. It is exactly what Mina faced, when she was a child – left alone and impoverished when her parents died. To her good fortune, she was able to become a teacher.

Could I be a teacher too? Perhaps if I could earn some money and save it, I might finally be able to attend university: the dream that was cruelly snatched from me by Pa's death.

It seems such a real prospect, and writing this, I feel hopeful. But then I think of Mina's darned blouses, her cautious way with money. I remember her descriptions of her life before her engagement to Jonathan. Can I imagine washing my own undergarments in a tub by a small fire? Darning my stockings? Living in one room?

I am used to this large house with my library, my own bedroom and the garden. I have only ever lived with servants to care for my needs. My putative future sounds exhausting and difficult and I am all too aware my plans could go awry. The truth is that I, the daughter of Charles Westenra, could end up in the workhouse or on the street.

_TELEGRAM, SEWARD, LONDON, TO VAN HELSING, AMSTERDAM. _ 5 SEPTEMBER_

_Patient greatly improved. Good appetite; sleeps naturally; good spirits; colour coming back.

6 SEPTEMBER 1894

Dr Seward came to see me yesterday, and again today. He performs a quick examination each time, but I think he can see that I am well and getting strong. Whatever has ailed me seems to have passed.

Today we took a stroll on the Heath. He was surprised to see how energetically I walked.

'I had not imagined you to be fond of the outdoors,' he panted, catching up with me at the crest of a hill.

'This Heath is my second home,' I said. 'If I cannot spend time here, I feel I am choking, unable to breathe.'

'Now, as your doctor, I must counsel you to return home and enjoy a restorative beverage.'

'As my doctor? Perhaps the prescription is more urgently required for the doctor than the patient! Let us climb one more hill, Dr Seward, and then I will acquiesce to your treatment plan.'

When we returned to the house, Dr Seward thirstily drank two glasses of cold water and I asked Beatrice to bring me a pot of tea. I offered some to Dr Seward, but he made his apologies and left soon after, stating that he had to return to Purfleet. As I watched his straight back moving away down the driveway, I found that I was sad to see him go. He is a serious man, but he is kind and I think his moral code is strong. In comparison to Quincey's quicksilver, lightly-come-lightly-go attitude (I have heard nothing from him in months), or Art's devious unpredictability, I find Dr Seward's company refreshingly simple. I feel if I were to confide in anyone, it might be he. But I must not forget that he is Art's friend before all else.

As I complete this journal entry, I find my thoughts straying to the Stranger in Whitby, as they so often do. My dreams are woven with remembered sensations and vivid flashes of memory come to me through the day. I have no word for who the Stranger was, nor for the sensations I experienced in those arms, but I feel sure I will never meet the like again.

As these thoughts come to me, I feel a fuzzing at the periphery of my vision.

I am sitting by the drawing room window. The sun is sinking.

I see a figure walking up the driveway.

Long and angular

Could it be The Stranger?

Come to claim me again?

No.

That figure is too tall - too tall to be human

It lopes.

The legs - jointed like a spider

It comes at me across the lawn.

The arms

So long -

grasping the window frame

Wrenching

The face

a blank black space

eyes like burning holes

A maw

widening

slavering

I cry

I crawl

The wide mouth pressed to the window

the glass billows

the breath, hot and fetid

I scream

Blackness.

_TELEGRAM, SEWARD, LONDON, TO VAN HELSING, AMSTERDAM._6 SEPTEMBER._

--Terrible change for the worse. Come at once; do not lose an hour. I hold over telegram to Holmwood till have seen you.

7 SEPTEMBER 1894

Through the darkness, I heard Mrs Staines's voice, whispering.

'The hallucinations were fierce, Doctor. She cried out over and over in her sleep, talking of a spider. And her hands were never still – plucking and plucking at the coverlet.'

I could open my eyes. I heard another voice. Deep. Kind.

'She is pale as chalk. Did she suffer any bleeding in the night?'

'From where?'

'Womanly bleeding. Or from anywhere else? A wound? From her nose, or mouth?'

There was no bleeding,' Mrs Staines again. 'Not that I saw, and I undressed her to put her to bed.'

With enormous effort, I raised my eyelids and blinked into the agonising bright light. I was in my bed.

I saw Dr Seward's concerned eyes.

'Well, Lucy, you have given us quite a scare. Mrs Staines has sat up all night at your bedside. She asked your Mother to send for me this morning and here I am. Now what can have happened? When I left you yesterday, you were bright and full of life, with the roses of health in your cheeks after our walk.'

I shook my head. I could not speak. He continued.

'I have sent a telegram to Dr Van Helsing. He will be with us tomorrow. I can see no reason for the sudden onset of these symptoms. I saw you myself yesterday afternoon and you were well.'

I closed my eyes again. Dr Seward stayed in the room, and I heard him writing at the desk, and then giving instructions to Beatrice to post a letter. When she had gone, he came to the bedside, and, seeing my eyes were open, sat down.

'I wrote to Art to tell him you were unwell again. I kept my language moderate – I do not wish to alarm him, for I know he is much occupied with his father.'

'Do you think he will come?'

'I am sure he will be here as soon as he can, Lucy, be comforted.'

I could not help myself – 'I do not want him to come,' I said fiercely.

'Oh Lucy, your selflessness does you credit. But it is my duty to let your future husband know how you are.'

I laughed harshly, which made me cough, and Dr Seward had to help me to sit up. When the paroxysm passed, he laid me back down on the pillows. He prepared to leave so I could sleep, but I caught at his hand.

'I do not know if I can trust you, Dr Seward. There is so much I could say, but I will not. All I will say is this. My body is my own. My own, I tell you. It does not belong to my Mother nor to Art. Nor to anybody. Body and soul, I belong only to myself.'

He stood by the bed, looking down at me. His face was impassive as always, but something moved in his eyes.

'Thank you, Lucy,' he said finally. 'I will keep that always in my mind.'

Dr Seward had some tea sent up for me when he left. I was relieved to discover that in putting me to bed, Mrs Staines had brought my journal up and put it on my bedside table. I am horrified by the ramblings I wrote in the depths of my delusion. Nevertheless, I have updated it and will conceal it beneath my mattress.

8 SEPTEMBER 1894

The night was, if anything, worse than the one before. The air was thick with the flapping of leathery wings, the hiss of hot, decaying breath and the scratching of sharp claws and teeth. In the morning, I opened my eyes to find Dr Van Helsing leaning over my bed, his face drawn with alarm.

He turned to Dr Seward, who hovered behind him. He beckoned and they tiptoed out of the room. Even though they closed the door, I could hear Dr Van Helsing's booming tones from the next room.

'My God! This is dreadful. There is no time to be lost. She will die for sheer want of blood to keep the heart's action, as it should be. There must be transfusion of blood at once. Is it you or me?'

'I am younger and stronger, Professor. It must be me.'

'Then get ready at once. I will bring up my bag. I am prepared.'

I had read of blood transfusion in Pa's medical books – it involves the transfer of blood from a healthy person to one who was lacking. I had no idea how such a thing might be accomplished. The two doctors left the room next door and went off downstairs for some minutes. When they returned, Dr Van Helsing spent some time laying out equipment on a table. I could not see what he was doing – he had chosen a spot beyond my eye line. At length, he came to the bedside holding a bottle and a small glass of some cloudy liquid.

'Now, little Miss,' he said in a sugary tone, 'here is your medicine. Drink it off, like a good child.'

I wanted to object to the way he spoke to me, but I was too weak. I managed to swallow the bitter liquid and lay back on the pillow. The two doctors took up their posts on either side of my bed and watched me with rapt concentration. It occurred to me that Dr Van Helsing had given me a narcotic of some description. I could feel lethargy stealing through my veins. I think I slept for a brief time, but then a few words pierced the deep fog of my consciousness.

'Come in, dear Arthur, come in!' Dr Van Helsing's voice was warm and affable. 'She is unconscious now. You may take that one little kiss whiles I bring over the table.'

Arthur? How was Art here? I fought with all my might to shake off the lassitude of the drug, but I could not move, nor open my lips to speak. I felt a shadow fall across my face, and with an enormous effort, I forced my eyes open. All I could see were his eyes – black, enormous, pitiless. He saw my own eyes open and smiled.

'Well, little Lucy,' he whispered, so low that the others in the room could not hear, 'there you are. How are you feeling? You look awful.'

Then he pressed his mouth against mine, forcing his tongue between my numb lips. Every fibre of my being recoiled in revulsion, but I was paralysed, unable to move, unable even to turn my head away. I telegraphed my hatred with my eyes, but he turned away, giving his attention to Dr Van Helsing.

The doctors came to my bedside, and I closed my eyes again. I heard the clinking of glass and metal. With low murmurs, Art was instructed to remove his coat and roll up his shirtsleeve. Was the transfusion I was to receive to come from him? The thought of his wicked blood flowing into my body horrified me. I struggled, but the drugs Dr Van Helsing had given me pulled me further down. At length, I felt a sharp pain in the crook of my arm. He had, I assumed, inserted a needle of some kind.

I heard Van Helsing's voice say, with evident satisfaction, 'He is so young and strong and of blood so pure that we need not defibrinate it.'

At this point, I gave myself up to true unconsciousness.

* * *

I must have slept the whole day, because when I awoke, the long rays of the late afternoon sun slanted in through the window. Dr Seward sat slumped in the chair beside my bed. He smiled to see me awake. He looked rumpled and tired, but he leapt to his feet and brought me a glass of cold water to sip. My mouth was arid and nothing has ever tasted so delicious. I felt crushed by a great weakness.

'You look better, dear Lucy.'

'Better than what?'

He looked uncomfortable with my teasing, but smiled thinly. 'You were very ill, Lucy. You seemed to show all the signs of acute anaemia.'

'But your tests showed I was not anaemic.'

'Whatever the cause, the transfusion seems to have lifted you.'

The word struck me as if he had dashed the glass of cold water in my face. The transfusion. Art's blood flowed in my veins now. It felt like the most brutal of invasions. I recalled how he had forced his kiss on me when I was drugged and unable to move or speak.

'Dr Seward – John – I know you drugged me, but I was awake, you know. I recall every detail of what happened before the transfusion.'

'Lucy, I would never doubt you, but the fact remains you have had a number of very vivid hallucinations.'

'You think I imagined it?'

'Not imagined...'

'Let me describe the scene to you. There, in the corner...' I indicated the table, '...you and Dr Van Helsing stood, preparing the equipment. Dr Van Helsing told Art he could come and take his kiss. Is my description of the scene accurate, Doctor?'

'It is,' he admitted.

'While your back was turned, Art...' As the memory returned of Art's kiss, I retched. Dr Seward grabbed a bowl and brought it to me. I coughed, causing agonies in my bruised throat, but nothing came up. At length I lay back on the pillows, exhausted. Dr Seward stood, looked out into the corridor and then closed the door. Then he came back and sat by the bed.

'Is there something you are concealing from me, Lucy? Is there information that might aid us in making a diagnosis?'

'Dr Seward, if I am completely frank, there are many things about my situation which are of great concern to me. But I do not think they have a bearing on my current ill health.'

'As your doctor, that should surely be my concern?'

'Are you my doctor? I have a doctor already. Dr Oliver, our family physician who has cared for me since the day I was born.

And yet here you are. Summoned by Art. Why should I put my faith in you?'

Art's name landed heavily between us.

'The trust between Doctor and patient...'

'Is such that you allow someone to kiss me without my consent when I have expressly said to you that I wish to have autonomy over my own body?'

Dr Seward shifted uncomfortably in his seat. 'You were unconscious...'

'How is that better? That someone may touch me as long as I am not awake to know of it? And as it happens, I was awake, even though I could not move.' I glared at him fiercely until he had the good grace to look away. 'So you see, Doctor Seward, there is a great deal I am not telling you. I have no reason to believe that you would respect my confidences. I think there is every likelihood that you would share any information I told you with Art, with Dr Van Helsing, with my mother...'

'Of course I would not...' he said weakly.

'Forgive me if I keep my own counsel on this matter,' I said coldly. 'Now, if you would be so kind, could you leave? I wish to call Beatrice to help me to wash and change.'

9 SEPTEMBER 1894

When Dr Seward returned the next evening, his face was drawn and grey with tiredness, but he smiled to see me up and about. When it came time to retire, I showed him to the bedroom opposite my own. I had had Eliza make up the bed and light a warm fire.

'I cannot possibly go to bed,' he said, although I saw his eyes linger longingly on the white sheets and soft counterpane.

'Very well, I will not attempt to offend your fine medical sensibilities,' I gathered up the counterpane and some pillows and took them to the sofa, which stood opposite the door. 'I shall leave this door open, and my door too. You may lie on the sofa, and if you open your eyes, you will be able to see me in my own bed. If I want anything I will call out, and you will come to me at once.'

Oh, how he wrestled with his conscience! But his weariness was so profound he could not resist. He took off his jacket and shoes and lay down. As soon as his head rested on the pillow, his eyelids fluttered closed, and his lips parted softly. His face was beautiful in sleep – vulnerable and young. I drew the coun-terpane over him and tiptoed to my own room to prepare for bed.

* * *

In the darkest hour, I awoke. I lay still, curled on my side, and tried to ascertain what had jerked me from slumber. The room was quiet and surprisingly dark. I recalled the pool of light from the lamp that Eliza had placed on the hall table outside my open door. Had someone extinguished it? Carefully, I angled my head to look. The narrowest sliver of light showed under the bedroom door. When I had gone to bed, my door had been open, as had Dr Seward's door opposite. Who had closed my door?

I made sure my breathing was as low and quiet as I could make it. I could not see anything, so I tried to sharpen all of my other senses. I could feel a small movement in the air, as if there was a breeze. It had been a damp, chill night, and the window had been closed when I went to bed. I allowed myself the smallest of sniffs, and sure enough, there was a hint of lemon verbena on the air.

As my eyes grew accustomed to the darkness, I could see his shape in the chair by the bed. The window behind him was open and told the story of how he had entered the room.

'You sleep so prettily, Lucy,' he whispered.

'Why are you here, Art?'

'I wanted to check on you. I was much weakened yesterday after I gave you my blood, but today I felt strong enough to ride down from Ring. I feel that we have come to a bad pass, dear Lucy.'

'How perceptive of you. How did you draw that conclusion? Was it the blackmail, or you trying to strangle me?'

'Bitterness does not become you.'

'I have no interest in what does and does not become me. All I ever wanted was my freedom – the freedom my father wanted for me. And you have stolen it from me.'

'When we marry, you will want for nothing. You can have anything and everything you desire – travel, adventure, beautiful dresses...'

'I would have had all of those without you!' I hissed, furious. 'You have trapped me and stolen what was rightfully mine. If there are any finer feelings in you Art, any at all, then persuade my mother to change her Will back. Give me what is mine – my freedom and my inheritance.'

'So you know about the Will.' This was a statement, not a question. 'Alas, Lucy, she has expressed her wishes most clearly.' He got up and walked to the window.

He drew in a long, ragged breath. 'And now my father is dying. I have been a disappointment to him in every possible way. Even now, on his deathbed, he can barely bring himself to look at me. He thinks I am superficial – a wastrel. I imagined, somehow, if I could bring my bride-to-be to him – a woman of good family, of breeding, of beauty and accomplishment, he might...' he gave a small, choking sob. 'What a mess I have made of all of this. It is too late. Too late.'

I wanted to hit him for his toadying self-pity; I climbed out of bed and crossed to face him.

'Art, you can weep all you like, but this situation is of your making alone. I will sacrifice my pride, my family name –

everything – to prevent you getting your way. You cannot blackmail and brutalise me into being what you want. I am not your property, some prize to be carried to your father. I will not stand for it.'

He turned to me, and I could see his features for the first time, as the faintest dawn light crept over the horizon.

'You are right, Lucy. Of course you are. You have always seen so clearly. Let me think about what I can do to end this regrettable situation.'

He put one leg over the windowsill, ready to climb down the trellis. I shivered in the cold breeze that came in through the window. I folded my arms to warm myself.

Art noticed this, and said, 'Why do you not ring for Beatrice? The house is rousing itself. You are awake now, and unlikely to sleep again. Get her to bring you some hot tea. It will comfort you.'

CHAPTER 18

'*I* brought you the good olive oil,' Rafaella said, unzipping her bag and handing me a bottle.

'You're an angel, and your timing is perfect. I've just finished the last bottle I had. Now, wine?' I said.

Rafaella sighed. 'Oh, yes. First, I endured the terrible flight, then the Underground. I feel I have been squeezed out of a tube of toothpaste.'

'Well, you're here now. We don't have to go anywhere this evening. Tomorrow is another day, and we can squeeze ourselves back onto the Tube and be tourists.'

'Perfect.' Rafaela folded herself into the corner of the sofa. 'So how's work, my dear?'

'Good. I've been sent back to the Enfield school where I did the month-long stint. I'm doing a maternity cover there now. I think they like me – they keep dropping hints about applying for a permanent post.'

'Do you like them?'

'I like the kids – they're feisty and funny and they challenge me, but they're never mean-spirited. The other teachers in the department are nice too.'

'So you could imagine staying there?'

'Well. Maybe.'

'And this... James?'

'You'll meet him tomorrow. He's driving up from Exeter.'

'That doesn't answer my question.'

'Which was? You just said, "This James?" That's not a question.'

'You are playing for time. Tell me – how is it going? Are we attending an English country wedding this time next year?'

'Whoa, slow down. It's going well. He's a great guy.'

'Ah, but you are not sure.'

'Why do you say that?'

'Because you tell me you are contemplating taking a permanent job in London.'

'I'm not really,' I couldn't hold Rafaella's penetrating gaze. 'Or maybe. Oh, I don't know. It's early days with James, and after Alex...'

'Speaking of Alex...'

'Do we have to?'

'He heard I was coming to see you. He came especially to visit me. He said he emailed you a few weeks ago, but you never responded. He asked me if he should ring you.'

'To which you said...?'

Rafaella did not reply – merely folded her arms and demonstrated the basilisk stare she'd given Alex. I laughed.

'So,' Rafaella said, 'should he ring you?'

'Of course not. I assumed that email was just a drunken, impulsive thing. Maybe he'd had a fight with Stacey...'

'He did have a fight with Stacey. She left. She's back in Swansea.'

'Oh.' Of everything I'd imagined might happen, I never thought ... 'What was the fight about?'

'About how he is not over you.'

I jumped up and then stood, indecisively in the middle of the living room.

'Oh, wine. We definitely need wine.' I headed for the kitchen.

I came back with a bottle and glasses and curled up opposite Rafaella.

'I'm going to change the subject. I don't want to talk about Alex, or hear about Alex, or even think about him. Tell me all your news instead.'

Rafaella obliged. She gossiped about her work at the art museum in Milan, her three brothers, and the love lives of her friends. I laughed till I cried.

'Oh god, what am I doing here?' I said, wiping my eyes. 'I miss you all so much. I miss Milan.'

'Milan will always be there. But if I am honest, you look so much better here than you did for your last few months there.'

'Well, that's not surprising. Alex was cheating on me, but I still had to see him every day at work. I was camping in your living room. It wasn't the best time.'

'It is more than that, *bella* Kate. Your eyes are bright. You have made this space your own, made some choices just for you. You have options. You could go to Devon to live with the lovely James. You could stay here and take a good job and study. You could travel to Mexico, or Bali, or the moon if you please. You could even come back to Milan, try to patch things up with Alex... ' It was Rafaella's turn to laugh. 'Oh Kate, your face! It is perfect. That is exactly the expression of horror I hoped to see.'

She followed me through to the kitchen and we began to prepare dinner.

'So what is it like living in the home of your mother?' she asked, looking around the small kitchen.

'Frustrating. It's so long since she lived here that I have no sense of her in the fabric of the flat, and my dad won't tell me anything about her time here. Gran doesn't know much at all, I find. She gave me those pictures,' I indicated the display on the hallway wall, 'but all I can work out is that Mum knew about Lucy living in this house and followed some of the same lines of enquiry I've found. She obviously knew a lot more than I did though... if all those pictures relate to the search. I still don't know what most of them mean.'

I looked over at the images. My eye was drawn to the garden with its imposing gate and the name – Proserpine – wound into the ironwork. I'd looked it up of course. Proserpine was the Latin name for Persephone, who was married to Hades, God of the Underworld. But why her name was on a gate, or where that garden might be, I couldn't imagine.

Rafaella's voice drew me back. 'This room – what it would have been in your grand old house?'

'On this floor, all the rooms were servants' quarters – so each of the bedrooms was probably occupied by a maid. On this side of the corridor, they knocked through the rooms to make the kitchen, living room and bathroom.'

'Difficult to imagine.'

I laughed, 'I've spent a lot of time imagining what the house must have been like back in the 1890s. That's easier than thinking about when Mum lived here.'

Later, as we ate dinner, I filled Rafaella in on everything James and I had learned about Lucy so far. She was horrified that Lucy's mother had disinherited her.

'How could she do that?' she said. 'What if Lucy had not wanted to marry this Arthur? What if he had abandoned her? Would he still have got all the property?'

'I suppose so.'

'Did Lucy leave a Will?' Rafaella asked suddenly.

'Would she have? I don't think so. She was only nineteen. Who writes a Will at nineteen?'

'I don't know. Someone who knows they are going to die? Who has property to bequeath, perhaps?'

I leaned over and picked up my laptop.

'James showed me where to search on the government website. If she did make a Will, we'll be able to see a probate record – maybe even get a copy.'

I opened the web page and typed in Lucy's name and date of death. No records came back.

'I thought it was unlikely,' I said, about to slam the lid on the laptop.

'Stop!' said Rafaella. 'Don't give up so easily. As a researcher, you should know better than that.'

'What do you mean?'

'Do not throw your hands in the air after one search. Broaden the dates. Perhaps there was a delay. Try different spellings of her name.'

'You're right, of course,' I said, although I felt sure there was little point. I broadened the years of my search until 1897, and tried "Lucie", "Lucey" and "Lucinda" as variants.

To my astonishment, a result popped up. Lucey Westenra's Last Will and Testament had been lodged for probate by Wholeman, Sons, Marquand & Lidderdale in 1895.

'That's the same solicitors' firm who lodged her mother's Will... and her father's!' I practically bounced with excitement as I waited for the page to load with the probate record.

'I wonder why they got her name wrong?' Rafaella said.

'Probably some clerk transcribing from a handwritten record. An easy mistake to make, I suppose.'

The page opened, and we read it.

Westenra, Lucey, Personal estate, 14 January 1895.

The Will of Lucey Rose Westenra late of Hillingham, in the parish of North End in the county of Middlesex, spinster, who died 19 September 1894 at Hillingham was proved at the Principal Registry by Beatrice Marks of Hillingham in the county of Middlesex, the sole executrix.

I raised my eyes from the screen and stared at Rafaella in shock.

'Beatrice? What property did Lucy have to leave to Beatrice?'

Rafaella, leaned over and pointed to a button.

'The Will is there. A copy of it has been digitised.'

My fingers trembled as I clicked and waited for the image to appear. And there it was. Faded but legible, and unmistakeably Lucy's handwriting.

The Last Will & Testament of Lucy Rose Westenra

I, Lucy Rose Westenra, being of sound mind and body, do make the following provisions upon the occasion of my death.

– That my funeral be a private affair, and that my mortal remains are not to be viewed by any other than my physician.

– That the coffin is sealed closed and placed in the Westenra family mausoleum at the parish church in Hendon, alongside that of my beloved father, Charles Westenra, at the earliest possible date following my death.

I do give and bequeath the library at Hillingham – both the structure and all the contents therein – to Beatrice Marks.

Signed this 18th Day of September 1894.

Rafaella touched Beatrice's name on the screen.

'Beatrice Marks? The maid who lived in your room? What does this mean?'

'I don't know. I just don't know. But it does open up a whole other avenue of research.'

Rafaella looked at me. 'You want to telephone to James, don't you?'

'So much.'

Rafaella stood. 'I am tired. I will get into bed, and you and

James can talk into the night.' She kissed me lightly on the cheek. '*Buonanotte* Katerina.'

* * *

AT ONE AM, James and I were still talking quietly.

'Okay,' he said, 'this is what we have. Our Beatrice Marks was born in 1875. In 1899, she married Cameron Locke. When they first married, they lived in the Bread Street Ward, but by 1911, they were back at Hillingham, living in the library.'

'That was shortly after the rest of the house had been converted into flats.'

'They had one child, Charles, born in 1900...'

'Do you think they named him after Charles Westenra?'

'It's possible. Anyway, Charles Locke was a late developer. Stayed living with his parents, working as an electrician, didn't marry till 1939. Then he and his wife lived in the library apartment with his parents, until Cameron, and then Beatrice, died.'

'And Charles and his wife had one child. Margaret, born in 1941.'

'Margaret, who according to every subsequent census and the electoral roll continued to live there,' said James. 'And still does.'

'Margaret.' I frowned and tapped my pen on my teeth. 'This is where I get confused.'

'The woman who lives in Flat 4. What's her name?'

'Mrs R. Baylis according to the label on her postbox.'

'Rita is short for Margaret.'

'Is it? I don't know. Could be. But why Baylis?'

There was a short silence while James typed and clicked. When he spoke again, his voice was tense with excitement.

'There's a Paul Baylis resident at number 4 in the 1981 census, but he's gone by 1991.'

'A short-lived marriage, but she kept his name?'

I sat back in my chair and stretched my arms above my head. I was cold and stiff, but wide awake.

'So, if we're right, Rita Baylis – who as we speak is sleeping about forty feet below me – is Beatrice's actual granddaughter?' I said.

'And as Beatrice died in 1954, when Rita was 13, Rita would remember her.'

'I just cannot believe that there's a real, living link to the story, and she's been here in the house all this time. She has to talk to us. She has to. How are we going to persuade her to speak to us?'

James yawned, long and loud.

'I don't know, my darling. But I do know that I'm due to leave in six hours to come and see you, and if I don't get some sleep, I'll be a menace on the roads.'

'Sleep, you wonderful, brilliant man. Sleep. I'll see you tomorrow.'

'Today. You'll see me today. Sleep tight.'

I glanced in on Rafaella, curled up, facing the wall in my bed. I wasn't ready to get in and lie beside her– my jumpiness would surely wake her. I went to the kitchen to make a cup of tea, choosing decaf, but there seemed little point. I was nowhere near being able to sleep.

I ambled back to my computer. The woman downstairs was, in all likelihood, a descendant of Beatrice's. But even more exciting than that, she'd lived in this building all her life. She had been here in the eighties, when Mum lived here. She must have known her, even if it was only in passing, and she might also know when and why Mum had drawn the replica of the house plans. At the thought of meeting her, of the possibility of new memories of Mum, I felt a fresh leap of anticipation.

I sat back at my computer and typed up everything James and I had learned about the Marks/ Locke/ Baylis family. I read back through all the notes I had made on Lucy story so far, and looked through all the documents I'd photographed and uploaded.

When I got to Rose Westenra's will, I paused. She had left the estate to this Arthur Holmwood. I searched Holmwood's name, trying it with and without his middle name and title. There was next to nothing, just a record of his being the only son of Lord Godalming. When I searched Lord Godalming's name, I found, as James had, a record of his family estate, Ring, in Hertfordshire. The name wasn't familiar – I had never heard of a stately home called Ring. I typed in Godalming/ Ring /Hertfordshire, and the top result came from a digitised book called *The Lost Great Houses of Hertfordshire*. The book had been written in the seventies and was long out of print, but someone had photographed and uploaded many of the pages. When I clicked through, there were paintings, drawings and engravings, but there were frustratingly few captions and they gave little information.

I peered at a black-and-white photograph of the house. It must once have been large, imposing and gothic, but in the photograph, it was a ruin with crumbling walls and no roof. A caption on this first picture baldly stated, "Demolished in 1937." There followed a series of engravings from various eras, showing the house in its heyday, with carriages on the driveway and its turrets and roof intact. A few watercolours showed the verdant hills of the park and the long stone wall that surrounded its hundreds of acres. I looked on Google Maps to see where Ring had been – the area was now a housing estate and a featureless retail park. No trace of the original grandeur remained.

I flicked through the next few pages, stifling a yawn – I was finally getting tired – when a late Victorian engraving stopped me in my tracks. "The Garden of the last Lady Godalming", the caption said. The image showed an orderly plot surrounded by hedges and bounded with a high, wrought iron gate. Wound into the ironwork was a name – Proserpine. I spun around in my chair so fast, I nearly fell off. There was Mum's drawing of the overgrown garden, those same gates... how could she have...?

It took me a few seconds to realise that Mum could not have seen the real garden if the house was demolished in the nineteen thirties. Like me, she must have found engravings and drawings. But what had sparked her interest?

I knew Proserpine was held captive by Pluto in the Underworld. I wondered about the goddess' link to horticulture, so threw the word "garden" into a search. A poem by Algernon Charles Swinburne was the top result: "The Garden of Proserpine".

The words swam before my eyes. I wasn't really up to analysing poetry at three am. But after a few slow reads, I got the gist – Proserpine's garden was the garden of the dead.

> *No growth of moor or coppice,*
> *No heather-flower or vine,*
> *But bloomless buds of poppies,*
> *Green grapes of Proserpine,*
> *Pale beds of blowing rushes*
> *Where no leaf blooms or blushes*
> *Save this whereout she crushes*
> *For dead men deadly wine.*

"Bloomless buds of poppies". "For dead men deadly wine". What was Swinburne saying? Was Proserpine's garden filled with deadly plants? Had Lady Godalming cultivated a poison garden?

LUCY WESTENRA'S SECOND JOURNAL

I opened my eyes to blinding light – sunshine poured in through the window. It did not look like early morning.

'What time is it?'

Dr Seward, sitting by my bed, glanced at his watch. 'It is just past five o'clock.'

'In the afternoon?' He nodded his assent. 'I have lost twelve hours, doctor.'

'You fell ill again in the night, Lucy. Dr Van Helsing arrived here at around eight this morning. He came to wake me and together we came into this room. You were prostrated across the bed – paler than I have ever seen you, and quite insensible. Clearly you suffered a relapse and were unable to cry out.'

'I – I have no memory of that,' I was deeply troubled by this turn of events. 'I was well when I went to bed, as you know, and I was still in good health when I woke in the night.'

'You woke in the night? Why did you not call out to me?'

'Because Art was here.'

'Art?' Dr Seward's brow wrinkled in confusion. 'Lucy, he was not here. He is at Ring with his father, as you well know.'

'He was here,' I insisted. 'He came to see me in the night. He sat in the very chair where you sit now.'

'At what time did he visit?'

'It was dark. The very dead of night. But he stayed almost until daybreak.'

Dr Seward frowned. 'But how did he enter the house? None of the servants mentioned seeing him.'

'He came in through the window.'

The doctor raised an eyebrow. 'The window?'

I could see he was humouring me.

'Do not treat me like a child, Dr Seward. I know what happened. Art came in through the window. It is quite possible to climb in, using the trellis outside, if you know how to do it. He sat in the chair and we spoke.'

'Hallucinations can be very powerful. Very believable...'

'But I was well last night! You saw me yourself, when we both went to bed. I was quite in my right mind.'

'You were, but...'

'What could have happened to me in the night that so altered that?'

'Illnesses can change and progress...'

'I am not mad, Doctor. Art was here. Then, when dawn broke, he left, climbing out of the window.'

'Lucy, I can assure you that Art is at Ring. I have had a telegram from him today, asking how you are. He has not been here.'

I felt increasingly desperate. How could I make him believe me? A thought struck me. 'Beatrice!'

'Beatrice?'

'I rang for her at around six this morning and asked her to bring me some tea. It was not long after Art left. She will tell you I was well, that I was not hallucinating then. If I was well at six, then I was not ill in the night, is that not so?'

I scrambled from the bed. I did not wait to find slippers or a robe. I rushed from the room barefoot and ran down to the kitchen. Dr Seward followed me, calling my name.

The kitchen was empty.

'Beatrice!' I called, pushing open the door to the scullery.

She was kneeling on the floor and she looked up, startled as I burst into the room. Her face was pale and her eyes swollen and red with crying.

'Oh Miss Lucy, I'm so sorry,' she sobbed. I frowned in incomprehension, and then my gaze took in what rested before her.

On a folded blanket, little Missy the cat lay on her side. Her eyes were open and her lips drawn back to reveal her teeth, but her body was stiff and contorted, as if she had been frozen in a moment of excruciating pain.

'Missy!' I cried, falling to my knees. I pressed a hand to the soft fur of her side, but it was cold, and her little heart was stilled.

'I found her in the bushes outside, Miss,' said Beatrice between sobs. 'She was already dead when I found her. She were fine this morning, wanting her little treats, playing with a bit of string. I don't know what could have happened.'

Dr Seward had caught up with me, and he came into the room. He took in the scene and knelt beside me. He drew Missy's little body closer and ran his hands over her limbs. He gently turned her face towards him and looked at her eyes and mouth.

'I cannot be sure, but I suspect she has been poisoned,' he said gravely. 'Does the gardener use rat poison perhaps, or are there any poison traps you have set in the house?'

'Not in the house, sir,' said Beatrice, and the gardener does have some, but it is locked in the shed. How could Missy have got hold of it?'

'Rat poison is bitter. She would have been unlikely to eat it on its own. But perhaps she ate a dead creature, a mouse or rat that had been poisoned?' Even as Dr Seward spoke, his tone was hesitant. I turned to look at him.

'Doctor Seward? You sound unsure.'

'I am indeed, Lucy. It does not look quite like arsenic poisoning. We had a problem with vermin when we first took over the asylum. I saw a great many rats who had ingested arsenic and their death rigours were not quite...' he paused. 'It is her eyes. Her pupils are dilated as wide as they can go. They start almost from her head. As if she has seen something awful.'

12 SEPTEMBER 1894

Dr Van Helsing has returned and has demanded a place to work within the house and Mother, without consulting me, has offered my library.

At some point in the afternoon, I heard the front doorbell ring, and voices in the hall below. Dr Van Helsing burst into my room then, without knocking, a big box in his arms. He placed the box on the bed – it was covered in stamps and stickers and had clearly come from abroad. He raised the lid and lifted out great bunches of flowers –white clusters of tiny blooms surrounded by glossy, dark green leaves.

'These are for you, Miss Lucy,' he said.

'For me? Oh, Dr Van Helsing!' I smiled sweetly.

'Yes, my dear, but not for you to play with. These are medicines.'

He brought a bundle of the flowers over to me and I took them, sniffing to see if they had a scent. They did, but it was pungent and savoury.

'Oh, Professor, I believe you are only putting up a joke on me. Why, these flowers are common garlic.'

He did not take my playful admonishment well. He frowned and then barked, 'No trifling with me! I never jest! There is grim purpose in all I do.'

I stared at him. Why did he persist in making these faux portentous, mysterious statements? He was clearly convinced of something, but I could not understand why he did not simply tell us his diagnosis.

He drew the flowers from the box. I could see they were woven into garlands. He began to drape them around the edges of every window and door, and around the head of my bed. Then he took a handful of the herbs, and crushing them in his hands, used them to rub around the window frames and on the doorjamb, and even along the lintel of the fireplace. It looked to me as if he were performing some kind of mystical rite – such as the ancient pagans might undertake. It was strange behaviour from a man I had thought to be a devoted Christian.

I was not alone in my misgivings – I had never seen Dr Seward disagree with his mentor before, but he said, 'Well, Professor, I know you always have a reason for what you do, but this certainly puzzles me. It is well we have no sceptic here, or he would say that you were working some spell to keep out an evil spirit.'

'Perhaps I am!' Van Helsing did not look at him – he was too busy fashioning another, smaller garland of flowers.

The gentlemen left the room and Beatrice came in to help me to get ready for bed. When I was settled, Van Helsing came in and draped the garland he had made around my neck, as if I had won a race. I tried my best not to smile, even though I could see Dr Seward's perplexed face over his shoulder.

'Take care you do not disturb it; and even if the room feel close, do not to-night open the window or the door.'

I made a solemn promise, even though I found the rigmarole

preposterous. I followed this with fervent, girlish thanks. I sensed he expected these as his due, and indeed, they proved effective, because shortly afterwards, the two medical men departed, and I heard them rattling down the driveway in Dr Seward's carriage.

I found that I was surprisingly tired, and even though the air in my room was thick with the pungent fumes of the garlic, I soon drifted off. Some hours later, I awoke to see a shadowy figure moving around my room. I sat up.

'Art?' I whispered sharply.

To my astonishment, I heard Mother's voice. 'No dear, it is I. Go back to sleep. I merely came in to check on you.'

I lay down obediently and put my head on the pillow. She sat in the chair beside my bed for a few minutes. I heard her sniffing suspiciously, and then she gave a small snort of disgust. She waited a few minutes until she was sure I was asleep, and then she gently lifted the heavy garland of garlic flowers from around my neck. I heard her rise and move around the room. I opened my eyes a crack and saw she was stretching to pull the flowers from the windows and the doorframe. She raised the sash and threw them all out of the window. She peered down at me and I continued to feign sleep. Once I heard her leave the room, pulling the door to, I allowed myself a small smile. Dr Van Helsing had met his match. However weak and ill Rose Westenra was, she would not allow cheap flowers in her house.

The fresh night air rushed in through the window and I heard an owl hoot. I closed my eyes and felt sleep rushing in to claim me once more. Flowers filled my dreams– the profusion of tiny white garlic flowers, the reeking lilies which had lain on Pa's coffin, and a dark purple flower, shaped like a helmet. It seemed to me that this last flower hovered above my face. It was as if someone was holding the bloom above me – who was it? Mother again? Was she in my dreams because she had lately been in my room? In the dream, I could not see the person's face, although I caught a trace of leather, as if the hand wore a glove. The flower moved above my eyes, swaying from side like the watch of a mesmerist.

Then the flower dropped out of sight, and I felt a finger – gloved as I had imagined, slide beneath the ribbon I had tied about my neck. I wore it habitually to cover the marks Art had left with his nails. The gloved finger in my dream drew the ribbon away from my throat, and I experienced the lightest touch, like flower petals on my skin. As I say, it was the strangest dream, and after it ended, I drifted back into deep sleep. However, I could still feel the trace of that touch on my skin.

13 SEPTEMBER 1894

When Dr Seward entered my bedroom the next morning, I was standing before the glass. He rushed to my side.

'Oh Lucy,' he said, and there was a sob in his voice. 'We almost lost you. You were so ill when we found you this morning. Let me guide you to bed.'

'No,' I brushed aside his fluttering hands.

He came up behind me and regarded my reflection in the mirror. I had loosened the ribbon I wore around my neck. I heard him gasp in shock. There was an angry red weal across my throat, as if I had been burned, or as if hands had gripped me round the neck.

'What has caused that? Did someone try to strangle you?'

'No. Maybe. I cannot remember...'

He leaned closer to look at the mark. 'I see no finger marks. It is not a burn from heat either. It looks like some kind of reaction to a chemical agent.'

Dr Seward persuaded me away from the mirror and we sat.

'What happened last night?' I asked.

'When we came in, and all the flowers had been removed by

your mother – you were pale, so pale, and your heart beat but slowly.'

'As before?'

Dr Seward glanced nervously toward the door. Dr Van Helsing was nowhere to be seen, but I could hear the bellowing sounds of his voice from down the corridor, interspersed with Mother's thin, imperious tones. I could not make out what they were saying, although I did hear Dr Van Helsing use the words "absolutely forbid" and "medical advice". Mother responded, and it seemed the argument would run for some time.

'Not... not quite as before. Dr Van Helsing was convinced we were seeing the same symptoms again, but I have continued to test your blood, almost daily, Lucy, and you show no signs of anaemia.'

'But Dr Van Helsing believes blood loss to be the cause of my illness?'

'He has an idea in his head and it is fixed...'

I could see Dr Seward wrestling with himself. He did not want to undermine his mentor. Hesitantly, he spoke.

'I have seen this phenomenon before. It is always a danger for scientific men. If you approach a case having decided you know its cause, all the evidence you uncover will support your theory.'

'Was that not the opinion of Francis Bacon?'

'I beg your pardon?'

'I read his views in the *Novum Organum*. He suggested that human understanding will draw all things to support an opinion when it has once been adopted. I was most struck by that point. We all do it – I know I am as guilty of it as anyone.' Dr Seward nodded. 'And you think that this is the error Dr Van Helsing is making? He is convinced that my illness is due to loss of blood, and cannot see other symptoms, even when they are presented to him?'

'I am afraid so.'

'And you? What do you believe?'

'I am no closer to knowing the real cause of your illness, but I quickly realised your heart rate was slow. I injected you with a small dose of digitalis. It brought your heart rate back to normal, and we soon saw colour return to your face. Your sleep changed from a deadly coma to restful slumber, and then you awoke.'

'But...' I frowned in confusion.

'But what caused it? Oh Lucy, I wish that I knew. I think...' he rose and went to stand by the window.

'You think...?' I urged him to continue.

'I am loath to offer my opinion, Lucy. I am so afraid of committing Francis Bacon's error. The evidence before me suggests one thing, but I am conscious that I may be neglecting other signs because they do not suit my theory.'

'What is your theory?'

'It was the death of your little cat that gave me the clue. Her eyes. Her wide-eyed death stare reminded me of your own eyes, when you were in the grip of illness.'

We looked at each other. I could feel pieces of the puzzle dropping into place with horrifying, cold precision.

'Beatrice,' I said, my voice as calm as I could make it. 'Beatrice said she gave Missy her treat...'

'I asked Beatrice. She said the cat loved a little saucer of cold, milky tea.'

'And the tea came from...?'

'What was left from your tray from that morning. I asked Beatrice, where she kept the tealeaves. She told me the household has two kinds of tea: Lady Grey, which your mother prefers. "And there's the special one for Miss Lucy."'

'I found a brand of tea in Whitby that I liked – I brought some packages back with me.'

He nodded. 'I asked Beatrice to bring me your package of

tea, along with a basin. I tipped out the tea. Among the leaves, I found this.'

He reached into his pocket, withdrew his handkerchief and unfolded it. Inside, there was a small, shiny black berry.

'What is that?'

'I was not sure. I took some of these berries to Purfleet, so I could further analyse them. I tasted the smallest part of one. It caused my heart to race, my eyes to start from my head and my mouth to dry out. And I saw... visions. Further reading suggested that the symptoms you have experienced – dilated pupils, sensitivity to light, a severely dry mouth and throat, slurred speech, urinary retention and hallucinations – all are indications of belladonna poisoning.'

'Belladonna? Deadly Nightshade?'

'Indeed. It would make you very pale and weak, which is why Dr Van Helsing diagnosed blood loss as the cause of your malady.'

I shook my head, trying to grasp this new idea. Belladonna. I may have been poisoned. But how...?

'How could it have got into the tea?'

'Beatrice says she opened this package of tea a few days after you came back from Yorkshire. It is possible, although highly unlikely, that the tea you bought in Yorkshire was contaminated when it was packaged. I have written to the company to ask them if there have been other instances of this. But the fact remains that I only found berries in the open package of tea. There were none in any of the other packages you brought back from Whitby.'

"But I have not had any of the tea since yesterday morning, and yet I still fell ill last night.'

'Did something happen in the night, Lucy? Anything at all?'

'I remember Mother coming in to check on me, and I recall her removing the flowers and opening the window. And then...' I faltered.

'And then?'

'I slept. I dreamed – feverish, strange dreams of flowers.'

'Flowers?'

I recounted the dream of the purple flower, the leather-gloved hand.

'It's peculiar, I'll grant you. I know that people believe there is symbolism in dreams. What would the purple flower mean? And why would I dream of someone touching my throat with it? Can my dream have caused this rash? 'I touched my neck gingerly. 'Could a dream be so vivid?'

'Unless it was no dream.'

'What do you mean?'

'There are certain flowers that are so poisonous that they could well cause both the rash and your swooning symptoms.'

'Such as?'

'Oleander, possibly, or Monkshood.'

'Monkshood?'

'Also known as Wolfsbane. I know little about these toxins – only what I have read as part of my studies. They are fiercely poisonous, however. I recall a case of a gardener who pulled some Wolfsbane out by hand and died some days later, merely from having touched the plant.'

'So what you are saying is that I may have been poisoned, more than once, and by different poisoning agents?'

'That does seem to be the likely cause of your repeated relapses.'

'It is unlikely that this is accidental.'

'Indeed.'

The silence grew between us. Dr Seward waited for me to say the words myself.

'You believe someone is trying to kill me?'

'I do not wish to rush to conclusions, but … yes, I think it is possible.'

'So do I,' I said quietly. 'And I know who it is.'

'You do?'

'It is Art, Dr Seward. Arthur Holmwood is the only person I can think of who would wish me dead.'

'Art?' his face tightened in shock. 'But why? He loves you, Lucy...'

'He does not love me.'

In halting tones, I told Dr Seward how Mother had settled the estate on Art, and about his blackmail of Pa.

'I challenged him. He knows that if I expose his fraud, either now or once Mother had died, he will suffer damage to his reputation, or worse, face a challenge in the courts and lose his right to the money. When I confronted him, I think I may have signed my own death warrant.'

An idea came to me and I gasped.

'Remember when you first came to our "At Home"? Art told Rosamond Nash about his mother's garden at Ring. He has the knowledge to poison me, the means to do so, and a motive. But what I do not understand is why he has brought you in, a friend of his, to be my medical practitioner? Surely in this way, he risks exposure?'

I stopped when I saw Seward's face. It was brick-red, suffused with impotent fury and dawning comprehension.

'He takes me for a fool,' he said. He was not speaking to me, but addressing the air in his blind anger. 'A fool, or his obedient lapdog.'

'John,' I said, forgetting myself and using his Christian name. 'What do you mean?'

'He has never had any respect for me as a man, or as a doctor.'

'Oh, John.'

'I was genuinely surprised when he asked me to take on your medical care. After years of teasing and ridicule, I was naïve enough to think that I had finally earned his respect. But I see it now. I am here to act as his willing accomplice.'

'What do you mean?'

'I am to tend you, and watch you die of some undiagnosed malady, and then stop anyone asking questions when it happens.' His eyes widened with sudden shock. 'What is the date, Lucy?'

'Why, the thirteenth of September.'

'I first came to see you when you fell ill at the beginning of the month, did I not? The first or second of September?'

'I believe that is so.'

He dashed his hand against his forehead and paced the room in a fury.

'If a patient has been under the care of a doctor within fourteen days of death, then that doctor can issue a death certificate. No postmortem nor coroner's inquest is necessary.'

I went to him and put my hand in his.

'He has taken us both for fools, John, but he is wrong. We know now, and we will prevail.'

'We will, Lucy. We will take what we know to Dr Van Helsing, in the first instance, and then to your Mother...'

I felt cold fear. Art still had the story of Quincey and me as leverage. I knew he would not hesitate to tell Mother, and the consequences of that did not bear consideration...

'Mother? She is so frail. I do not think she is strong enough for a shock like this.'

'What is our alternative, Lucy? Shall we let him kill you and steal your inheritance?'

'Of course not. But let us begin by speaking to Dr Van Helsing. We need his support and his gravitas. Perhaps between the three of us, we can prevent Art from any further attempts.'

'Very well. But Lucy, I would suggest...' he hesitated, '...that I speak to the Professor alone.'

'Alone? Why? It is my life that hangs in the balance.'

'I know. But Professor Van Helsing's views on the fairer sex are...' he hesitated.

'Archaic? Insulting? I know. Perhaps now is the time to change his mind.'

'You will not change it Lucy, but...'

'I will speak to him. I will present my own story. Let me have at least that, John. I have been robbed of all else.'

His shoulders sagged and he bowed his head.

'Very well, Lucy. When he returns to the house, we will speak with him together.'

'Well then, let me dress, the better to present my case.' I smiled at him.

He bowed and, as he turned to go, released my hand. I realised that our hands had been intertwined for many minutes. I felt suddenly shy at this moment of unheeded intimacy. As he left the room, a blush warmed my cheeks.

Later

We asked Dr Van Helsing to join us in my library in the early afternoon. Getting dressed had exhausted me. I was forced to sit, as my quivering legs were not strong enough to hold me up. I caught a glimpse of my face in the glass of one of the cabinets. It was gaunt, and my upper lip had drawn back to reveal my teeth. I had left my throat bare, so that the Professor would be forced to see the ugly, weeping weal that encircled it.

Dr Seward laid out his case for believing my symptoms were related to poisoning. Dr Van Helsing began by listening, but just a few sentences in, I could see he had stopped paying attention, and was merely looking for an opportunity to halt the flow of John's words and interject. To his credit, John persevered, speaking strongly and, I thought, rationally.

'As my pupil, you should know better than to perform a single experiment with yourself as subject,' Dr Van Helsing growled. 'This is not science, Friend John.'

'I was not the experiment, Professor, I was the control,' John said passionately. 'Lucy's symptoms so clearly echo what we know of belladonna poisoning...'

'Have you seen belladonna poisoning?' Van Helsing barked.

'I have read of it...'

'I have seen it, and the victim died a most horrible death. This is not what ails Miss Lucy!'

Van Helsing was so forceful, I thought John would back down, but he persevered. He spoke about my most recent collapse and indicated the burn mark on my throat.

'Wolfsbane?' Van Helsing all but guffawed. 'Now you are searching for the most fantastical of possibilities, John. How should Wolfsbane have floated into a house with the doors all sealed, and touched Miss Lucy upon her pretty throat?'

John and I looked at one another. It was time for me to present my part of the case. I stood, a little unsteadily, and walked over to Van Helsing.

'Professor, I have reason to believe someone wishes me ill. I think they have been reaching my bedroom through the window. This has happened on more than one occasion.'

I expected him to reject my suggestion, but instead his eyes flared with excitement.

'Indeed, Miss Lucy? You believe this to be true? I believe it too! I believe it with all my heart. But I must ask you. Have you seen this – this creature who will harm you?'

'I have. I have seen him in my sleeping and waking.'

'In what form does he come to you? Is it as a bat? A bird? Or another creature? Or does he take the form of a man? What of his eyes? Are they red? And his teeth? Have you seen the fangs of which I have read? Can he pass through walls as they say he can?'

I took an involuntary step back. His stare burned with the light of the fanatic. I glanced past him at John, who frowned in incomprehension. This clearly meant nothing to him either.

'My assailant is not a spirit, nor is he a creature, Dr Van Helsing. He is a man, and a man whom we all know well.'

Van Helsing looked confused, 'Do you mean to say he can

shift his shape and impersonate one we know? There would still be clues – the glowing eyes, for example...'

'This is no shape-shifter!' To my chagrin, my voice had become shrill. 'I speak of Arthur Holmwood, Dr Van Helsing. It is he who wishes me dead.'

There was a shocked silence, and then Van Helsing roared with laughter.

'Oh Miss Lucy,' he said, wiping his eyes. 'Has there been a lover's tiff? Did he forget to bring you a little gift? Or was he remiss on commenting on a new bonnet?'

'No, I...!'

'They say that hell hath no fury, and that is true. Well, this too will pass. The fine young Mr Holmwood will come and make pretty apologies, and then the lovers shall kiss and make up. It is usual, is it not, these – how do they call it – "jitters" before the wedding day?'

'Lucy does not have jitters, Professor,' John stepped in. 'She has real foundation to think that Art wishes to cause her harm.'

'This is feminine logic,' Dr Van Helsing burst out, 'and John, you should know better.'

'Feminine logic?' I felt anger blaze in my breast. 'By this you mean no logic at all, Professor? Is that what you think? You do not know Arthur Holmwood. You do not know what he is capable of...'

'On the contrary,' said the Professor. For the first time in this conversation, he was angry. 'I do know Arthur Holmwood, though we have met but few times. I know a man so handsome, so noble. He is just exactly the same age as my son would have been. He has the same golden hair and fine eyes and tall straight back. Just like my own boy, had he not sickened and died...' His voice cracked and he broke off, before continuing, even more passionately. 'Arthur Holmwood is the heir of a fine, old family, and he tells me so much of his great love for you, Miss Lucy. How can you imagine he would ever wish you harm?'

His love for Art shone through his eyes. He accused us of flawed logic, but he was blinded by Art's charm. I could see already that nothing would persuade him. I could show him Mother's Will and the entries in the ledgers of Westenra and Co., and he would not be moved.

He was still agitated, pacing up and down the carpet of the library. Then he spun around and turned on John.

'And you, Friend John, you most of all should be mortified of yourself.'

'He has been only a support to me,' I interjected, but he ignored me and stalked over to John, leaning in to bark in his face.

'When Miss Lucy was so deeply asleep, you know what you confessed to me.'

John's eyes flared in alarm.

'Professor...'

'You have your own motive for this ugly attack on your so-called friend Arthur, do you not? For you love her. You would win her for yourself. I am ashamed of you.'

'That is not...'

'Enough!' the Professor roared. 'Enough. I cannot listen to this disloyalty anymore. John, you will return to your own home and consider what kind of man would do as you have done. I alone will take the care of Miss Lucy and watch over her through the dark hours. I am certain, more certain now than I have ever been, of the cause of her malady. As I wait up in the nights, and guard her with the garlic and with other signs I will place in her room, my thesis will be proved correct. You shall see!'

And with that, he stormed from the room, slamming the door so it rattled in its frame.

CHAPTER 19

⁂

5 MAY 2024 – KATE

*D*ear Mrs Baylis,

I spoke to you briefly the other day – I'm Kate Balcombe and I live upstairs from you, in Number 8. The flat I live in originally belonged to my mother, Noni Rosen, who lived here in the early 1980s. Perhaps you knew her?

When I knocked on your door, I mentioned that your flat was once the library in the original house. I've been doing some research, and I learn that in the 1890s, the then owner of the house, Charles Westenra died, and he left the library to his daughter Lucy, as a separate entity...

I laid out everything I knew about Lucy, and about the fact that the flat had then passed to Beatrice. I explained that my bedroom must once have been Beatrice's room, and that I'd found a letter under the floorboards.

The letter was entrusted to your grandmother, so I thought it might be of interest to you. I'd be happy to show it to you, along with all the other information I have found.

I signed the letter, then slipped out of the flat and down the stairs to the hallway. There, I put it into Mrs Baylis's post-box. I stood in the cool and silent foyer. If Rita was indeed Beatrice's granddaughter, it was unlikely that she was ignorant of the origins of her flat. So why, when I'd asked her, had she said she didn't know anything about it?

When I got back upstairs, Rafaella was in the kitchen brewing coffee.

'Not much sleep?' she said, by way of greeting.

'No, but it was completely worth it.' I accepted a cup of coffee and quickly filled Rafaella in on what James and I had learned the night before about Rita.

'Astonishing!' Rafaella said, 'Do you think she will speak to you?'

'She wasn't friendly when I went to her door the other day.'

'But she is the living link to the story of Lucy,' Rafaella said. Her eyes widened. 'Your flowers!'

'Flowers?'

'You told me of the flowers left at Lucy's grave. Perhaps your Mrs Baylis is the one who sends them. As a thank you for her family's good fortune?'

'Oh my god, you're right! That would make perfect sense!'

Despite my excitement, I stifled a huge yawn.

'Don't fade on me now,' said Rafaella. 'I wish to be a tourist all day. If I don't finish the day outside the Tower of London wearing a Union Jack hat, I will consider it wasted!'

I laughed. 'A hot shower and a bacon sandwich and I'll be raring to go!'

James arrived at ten. He also looked weary. I filled him in on what I had learned about Lady Godalming's garden at Ring, and the Swinburne poem.

'It's hard to know what to make of it,' he said cautiously, 'but amazing that you've found another link to one of your mum's drawings.'

Within minutes, he and Rafaella discovered they were both fans of Inter Milan, and they chatted about football on the Tube on the way into town. Rafaella set a blistering pace around the tourist attractions in central London. By two o'clock, my vision was blurring. Rafaella laughed as I stifled another jaw-cracking yawn.

'We have tickets to the jazz tonight, so I will show mercy. Shall we go back to your flat for a rest before the evening festivities?'

'Please,' I said.

Once in the flat, I left James and Rafaella chatting in the kitchen and went to my room. As soon as I lay down on the bed, I tumbled into a heavy sleep.

Some time later, I jerked awake with James's warm hand on my shoulder.

'You've been dribbling on your pillow. Very sexy,' he said.

'Sorry. Is it time to go?' I sat up, groggy.

'Not yet. It's only just past five.'

'Really? Why did you wake me?' I rubbed a hand over my face. 'Let me go back to sleep.'

'Well you can, but your Mrs Baylis is in the living room, so...'

'Oh, my god. She's here?'

I jumped to my feet, turning aimlessly this way and that. I caught a glimpse of my reflection in the mirror. My hair stood in a crazy halo around my head. James laughed.

'Why don't you go to the bathroom and gather yourself? Rafaella's charming Mrs Baylis with coffee and biscotti. You can take a minute.'

A few minutes later, I walked into the living room. A petite, fine-boned woman sat on the sofa, cup in hand. She was neatly dressed in a jumper and tailored trousers, and her hair was freshly coiffed. She could have been any age from her mid-sixties, although I knew she had to be over eighty. She regarded me with the bright blue, narrowed eyes, which I'd seen peering around the door of Number 4. It felt odd to see the whole woman.

I went over and offered my hand. Mrs Baylis's grip was firm and strong, although her hand was tiny.

'I got your note. Thank you. Very interesting.'

'I'm so glad you came,' I said, sitting down opposite her.

'I can see now that you're Noni's girl,' she said.

I felt tears start in my eyes. 'Can you?'

'Same eyes. Her hair was longer, obviously. Are you also an artist?'

'No,' I said regretfully. 'Did you know her well?'

'She was a good neighbour. Very friendly.'

I waited for her to say more, but she didn't.

'I have some drawings she did,' I said, pointing to the display on the wall. 'They seem to suggest she was also interested in Lucy Westenra and the history of the house at that time.'

Rita Baylis glanced at the pictures but her eye didn't linger and she didn't ask any questions. She turned back to me expectantly.

'Well?' she said.

'I'm sorry?'

'The letter you found?'

'Oh, yes, of course,' I said.

I went back the bedroom. I hesitated, looking at the real letter, now carefully preserved in a sealed plastic wallet. I left it on the desk and instead, picked up a photocopy of all the pages, along with the transcription of the shorthand. I came to sit beside Mrs Baylis on the sofa and handed her the papers. Mrs Baylis put on the reading glasses, which hung on a chain around her neck. She spent some moments reading Lucy's instructions to Beatrice on the outer wrapping, then she picked up the photocopy of the shorthand letter. I expected her to put it to one side and look at the transcript, but instead she seemed to read it easily. When she had finished, she handed it back to me. She seemed neither surprised nor shocked.

'Thank you,' she said, 'that was interesting to read.'

'You read shorthand?' James said, surprised.

'I was a headmaster's secretary for forty years,' Mrs Baylis said crisply, without looking at him.

'Do you have any idea why your grandmother never posted the letter?' I asked. 'Did she ever speak about it?

'I do know a little about what happened,' said Mrs Baylis, 'I think it's likely events moved fast. Perhaps things changed, and the letter wasn't necessary.'

'Things changed?' I was shocked by the woman's calm demeanour. 'Do you have any idea what happened to Lucy? What she died of?'

'No.' Mrs Baylis said abruptly.

'Er...' James interjected, '... actually I may be able to help with that. I forgot to say that just before I left to come here this morning, the post came. I think Rose and Lucy's death certificates have arrived.'

'Really? And you're only just telling me that now?'

'Sorry. I threw them on the back seat of the car and forgot about them. I'll run down and get them.'

While James was gone, I turned back to Mrs Baylis.

'Do you have many memories of your grandmother?'

'I was only a girl when she died, but I do remember her. She was small and wiry, like me. Very strong. She went into service when she was about twelve, as many girls did then.'

'Did Beatrice... your grandmother... did she ever talk about that time? About Lucy?'

'Of course she did! Lucy left her the library. She changed the course of our lives.'

'Ask about the flowers,' Rafaella urged.'

'What flowers?' Mrs Baylis frowned.

'We visited Lucy's grave, and someone has flowers delivered there once a week – white roses. Is it you?'

'Flowers?' Mrs Baylis's blank expression did not appear to be feigned. 'I don't know anything about flowers.'

I exchanged a glance with Rafaella who shrugged.

'What did Beatrice tell you about Lucy?'

'She said she was a strong-willed girl. Very spoiled when she was young. Wilful. Her father gave her everything. But she came good in the end, Nan always said.'

'Came good? What does that mean?'

'Not sure I know,' said Mrs Baylis.

She put her coffee down and took a tissue from her cardigan pocket to dab her lips. Before we could ask her anything else, James came back in with two brown envelopes in his hand. I noticed that Mrs Baylis regarded James with thin-lipped contempt. For some reason, she didn't like him. James handed me the envelopes, and I opened them with trembling fingers.

While I did so, Rafaella picked up the conversation smoothly.

'A library,' she said to Mrs Baylis, 'That must have been an interesting place to grow up.'

'It wasn't designed for living in,' Mrs Baylis sniffed. 'My grandad Cameron panelled over the shelves and made wooden partitions to divide it into separate rooms. When they did the conversion of the rest of the house, he had a bathroom and kitchen installed at one end. Tiny, poky rooms. And dark.'

I now had both certificates spread out on my knees.

'Rose died of heart failure, according to this, and Lucy died of "loss or waste of blood". I don't even know what that means.'

'Could it be a gynaecological complaint?' asked Rafaella. Or... a miscarriage?'

'It wasn't that,' said Mrs Baylis. We all turned to look at her. 'As I say, there was a lot going on at that time.'

'Well, of course there was,' I said, holding up the death certificates. 'With two deaths in the house... it's almost as if this place was cursed.'

'You don't know the half of it,' said Mrs Baylis. 'There weren't two deaths at Hillingham that year. There were three.'

LUCY WESTENRA'S SECOND JOURNAL

1 SEPTEMBER 1894

I was to be left in Dr Van Helsing's sole care for some days. I felt horribly alone. To whom could I turn? I wrote a desperate letter to Mina in shorthand and told her of my illness and my fears. There was no time to lose, so as soon as I finished it, I addressed it and went looking for Beatrice so that she might go and post it. I opened my bedroom door, and Beatrice was just outside, talking to Mrs Staines. They had their heads close together, and Mrs Staines had a hand on Beatrice's sleeve.

She was speaking softly but urgently, and I caught the words: 'Dr Oliver said you must not....' the rest of her words were lost.

Beatrice nodded, her eyes wide and worried.

I stepped out, 'Beatrice,' I said, 'Could you possibly…?'

'I'm afraid Beatrice is needed to sit with your mother, Miss,' Mrs Staines said firmly.

'Of course,' I said. They both looked pale and worried, and they hurried off along the corridor to Mother's room.

Back in my room, I grabbed another sheet of notepaper, wrapped it around the letter and wrote on the outside:

B,

Please post this. I implore you, do not show this to my mother or to any other.

L.

I crept down to Mother's bedroom and tentatively opened the door. I was shocked at her appearance. Her lips were bruised a dark blue. Beatrice sat at the foot of the bed, her eyes wide and a little scared. I handed her the letter, and watched her read the words I had written, mouthing them to herself.

'Post it when you can,' I whispered. She nodded, slipping the envelope into her apron pocket.

I sat by Mother's bedside and held her cold hand. After a while, Mrs Staines came in with a warming pan to place at the foot of the bed. I stepped out into the corridor to speak to her.

'She seems much worse,' I whispered.

'She was better this morning. She read her letters and the newspaper, and spoke about them. She was quite bright. You know how she loves a little gossip, but perhaps she over-exerted herself.'

I smiled. 'She does enjoy gossip.'

'There was a story in the paper about a wolf escaped from the Zoological Gardens. Well, that quite captured her imagination.' Mrs Staines patted my cheek and bustled off back to the kitchen.

In the evening, Dr Van Helsing came to my room once I was settled in bed. He had had another box of the garlic delivered and he performed the ritual of festooning the bedroom with the garlands. He did it with great seriousness, and I tried not to laugh.

Once he had finished to his satisfaction, he placed a wreath around my neck and took his place in the chair beside the bed. I had no desire to make conversation with him, so I curled up with my back to him and feigned sleep. The curtains were imperfectly drawn, and I could see a sliver of the inky night sky in the gap between them. I gazed at the single star that was visible. It glittered coldly, millions of miles away.

Art is determined and ingenious. John's advice is all very well, but I cannot starve myself indefinitely, nor can I cease to drink, and even if I could, Art has proved that he can cause mortal harm merely by touching me. I realise now that there is a real chance that he will succeed in his mission to kill me.

17 SEPTEMBER 1894

After three days and two nights where I suffered no relapses, Dr Van Helsing relaxed his guard. He arranged the garlic and then sat down, looking around the room with considerable satisfaction. He folded his hands over his belly.

'Now my sweet Miss Lucy, you cannot disagree with my methods anymore, can you? For look how well you are. Since I have placed the garlic and stood guard over you, no ill has befallen you.'

There was no point in arguing with him.

'No indeed, Doctor,' I said meekly.

'Tomorrow, I must travel to Antwerp. There is an event that I must attend. I tried to make my apologies, but the host would not take my no for his answer. I will send a telegram to Dr Seward, to make sure he will be here to sit with you tomorrow night.'

'I have every faith in Dr Seward,' I said, and then diplomatically closed my eyes to feign sleep.

* * *

Dr Van Helsing left early the next morning. It was a warm, bright day and I enjoyed a quiet day in the garden. When I went downstairs that evening, I met Mother on the stairs, She looked well herself, and in good spirits.

'Shall we go in to dinner?' she asked. 'For once, I have an appetite.'

'We are expecting Dr Seward,' I said. 'Should we not wait?'

'Are we?' she looked put out, 'Well, I suppose we could postpone until seven or so.'

Seven came and went, and there was no sign of John's carriage. I peered down the driveway into the gathering gloom.

'I really cannot wait any longer,' said Mother impatiently. She was starting to tire. 'Your Dr Seward has obviously been delayed. Let us eat. If he arrives soon, he may join us. If not, Mrs Staines can keep a plate warm for him.'

We went through to the dining room, and Mrs Staines served the soup. I could not risk eating it, so I crumbled bread on the side of my plate. Mother did not seem to notice my lack of appetite. She ate slowly, taking the time to steady her hand before each mouthful.

Without preamble, she said, 'Have the leaves on the trees begun to turn yet? On the Heath?'

'I don't know,' I said, 'I have not walked there for some time. Why?'

'I love the autumn colours. I do believe it is my favourite time of year. Spring can be a little vulgar in its joyful abundance, but the autumn colours – so rich, so elegant. I loved to stand at the top of the hill and see the trees spread out below, red and gold and orange.'

'I love it too,' I said, surprised. I had never known her to express interest in the natural world. 'Perhaps tomorrow, if the weather is fine, we might ask Watkins to drive us to the top of the hill?'

'Perhaps,' she said, although she looked unsure.

'You could be wrapped in rugs,' I said, warming to the idea. 'I know just the spot, near Jack Straw's Castle. From there you will be able to see every beautiful tree north of London.'

'I should like that.' She smiled then. 'I have a clear memory of you, Lucy, as a very small girl, on just such a day. You were perhaps four or so. Your hair was so bright in the sun. You were running across the grass on the Heath, your skirts flying. You found a pile of leaves and you threw yourself straight into them. I tried to stop you, to make you walk demurely, but you loved the heaped-up leaves so much. You flung yourself into them over and over. And then you gathered a great bunch of them and insisted on bringing them home. Mrs Staines threw them away after you'd gone to bed, and you were quite incandescent with rage.'

This anecdote was like many such she had told over the years – tales of how disappointing and unladylike I was. But she did not wear her habitual frown. She was smiling at the memory.

'You are an original, Lucy,' she said, looking at me. 'Never let it be said you are of the common herd.'

'Thank you, Mother.'

'And now I must go to bed,' she said, putting down her spoon. 'Please apologise to Mrs Staines for me. I am too tired to eat any more.'

'Shall I ask her to bring something up to you?'

'No thank you, my dear. Although you should eat a little more. You are too thin and you are looking pale. No girl wants to look consumptive in her wedding portrait.'

She was still her acerbic self then. I stood and offered her my arm. She leaned on me as we made our slow way upstairs. Eliza followed, and Mother waved me away.

After she had gone to bed, I watched the window, hoping to see the lights of a carriage swinging into our driveway, but the darkness remained undisturbed. I was afraid to go to bed without John in the house, but I was weak and tired.

Feeling foolish, I took up a poker from the fireplace and walked cautiously around the house, checking doors and windows. Mother was restlessly asleep, but she did not wake when I went in to check her windows.

Eventually, exhausted, I came to my own bedroom. I checked and double-checked the fastenings on the window. I pulled the curtains tightly closed, but then hesitated and opened them again. Better to have some warning if an intruder came. I undressed and readied myself for bed.

* * *

These events are written down very much after the fact, but I will try to tell them in the order they happened.

It was an unsettled night, and with every gust of wind or creak of a branch, I jerked to full alertness. The clock chimed midnight. I was certain now that Dr Seward was not coming. I rose and looked out of the window into the unbroken darkness.

The door of my bedroom opened, and I spun around, my heart pounding. Mother stood in the doorway, candle in hand.

'Lucy? What are you doing out of bed?'

'I cannot sleep. Dr Seward has not come, and I...'

To my mortification, tears sprang to my eyes. The tension of the past days overwhelmed me, and I sank to my knees and sobbed. Mother came into the room and stood over me.

'Oh, Lucy. Come, my dear girl, get up. I am not able to get down there to comfort you.'

I stood unsteadily, and said, surprising even myself: 'Will you get into bed with me, Mother? I do not think I can bear to be alone.'

I was certain she would refuse, but she nodded. She put the candle down on the bedside table and slipped between the covers. She was half sitting, propped up on the pillows, and she still wore her dressing gown. She looked self-conscious, but she opened her arms to me, and I crawled in beside her and rested my head on her breast. I do not believe I had ever lain in her arms like this. Even when I was a tiny child, she had entrusted my care to a succession of nursemaids. Any affection I received had come from them, or from Pa.

The tears did not stop, and I could feel them trickling down my cheek and soaking her nightgown, but she did not push me away. I could hear her poor, weak heart beating threadily and irregularly.

'Now then, Lucy,' she said, and while her voice was not tender, I knew she was doing her best to comfort me. 'Why the tears? You are to be married. Your life is ahead of you.'

I did not plan what happened next, but I was unable to suppress the words. I sat up and turned so I could face her and we could look into one another's eyes.

'I do not have my life ahead of me, Mother. For someone is determined to end it.'

'Don't be preposterous,' she said. 'Who would wish to harm you?'

'Art. Art would.'

'Stop it!' she said shrilly. 'You speak of your future husband. The man you love!'

'I do not love him. I hate him. He has blackmailed me into accepting his proposal. I know about your Will, Mother. I know you have settled everything on Art. And now you have done that, I am surplus to requirements. He has been trying to poison me, and I think it is likely he will succeed.'

'You wicked girl!' her face was pale and her breath wheezed in her chest. 'Poor Arthur is at his father's deathbed, and you have made up these lies – I do not know why. You are vindictive and cruel. Would you kill me? Would you see me die right now, before your eyes?'

'I do not wish you to die,' I said, and again the tears began to roll down my face. 'But I could not keep this secret any longer. John – Dr Seward believes me...'

'Dr Seward is a fool! Art has told me often that he is weak and silly.'

'Yet he asked John to be my doctor.'

'And this is how you repay his concern? With lies? And what is this "John"? Are you and Dr Seward now so intimate that you are on first-name terms?' Her sneer was full of suspicion.

'He is my friend, and he has evidence – real medical evidence – of what Art has done.'

'And what of Dr Van Helsing? Does he believe this tale?' My silence gave her the answer she wanted. She nodded with satisfaction. 'I can only surmise that you have lost your mind, Lucy. You are suffering from some sort of brain fever. I am going to insist that you cease this nonsense. I hope to live long enough to see you married in ten days' time. And I very much hope that you will not disgrace me with any further outbursts. Once you swear to honour and obey Arthur, you will be under his care and rule. I hope he does a better job of disciplining you than I have done.'

I stared at her. Sadness and anger fought for supremacy in my breast, but there was no surprise. She had never taken my side. I could see sweat on her hairline and her lips were drained of colour; I knew that our argument had taken its toll.

She took my silence for acquiescence. 'Well then,' she said. 'Let us say no more of this.'

I think she would have liked to get up and leave the room, but she did not feel strong enough. She slid down under the covers and turned on her side, towards the door and away from me. I remained where I was, sitting on the edge of the bed. She was feigning sleep now, to avoid speaking to me. What had I expected? That she would believe me? I sat in the gloom, staring at the window and listening to the noises of the night.

A sudden sharp flare at the window made me gasp and fall back. I was momentarily blinded. Someone was at the window, holding a light.

'It is him,' I said. 'He has come.'

Mother turned to look at me, but before she could speak, his voice echoed into the room.

'The window is locked, Lucy. Open it. Open it now!' He sounded unhinged and furious.

'No!' I shouted, my voice cracked and high. 'Go away!'

In the light spilling from his lamp, I could see the glint of his bright hair.

'Open the window, Lucy, or so help me, I will...'

'No!'

I saw the white flash of his teeth, bared in a grimace, then he raised a fist and punched it through the glass. He reached a hand through the jagged hole and opened the catch, then forced the sash up and clambered into the room.

He stood in the middle of the floor, panting with effort, his bright hair tumbled over his forehead, blood dripping from his gashed hand onto the carpet. He strode to the door and turned the key in the lock and then came back to stand at the end of the bed.

'Art,' I said, 'What are you doing here?' The room was dark and he had not noticed Mother. I reached a hand behind me to quiet her.

'My father is dead, finally. He lingered for days. So I stand before you as Lord Godalming.'

'I am sorry for your loss,' I said quietly.

He took a handkerchief from his pocket and wrapped it around his bleeding hand.

'Well, some say loss, others may say gain,' he said. 'I have lost a man who found me a profound disappointment. I have gained a crumbling house, an estate that cannot pay for itself, and a mountain of debt the size of Scafell Pike.'

'Art...'

'I am disappointed in you, Lucy. You're such a fine-boned, delicate wisp of a girl. Yet here you still are. I did not imagine I would have to get my hands dirty. I thought a few days of the tea would do it. But it seems you are more resilient than you look.'

'Art, I am begging you...'

He took a step closer to the bed. 'Oh Lucy, I am weary. I just want this all to end. If only you would have cooperated – but you are stubborn. Your miserable old bitch of a mother will be dead soon. I'm sorry to say the likelihood is that your death will hasten her end. But there you are. The Westenras will all be together in Heaven, God willing.'

He reached into his pocket and I saw the flash of a blade in his hand. I gasped.

The next moment seemed to last a split-second, but also an eternity. Mother sat bolt upright in the bed behind me. Art, shocked, let the knife fall from his hand. He looked frightened, but then his face settled into an ugly sneer. I turned to look at Mother. Her pale blue eyes started almost from their sockets. She stared at him, unblinking. I could see realisation dawning. She saw that Art, whom she had so loved, held her in unconcealed contempt. And worst of all, she knew now that I had told the truth, and that she had brought this upon me.

Her mouth opened wide, and I expected her to scream, but instead, she let out an unearthly gurgling sound. We all froze in a horrified tableau, and then Mother's eyes rolled back and she slumped sideways. I lunged to catch her and her head struck my forehead. She fell across my chest, heavy, inert and still.

I rolled her off me and onto the pillows. Her mouth gaped open in a silent cry and her eyes stared sightlessly at the ceiling. Art and I looked at one another. He was shaking uncontrollably. I opened my mouth to speak, but I was interrupted by hands pounding on the door of the bedroom and rattling the doorknob.

'Lucy? Miss Lucy?' it was Beatrice's voice, high with fear. 'Are you all right? We heard breaking glass.'

'The door is locked, Miss Lucy!' Eliza cried.

Art snatched up the blade and bounded over to the bed. He pressed it against my throat and whispered urgently.

'Go to the door and say your mother has died. Let them in to see her and then send them downstairs to get brandy for them and for you.'

'I will not...'

'So help me, you little whelp, I will slit your throat first and then kill them all. Do as I say.'

He stared into my eyes until I gave a small nod. Then he stepped behind the heavy drapes that framed the windows. I stood unsteadily and went to the door, turned the key and opened it. Mrs Staines, Beatrice and Eliza stood framed in the dim light of the corridor. Mrs Staines held a lamp.

'My Mother...' I said. '... she has died.'

Mrs Staines pushed past me into the room and crossed to the bed. She held the lamp high and pressed two fingers to Mother's throat, seeking a pulse. It was a futile gesture – Mother's empty eyes told the story. Eliza and Beatrice crowded in behind her, clutching one another and trembling. Mrs Staines completed her examination, gave a single nod and crossed herself. Eliza burst into noisy tears and pressed her face into Beatrice's shoulder.

'What happened?' Mrs Staines turned to me. 'Why is she in your room?' She looked at the broken glass on the carpet.

'She came to check on me and got into bed beside me. The... wind smashed a branch against the window. I think the fright...' Eliza's sobs reached a new pitch.

'Quiet yourself, girl!' said Mrs Staines sharply. She took a step closer to the window. She was within feet of Art and his knife, concealed behind the drape.

'I feel faint,' I said quickly, and sank onto the edge of the bed. 'And I need a moment to pray beside her – alone. Perhaps you might go down and fetch us all some brandy to steady our nerves? The decanter is in the dining room. You all three should have a glass and then bring one to me.'

Mrs Staines hesitated. Eliza's sobs were now hysterical, however, and I saw my chance. I spoke firmly.

'Please do as I say. I need a private moment with my Mother.'

Mrs Staines frowned. She took a moment to straighten Mother's head on the pillow and cross her hands over her breast. Then she gathered Eliza and Beatrice under each arm and left the room. She drew the door closed behind her. I heard their steps and Eliza's weeping as they went down the corridor and moved to the stairs. As soon as the sound faded, Art emerged from behind the drapes and locked the door. A sudden horrible thought came to me.

'Oh God. I have sent them to be poisoned. You have poisoned the brandy.'

'Not poisoned. Drugged. The last time I was here, I took the opportunity to tip a quantity of laudanum into the decanter. They will sleep, but they will not be harmed.'

He began to walk towards me then. In the dim light, all I could see was the glint of his eyes and the blade of the knife he held at his side. I backed away until I collided with the bed. I reached a hand behind me to steady myself and touched Mother's cooling, still hand where it lay over her breast.

So this is how it ends, a small calm voice said in my mind. There was so much more I wanted to do. My vision clouded, and I felt my legs weaken. The darkness rushed in and I felt myself beginning to fall, fall, fall.

CHAPTER 20

5 MAY 2024 – KATE

I sat with my hand pressed against my mouth. Questions were begging to burst forth, but I forced myself to be quiet, to let Mrs Baylis speak in her own time.

'Three people died?' James asked, leaning forward, elbows on his knees.

She jerked around at the sound of his voice. She seemed to come to her senses suddenly, and I saw the shutters come down.

'Well, yes. Mr Westenra, then Mrs, then Lucy. Tragic.' Mrs Baylis dropped her gaze to her lap.

'Charles died in 1892, though,' I said, and I could have kicked myself, because Mrs Baylis abruptly gathered up her handbag and stood up.

'It's getting late,' she said. 'Thank you for the coffee. Sorry I couldn't help more.'

She walked to the door. I ran after her.

'I'll walk you back downstairs, Mrs Baylis.'

She didn't say no, so we descended the stairs together.

'It was so lovely to talk to you.' I tried to keep the pleading out of my voice. 'I'd love to chat more. To learn about the house, how it was back then. We're so lucky to have met you, an actual living link to the past...'

'Yes, well,' Mrs Baylis said, 'I'm not a fossil yet.' She seemed a little calmer, now she was alone with me and was no longer the subject of scrutiny.

'Definitely not.' My mind raced, trying to find a way to stop her going into number 4 and shutting the door forever. 'Tell me, have you ever seen a photograph of Lucy?'

'A what?'

'In my research, I found a family portrait that was taken on the steps of Hillingham. Charles and Rose, with Lucy when she was about fifteen. I'd love to show you.'

We were standing on the landing outside the library's heavy wooden door. Mrs Baylis scanned my face with her bright, penetrating gaze.

'Your friend goes back to Italy tomorrow, doesn't she? And your young man tells me he's off back to Devon.'

There was a little sneer that accompanied the words "young man". I chose to let it go. Then inspiration struck.

'Did James tell you his last name is Harker, by the way? He's the great-great-grandson of Mina Harker, Lucy's friend. The one to whom that letter was written.'

Mrs Baylis's eyebrows shot up in shock.

'He is? Well.'

She looked confused, as if she had made up her mind about something and was being forced to reconsider her position. She turned to the door and unlocked it.

'Would you like to see the photograph?' I burst out.

Mrs Baylis turned.

'If you make sure there are some of those Italian biscuits, I'll come for coffee on Monday evening, once your friends are gone. I'll see it then.'

She went in and closed the door and I was left staring at a deep crack in the wood of one of the panels. I touched it briefly, then went back upstairs.

LUCY WESTENRA'S SECOND JOURNAL

TELEGRAM, ARTHUR HOLMWOOD, RING, TO QUINCEY MORRIS, MAYFAIR, LONDON. 17 SEPTEMBER

Have not heard from Seward for three days, and am terribly anxious. Cannot leave. Father still in same condition. Send me word how Lucy is. Do not delay.-- HOLMWOOD.

18 SEPTEMBER 1894

I awoke.

A miracle, to wake, to draw breath and to see the light. To be alive. I was in a bed – not my own but the bed in the room across the corridor. My damp hair was loose and fell across my face. I lifted my head from the pillow, and saw Beatrice's pale, pinched face looking at me from a seat at the end of the bed. She gasped, then squeaked and ran from the room, calling.

'Dr Seward! Dr Seward!'

I struggled to sit up, and as I did so, felt the crackle of paper. A sheaf of folded pages had been slipped inside the neck of my nightgown and rested against my breast. I drew the pages out and unfolded them. They were somewhat crumpled and water-stained, but, to my great surprise, they were written in my own hand. I had no recollection of writing anything.

The words on the first page began:

17 September. Night.--I write this and leave it to be seen, so that no one may by any chance get into trouble through me. This is an exact record of what took place to-night. I feel I am dying of weakness, and have barely strength to write, but it must be done if I die in the doing.

I frowned. The last thing I recalled was that I had lost consciousness as Art advanced towards me with the knife. I had been convinced I would die. How had I not? And how had I then awoken and written this document – which was long and complex – without recalling doing so at all? I began to read the pages. They told a story that I did not recognise.

Apparently I had been awake and had heard a dog howl outside, and then seen a bat flapping at the window. I had gone to my bedroom door and called out to see if anyone was there, Mother had come in and got into bed with me – that part at least was true – and then all of a sudden, the window had been smashed by the head of a great, grey wolf. The shock of this brought about Mother's fatal heart attack. I frowned at this. How would a wolf have reached my bedroom window, on the upper storey of the house?

Shortly thereafter, "the maids" had come to the door. I was even more puzzled by this section, as I did not name them, and I said that there were four women rather than three. I sent them to get a drink, and they were drugged. Apparently, I had then returned to the bedroom to sit with Mother's dead body. This paragraph concluded this unlikely tale.

The air seems full of specks, floating and circling in the draught from the window, and the lights burn blue and dim. What am I to do? God shield me from harm this night! I shall hide this paper in my breast, where they shall find it when they come to lay me out. My dear mother gone! It is time that I go too. Good-bye, dear Arthur, if I should not survive this night. God keep you, dear, and God help me!

I was still puzzling over the pages when John burst into the room.

'Lucy,' he said, and fell to his knees beside the bed, opening his arms to me. 'My poor girl,' he murmured into my hair, and something in his tone brought back the true horror of the night before. I jerked away.

'Mother!'

'She has indeed passed away,' he said gently. 'We have carried her to her own bedroom. I consulted with Dr Oliver. Her death was not unexpected, so I have been able to issue the death certificate without need for a post-mortem or inquest.'

Mother was dead. I was nineteen years old and an orphan. I should weep for my dead mother, should I not? But my eyes were dry and there was a numb weight in my chest.

'What has happened to me?'

John gestured to the pages in my lap. 'Your account tells the story so far as we can tell. When we arrived, the servants were indeed drugged in the dining room. Your Mother, God rest her soul, was dead in the bed beside you, and you, dear Lucy, were almost drained of life yourself.'

'Drained?'

'This time, Dr Van Helsing's diagnosis seemed accurate. You

were severely anaemic, as if a great deal of blood had been drawn from you. We warmed you in a hot bath...' He looked uncomfortable, and I realised he was admitting that he had seen my naked form. I touched my hair. That explained why it was wet. John continued.

'Dr Van Helsing insisted that once you were revived, we replace the papers in your bosom, just as we had found them, lest on waking you should be alarmed that they were gone. There was no doubt you needed a blood transfusion, and soon. We were very lucky that there was someone able to help in our moment of greatest need.'

'Someone?'

John glanced at the door, and my gaze followed him. Framed in the open doorway, I saw the tall, lean figure of Quincey Morris.

'Well then, Lucy,' he said, strolling into the room and sitting on the edge of my bed. He took my hand. 'You gave us quite a fright this morning, my girl.'

I stared at him mutely. His hair was longer, almost touching his shoulders, and streaked with blond from the sun. His skin was darkened by his months in Europe and there was a scattering of freckles across his handsome nose. I looked into his gold-flecked eyes, and let my eyes roam down to his strong, brown hand, which held my own. I felt nothing. I did not know him at all.

No, that is not quite true. I knew him, in that every inch of his skin was familiar to me. But I no longer knew myself. The carefree, arrogant girl who had lain with him and taken her pleasure was dead. Lucy Westenra may still be breathing, but I was a different, harder woman than that girl. Over Quincey's shoulder, I could see my reflection in the tall glass. My face was thin, haggard and deathly pale, my lips drawn back from my teeth, which looked large and yellow. My eyes were hollow and my hair wild. I looked like a ghost of my former self.

'Why are you here?' I asked.

'I got back from Spain earlier this week,' he said. 'Art telegrammed me and asked me to come and check on you.'

'Art?' I frowned. Shadowy, terrifying memories surfaced from the night before. 'He was here last night.'

Quincey squeezed my hand. 'He wasn't, my dear. He was at Ring. His Father...'

'... Is dead. He told me so, last night.'

Quincey and John exchanged a look.

John said quietly, 'Lord Godalming is still with us, so far as we know. Although he is gravely ill. That is why Art cannot be here.'

I looked sharply at him. 'Can I speak to you alone, John?'

Quincey patted my hand and excused himself.

'He was here last night,' I said urgently. 'Art. He came in through the window. He smashed it. He quite literally frightened Mother to death.'

'But the wolf... What about the wolf? You wrote about it in those pages...' John pointed to the pile of papers, which lay on my bedside table.

'There was no wolf. I did not write those words.'

'But Lucy, they are in your hand...'

'I did not write this. I recall none of the events mentioned in these pages. What I do remember is this. Art came. He gave Mother such a fright that she died. Mrs Staines, Beatrice and Eliza came to the door and he forced me to send them away. And then... I think I blacked out. From fear. Beyond that, I do not know what happened. From your account, I lost a lot of blood.'

I climbed unsteadily from the bed and walked to my wardrobe. Drawing the curtain across to conceal myself from the rest of the room, I looked into the mirror on the wardrobe door. I pulled up the sleeves of my nightgown; there were now bruises in the crooks of both elbows where the doctors had inserted the needles for the transfusions. I pulled my nightgown off and stood naked before the glass.

'I have bruises on my shoulders, ribs and thighs.' I called to John.

'We might have caused those, carrying you to the hot bath and reviving you,' he said.

I ran my hands over my body, turning to look at my back view and lifting my hair. Everything ached, and my body felt strange and unfamiliar. I knew that while I was unconscious, I had been touched and used in ways I could not understand. This act of self-examination felt necessary, as if I could in this way reclaim my body. I checked each inch of my skin. I found, high on each inner thigh, two deep, thin cuts. They looked as if they might have been made by a scalpel or a sharp blade. They had sealed over and scabbed, but I guessed they must have bled extensively when they were fresh. On my throat, the two wounds where Art had scratched me with his fingernails some weeks before, had been reopened. These too had scabbed over, but they looked fresh and much deeper than before.

'I believe he bled me.' I said, half to myself.

I looked up and with a shock, realised I could see John's profile in the mirror. The angle of the wardrobe door meant that my image was replicated onto the window, and he was staring at this shadowy vision of my naked form. He did not look like a dispassionate medical man. He looked mesmerised. He looked hungry.

Horrified, I grabbed my nightgown and pulled it back on. He drew himself to attention and regained his professional demeanour.

'We observed the wounds on your neck. Dr Van Helsing seemed to draw some satisfaction from what he saw, as if they confirmed his mysterious thesis.'

'And no doubt this rambling account...' I indicated the pages that had been tucked into my breast, '...supports his belief that what has been happening to me is of supernatural origin.'

'You are sure you did not write this?'

'Since I lost consciousness last night, I have not awoken until half an hour ago. I must have been drugged. I certainly could not have written anything.' I picked up the pages and looked at them more closely. 'This is not my notepaper, John. Nor is the ink my usual colour.' Realisation came. 'He has had Bevington, the forger, write it. He thought I would be dead and unable to contradict the version of events contained in these pages.' I sank onto the bed. 'I do not know why I am not dead. He must have been interrupted, or lost his courage.'

I began to shake then, uncontrollably and my teeth chattered. John approached and I held up a hand to ward him off. I could not bear to be touched. Art had violated my body. Not knowing what he had done was worse than the cuts and bruises and unexplained aches. He had stripped me naked and done his best to kill me.

John backed away and sat down. We sat together in silence. I did not know if he believed me anymore, or whether he thought I was deranged. Most of all, I was disconcerted by the look of unconcealed lust I had seen in his eyes. I had come to like and trust him, yet now I felt less certain. But where else could I turn?

'He will not stop, John. He will not stop until I am dead. I need you to believe me.'

The silence between us was even longer. Finally, he spoke.

'I believe you.'

'So let us give him what he wants.'

'What do you mean?'

'I must die.'

'What? Lucy, no!'

'I cannot just wait for him to complete his evil work. We have seen, time and again that he will not give up.'

'There is another choice.'

'What is it?'

'Marry me, Lucy. I will leave the asylum. We can go away – anywhere you like. We can build a life somewhere else – Canada perhaps, or Europe. I will keep you safe.'

I sighed, 'Oh John. Is that what you would want? For me to marry you under duress? Out of fear of another? And where would we go? He knows I know of his transgressions, and I do not believe he would let it lie. He would come after me. We would be watching over our shoulders for the rest of our lives.'

We talked then, for an hour or more. I pleaded, begged, explained. Eventually, he let his head drop into his hands. When he looked up, his eyes were red-rimmed, and he looked tired but determined. He gave a single, exhausted nod.

I rested my hand on his. 'Thank you, John. Thank you.' He nodded, then stood, his shoulders bowed. 'Can I ask you to do something for me? Can you bring me pen, ink and paper?'

'Of course. What do you wish to write?'

'My last Will and Testament.'

* * *

My Will, now I have written it, is pitifully brief. How little I have that is my own. I have made sure it contains explicit instructions for a speedy and private funeral and stipulates that my body should not be viewed and my coffin be sealed. I have said that I wish to be placed in the mausoleum in Hendon, along with Pa and Mother.

I have given John a copy of the Will, and he has promised that he will lodge it with Mr Marquand. I placed another copy on my desk, in plain view. I had the idea of leaving a journal for them to find, so I found an old school exercise book and jotted some brief entries in it, of the sort Van Helsing might expect an empty-headed young girl to write. This I also left in plain sight. Now I went through all the correspondence in my desk. The letters Mina had written were impressively innocent, and we left them where they were. I gathered any envelopes in which she had written secret messages. I have tucked them into this journal and replaced it in its secret place in the library, where I hope it will always remain concealed.

Later

I used talcum powder to whiten my face. I reclined on my bed, and carefully placed the pages with the 'account' back in my breast. John went to call Dr Van Helsing. He had told me of the symptoms Van Helsing had observed during my illness and I took care to imitate them. I lay with my eyes closed, and when the door opened, I breathed stertorously. Dr Van Helsing stood close to the bed and I could hear him mutter sadly. He took up my wrist to feel my pulse. I am sure fear made it race, for he whispered to John.

'Her heart is fluttering, trying to move her poor blood.'

'She is very weak,' said John sadly, 'and her sleep has been restless.'

I took this as my cue and moved my head on the pillow, frowning, as if my dreams plagued me. I reached for my own throat and pawed at it. Then I slipped my hand into the neck of my nightgown and drew out the pages. I tore them through once. Van Helsing gasped and plucked the pages from my fingers. I continued to perform the action of tearing, as if shredding the pages to nothing.

'Professor,' said John, his voice thick with emotion, 'I fear we may lose this battle. She is so delicate, and it seems likely the physical strain, coupled with the shock of the loss of her mother, will be too much for her.'

'You may be right, friend John. We will keep watch with her through the night, but it may well be the last night through which we must do so.'

I let out another heaving, wheezing breath then I opened my eyes and gazed at Dr Van Helsing.

'Oh doctor,' I whispered. 'I feel so weak.'

'You are quite fine, sweet little miss,' he said, with faux jollity. 'Why, we are taking the very best care of you! You will be up and frolicking in no time at all.'

I stared at him. I had heard him say to John, seconds before, that he doubted I would see another day. He was happy for me to die unprepared, rather than speak to me frankly.

'No, Dr Van Helsing,' I said, keeping my voice soft and breathy. 'I feel the darkness closing in.' He opened his mouth to contradict me, but I continued. 'I have but one wish. Bring Arthur to me. Let me lay eyes on him one last time. I beg you.'

'Oh Miss Lucy,' he said, and his eyes filled with tears.

'Please,' I said, letting my head fall back on the pillow. 'Send for him now. I implore you.'

The Professor nodded, patted my hand and left the room.

Art arrived at sunset and was brought into my room. He looked haggard and tired. He wore a black armband, and I heard Quincey, John and the Professor offering condolences to him for the loss of his father. I had perfected the semblance of a semi-conscious doze, which allowed me to keep my eyes lidded but open. The men assumed I was insensible and spoke around me freely.

'I cannot believe how much she has deteriorated,' said Art, his voice cracked and hoarse with grief. I had to admire his acting. 'When I last saw her, I had thought her quite recovered.'

'Sadly, there is nothing more we can do,' said John. 'Her system has suffered a great many shocks.'

'May I have some time alone with her?' Art said. I felt my pulse begin to race, and I let out a harsh, rattling breath.

'She is so weak,' John said in his most formal medical tone, 'I cannot risk her suffering a sudden turn for the worse. I will sit here by the window. You may speak to her in confidence. I will not listen.'

His ruse worked perfectly. Art sat by my side and held my hand in his, but he did not speak, nor threaten me. He did not dare. His presence proved too much for me, however. I could not resist opening my eyes. I wanted to look into his face one more time – to imprint his features on my memory.

I allowed my eyelids to flutter and open and turned my head on the pillow to look at him.

'Art,' I breathed, 'there you are.'

'Here I am,' he said.

I heard John clear his throat and turned my head the other way to look at him. He frowned a warning. I ignored him. I smiled weakly, then turned back and glanced down at Art's arm.

'You wear a black armband,' I said.

'My Father has died.' I could see him searching my face, looking for a flash of memory. Would I reveal that I already knew this? I kept my expression blank.

'I am so sorry.'

'I too am sorry for the passing of your Mother.'

'Her death was quick. Although it is always a shock for those left behind.'

'Indeed.'

'So here we are, two orphans,' I said, squeezing his hand weakly. 'At least we have each other.'

'Oh Lucy,' he said. I could see to my immense satisfaction that I had made him uncomfortable. He could not know whether in my last delirium, I was being sincere, or if I was threatening him. And with John in the room, he could not respond.

'I cannot wait, Art,' I breathed. 'Soon I will be by your side for all time. For the rest of your life, I will walk beside you, returning the love you have given me, measure for measure.'

His face was a kaleidoscope of emotions – confusion, anger,

and, I was delighted to see, a fleeting sneer of fear. I feigned exhaustion and sank back onto the pillows, releasing his hand and closing my eyes.

Art and Dr Van Helsing took the first watch of the night and I listened to the quiet murmur of their voices. Van Helsing's affection for Art was fawning and nauseating, he called him "my boy," and "my son", and on several occasions commented on Art's resemblance to his own dead child. Art played up to it and acted the heartbroken suitor and bereaved son. At one in the morning, John came in to take over the watch. At first, Art insisted he should stay with me.

'You are exhausted, Art,' said John, patting his shoulder. 'We will need you well rested in the morning. We cannot risk the chance of any of us breaking down for want of rest, lest Lucy should suffer.'

Van Helsing urged him too: 'Come, my child. Come with me. You must not be alone. Come to the drawing room, where there is a big fire, and there are two sofas. You shall lie on one, and I on the other, and our sympathy will be comfort to each other.'

Through my half-closed lids, I could see Art struggle with their insistence. He was clearly tired, but I think he had hoped for some time alone with me to complete his gruesome task. A pillow over my face would do the job quickly. However, he was too wary to insist, lest it appeared suspicious. He reluctantly went out with Van Helsing.

19 SEPTEMBER 1894

John locked the door and lay on top of the covers beside me. We slept as much as we dared and were both woken by the first rays of dawn. When I stirred, I was looking into his eyes. He did not speak, but reached out a hand to touch my cheek lightly. I trembled at his touch.

The curtains were open, and I turned over to look out at

the sky, an incomparable cerulean expanse. Such beauty on this, the last day of my earthly life. John fetched a drink of water for us both. I rose and went to my dressing table. I brushed out my hair so it lay over my shoulders, bright and light. I powdered my face until it was pale, and then put on a fresh, pure-white nightgown. I was back in bed when John returned.

'They are still asleep downstairs,' he said. 'It is for the best. Now, I will give you the draught, and once you feel yourself beginning to fade, I will call them.'

I nodded and gripped his hand tightly. He crossed to the desk where he mixed his ingredients in a small glass beaker. He carried it over to me carefully, as if it were dynamite. The liquid was cloudy, and he stirred it with a small silver spoon. I eyed it with fear.

'What is in it?'

'It contains morphia, and a minute amount of poison gathered from the puffer fish, found off the coast of Japan.'

'How did you know of it?'

'I read an account of its effects in the records of Captain James Cook. On one of his voyages to the Orient, his crew and the animals on board suffered poisoning with this toxin after eating puffer fish. When I travelled to the Far East, I made a point of learning about it from a doctor in Japan, and out of curiosity I brought a small amount back with me.'

I glanced out of the window. The sun was rising.

'We are running out of time, John.'

I indicated that he should place the beaker on the bedside table, then I sat up and grasped both of his hands tightly. He stared at me and his eyes burned with something intense. Then, without warning, he leaned in and kissed me, long and deeply. My eyes widened in shock, and I was about to stop him and speak. But he broke off the kiss and reached immediately for the beaker.

'Now, drink it off,' he said, 'I fear they may wake and come in before we have done what is necessary.'

I took the vessel obediently and gulped down its contents in one mouthful. The taste was bitter and foreign, and I gagged at it. John frowned and immediately handed me a glass of water, which I swallowed as quickly as possible. As soon as the deed was done, I began to tremble uncontrollably. Whether it was the immediate effects of the poison or mortal fear, I did not know.

John took the beaker and spoon from me and placed them back in his medical bag. Then he sat on the side of the bed and took my wrist in his hand. He kept a careful watch on my pulse.

The first thing I noticed was an unaccountable weakness. I was forced to lie back on the pillows, and my eyelids drooped with tiredness. My limbs felt heavy and feeble. Then I sensed a tingling in my fingertips and lips, and my mouth began to fill with saliva. Rushes of nausea came, and my stomach cramped so that I cried out. All the while, John kept a hand on my wrist. He touched his other hand to my forehead, which was beaded with sweat. Then, without warning, he dropped my wrist and stood.

'It is time,' he said.

He straightened his waistcoat and headed for the door. I turned onto my side and curled around the pain in my stomach. I could hear John's footsteps as he ran along the corridor and down the stairs. It probably took no more than a minute for him to rouse Dr Van Helsing from his sleep, but it felt like an eternity.

By the time they came into the room, my vision had begun to blur and warp. The saliva in my mouth had spilled down my chin. My limbs felt as if they were pinned to the bed. I could no longer move my legs, and my hands twitched uselessly on the covers. Dr Van Helsing came in and looked down at me. I stared up at him with unfocused eyes. He touched his fingers to the pulse at my neck and gave a hissing in-breath.

He turned to John and said, 'She is dying. It will not be long now. Wake that poor boy and let him come and see the last; he trusts us, and we have promised him.'

John nodded and flew back out of the room. Within a few moments, he had returned with Arthur, whose hair was mussed and face was soft. He must have been deeply asleep. He was able to slumber innocently while I lay dying in the room above.

I managed to flutter my eyes open and said, in a slurred whisper, 'Arthur! I am so glad you have come!'

He stooped to kiss me, but Van Helsing took his elbow and drew him back.

'No. Not yet!' he said, 'Hold her hand; it will comfort her more.'

I could have laughed at the Professor's attempt to stage-manage this touching scene. Art kneeled by the bed and took my hand in his. Or at least I assumed he did – my hands and feet were numb, so I was unable to discern his touch.

I lay back on the pillows and closed my eyes. As the cramps rolled through my body and saliva flowed over my chin, I had a moment of crystal, agonising clarity. This man, this viper, kneeling beside my bed, muttering prayers, had robbed me of everything. He had killed my mother and stolen my home, my future and my innocence. My life. The anger rose in me like a tide, so powerful I thought I might vomit. But instead his name burst forth from my lips like the guttural howl of an animal dying in a trap.

'Arthur.'

With the last of my consciousness and strength, I lurched up towards him, growling. My arms were useless, but in my delirium, I imagined I could bite him, or tear at his face with my teeth. Van Helsing moved much faster than one would expect for a man of his age and bulk, and he pulled Arthur away from me by the scruff of his neck.

'Not for your living soul and hers!' he cried. Arthur lay

sprawled on the floor, his eyes wide with shock. I think in that terrible instant, he had seen the murderous intent in my eyes. As for me, I had slipped sideways and lay with my face pressed into the sheet, unable to move. Van Helsing lifted me tenderly and set my head back on the pillow. I felt the last seconds of my consciousness slip away from me.

'Thank you,' I whispered. The words were for John, but Dr Van Helsing's nod showed me he thought I intended them for him. My eyes closed, and I felt the blackness wash over me.

CHAPTER 21

7 MAY 2024 – KATE

'So did you have a good weekend?' Mrs Baylis asked, sipping her coffee.

'We did, thank you. I think Rafaella had fun, and that's the main thing.'

'She's a nice girl.'

'She is.'

'She told me you were friends when you lived in Italy?'

'Yes. We lived near one another in Milan.'

'Is it a nice place?'

'Beautiful.'

'Why did you come back here?'

I laughed, 'You're quite the interrogator, Mrs Baylis.'

'Call me Rita. Why did you come back?'

'A relationship ended. Are you satisfied now?'

Mrs Baylis grinned triumphantly. 'Always a man, isn't it? Ruining things.'

It was my turn to scrutinise her.

'Am I right in thinking you're not too fond of the male sex, Rita?'

'Why do you say that?'

'Well, I couldn't help noticing that you maybe... didn't warm to James when you met him.'

Rita gave a shrug and reached for a biscuit. She didn't deny it. I pushed on.

'He's the sweetest, kindest man. I can't believe he could have done anything to offend you, not in the ten minutes before I came into the room.'

'Yes, well.' Rita folded her hands in her lap and her lips into a tight line. 'I'm sure he's very nice. But I've not had the best experiences with the whole lot of them.'

'Men?' Mrs Baylis gave a short nod. 'Was it... Mr Baylis?'

'Hah! What a mistake he was. He came into my life when I was twenty-nine. In those days it was old to be a spinster. I thought I'd missed my chance and then there he was. Well, I learned soon enough that he liked a drink. He had a temper and was very quick with his hands. Then he tried to force me to sign the flat over to him. We... I kicked him out and changed the locks.'

Her tone was harsh, but I detected a tiny crack in the bravado. According to the census records, Rita had parted company with Paul Baylis more than 40 years before, but the pain still seemed fresh for her.

'I'm sorry to hear that.'

'Your Lucy – I don't think she liked men much either,' Rita said suddenly.

'Really? Did your grandmother tell you that?' I leaned forward eagerly.

Rita ignored the question. 'My Nan said Lucy had plenty of admirers. But she always said she wanted to go to university, to learn and travel. Not to get married. I met one of her suitors when I was a little girl, actually. Of course, he was a very old man by then.'

'You did?'

'He was a doctor. Very highly regarded. I think he was a bigwig at one of the fancy universities – Oxford or Cambridge. A Professor Seward. He came to see my Nan out of the blue once. He was in the neighbourhood – his wife was visiting her family. Tall he was, with a wonderful head of grey hair. He and Nan spent ages in the corner, whispering to one another. She cried when he left, but she said she was happy he came.'

'So his wife was a Hampstead local?'

'Yes... she grew up around the corner. Lovely lady. Her name was Rosamond, I think.'

I put my cup down and reached for the folder I'd placed on the coffee table.

'You said you'd like to see Lucy's photograph.'

I handed over a printout of the image I'd found of the Westenra family standing on the steps of the house. Rita stared at it for a long time.

'Well,' she whispered, 'it's quite something to see them for real. and to see the house as it was then.'

She held the image close to her eyes, scrutinising every detail. She raised one finger and traced the tumble of Lucy's fair hair over her shoulder.

'She was blonde then,' she murmured. 'Fancy that.'

'I beg your pardon?'

'She was blonde. I didn't know that.'

'You said she was blonde *then*. As if there was a time when she wasn't?'

'Did I? I didn't mean to.' Rita handed the picture back. 'Well, thank you for showing me. I must be getting back down to my flat. It's time for my television programme.'

* * *

347

LATER, I spoke to James on the phone.

'She knows more than she's letting on,' I said.

'She's a tough nut, though. She's not going to tell you anything she doesn't want to. Unless you torture her.'

'I'm not sure where the Geneva Convention stands on brutalising octogenarians out of historical curiosity. I'm guessing it would be frowned upon.' I sighed. 'The fact is, it isn't even my story. I just found Lucy's letter. Beatrice was Rita's grandmother. I can't be angry with her for not telling me. But I keep thinking about Lucy's death certificate. Does that cause of death not bother you? Loss or waste of blood? It's very suspicious. I still think there's a very real possibility that Lucy was murdered.'

'That's quite a leap.'

'Is it, though? She thought she was in danger. She wrote a letter saying so.'

'There is one other option,' James said. 'Why Rose left the estate to Holmwood. Why Lucy died so young. Why the letter.'

'And that would be?'

'That Lucy wasn't... well in the head.'

I gasped. 'Seriously? You're going for "the woman was mad" as your explanation?'

'I didn't mean it like that. Her letter just sounds...'

'Be very careful what you say now.'

James paused and then said quietly: 'Improbable. Paranoid, maybe? What if she *was* mentally unwell? Having delusions? Maybe she even did herself a mischief?'

'You mean suicide?'

'It's not entirely impossible, is it?'

I drew my knees up and wrapped my arms around them. 'Not impossible, no,' I conceded. 'But wasn't suicide frowned upon in those days?'

'Well, less so than in previous generations. I think they had begun to understand the link between suicide and mental illness by then. In generations before then, if she had committed suicide, she couldn't even have been buried in consecrated ground.'

'Well, she was,' I said. '*Vade retro satana,*'

'What?'

'On Lucy's tomb. "*Vade retro satana*". Go back, Satan. A Catholic formula for exorcism.'

'So whoever put up that plaque perhaps thought Lucy was inhabited by an evil spirit?'

James let a long silence develop, and then he spoke gently.

'I know you don't want to hear this, Kate, but I think we've hit a dead end. I've been combing the records for any other reference to Arthur Holmwood, but the family line just seems to vanish after him. If he did inherit the Westenra estate, he didn't do anything with it. He wasn't the person responsible for redeveloping the house into flats.'

'I know,' I said. 'But the truth feels so close. I just want to know what happened to her.'

'From my limited experience, historical research is full of dead ends. It just takes one missing document and suddenly nothing makes sense. And I think for women, it's even harder.'

'What do you mean?'

'Well, they generally didn't get to tell their own stories. Men wrote histories, led countries and armies, ran companies, left documents and artefacts. Chances are, Lucy's story is just lost.'

There was something in his voice – a semitone note of finality, as if the case were closed. I felt a snap of irritation. His family records were complete. His narrative was laid out – except of course for Mina's story. Yes, another vanished woman slipped beneath the waves of history.

'But why? Why should it be lost? Why should I just throw up my hands and give up?' I was conscious I was raising my voice. I stopped myself. 'I have to go. Chat soon.'

'Okay.' I could hear the surprised hurt in his voice. I hung up.

LUCY WESTENRA'S SECOND JOURNAL

I woke with John's hand down my throat. He had rolled me on my side, and was pushing his fingers into my mouth, forcing me to gag. I retched, and a thin trickle of liquid ran from between my lips.

'Come on, Lucy, more!' he said in a fierce whisper, pushing deeper.

My body convulsed again, and more liquid poured out of me and onto the folded cloth he had placed beneath my head. John grasped me by the shoulders and pulled me into a sitting position. As soon as he released me, I flopped to one side, unable to hold up my own weight. He propped me up on the pillows and slapped my face sharply. I gasped.

'Good girl,' he said. 'Good girl. Keep your eyes open. We have the worst of it out of you. Now I need you to eat this.'

He prised my mouth open again and pushed in fragments of something. It tasted bitter and gritty. I grimaced and tried to clamp my lips closed.

'Eat it, Lucy,' he said, again forcing his fingers between my teeth. 'It is charcoal, and will absorb the rest of the poison in your stomach.'

Reluctantly, I allowed him to push the disgusting stuff into my mouth. I swallowed it as best as I could with sips of water from a glass he held to my lips. My head spun. The nausea came in waves, and the stomach cramps were agonising.

I do not know how much time passed. I faded in and out of consciousness, and whenever I opened my eyes, John was there, monitoring my pulse, asking me questions, checking how much sensation I had in my extremities. It must have been several hours later when I was finally able to open my eyes fully and focus on him.

'What happened?' I asked, in a hoarse whisper. 'Do they believe...?'

'You died,' he said, and a small smile twitched at the corner of his mouth. 'You died so convincingly that Dr Van Helsing called Art to come and kiss your forehead, and then they said heartfelt prayers over you. Art... well, I could see that he was desperate to get out of the room. I think the reality of what he had done was rather grimmer than he had expected. He wept like a child, and Van Helsing led him away, offering fatherly comfort. They seemed happy for me to declare the time of death and take over. I had to let Quincey in to witness that you were dead, and the servants came in to pay their respects. But as soon as I could, I ushered everyone from the room and locked the door.'

'The servants,' I said, weak with guilt and misery. I thought of Mrs Staines, Beatrice, poor, sweet Eliza – all already reeling from Mother's death. What would become of them?

'I am afraid they wept most bitterly. They are heartbroken.'

'I beg you, John, when this is over, do what you can to make sure they are treated fairly.'

'I will do my best for you, Lucy, as I do in all things.' He sank on his knees then, at the edge of the bed, and clasped my hand in his. 'Lucy, seeing you then, insensible, your eyes open and staring ... you truly looked as if you were...' He rested his forehead on our joined hands, and I felt his tears, hotly running between my fingers.

'But I am not,' I drew my hand away. 'I am alive. And soon they will wonder where you are, and why you are still in here with my corpse. You need to go. I think I am strong enough to move.'

John drew a ragged breath, raised his head and wiped his eyes. He stood.

'I have already drawn their attention to your Will. They know your wishes for a speedy burial. Art was quick to agree. He is desperate to have the whole business over with.'

'Is the room ready?'

He nodded. I tried to sit up and swing my legs over the edge of the bed, but the nausea was overwhelming. I retched into my cupped hands, and a thin stream of black, evil-smelling liquid poured from my lips. I stared at it in horror.

'It is the charcoal,' John said soothingly. 'It is doing its job, absorbing the poison. You will not be able to walk. I will carry you.'

He went to the door and unlocked it. He eased it open and peered up and down the corridor. Then he passed through and disappeared for some minutes. When he came back, he was carrying a long, thin bolster, which I recognised from one of the guest bedrooms. He slipped his arms beneath me and lifted me from the bed as if I weighed nothing. He placed me in a chair, then put the bolster in the bed and covered it with the sheet, drawing it right up. It did indeed look as if there was a body, its face covered, lying in the bed.

'On no account must anyone come into this room alone to see my body,' I said weakly.

'I will lock the door and keep the key with me at all times.' John promised.

Then he scooped me up once more, and, after checking that the corridor was empty, carried me quickly along to a small, never-used room. It had been intended for a valet or nursemaid to sleep close to their charge. It was usually sealed up, but during the course of the previous night, John had prepared it as my sickroom. I had instructed him where to find the key in the key press in Mrs Staines' pantry. The narrow bed was freshly made up, and he had a table with the medicines he would need to effect my recovery from the toxic draught. There was a carafe of water and a little basket of apples and biscuits if I felt well enough to eat. He put me in the bed and encouraged me to sip some more water.

'Sleep now, Lucy,' he said, touching my cheek tenderly. 'It will take some days for the poison to pass from your body entirely. In the meantime, I will move forward with the funeral plans.'

He hesitated, as if he would say something further, but then thought better of it. He let himself out of the room, locking the door after him.

I lay for a moment, conscious of every precious breath. That I was still able to draw air into my lungs was a miracle. Every part of me hurt and I took careful inventory of my agonies. My head throbbed and my neck felt bruised. My ribs creaked and my stomach burned. Yet the most searing pain was in my left hand. I raised it above my face to examine it. The knuckle of my ring finger was bloodied and puffy and the nail of that finger had been snapped near the quick. Dark bruising had swelled around the gold band which encircled it. The setting rose up in four empty claws – the stone was gone. I imagined Art, weeping crocodile tears over my dead body, then, as soon as John's back was turned, using all his strength to try and wrest the engagement ring from my dead finger. He had failed, and had had to pluck out the Godalming ruby like an eye from its socket. He was welcome to the repulsive thing. I closed my eyes then, and slept.

* * *

When I awoke, I had a fierce thirst. It took prodigious effort, but I was able to sit up and sip at the glass John had left by my bed. The water made me retch, but I managed to keep it down. There was no clock in the room, although it was still daylight.

I heard footsteps in the corridor outside and froze, wary even to breathe. A key rattled in the lock and I gasped, pressing myself back against the wall. I let out a ragged sigh when John slipped in, drawing the door closed behind him. He locked it and came to sit beside me on the bed.

'You look immeasurably better,' he said, taking my pulse and looking into my eyes.

'I feel as if I might live,' I said wryly, 'which comes as something of a surprise. I was not at all sure of that fact this morning.'

'You see now that you must trust me,' John said softly, and stroked the skin on the back of my wrist with one finger. I drew my hand back.

'What has been happening?'

'Art left as soon as he decently could, to return to Ring for his father's funeral. Quincey has gone with him. We have written to your Mother's solicitor, and he is coming to see us tomorrow.'

'Her Will shall come as a surprise to some,' I said.

'The Undertakers have come. I have paid them a handsome stipend. Your Mother has been placed in her coffin, and they have put your coffin in your bedroom. I said that I would put your body in there myself.' He hesitated. 'Lucy, Dr Van Helsing has expressed a wish to see your body laid out this evening.'

I shivered at this. We had spoken about the likelihood that I would need to be viewed. I nodded.

'When?'

'I think it best that we do it after dark. By candlelight, it will be easier to...'

I glanced at the window. The sun was sinking, blood red.

'Very well.'

John brought a bowl of warm water and a cloth, together with a small looking glass. I washed my face and tidied my hair. When it was fully dark, we slipped down the corridor into my bedroom. It was transformed and I trembled to see it. My bed had been pushed against the wall, and a dark, polished coffin sat on trestles in the middle of the room. Floral arrangements had been piled on the floor beside it. A corona of candles shed a dim glow, and the drapes were drawn. John removed the bolster from the bed and concealed it in the wardrobe. I stared at the scene for a long moment, then steeled myself and turned to John.

'Let us begin,' I said.

He grasped me by the waist and lifted me up. He laid me gently in the coffin. I could feel the cold, hard wood through the satin lining. The sides pressed in on me, and it took all my courage not to cry out and bolt. I lay still until I could get my breathing under control and the trembling in my limbs had stilled. Then John draped the winding sheet around me and arranged flowers on top of me so they concealed much of my body. These would help to hide any movement in my breast. I opened my eyes to see John's concerned face looking down at me.

'Are you ready?' he whispered.

I allowed myself a tiny nod, and he draped the corner of the winding sheet over my face. He stepped back then. I could sense he was still in the room. I willed him to go and fetch the

Professor so this ordeal could end. But then he spoke, his voice hoarse.

'I love you, Lucy. I hope my actions have shown how deep my devotion is. I want you to know that I have done everything for you that I can, and...'

He broke off then, and I could hear his breath, ragged with emotion, catching in his throat. I remained silent and motionless. After a few moments, I heard his footsteps cross the floor and the door opened and closed.

In the minutes that I was alone, I drew deep breaths and tried to steady my rising panic. The cloth over my face brought on a rush of claustrophobia. I silently begged John to hurry. It seemed to take hours for him to return with the Professor. As soon as I heard the door open, I held my breath. The Professor crossed to the coffin and lifted the corner of the sheet from my face, folding it back. I allowed myself only the shallowest of aspirations through my nose.

The Professor gave a grunt of sorrow, and I heard him say to John, 'Remain till I return.'

He stepped from the room. In the moment that he was gone, John reached beneath the flowers to grasp my hand and squeeze it. The Professor returned, and I felt him place something beneath my chin. The rich savoury scent let me know immediately that it was a nosegay of his ubiquitous wild garlic. Then I felt a touch on my mouth and it took all my strength not to recoil. He withdrew his hand, but I could still feel something – he had placed an object, cold and metallic, across my lips. Then he draped the cloth over my face once more.

He turned to John, and I heard him speak in a brusque, business-like tone.

'If it were in my power, I would ask you to bring me, before night, a set of post-mortem knives.'

John's gasp was audible, and his voice was high and nervous.

Must we make an autopsy? It seems unnecessary, does it not? We were present at her death. There can be no doubt...'

'Not an autopsy. If I could, I would operate, but not as you think. I would cut off her head and take out her heart.'

I heard John let out a strangled gasp. My own heart pounded in my breast, so loudly I was surprised the men could not hear it. A rustle of cloth suggested that the Professor had put his arm around John's shoulders.

'I would do it, but I can see it is too late. He, the evil one, has laid claim to her already. See how he has placed his mark of wantonness upon her! Her lip is red and her bosom swells voluptuously. She is lost to us now, and there is nothing we can do but hope and pray that somehow, she may rest in peace.'

'But why would you mutilate her body?' John said. 'It is monstrous.'

'Friend John, I pity your poor bleeding heart. There are things that you know not. John, my child. I may err, but I believe in all I do.'

He believed in what he did? And this was sufficient motive to perpetuate this atrocious act?

He continued: 'Friend John, will you not have faith in me? There are strange and terrible days before us.'

John let out a small strangled noise. It was not a word, but the Professor took it for assent. He clapped John on the shoulder and left the room.

John followed him to the door, saw him out and locked it. Then he rushed over and helped me out of the coffin.

'Oh God. Oh God,' he said. I could see his hands were trembling. 'Oh, Lucy. What have we done?'

His face was sheet-white and sweating. Panic had overwhelmed him. I gripped his hands tightly.

'Calm down, John,' I whispered. 'He is a devout Christian. He should be relieved that I have passed into God's hands and that I am safe in heaven. But for some reason, he does not believe this.

You must have some idea of his thinking. What does he believe caused my death?'

'He has not said. He has been cryptic.'

'This is what we will do,' I said quietly. 'Let me return to my secret room and rest for a few hours. When the Professor and all the servants are asleep, come and fetch me and we will go to my library. We will gather all the information that we know and see if we can work out what is in the Professor's mind. You need to know, so we can be prepared if he decides he does want to do this post-mortem.'

John's assent was reluctant, so I sought his promise that he would come for me as soon as the house was quiet. Then I crept back to the little room, crawled into bed and fell deeply and instantly asleep.

* * *

In the quietest hour of the night, John and I sat at the polished desk in the library, books and notes piled around us. I jotted down what I could recall from conversations with the Professor.

I did my best to consider what he had said in the weeks in which I had been under his care. He was convinced that my illness came from loss of blood, even though there had been no blood to be found on my body or in my bed. Despite the fact that he was a doctor, he had performed no medical procedures, nor prescribed me any medicine. Indeed, the only substance he had prescribed was garlic, and his principal method of treatment seemed to be prayer. All of this indicated that he believed my illness came from some supernatural source. He appeared to believe that God – and indeed only his version of the Christian God – would be able to protect me.

Did he believe I was possessed by a demon? He had neither recommended, nor tried to perform an exorcism. And even if I was, surely praying over my body would be enough to drive out the demon, if I were dead? His wish to mutilate my corpse suggested something else – whatever he thought had caused my death was still resident within my body, even if the life had left it.

I took an inventory of which of my books had captured his interest. Fortunately, he was not a tidy man, and had left the volumes he was consulting scattered across the desk. *The Book of Were-Wolves* by Sabine Baring-Gould lay on top of the pile. I picked it up, and it fell open where he had inserted a bookmark between the pages. At the top of the page, I read the words: "… formed the resolution to bathe her face and her whole body in human blood so as to enhance her beauty." I gasped in surprise. What gory fantasy had the Professor been reading?

I turned back a page and read the story of an aristocrat called Elizabet Bathory, who, in 1604, discovered that bathing in the blood of young women made her skin whiter and more transparent. She lured unsuspecting girls to her castle and tortured them to capture their blood, believing it brought her closer to immortality. This story was both grim and fantastical – I knew that Baring-Gould believed the stories he quoted in this text to be true, but surely this one must be make-believe or a folk-tale?

The next book in the pile was *The Folk Tales of the Magyars*, and this bristled with the Professor's bookmarks. When I checked each page he had marked, they all mentioned the use of garlic in charms and incantations against evil.

There were a number of scientific and medical books in the pile – one with detailed illustrations on how to effect a blood transfusion. I shivered at the images. I was glad I had not been awake when the procedure had been performed upon me.

The last volume was so slim I nearly missed it. It was almost a pamphlet, consisting as it did of fewer than fifty pages. The cover was faded and worn – I guessed that it was old, and indeed when I looked at the title page, I saw it had been published some seventy-five years previously. I frowned at the author's name – it was familiar, but I struggled to recall where I had heard of it before: John William Polidori.

I did not think he was a poet or writer – yet his name seemed in some way linked to my knowledge of poetry. I was about to turn to Seward and ask him if the name was known to him, when the answer came to me. Perhaps it was seeing Seward, a medical man, bent over his work, for I recalled that John Polidori was a doctor too – the friend and physician of Lord Byron. He was with Byron in June 1816, at the Villa Diodati on the shores of Lake Geneva. One rainy evening, he, Byron, Shelley and Shelley's wife Mary entered into competition to see which of them could write the best ghost story. I had, of course, read the most famous text to have emerged from this contest – Mary Shelley's *Frankenstein; or, The Modern Prometheus*.

I opened Polidori's slim book. Reading the introduction, it was clear this was Polidori's contribution to that famed competition – his own ghost story. This tale was a mere 40 pages long, so I settled down to read it. Perhaps, Polidori, as a doctor, had had some medical insight that the Professor found useful?

Words in the very first paragraph chilled me to the bone:

The superstition upon which this tale is founded is very general in the East... of the dead rising from their graves and feeding upon the blood of the young and beautiful.

The volume fell from my nerveless fingers, and I gasped. John looked up from his labours and leapt to his feet when he saw my shocked expression.

'What is it, Lucy?'

Wordlessly, I pointed to the slim book that lay on the carpet. He came over and picked it up.

'That is what he thinks,' I whispered. 'This is what your Professor, the great scientist, believes I am.'

'What?' John looked at me, puzzled.

'He believes, that I have been the victim of... that I will become...' I choked.

'Lucy... what are you saying?'

Again, I pointed, and John looked down at the title of the book in his hands.

'*The Vampyre?*' he said, his brow wrinkled in confusion.

We went to the sofa and with the volume between us, we read Polidori's gruesome little tale. It told of a nobleman, Lord Ruthven, who feeds on the blood of his victims. He makes friends with a young man called Aubrey, who becomes his travelling companion. Ruthven slays a young Greek woman called Ianthe, with whom Aubrey is in love, but then is in turn slain by bandits. As he lies dying, he makes Aubrey promise that he will not tell of the circumstances, nor the facts of his – Ruthven's – death for a year and a day. Aubrey makes this vow and then returns to England and his beloved sister. To his great surprise, he encounters Ruthven in London, risen from the dead. Ruthven makes him promise to keep his oath, and Aubrey suffers a nervous collapse. Upon his recovery, he learns that his sister is to be married to Ruthven. He tries to prevent this and fails, and dies from a ruptured blood vessel in the brain. Ruthven weds Aubrey's sister and then devours her.

As we turned the last page, John turned uncomprehending eyes upon me.

'This is a silly and fantastical story,' he said.

'Agreed, but yet this, along with the other books I find the Professor has been studying, leads me to an inescapable conclusion. He believes that there is a vampire, a blood-feeder, of the same sort as Lord Ruthven, currently abroad in London. He believes that I have been its victim on more than one occasion, and that its ministrations have ultimately led to my death. And now that I am dead, he believes I will rise from my grave, undead, to drink human blood in my turn.'

'How he has drawn these preposterous conclusions?'

'Francis Bacon. The *Novum Organum*. Human understanding will draw all things to support an opinion when it has once been adopted.'

20 SEPTEMBER 1894

We sat in the library, watching the sun rise across the bleak garden. Shortly after eight, we heard the rattle of a carriage on the driveway and John went out onto the stairs to see who it was.

'There is a carriage and a man with impressive grey side-whiskers.'

'That will be Mr Marquand, Mother's lawyer. He must be here to discuss her Will, and mine.'

John looked at me reluctantly. 'I had better go.'

I knew John, Art and Van Helsing would all be occupied with Mr Marquand, so I took the opportunity to gather some items from my bedroom, preparing for my flight that night. I packed a few changes of clothes and a shawl into a small travelling case. I collected together all the money I had – an insubstantial sum in bank notes and coins – and put it in an embroidered purse. It would be enough for a train ticket to Exeter, and not much more. Once I arrived, I would have to rely on Mina and Jonathan's kindness. This I wrapped in the shawl and hid at the bottom of my travelling case. I hesitated over my jewellery, hoping that there might be some items I would be able to sell, but I soon realised that if anything valuable were missing, blame would fall on Beatrice. Reluctantly, I left it all.

When John came back, he spirited the case and me back to the secret room.

'It is done,' he told me. 'I have laid rocks wrapped in cloth in the coffin and nailed it shut.'

He promised to return as soon as the household was asleep.

As I waited, I could not help but dwell on what I was leaving behind. I would have loved to take some books, but how to choose? To take one volume or two would mean foregoing the many more that had been my joy and my lifelong companions. Exhaustion washed over me suddenly. I was still weak from the poison and the trials of the last few days. I curled into a ball on the narrow bed and let sleep claim me.

I woke, finding myself in the pitch dark. Confused, nauseous and dizzy, I lit a candle with shaking hands. My journals. How could I have forgotten my journals? They were still behind the panel in the library. I could not risk leaving them there.

I was about to dress, ready for my departure, when the door of my tiny room swung open. John stood in the doorway. He stepped into the room, drawing the door closed behind him. He swayed close to me in the narrow space, and I smelled the sweet perfume of brandy on his breath.

'Lucy,' he said, his voice rough and deep. I had never before heard him speak in this tone. 'My own Lucy Westenra.'

'John,' I said, keeping my own voice as clear and business-like as I could, 'I need you to fetch my journals for me, from the library. I will tell you where to find them. While you do so, I will dress...'

'Do not dress, Lucy, not yet.'

He dropped a hand, heavy and clumsy with alcohol, onto my shoulder. I tried to step back, but my legs were pressed against the bed. There was nowhere to go. He pulled me to him and pressed his wet mouth onto mine. I struggled to free myself, but he held me tightly.

'Oh Lucy,' he breathed hotly against my lips. 'The risks we have taken, the secrets we share. I have never felt so close to anyone. I want you. I want to...'

'No, John,' I said, pushing my hand uselessly against his chest. 'I do not want this. I thank you for all you have done, but...'

He drew back a little, and I saw a sneer pass across his features.

'So you will not do for me what you did so willingly for Quincey?' I froze. He grasped my wrist and drew my hand to press against the front of his trousers. 'Quincey is in his cups downstairs. Once Art and the Professor had retired, he drank most of a bottle of rum and he has become quite maudlin – and most descriptive of the pleasures he enjoyed with you. Quincey has had many women – many – but you seem to have made quite the impression upon him. His description of your sweet breasts alone...' He pushed his hardness against the palm of my resisting hand.

'John,' I said, 'please.' I tried to pull my hand away, but he would not release me.

'You are full of surprises, Lucy,' he growled. 'You look so pure. So innocent. And yet you open your legs for a wastrel like Quincey. Why did you not make *him* your lapdog? Why not get him to do your bidding as I have done?'

I did my best to keep my voice low and calm. He was swaying dangerously now. I could see he was very drunk indeed.

'John, I needed your help, and you gave it. I am immensely grateful for all you have done. You have shown such courage and integrity. What happened with Quincey was so long ago...'

'So you admit it happened? You filthy whore. I did everything for you. I would have given everything up for you. Everything.'

His face was brick-red with fury, alcohol and arousal. I had made a fatal error. I should have denied it. Perhaps he would have believed me. As it was, he was now enraged and inflamed. He released my wrist and grabbed at me, pulling me to him.

With one clumsy hand, he reached down to tug up the hem of my nightdress.

I acted on instinct. My hand was still between us, and with one furious blow, I hit him between his legs. He gasped and fell back, bumping into the door. It swung open. He crumpled to the floor, holding himself and breathing noisily. I did not hesitate. I leapt over his outstretched legs and fled down the dark corridor. The door of my bedroom was closed, but I opened it and slipped inside. The coffin lay on its trestles, gleaming dark and now mercifully sealed closed. The air was thick with the scent of flowers. I dragged the curtains aside and pulled up the sash of the window. I listened for a second, expecting to hear John coming after me, but there was no sound. Swinging a leg over the sill, I climbed out onto the trellis. I pulled the window closed behind me. It might slow him down. I scrambled down to the ground and took off as fast as I could, running down the path, through the side gate, across the road and onto the Heath. It was a moonless night, and I was grateful to reach the shelter of the trees. I hid behind the trunk of a big oak and looked back. No one emerged from the house to follow me.

I waited there for some moments, shivering. I was wearing nothing but my thin nightgown. My feet were bare. My bag, my clothes and my money were in the room with John. I was as vulnerable and exposed as I had been that night on the cliffs at Whitby.

I was overcome with an intense weakness. My body was still poisoned. With slow, agonising steps, I hobbled along the paths of the Heath until I reached the clearing where Quincey and I had lain together.

The grass had grown long and soft, and I sat down, looking at the gnarled trees that surrounded me, stooped giants, forming a guard around this secret place. One willow tree in particular had a wide, bulging trunk and branches, which hung low to the ground. I rose and walked over to it. To my surprise,

I saw that the trunk was split open, and the tree, though living and covered in leaves, had a great hollow in its base, big enough to accommodate a child or a small adult. I got down on my hands and knees and crept in. The sandy earth inside was dry and clean – this was not the present home of any animal. I was able to sit up towards the back of the hollow. Could one call it a cave if it were inside a tree? With the low branches heavy with summer leaves, I was sure I was invisible, hidden from casual passers-by. I curled myself into a tight ball and fell asleep.

CHAPTER 22

⤬

I was washing dishes when my phone rang. It was a mobile number I didn't recognise, so I let it ring out. A few moments later, a message notification buzzed. Drying my hands, I dialled voicemail.

'Hey.'

My stomach lurched. It took just that one word. Alex. There was a long silence on the line. I could hear chatter and traffic in the background.

'Hey babe,' the voice resumed. 'As you can see from the number, I'm back in the UK. In fact, I'm just down the road, at the Starbucks in Golders Green. Ha,' he laughed lightly. 'Starbucks. Me. I know. So... um... maybe you could come and rescue me? I'll be here for the next hour or so. I'd really love to see you. Bye. Bye.'

He didn't cut the call immediately, and I could hear him breathing for a moment as if he was considering saying something else. Then he clicked off. I stared at the phone in my hand.

I walked back to the sink, finished washing the dishes, then carefully dried each item and put it away. I wiped the counters and neatly folded the dishtowel. Then I rang James.

'Good morning,' he said, surprised. 'Everything okay?'

'Um... not really. Alex just called.'

'Alex? Your ex?'

'Yeah. I didn't pick up. He left a message. He's down the road and wants me to meet him for coffee.'

'Well,' said James, and then stopped. He waited for me to speak.

'I wanted you to know. I didn't want to lie,' I finished lamely.

'Are you going to go?'

'I think so. Yeah.'

'Thank you for telling me,' said James eventually, and his voice was small and sad. 'Kate ... I know this thing between us is new. But so far, for me anyway, it's been... so great. You make me very happy. I just want to say that you deserve only good things. And whatever those are... I want you to have them.'

'Thank you.'

'I.... I...' James said, but whatever it was he wanted to say, he didn't seem quite able to get it out. 'Look, call me later, one way or another,' he said. 'I'll be here.'

I saved Alex's UK number to my phone and sent a quick text: "See you in half an hour". I brushed my hair, but made no other effort with my appearance. Then I walked down the hill.

As I approached the coffee shop, I saw him sitting on a sofa by the window in a patch of sunlight. His hair curled over his collar. He had two espressos in front of him and was frowning at his laptop screen. I stared at him and experienced an odd disconnect. He looked simultaneously familiar and utterly unknown – a recognisable stranger. I knew if I sat down on the sofa beside him, I would know the warmth of his arm beside mine, the texture of his hand, the smell of his skin. I took a deep breath, walked in and slid into the upright seat across the table.

'Hi.'

He looked up at me, and his eyes flared with happiness. He half-stood and leaned over the table. I turned my head a fraction too late and his kiss landed on the corner of my mouth. He sat back down and pushed one of the coffees towards me.

'You look great.' He reached across again and touched my hair. 'I like it longer. It suits you.'

'What are you doing here?'

'I emailed you. You didn't reply.'

'So you flew eight hundred miles?' He shrugged and risked a small smile. 'Seriously, Alex, why are you here?'

I watched emotions play across his face. I could see him weighing up whether to be sincere, to abase himself and beg for forgiveness. But it just wasn't in him.

'Oh, you know, thought I'd swing by the old country. Go and see Mum. Italy's done. I'm going to take a few weeks here before I look for my next post. I'm thinking about South America next.'

'That's not fair,' I blurted. 'I begged for us to go to South America about a million times over the years. You always said no.'

'Well, that's why I'm here. I don't want to go alone, Katie,' he took my hand between both of his, 'I came to ask you to go with me.'

Someone across the coffee shop laughed loudly. The coffee machine hissed and clanged. I looked down at our joined hands. Alex pressed on.

'I've had a lot of time to think. I know Rafaella told you it didn't work out with Stacey. And I wanted to say... I'm sorry. It was a mistake. She was a mistake. I made a catastrophic error. I took you for granted – took what we had for granted. And it wasn't until I lost it that I realised...'

He was searching my face for a response, but I did my best keep my expression blank. How long had I waited for him to say this? How many nights had I lain, curled around the pain, aching for him to express just these feelings? My heart was pounding so loudly I could hear it pulsing in my ears. Alex released my hand and reached for his laptop. He spun the computer around so it was facing me.

'This language school in Rio is looking for two English teachers, as it happens. Accommodation included. Six weeks of summer school, and then we could go on a road trip. Maybe take in Bolivia and Peru... Argentina...'

I imagined rattling along in a rickety bus, my backpack wedged under my seat, coming to another strange new town at sunset, as we'd done hundreds of times all over the world.

'I would love to go to Argentina,' I said.

Alex's eyes widened. He smiled slowly and put his hand over mine.

'It'll be so amazing,' he said. 'We're going to have such a...'

'No.'

'No?' a frown creased his brow. 'What do you...?'

'Not with you. I'm not going with you.'

The answer came as much of a surprise to me as it did to him. That said, I must have sounded convincing, because he slumped back in his seat. He folded his arms and then said petulantly, 'So is there someone else?'

'There is, as it happens, but I'm not saying this because of him. I've started to make a life here. I've started building a career. I've found things that interest me.' And then, with my voice growing stronger. 'I have plans.'

Alex let a long silence lapse between us, and then he leaned forward.

'What if I stayed in London?'

It was my turn to look surprised.

'You hate London.'

'But I love you.'

'Do you though?' He looked shocked, but before he could answer, I forged on. 'Alex, you turned up out of nowhere, uninvited. You haven't asked me a single question about my life here. You just throw out an apology and make a grand gesture. This is real life, Alex, not a movie.' He looked stung by this and opened his mouth to protest, but I kept going. 'You're offering me a slightly adapted version of the life we used to share. But you know what? That life wasn't working. Stacey was a symptom, not the cause. I wish you all good things...' I realised I was echoing James's words to me. '... but my future doesn't include you.' I leaned across the table and kissed his cheek briefly. 'Have a fabulous time in Brazil, Al,' I said. 'Send me a postcard.'

I walked quickly back up the hill. I was panting when I turned into the gates. I got as far as the steps of the house and sank down, sitting on the cold stone and drawing my knees up to my chest. I looked down at my hands, which were trembling. Glancing at my watch, I was astonished to see that I'd been with Alex for less than half an hour.

It took a few minutes for my breathing to regulate. I felt oddly light-headed – the kind of vertigo I remembered from standing in a high place, looking down into a chasm – part fear, part elation. I stood then and went into Hillingham Court.

By the time I'd taken off my jacket and made a cup of tea, I'd found a place of deep calm. I texted James.

'He's gone.'

He called immediately and I told him the bare bones of the conversation Alex and I had had.

'When you next see me,' he said, 'I'll show you the grey hair I grew especially for you in the hours since we last spoke.'

'It can only make you look more distinguished,' I said. 'I'll call you later. Have a good day.'

I was about to hang up when he spoke quietly.

'You too, Kate. I love you.'

LUCY WESTENRA'S SECOND JOURNAL

Wracked with the poison and with grief, sadness and fear, I slept through the night and all of the next day. When I awoke at dusk, I realised that my funeral had taken place. Together with Mother's, my coffin would had been placed in the mausoleum in the churchyard at Hendon. Lucy Westenra was dead and buried.

In the rapidly cooling evening I crept from my hollow tree, stiff, shivering uncontrollably and desperately thirsty. I crouched in the clearing for a long time, listening. I could hear no voices or footsteps. I stood cautiously and tried to rub some warmth into my numb and frozen limbs. My thirst clamoured, and I recalled that there was a small stream that ran along the bottom of the hill. Moving cautiously, I began to flit from clearing to clearing, stopping every few steps to listen. At one point I had to crouch behind a bush as a bearded man carrying a tool bag sauntered past, whistling. He was, no doubt, on his way home to a hot dinner. How I envied him his food, his warm coat and his stout boots.

I reached the stream and knelt on the muddy bank, scooping

water from the thin trickle into my mouth. It was gritty and tasted of mud, but I did not care. I gulped it down, then crept back into the undergrowth. Now I had had water, I was aware of the hunger that gnawed at my insides. I had never truly known deprivation, only momentary lack and the delightful anticipation of a meal. This emptiness with no hope of relief was agony.

How was I to find food? If I approached anyone, they would want to know who I was and why I was there. I would be vulnerable to violence and violation. I would be unable to flee, barefoot, weak and hungry as I was. I turned back up the hill and began a slow progress back to the sanctuary of my hollow tree. It was almost completely dark, and I had to cross an open stretch of grass. It was soft under my bruised, aching feet, and I sank to my knees and ran my fingers over the soft blades. The fresh green scent made my mouth water, and I grasped a handful and tugged. I crammed the grass into my mouth and chewed. It was tough and tasteless. I managed to gnaw and swallow a few more mouthfuls. My stomach cramped, but I persevered. At least it was something. I knew if all I had to live on was grass I would soon starve, but at least it gave me enough energy to reach my temporary home.

As the sun dropped even further, the cold began to roll up the hill towards me and I shivered uncontrollably. I was likely to die of exposure before I perished from hunger. It was almost October, and the nights were already chilly. I scooped up as many dry leaves as I could find in the clearing and piled them into my hollow tree. Then I crawled in after them and buried myself under the leaves, hoping they would offer some little protection from the elements.

Somehow, in the next day or so, I needed to find some way to keep warm, sources of food, and, most urgently of all, shoes. Without shoes, I could not make any kind of escape. I thought of my bag, packed with my few possessions, and my small stock of money, still in the valet's room. Without it, I had no hope of reaching Mina in Exeter. But even though I was within half a mile of Hillingham there was no way I could return there. No doubt, Van Helsing, Art and John were still in residence. I was also in constant danger here in the Heath and in the streets of Hampstead. I would inevitably be seen by someone who knew me.

As if conjured by my thoughts, I heard a voice, faint on the breeze. A man, calling. Perhaps someone who had lost a dog? He drew closer to my hiding place, and with a shiver, I recognised both the voice and the name he called.

'Lucy!' shouted John, 'Lucy, where are you?'

He sounded hoarse and desperate. I buried myself more deeply under the cover of leaves and prayed that no glimmer of the white of my nightgown showed through.

'Lucy! I'm so sorry. Lucy come here. Let me help you. I was stupid. Forgive me. Please!'

He entered the clearing and I could dimly see the legs of his trousers and his mud-encrusted shoes. I prayed he would not spot the hollow in the tree through the hanging willow fronds.

'Lucy,' he cried again, and a sob cracked his voice.

He seemed to slump. Then, to my relief, in a nearby clearing there was the crack of a stick, and a bird took flight with a noisy flutter.

'Lucy?' John called, faint hope animating his tone. He set off towards the sound.

I lay listening to his fading footfalls. What would he have said if I emerged? That he was sorry? That he had been drunk? Both were true, but drink had not altered his behaviour – it had revealed his true nature. He had expected to have me as his reward for helping him. I could not trust him. I was truly alone.

* * *

The hours of the night seemed endless. I shivered uncontrollably, and when I did drift off, nightmares jerked me awake. Finally, light finally crept in through the entrance of my small hiding place. As the sun rose, so did the temperature, and, exhausted by my long and wakeful night, I was finally able to sleep.

The sun was at its highest point when I stirred again. It seemed, as I hovered between the worlds of dream and reality, that an unusual sound had roused me. I opened my eyes and lay still. What had I heard? After several long seconds, I heard the sound again – a faint cry. John again? The voices were higher pitched. Was it weeping? No, it was laughter – the merriment of children. They were some distance away, down the hill, squealing and chattering.

I heard one voice, louder than the others say – 'I shall count to fifty. Then I am coming, whether you are ready or not. One, two...'

'Cover your eyes, Clara, you cheat!' Another voice spoke furiously.

'I am!'

'With both hands. And turn your back.'

There was some further wrangling and then the first voice – Clara, I surmised – began to count, loudly and slowly.

'One, two, three...'

I heard the sound of running feet – several children scattering in all directions, looking for hiding places. I shuffled further back in my hollow tree, sat up and wrapped my arms around my knees.

I heard them whispering and laughing, arguing about who could hide in which bush. They seemed mostly to have chosen hiding places close to where Clara stood counting. But my heart sank as one determined set of footfalls grew louder and louder. I heard panting breath in the clearing. He or she stood looking around, and I willed them to choose the dense clump of azaleas or move into another clearing. But then light pierced my little hollow as they parted the fronds of the willow and gasped to see the hole in the trunk.

The small body of the child blocked the light as they crawled into the hollow, so I could not see a face, but from the shape of the head and clothing, I could see it was a girl. She looked as if she was perhaps seven or eight years old. I huddled back, but the space was tiny, and as she reached out a hand, she came into contact with my bare foot. She gave a small scream, which she quickly stifled, checking over her shoulder.

'Don't worry,' I whispered, 'I too am hiding.'

She crept in a little closer and squinted at my face in the gloom.

'Are you playing a game?'

'I am. So far no one has found me.'

She looked me up and down, taking in my white nightgown and tangled hair.

'Are you a fairy?' she asked suspiciously.

'I don't think so,' I replied seriously, 'I do not have wings.'

'You are very pretty though,' she said, and reached out a hand to touch a strand of my hair.

'Thank you.' I shrank from her. Perhaps she saw a fairy, but I was dirty and my mouth tasted foul.

'I am called Alice,' she said, 'I am here for a picnic with my mother and father and all my cousins. What is your name?'

I was about to reply, but then I imagined her going down the hill to her parents and saying she met a fairy called Lucy on the Heath. They may believe it to be a childish fancy, but if they did not, and if they told anyone...

'I have no name,' I said.

'I shall call you the Beautiful Lady,' she said solemnly. She stumbled over the word 'beautiful'.

'Thank you,' I said. My voice was rusty from lack of use – I had not spoken a word for two days. It caused me to cough.

'Are you sick?' Alice asked.

'Not sick, but a little weak.'

'Are you hungry?'

'Very.'

She reached into the pocket of her pinafore and brought forth a biscuit.

'I saved this from the picnic. You can have it.'

It took all my self-control not to snatch the biscuit. I took it from her hand gently.

'Thank you,' I nibbled on a corner. The sweet crumbs made my mouth flood with saliva.

'This is a good hiding place,' Alice said. She sat down and wrapped her arms around her knees, in imitation of my pose.

'It should be our secret,' I said. 'Let us not tell anyone. Otherwise everyone will want to hide here.'

'I won't tell,' she said seriously, 'If I did, Clara would come, and she'd make it hers and tell me I wasn't allowed to play in it.'

The biscuit was gone. It had done little to dull my hunger. My hands shook. Alice reached out and touched one of them.

'Are you still hungry?'

'A little.'

I haven't anything else,' she looked sad, 'but I did see some brambles growing over there.' She waved in a vaguely westerly direction. They're old, because it's nearly winter, so they're probably not very nice, but it's something, isn't it?'

'It is something,' I agreed.

'Alice!' Clara's voice called crossly from down the hill. 'Alice! I can't find you and now Mamma says we have to leave.'

'You had better go,' I said. 'Make sure Clara tells everyone that you were the winner of hide and seek.'

'Oh, she won't. But I know I won, and that's good enough.'

She gave me one small, serious nod, and then scrambled backward out of the hollow.

'Goodbye, Bloofer Lady,' she whispered, and I heard her footsteps fading away as she scampered down the hill.

It took all my willpower to wait for sunset, but as soon as the sun dipped, I crept from my hiding place. I crouched in the shadow of the tree for some minutes, listening. Other than the sounds of birds roosting and the whisper of the wind, all was quiet. Keeping close to the bushes, I crept around the edge of the clearing. It took a little searching, but I found the patch of brambles Alice had described.

I had just begun to pluck berries and eat them when I felt a hand on my elbow.

'Are you a nice lady?'

I froze, then turned slowly and looked into dark eyes. The child's face was so thin that her eyes were enormous – sunken into hollows in her skull. She was wearing a ragged pinafore dress and, like me, was barefoot.

'I... think so,' I said carefully.

'Pa's gone out to look for work. He says I'm to stay away from the lodgings till he comes back. I was just so...' she hesitated.

'Hungry?'

'We've no food at home. And no money. Pa spent the last of what we had on gin. He told me to find a nice lady and ask her for a crust.'

'I don't have a crust for you. I do not have one for myself either.'

She crumpled then. A tear rolled down her thin cheek.

'My stomach hurts something fierce,' she said.

'Mine too,' I took her hand. 'I cannot give you bread, but here is something we can eat.'

I plucked a berry and offered it to her. She took it and popped it in her mouth. She winced at the sourness, but ate it gratefully. The next one I found for her was sweeter, and she smiled hesitantly. The poor little mite was ravenous, and once she got the knack of spotting the berries among the foliage, she dived in, not heeding the thorns and twigs. I had to caution her to slow down, for her thin arms, shoulders and neck were soon covered in scratches. She plucked and devoured the fruit as if she had not had a meal in days.

After some minutes, we had exhausted the crop. She looked around for more, and then sank, disappointed to the ground.

'I am very tired,' she said. Her mouth was stained purplish red. She looked about, spotted a nearby furze bush that hung close to the ground, and crawled towards it.

'What time will your Father be home?'

'Not till very late. I think I will hide under here and sleep a while, until it is time to go home.'

'Are you sure?' I asked, but her eyes were already closing. She pillowed her head on her thin little arm and sighed.

Oh, that I could scoop her up and offer her sanctuary– a home, warm food, love and safety! But I had none of these things myself. I stroked her tangled hair from her face. I piled some leaves in front of her hiding place, the better to conceal her.

I returned to my base in the hollow tress. Using my teeth to rip, I tore long strips from the bottom of my nightgown, I used these to bind around my feet for protection. The berries and Alice's biscuit had given me a small reserve of strength. It was time to move on. I began to walk, making my way South and West. I would, I knew, soon leave the Heath and reach the fields of Temple of Fortune Farm.

Sure enough, I came upon a hedge. I found a gap and scrambled through it, and then I was in a field. It had been harvested and ploughed over. I crept along in the shadows and passed into the next field, and the next. I found a trough – it looked clean enough, and I scooped a few handfuls of water into my mouth and used more to wash my hands and face.

I was not familiar with the layout of the farm, so it was sheer luck that I stumbled upon the orchard. Searching though the grass in the dark, I discovered a few autumn windfall apples. I picked them up carefully, and they were mercifully free from wasps or worms. I devoured them gratefully. Now, if only I could find a farm outbuilding where I could sleep, I should consider myself a princess among women.

The night was black, and the byre at first seemed only to be a patch of deeper darkness, but the rich, fecund smell reached me on the breeze, so I made my way towards it. I felt along the side of the building until I came upon a door, eased the bolt back and slipped inside. The warmth hit me like a wall. There were ten or so cows, packed in close. They shifted when they heard me come in and let out low sighs. They did not seem particularly interested in me. I crept around behind them, and, by feel, located a pile of dry straw in the corner. Groping around me, I found a piece of rough sacking, which I spread over the straw. I sank down on it. After two nights in the hollow tree, a makeshift bed in this smelly, warm place represented the most unimaginable luxury.

My eyes became accustomed to the darkness within the room, and I could soon make out the broad barrel body of the cow next to me. She was creamy white and in the gloom, I could see her heavy udder swinging beneath her. I edged closer. I had never seen a cow close up before and I was in awe of her immense size. I put a cautious hand on her flank. She twitched her ears, but otherwise ignored me. I stroked her rough hide and gradually let my hand trail down her side. She stamped one hoof, and I paused, but she did not seem especially disturbed. What I knew of the milking of cows was merely what I had read in books, so I had no idea how to begin. What a patient, dear old girl she was. She stood without moving or kicking me, while I tugged and pulled until, to my astonishment, I managed to produce a hot jet of milk from her. After a few more clumsy attempts, I was able to aim the stream into my mouth. Oh, how delicious it was! Creamy, rich and warm, I could feel every drop as it ran into my aching, empty stomach. I was quickly replete, and like a sated baby, tumbled onto my makeshift bed and slept.

'Oy!' the voice was high and sharp and jerked me awake. 'You can't sleep 'ere!'

A figure loomed over me. I sprang to my feet. In my confused, half-awake state, I registered that the figure was smaller than me – just a boy, maybe ten years of age or less. Nevertheless, he reached out and grabbed my arm. His grip was strong.

'We won't have vagrants, you 'ear me?' he snarled. 'My Pa's just outside. Just you wait till 'e...'

I did not wait to find out what his Pa would do. I yanked my arm out of his grip and lunged for the door. I expected him to fight me, but to my surprise, he fell back with a cry and grasped his throat.

'You scratched me, you witch!' he yelled. He kept shouting, but did not follow me as I bolted for the door and out into the dim dawn.

Despite his protestations, there was no sign of his father. I turned back the way I had come, and running as swiftly as my roughly bandaged feet would carry me, I crossed from field to field until I reached the line of trees that marked the edge of the Heath. I found a dense clump of furze bushes and crept beneath them, lying flat on my belly.

I did not know whether the boy had seen me clearly, nor what he would say. In just a few hours, I had been spotted three times. I resolved to be more cautious. Even though the farm offered opportunities for food and shelter, the risk of being seen or caught was multiplied.

When night fell, I crept back to my hollow tree and spent another night shivering and jumping at every sound. At dawn, I hunted for more brambles, but found pitifully few. I dreamed of a fire, of warm water with which to wash. I had to face the truth, if I stayed on the Heath much longer, nature would do Art's work for him.

I was forced to laugh at the irony. I had risked all to claim my freedom. And here I was, with all the freedom in the world, and I had never been more trapped. Within a month or so, winter would set in. If the cold did not kill me, the hunger would. Dressed as I was in a stained nightgown, my feet bound in filthy rags, I could not travel far, and unless I could remove myself from this area where I was known, I could not reveal myself and ask for help. And to whom could I go for help? I could not approach strangers and tell them who I was – their first action would be to contact Art. With no money, nor the ability to write and send a letter, I could not reach Mina, the only person in the world I trusted.

Or was she? Was there someone else from whom I could seek help? I sat in my tree for long hours and considered my options. As the sun began to sink, I emerged cautiously, and set off to put my plan in motion. It was risky, but I had no other option.

24 SEPTEMBER 1894

It was almost night when I arrived. I stood at the side gate, keeping watch. The house was in darkness. Now that a few days had passed, I had guessed that Van Helsing, Art and Seward would have left, and the absence of movement or carriages told me my guess was correct.

I lifted the latch, pausing to listen, and padded silently up the side of the house. It already looked forlorn and abandoned. I looked up at my bedroom window, but it was closed and shuttered, as were all the upstairs windows. I crept further along, coming to the corner of the house. I peered round, expecting to see light flooding from the scullery door, to hear the bustle of Mrs Staines cooking, and to smell food, but there was only a faint glow, as if a single candle burned inside. I was about to step forward when the door opened and a figure came out with an enamelled basin and went towards the kitchen garden. I pressed myself into the ivy and squinted to see who it was. With a sigh of relief, I spotted Beatrice's long plait swinging over her shoulder as she bent to pick some spinach.

I was so happy to see her that before I could consider her possible response, I stepped out onto the path and called her name. She jerked upright, spun around and peered into the gloom. When she saw me, the basin she was holding tumbled to the ground with a clatter. She stood frozen, staring. In the silence, I heard what sounded like running water. After a moment of confusion, I realised she had wet herself. I stepped forward. She screamed and stepped back.

'No,' she said in a wheezing whisper, 'No. It's because of the letter, isn't it? I was going to post it. I was. But the foreign gentleman stopped me. He wouldn't let me leave the house. I still have it, Miss. I hid it in my room, under the floorboards. I can get it. I can post it if you'll leave me be…'

'Beatrice, do not fear. It is I. Lucy. I am no spirit. I am alive. I promise. Here –' I held out my hand. 'You can touch me and see it is so.'

'They put you in the tomb.'

'The coffin was empty.'

I was lucky that it was Beatrice I encountered, and not Eliza. Eliza was a superstitious girl, prone to drama. She would have fainted dead away at the first sight of me, and nothing would have persuaded her that I was alive. Beatrice, on the other hand, stood for a long moment and then took a tentative step forward. She reached out a trembling finger and touched my hand. She added a second finger and traced the scratches and grazes among the dirt. Then she stepped closer and gripped my hand tightly in both of hers.

'Miss Lucy,' she whispered, and tears rolled down her cheeks.

She took me into the house. The kitchen was in darkness except for a few candles, and the air was cold. The table was scrubbed and empty – I had never seen it so before. It was always piled with vegetables, or dusty with flour as Mrs Staines prepared yet another meal.

'Where is Mrs Staines?'

'Mr Holm-... Lord Godalming dismissed her. Dismissed us all.'

'He what?'

'Sent us packing. Gave a week's pay in lieu of notice. Eliza has gone to her brother in Bromley, and Mrs Staines went back to her family in Margate. I don't know where Mr Watkins went.'

'And you?'

'Got nowhere to go. I came here from the orphanage. And he can't force me out, because now I own the libr...' she paused, horrified. 'Except I don't, do I? You're not dead.'

'I am dead, Beatrice,' I assured her, 'to all but you. I am dead, and I will not be returning. The library is yours. How did he react when he found out?'

'He was fair furious,' she said, and she opened her eyes wide and round. 'He raged and shouted, but the solicitor man...'

'Mr Marquand?'

'Mr Marquand, yes. He just sat and let Lord G scream. He looked down at his papers, and did not move, and then he said, "It is the law, my Lord, and according to the law, the library was Miss Lucy's property to dispose of as she would." And Lord G said he'd ruin me in court, and then he walked out and slammed the door so hard it cracked.'

'Can he do that?'

'Mr Marquand said that to do that, Lord G would have to be able to pay a solicitor and a barrister, and...' she stopped. She had shocked herself with her forward talk.

'And he... cannot?'

Beatrice picked up a candle and beckoned to me.

'Come, Miss,' she said.

She guided me to the main atrium. By the light of Beatrice's candle, I saw that the portrait of Mother was missing, as were all the other paintings that usually lined the walls. Beatrice opened the door to the drawing-room, and I gasped. The room resembled a mouth from which teeth had been brutally extracted. Paintings, ornaments and items of furniture were missing, and the room had been left in a state of disorder. Had we been robbed?

The solicitor said he shouldn't take anything – not until the pro...' she searched for the word.

'Probate?'

'That's it. Until the estate is settled, he can't sell the house, nor touch the money in the bank. But he didn't listen to the solicitor. Came in with a man with one of those jeweller's eyepieces, and they picked out all the things they thought was valuable. Mrs Staines tried to stop him, but he just ignored her.'

'In the whole house?'

'Except the library,' said Beatrice. She looked mortified. 'Your gowns too, Miss, and your jewellery, and all that belonged to your Mother, God rest her soul. This was yesterday morning. They loaded it all on two carts and took it away.'

I sank down on a chair. 'He is desperate for money – quick money. And perhaps that means he will not be able to pursue a court case.'

'If he does, Mr Marquand has said he will stand for me, and without fees.'

I smiled weakly, 'Well then. There is still good in the world.'

Beatrice offered her hand to me. 'Come on, Miss. Let us get you clean and warm and fed. Then you can tell me the story of how this all came to pass.'

An hour or so later, I had luxuriated in a hot bath and put on one of Beatrice's warm flannel nightgowns. We sat at the kitchen table with a single candle between us, and I wolfed down bowl after bowl of warming vegetable soup. Once I was replete, I moved my chair closer to the fire, and told Beatrice some of my story. I omitted Art's blackmail, and merely said that he was forcing me into marriage, and that once he knew he had inherited the property, he had seen no further use for me. I told her that John and I had faked my death, but that he had attacked me on the night before the funeral.

'Oh,' she breathed, 'That explains it.'

'What?'

'Oh Miss, Dr Seward has been a broken man. He fair wept for the whole day of the funeral, and he has returned to the house each day since. I was not sure what he was looking for, but now I know he was looking for you.'

'What time does he come?' I said, starting to my feet.

'In the mornings sometimes. You are safe.'

'Thank you.' I sank back onto the chair.

'Although...' she said hesitantly, 'Lord G is a bad man, Miss. I see that now. There's a cruelty to him,' she grimaced in disgust. 'But Dr Seward... well. He's always been kind, Miss. To you and to everyone. And he does seem terrible upset.'

I did not reply. I could not trust John. Tempting, as it was to stay in the house, I needed to find my bag, with its change of clothes and my money, and depart as soon as possible.

'I need to go and find some things, Beatrice,' I said, standing and reaching for the candle.

'I'll come with you!' she stood too.

'No, thank you, Beatrice. I need to look alone.'

The corridor between the bedrooms was shadowy and dim. The oriental silk runner that had covered the floor was gone, as were the paintings. The floor was dusty, and the board creaked beneath my bare feet. I opened my bedroom door. The bed had been replaced in its usual spot, but was stripped to the mattress.

The wardrobe stood open and empty, and my dressing table had been swept clear. I would need to search it more thoroughly to see what was gone, but for now, I drew the door closed. It was too painful to see. I continued down the corridor to the secret room. I tried the handle, but it was locked. I went back downstairs to Mrs Staines' pantry. The key press hung on the wall, but when I swung it open, it was empty. Someone had removed all the keys.

I found a small toolbox under Mrs Staines' desk. Within, I found a short crowbar. I took it upstairs and inserted it into the crack of the door beside the lock. I had little strength, but with some pushing and pulling, I heard the edge of the door crack and splinter. With a few more sharp yanks, the lock sprung free, and I was able to open the door.

It was empty. The bed had been stripped, and the little table where my food had been kept had been removed. There was no sign of my bag. John had eradicated all evidence, but in doing so, he had robbed me of my means of escape.

Curiosity had obviously got the better of Beatrice and she came up behind me, a lantern in her hand.

'Was this where you were hiding, Miss?'

'It was. But Dr Seward has removed everything that was here. Has he left anything elsewhere in the house?'

'No Miss, he took all his things away with him in his carriage yesterday.'

'Was there a travelling case?'

'There were several. He stayed here for quite a few nights before you...' she did not know how to finish the sentence. 'I just thought they were his things. And of course the Professor – the foreign gentlemen – took all your papers.'

'He what?'

'All your letters, Miss – those in the desk in your bedroom. He said he was going to talk to Mrs Harker about them.'

'Mina?'

'Your friend in Exeter? He has gone there, I think. To see her.'

'Dr Van Helsing has gone to see Mina?'

I sat down on the edge of the stripped bed. Mina would now know of my "death". How sad she would be. And if Van Helsing had gone to Mina, then they all knew of our connection. Mina's home in Exeter was no longer the remote refuge I had imagined it would be.

Beatrice made up a bed for me in Eliza's room – we thought it best to be close together, in case there were unexpected visitors in the night. I slept late and breakfasted well. I felt as if, at last, the poison had passed from my body.

26 SEPTEMBER 1894

No one came to the house yesterday nor today. I spent the days writing a long letter to Mina, telling her all that had happened, and pleading with her to send me a little money – just enough so that I could buy a simple set of clothing, and for the price of a ticket to Exeter. I did not know where else I might go. I gave it to Beatrice in time for the last collection, and she went off to post it.

While she was out of the house, I took the key to the library and opened the door. To my great relief, it was undisturbed. I went immediately to the wall by the window and pressed the hidden catch to open the panel. My journals, including the one in which I write these words, were still there. I took them and closed the panel. It has taken me some hours to record everything that has happened over the last days, but I have now done so. For now, I will keep the journal with me, for who knows when I might need to flee this house?

CHAPTER 23

*L*ater that evening, I sat looking out over the dark Heath. So Alex and I were over forever. I expected to feel more – grief – even anger. But I felt very little. Perhaps it was the numbness that follows a shock amputation and the pain was yet to come, but for now, I felt quietly content, as if an end had been correctly and satisfactorily reached. Alex was in the past, on my terms at last.

I made some soup, and sat down to watch something on Netflix. To my surprise, there was a knock on the flat door. I hadn't heard the downstairs buzzer, so it had to be someone from inside the building. Rita? My heart lifted in hope. But when I opened the door, I reared back in surprise. Alex stood there, grinning.

'Oh.'

'Oh?' he took a step forward, leaning in as if to kiss me. I leaned back, out of his reach.

'How did you get in?'

'Someone was coming out just as I arrived. I slipped in.'

As he stepped past me, I smelled the beer on him. I followed him through to the living room.

'So this is your mum's place? I always wanted to see it. Nice bit of real estate you've got. In Hampstead, no less.'

He sat down on the sofa and spread his arms along the back, knees wide. I stayed where I was in the doorway. He gestured for me to join him but I didn't move.

'What are you doing here?'

He frowned then and his mouth twisted into something that looked like anger.

'I just... I couldn't really understand what happened this morning. I mean... eight years. Eight years, Kate. How can it be over in five minutes like that?'

I let out a bark of laughter.

'Seriously?'

He looked hurt at this response and raised his hands in a placating gesture. But my blood was up.

'It's scarcely five minutes, is it, Alex?'

'I know, but...'

You don't get to walk in here and rewrite history. You left me, Alex. You. Left me. Six months ago. I lost my home. My job. My friends.'

'I didn't make you leave...'

'How could I have stayed?' I was yelling now, and then to my horror, I was crying. And then I couldn't stop.

It was if the wound had been torn open and the agony was fresh. The sobs ripped through me, ugly and guttural and I battled to draw breath. The humiliation of the day I'd arrived back from work early, finding Stacey standing in our living room, wrapped in a towel. The hideous, sleepless nights in Rafaella's family home, those dark, dark early days in London. The sheer enormity of my loss.

Alex leaped to his feet and drew me into his arms. He

cupped the back of my head with one hand and murmured incoherently in my ear.

'Oh babe. I'm so sorry. So, so sorry. It was the worst mistake of my life. I just want to fix it. Please tell me how to fix it. Please.'

I was suddenly conscious of the warmth of his hand, pressed lightly on the nape of my neck. Every nerve in my body lit up, and instinctively, I rested a hand on his hip. I recognised the jeans he was wearing just by touch. They were faded and soft, with a small rip on the left front pocket. I'd hooked my thumb in the belt loop as we'd walked through sunny streets, arms round each other's waists. I'd unbuttoned them and pulled them off him, tumbling on our bed. I'd washed them hundreds of times, folded them and dropped them into his drawer.

Oh, the smell of him. He radiated heat – he had always been hot-blooded. We breathed in unison for a long moment. He was narrow and wiry– the opposite of James's tall bulk.

James. Oh god. James.

Alex drew back slightly. I knew what was coming next – sweet, soft kisses, and then, inevitably... I extricated myself clumsily, stumbled away and stood in the kitchen doorway, in the comfortingly bright neon light.

'You can't be here.'

'Why not?'

I drew myself up and said, with as much conviction as I could muster: 'because I don't want you to be.'

He tipped back on his heels, and I wondered for a brief moment just how drunk he was. A dangerous light ignited in his eyes.

'You don't want me to... or your "boyfriend" wouldn't want me to?'

He put heavy quote marks around the word boyfriend. Did he think I was lying about seeing someone? He came towards me and I raised my hands to ward him off.

'Please Alex. Go. Now. I'm serious.'

He nodded and dropped his head as if in contrition. He went towards the front door then, and turned back.

'Will you walk me out at least?'

I nodded. It was probably best to make sure he left the building. I scooped up my keys and followed him down the narrow staircase. On the second-floor landing, he turned to me.

'Kate, this breaks my heart. Are you sure...?'

I hesitated for a fraction of a second. Not because I was uncertain, but because I didn't know how to make myself clearer. But Alex saw an opening. He came at me then, grasped my face between his hands and kissed, me, hard and deep. He walked me back forcefully until my back struck the door of the hidden utility room. The door burst open and Alex pushed me into the narrow, dark room, up against the nearest wall. He pressed himself against me so I could feel his hardness against my stomach. He was strong, I knew that, and he seemed convinced that his ardour and certainty would sweep me away. I wriggled away, furious and lunged for the still-open door. He reached out and grabbed my wrist. His grip was too tight for me to break without a struggle. With a chill, I realised he wasn't playing. He pulled me in again. He was much stronger than me.

'I will scream,' I said, my voice loud enough to echo down the stairwell. 'I will scream 'til the neighbours hear.'

'Kate?'

Alex's eyes widened at the voice echoing up the stairs. We both turned to look. Rita was standing in the doorway of the little room. She held a phone handset, raised.

'I've dialled 999,' she said crisply. 'I just need to press the green phone button.'

I glanced at Alex. His face had a sweaty grey sheen, as if he had just awoken from a bad dream.

'Oh god,' he muttered. Then he fled out of the room past Rita and down the stairs. I heard the front door open and close with a bang behind him.

On wobbly legs, I walked out of the little room.

'Thank you.'

'Not at all. Are you all right?'

I nodded dumbly.

'Well, then. Off to bed with you.'

She made her way back down the stairs and I heard her heavy door close with a firm click.

I climbed back up to my flat. Once inside, I double-locked the door. Still shivering, I got into bed and rang James. He answered on the first ring, and his deep, calm voice broke me. I began to sob. He listened as I recounted what had happened.

'Do you want me to drive up to you? I'll leave now.'

'Don't be crazy. You've got work tomorrow. I'm fine. Honestly.' I almost believed myself.

'Do you think he'll be back?' he said, his voice tight with tension. 'You should probably report him to the police.'

'He won't be back.' I said. 'I think he was horrified at himself, and anyway, Rita was right there.'

'As long as you're sure,' James said hesitantly. 'You're not working tomorrow, are you? What are you doing with the rest of your day?'

'Finishing other unfinished business. Listen, can I get on the train and come and see you this weekend?'

'I'd like that,' he said.

I took a deep breath. 'I love you James.'

'Well then,' he said. I heard the quiet smile in his voice. 'That's most convenient. I love you too.'

LUCY WESTENRA'S SECOND JOURNAL

I stood before the small glass in Eliza's room, brushing and plaiting my hair. A meal and a good night's sleep had restored me and I felt a tiny green shoot of hope for the future.

There was no knock. The door was pushed wide and John's tall frame filled the doorway. I backed away from him. I felt an almost animal panic. The room was narrow, and there was no way past him. I darted a glance at the window, even though I knew I could not flee that way without falling to my death.

'Lucy,' he said, and his face contorted with pain at my panic.

'Get away from me.'

'Lucy, please listen. I am sorry. I am so sorry. I would never hurt you. I...'

'You did hurt me.'

His head dropped, and I thought he might be about to weep. How had he found me? With a cold plummet of fear, I realised. Beatrice. I had been betrayed. My anger burned brighter than my fear, and I rushed towards him, my hands outstretched to push at his chest. He lurched, unresisting, out of the way. Beatrice was standing in the corridor, pleating her apron between nervous fingers, her face pinched and pale. I launched at her, fingers outstretched, ready to claw out her eyes.

'You witch!'

Beatrice screamed and John, suddenly galvanised, caught me by the arm and dragged me away from her.

'Lucy, be calm!' he said, struggling to contain my flailing limbs. 'Beatrice only did what she did so I could help you. We both want to help you. We are not your enemies. Please. Trust us.'

'Trust you?' I spat. 'Why should I trust you? First Art, now you. I have been left with nothing. Nothing!' I rounded on Beatrice. 'And you?'

'I... I...' she stammered.

'Art left her with nothing too. I have been giving her money,' said John. His voice hardened. 'The library was a pretty gift, but the girl needs to eat. When I came this morning, I could see she was hiding something. I pressed her to tell me.'

I looked to Beatrice. Her face was pink, and she was trying not to cry. The three of us stood on the landing, tension crackling between us. Then John spoke quietly.

'There is much that you do not know. Much has happened since you... well. If you are to escape safely, there are facts you will need to hear. Now, can we go down to the kitchen and talk calmly? Time is very much of the essence today.'

He frowned at me. Tension and pain had carved new, deeper lines between his nose and mouth and creased his brow. He is not yet thirty, I thought, and these events have aged him. He turned then and left. After a moment I followed him to the kitchen.

'Sit down,' he said shortly. 'Now. This is what has happened in the past few days. Dr Van Helsing sought permission from Art, as your heir, to go through all of your papers. They led him, unsurprisingly, to Mrs Harker, and he travelled to Exeter to see her. She was devastated to learn of your death. She has suffered her own loss too – her husband's business partner, Mr Hawkins, has passed away.'

'Poor Mina. She was fond of him.'

'He has left both Mina and Jonathan considerably better off – Jonathan has inherited the law firm and Mr Hawkins' house. That is where they are living now.'

I thought of my letter, which I had posted to Mina's old address. It would need to be forwarded. What delay might there be in her getting the news that I lived and was in need of her help?

John continued. 'Mina welcomed Dr Van Helsing and was most helpful. She has kept a journal apparently, and she had prepared a typed transcript for him.'

I gasped. What secrets had she unwittingly revealed?

'I have seen it,' said John. 'You told me what Mina said about owning the story. She has done so. The Lucy in those pages is the same sweet, obedient girl, in love with Art who appears in your own letters and manufactured journal. There is no whisper of scandal. She has protected you. The Professor seemed most interested in an account she had written of an incident where you walked onto the cliffs at Whitby in your sleep. It seemed to suggest you encountered a mysterious figure?'

This jolted me. I had thought Mina knew nothing of my liaisons with the Stranger.

John continued. 'More worryingly, Mina gave the Professor a transcript of the journal her husband kept on his travels to Transylvania. I understand that he was missing for some weeks?'

'Yes, Mina was very worried about him.'

'And he was then discovered in a weakened state, both physically and mentally damaged from an unknown ordeal?'

'That is true. Mina travelled to Buda-Pesth to meet him and

bring him home. They were married there. She wrote to me in confidence. She believed he had sustained a prolonged delusion, and that his mental health was precarious, if not permanently damaged.'

'I myself have not had sight of what Jonathan Harker wrote. However, the Professor does not suspect mental illness, but instead believes Harker's account to be the unvarnished truth. Harker claims to have suffered some form of supernatural attack, perpetuated by the nobleman with whom he went to do business.'

'And so?'

'This, coupled with the account of the shipwreck in Whitby...'

'The shipwreck?' I frowned. 'What does that have to do with anything?'

'The ship came from Varna, did it not?'

'It did. It was a Russian schooner, I recall. There was a mutiny. The crew murdered the captain and absconded.'

'That is not the version of the story I have heard, nor the one that Van Helsing fervently believes. He thinks that this ship brought Harker's mysterious Count to the shores of Britain, and that you were his first victim.'

I laughed. 'What a preposterous notion!'

'That may be, but all of this feeds into Van Helsing's belief that you were targeted, firstly in Whitby, and then subsequently in London, causing you to become ill and die.'

'So we were right? He thinks I was slain by a vampire?'

'He does. He saw your coffin put in the tomb, but this did not by any means set his mind at rest. Hence his visit to the Harkers.'

John took a deep breath. I sensed that this brought us to the real purpose for his visit.

And then, this week, there were... reports in the newspaper.'

'Reports? About what?'

He drew out a copy of the *Westminster Gazette*, pointing to a small item on an inner page, which bore the headline "A Hampstead Mystery". I skimmed the article. A few lines in, I gasped to read:

During the past two or three days, several cases have occurred of young children straying from home or neglecting to return from their playing on the Heath. In all these cases the children were too young to give any properly intelligible account of themselves, but the consensus of their excuses is that they had been with a 'bloofer lady.'

I raced through reading the rest of the article. Towards the end, I read these words:

"... some of the children... have been slightly torn or wounded."

I recalled the little girl, scratched by the brambles and the boy in the cow byre. I looked up at John.

'The Professor believes that you are this "bloofer lady."'

'I am,' I said. 'I mean... I have encountered children, and they may have spoken of me in those terms, but I never...'

'He believes you have risen from the dead and are traversing the Heath, feeding on children,' said John roughly. 'Do you see why we are in a terrible predicament?'

'But John, you are to tell him he is wrong. He is clearly deranged...'

'Last night, he dragged me across the fields to Hendon, to the churchyard. When we got there, I discovered that he has the key to your family mausoleum.'

'He what?'

'He took charge of the key from the undertaker, promising to give it to Art, but has kept it for himself.'

'The man is not sane, John.'

'He is so firmly convinced of the rightness of his argument that he cannot be swayed. I did everything I could to dissuade him from his course, but he forged on. He opened the tomb and then insisted on opening the lid of the coffin and prising open the lead lining. And of course...'

'The coffin was empty.' I finished.

'Which supports his argument that you are what he believes you to be.'

'And so what...?'

'He wants to return today. To see the coffin again.'

'Oh, John,' I said, dropping my head into my hands in despair, 'how do we put this madness to rest?'

John spoke hesitantly, 'What if, when we open the coffin, you are in it...?'

'What? No!' I sprang to my feet.

'If, in the light of day, he sees that you are in there, he will believe he is wrong. That he was mistaken.'

'You are asking me to lie in that coffin in my family mausoleum, beside the bodies of my parents...?'

'For minutes. Just minutes. It will not require more than that.'

'I will not do this. It is deranged.'

John reached across the table and gripped my hand. 'He will hunt you Lucy. He will not rest. I know him, and he is unswerving. What a terrible thing I did, asking him to come and consult on your case. I unleashed a monster.'

'Can you not just tell him the truth? Tell him that I am alive and we counterfeited my death?'

'At best, he will say I am under your spell. That you have enslaved me to do your bidding. And Lucy,' his eyes were pink with fear, 'If I have to press the point, it will emerge that I signed your death certificate, knowing you to be alive. I could be struck off for dishonesty.'

'What if I flee to Mina's...?'

'Jonathan Harker is equally convinced of this delusion. He is certain that what happened in Transylvania was real and that you too are a victim of this mysterious Count. You would not be safe in Mina's home. Jonathan would rush to tell Van Helsing you were there, or he might seek to harm you himself.'

I suppose I had known I could not go to Exeter, but to hear John say this was a most dreadful blow. The silence between us was long. Eventually I spoke.

'So what do you suggest?'

'There is no body in the coffin. This has confirmed what he so fervently wants to believe. He is even convinced that he saw a figure in white, flitting through the churchyard. I, of course, saw no such thing. We are to return to the graveyard at midday today. A funeral is due to take place. Once the mourners have departed, I will re-open the tomb. I will call Van Helsing in, and he will see you dead, within your coffin. I am sure I can convince him that we were deluded by our own fear last night. He will see you, and he will believe that he was mistaken, and this appalling episode will end.'

And then? What would happen then? I could no longer go to Exeter. Where else could I go? Whom could I trust? Those Hampstead families I might once have called friends would never take me in – without a doubt they would contact Art if I arrived on their doorstep. I had no other school chums – Mina had been my only real friend and confidante. And there was no use in going to Mr Boyden. His loyalty would be to the man now responsible for paying his salary. There was only one option – one so remote and outrageous, I scarcely dared consider it. I would not confide my plan to John.

'I will need my bag, with my clothes. The one that was in the small room upstairs. Where is it?'

I saw a shift in John's features then, something sly. He knew he had something with which to bargain.

'I have it,' he said, and then added hastily, 'although I do not have it with me now. But if you come to Hendon this afternoon and do as I ask, I will place it in the crypt beneath the church. And then you may do with it as you will.'

We glared at each other, furious. He has been changed by this dreadfulness, I thought. The shy young man who came to propose to me, who sat on his hat and cut his finger, was gone. This man was as iron – fierce and cunning. But I too had been forged harder. If I were to escape, to start again, I needed my tiny store of money.

'Minutes only,' I said between gritted teeth. 'And then I am gone, and you will never see me again.'

John said we had half an hour before we needed to leave. I fetched my journal from its hiding place and then went to find Beatrice in the scullery. Her eyes were red and swollen.

'I'm sorry, Miss,' she whispered.

'I'm sorry, too, Beatrice. None of this is your fault. You did what you needed to do, I understand that.' This released her tears, and she sobbed, holding tightly to my hand. 'I have to go now,' I said. 'I will not return. I really am sorry, Beatrice... my gift of the library was meant to bring you good fortune and a brighter future. Not pain and fear.'

She managed a weak smile. I dropped a kiss onto her wet cheek and turned to go.

I travelled to Hendon on the floor of John's carriage, curled under a dusty rug. I wore a white nightgown, like the one I had worn in the coffin and I had a shawl to keep me warm. When we arrived around eleven, the churchyard was deserted, but for a gravedigger preparing the ground for the midday funeral. He was engrossed in his task under a spreading yew tree, and it was a simple matter for me to slip from the carriage and creep around the back of the church. The gate to the crypt stood ajar, and I tiptoed down the steps and opened the heavy creaking door. The space was narrow, dark and dusty, and the tombs ancient, some of them dating back to Norman times. In all the years I had worshipped in the church, I had never entered this space. I looked around curiously. True to his word, John had left my travelling bag behind one of the tombs. I put my journals inside it, then settled down to wait on a plinth, set well away from the door.

John went to let himself into the mausoleum. The previous night, Van Helsing had merely moved the lid aside and prised back one corner of the lead lining. If I were to be able to climb inside quickly, there needed to be a wider opening, and the lid would need to be set aside. When he had completed his task, he came to find me.

'I am certain no one will disturb you here,' he said, 'but if by any chance anyone enters, conceal yourself. I will go and wait for Dr Van Helsing. When it is time for you to come, I will make some excuse to send him away, and fetch you. You will know it is me, for I will knock three times on the door before I enter.'

In the gloom of the crypt, there was no way for me to measure time. While the funeral party was in the church above my head, I could hear the muffled sounds of words and singing, but when they passed out into the churchyard, there was only silence. The mourners must have lingered, for the minutes seemed to drag. I was considering creeping to the door and leaving, when I heard three muffled raps on the thick wood. The door creaked open, and I saw the pale oval of John's face.

'Come!' he hissed. 'I have sent the Professor to my carriage to fetch an electric lamp. We have just moments until he returns.'

I climbed the steps behind John and we ran as silently as we could, close to the north wall of the church. John guided me through the open door of the mausoleum.

The windowless room was narrow and dark, and cobwebs hung in festoons from the ceiling. A coffin along the back wall was most deeply covered in dust – the resting place of my grandmother Niamh. Pa's coffin, dull but not dusty, lay at right angles to this, and on a shelf above him, a new, shining casket – Mother's – was covered in heaps of dead and dying flowers. The air was thick with the scent of this decay, which, I suspected, hid a deeper note of further degradation.

My own coffin was alone on the right side, resting on a stone shelf. The lid had been propped against the side, and John had cut and lifted the lead flange. I felt my legs tremble beneath me, but there was no time to dwell on the horror of the situation. John swept me up in his arms and lowered me carefully into the coffin, taking care not to cut me on the sharp edges of the lead. Then he folded the flange back as flat as he could, leaving one corner lifted so that my face was visible. He stepped back to examine his handiwork.

'Yes, this is how we found it,' he said, satisfied.

He hurried out to meet Van Helsing, who would be on his way back from the carriage with the lamp. On his way out, John pushed the door almost to, but left it just enough ajar that a sliver of light showed.

Both of my dead parents were mere steps away and I breathed the air of their final resting place. A deep chill settled upon my soul.

Just when I was sure my courage would fail, Van Helsing entered with John behind him. I heard his heavy tread as he walked over to the coffin and forced back the leaden flange. I had expected to hear him exclaim in dismay, but instead, he gave a grunt of satisfaction. I felt a cold trickle of unease. Slightly too late, John gave his own exclamation of surprise. If Van Helsing noticed, he did not react.

'Are you convinced now?' The Professor demanded. I felt the heat of his hand as he reached into the coffin. He pulled my upper lip up roughly to expose my teeth. It took all my willpower not to flinch. 'See,' he went on, 'they are even sharper than before. With this and this,' he touched my canine teeth, 'the little children can be bitten. Are you of belief now, friend John?

She has been dead one week. Most peoples in that time would not look so.'

He stepped back and lifted his electric lamp, the better to see me.

'Here, there is one thing which is different from all recorded,' he observed. 'She is so sweet that she go back to the peace of the common dead. There is no malign there, see, and so it make hard that I must kill her in her sleep.'

I heard John's sharp intake of breath. The Professor took the gasp for acquiescence.

'Ah, you believe now?'

'Do not press me too hard all at once.' John said. Then, hesitantly, 'How will you do this bloody work?'

'I shall cut off her head and fill her mouth with garlic, and I shall drive a stake through her body.'

I heard a thud and a clank, and realised he had brought a bag of implements with him and was placing it on the floor in preparation. He fully intended to perform this horrific mutilation here and now. He knelt heavily and began to rummage in the bag.

'Professor,' John's voice was high and cracked. He sounded like a terrified boy. I could almost hear his mind racing. 'What of Art? How will we explain this desecration to him?'

It was a desperate stab in the dark – anything to delay the Professor. Nevertheless, I felt fury rise in my breast – even in death, I belonged to Art, body and soul.

But John's gamble was correct – the plea stayed the Professor's hand.

'If I did simply follow my inclining I would do it now; but what of Arthur indeed? How shall we tell him of this?' He sighed again. 'I know that he must pass through the bitter waters to reach the sweet.'

I felt a shadow cross my face as he pushed the lead flange back down and then I heard him scoop up his bag. The two of them left the tomb, and, to my horror, I heard the door clang shut behind them and the key turn in the lock. I opened my eyes, and saw nothing; I had been plunged into inky darkness.

I forced back the flange and climbed from the coffin. Pressing myself against the door, I hoped against hope that some fresh air was making its way around the heavy wood. Each breath was unbearably thick with the stink of decay and the weight of the darkness. If John did not return, I might well suffocate. They would find me here, crumpled against the door, the oak scored with the scratches from my nails. If they came back sooner and found me alive, Van Helsing would think me one of the walking dead and would kill me anyway.

Panic rose in my chest, but it was matched with a roaring, blinding fury. I had been foolish enough to trust John again, even after he had tried to rape me and had bribed Beatrice into betraying me. His weakness and stupidity had dragged me into this invidious position. I would fight my way out with my claws and teeth.

Seconds – or hours – later, I heard the key in the lock, and John pulled the door open. He started to see me standing so close. With a snarl, I leapt forward, my nails aimed at his eyes. He gasped and lurched backward, raising his hands. He tripped over the corner of a gravestone and fell, sprawling on his back. I sprang at him and landed so that I was sitting astride him. He raised a hand to protect his face, but I batted it aside.

'So help me God, John... what have you done? What have you done?'

'I never believed he would...'

'You have gambled with my life!'

'He will not find you in the coffin again. He will not be able to...'

'Now you believe he will stop? You told me that he would hunt me across the wide world if he has to. And what of Art? What will Art do?'

'I have an idea...'

'I have had enough of your ideas,' I said. 'You brought this madman to my bedside. You brought this all upon me. I cannot trust you, John. You have failed me at every turn.'

I saw his face crumple at my words and I was disgusted by him – by his cowardice. I wanted to strike him, to bloody his face and inflict some of the pain I had suffered upon him. Worst of all, I believe he would have lain there and let me do it, so abject was he. I raised a fist, but in that instant heard the gate of the churchyard clank open. Someone – the Sexton perhaps – was coming. I scrambled to my feet. Years of attending this church and playing in the churchyard after services meant I knew every inch of it. Without a backward glance, I fled north, down the slope, over the low stone wall and into the fields of Sunnyhill Farm. I kept running, bent double in the shadow of hedges until I had passed through three fields. There, I found a haystack and crept beneath its shadow to wait for the sunset.

The sun began to sink, but I did not feel the cold. The deep, roiling well of wrath within me warmed my body and sharpened my mind. No more.

CHAPTER 24

12 MAY 2024 – KATE

*T*he next morning, I woke to a message from Alex.

Jesus, Kate, what an idiot I was last night. There's nothing I can say to excuse my actions. I was drunk and stupid. I am so sorry, and so embarrassed. Getting the train to Manchester to see Mum today, then flying out to Rio from there. Hope one day we can meet for a coffee as friends. Ax.

He would see the two blue ticks beside his own message, knowing I'd read it. I felt no need to reply.

I lay looking up at the ceiling, and then abruptly, a rush of nausea overcame me. I only just made it out of bed and along the corridor to the bathroom. After I'd been sick, I sat trembling on the cold floor. Eventually, I managed to get to my feet, wash my face and brush my teeth and stumble back to the bedroom. I curled in a tight ball under the duvet and closed my eyes.

At some point later in the morning, my phone rang. I picked it up to cancel the call, but then saw it was Rafaella.

'Hello? I answered, in a shaky, small voice.

'You came into my mind,' Rafaella's warm voice came to me. 'Is everything okay? You sound...'

'No,' I said. 'No. I'm not okay.' Haltingly, I told her what had happened with Alex the night before.

'The bastard,' Rafaella said. 'Are you all right, though? Can you call someone to come and be with you?'

'I thought I was okay. I really did. I spoke to James last night and I felt quite calm, but today...'

'The shock is delayed.'

'It's not that. It's just... I realise he could actually have hurt me. Could have raped me if he'd really wanted to.'

'It's Alex. Come on.'

'I know. But there was a moment... just a brief one, when I felt his strength. I sensed that if he wanted to, he could use it against me. And I wouldn't have been able to stop him.'

'I'm so sorry.'

'We trust men,' I said. 'But they can turn. Even the ones we love and think we know.' I sobbed then. Rafaella listened to me cry.

'I am sorry that this happened to you,' she said. 'I wish I could hold you. I wish also I could tell Alex what I think of him. I would tell him ....' she let fly with a string of Italian expletives that made me smile through my tears.

'Ridiculous, isn't it?' I said. 'I've travelled all over the world, walked alone through dangerous cities, slept in tents on mountainsides... and when the bad thing finally happens, it's someone I thought I could trust, in my own home.'

'What do you need to feel safe?' Rafaella asked. 'Do you want to ask James to come and be with you? You know he would.'

'I know. But I have to sort this out myself. I need to find my own answers.'

After I said goodbye to Rafaella, I pulled my laptop towards me and opened Google. Something settled in my chest – a need to change something. To do something decisive. "Postgraduate funding," I typed. I spent rest of the morning researching and making notes.

I know Dad doesn't answer his phone during work hours, but he takes his lunch between twelve-thirty and one. Checking my watch, I dialled his number.

'Kate,' he said.

'Dad,' I began in a rush. 'That cheque you gave me. Thank you. I don't know if I ever said thank you properly.' I took a deep breath. 'So... I know you think I've spent the last few years just bumming around the world, but, well... it turns out I've got a huge amount of experience, and it's all quite diverse. I've taught people with vastly different skills, from different cultures in all sorts of environments. So, I started to think... what if I did a further degree? Could I draw all of my experience together? Like... a Master's in Education, where I could write a dissertation on pedagogy around the world?'

When the idea had come to me, it was as if a door had cracked open and I could see some light. It felt right and possible. A choice for me. My own path.

There was a long silence, and Dad said, 'And then?'

'Well, it might lead to a better-paid job. But maybe more research. More study. A PhD, maybe? The research I've been doing on the people in this house... it inspired me. Gave me courage. I think research is something I could be good at.'

'Well,' he said. 'Well.' He sounded winded with surprise. 'Kate... I will do anything... anything at all to support you in this. More money... a place to stay...'

'Dad, you've done more than enough. I can get a loan to study. The school trust where I'm working right now will give me time off for the course and they might even subsidise it.

Your cheque will make all the difference to me. I just wanted you to know.'

'My dear,' he said. 'I'm delighted to know. Just delighted. But you should know the money wasn't from me.'

'What do you mean?'

'When you rang me to thank me for the cheque, I tried to tell you, but you were too quick to get off the phone. Some months ago, I received a letter from the bank. They'd found an account in your mother's name. She opened it when you were born, and she'd put by a few pounds a month. She didn't get a chance to save much, but it's been sitting there earning interest since she died.'

'So ...'

'Your future plans are a gift from Noni, my dear.'

* * *

A FEW HOURS LATER, I stood outside Flat 4. I took a deep breath, stood tall and knocked firmly. I heard Rita's footsteps approaching, and then a pause. The door cracked open, as it had before, still restricted by the chain.

'Kate,' Rita said, not in greeting but as a statement of fact.

'Yes, me again.'

'What do you want?'

'First, to say thank you for last night.'

'You said thank you then. It's in the past. I don't think he will be coming back.'

'No.'

Rita went to shut the door, but I looked at her pleadingly.

'I know you want me to leave the whole Lucy thing alone, and I don't blame you. It's ancient history and I have no right to be digging.'

'But?' said Rita sardonically, 'There's always a but.'

'No but. Lucy's story isn't mine. I'm rubbernecking at something that happened 130 years ago because I thought it might bring me closer to my mum. I have no right to do that. But you do. The letter...' I held up the plastic Ziploc bag. 'This is the original. I want you to have it. It was in Beatrice's room. So it should belong to you.'

'No, it shouldn't,' said Rita.

'I beg your pardon?'

I was shaken. I'd expected Rita to take the letter and close the door.

'If anyone should have the letter, it's your Mr Harker. Mina was the intended recipient, and he's her descendant. Beatrice was a silly girl. She should have sent the letter. If she had, things might have turned out very differently.'

'What things?'

Rita slammed the door closed. I took a step back in shock. Was this it? Had the old woman clammed up again? I couldn't bear it if... But then I heard the rattle of the chain releasing and the door swung wide open.

'You'd better come in,' said Rita. 'Welcome to the library.'

LUCY WESTENRA'S SECOND JOURNAL

As the quiet of evening settled across the valley, sounds came to me across the fields. I could hear chickens clucking, and a woman's voice, talking soothingly as she fed them. I crept out from beneath the haystack, and keeping once more to the shadow of the hedges, followed the sound of her voice.

She was a tall, broad-backed woman standing, hands on hips, as the chickens pecked around her feet. In one swift movement, she bent and scooped up a hen – a scrawny white bird. She tucked it under her arm. A blood-stained cleaver was imbedded in the top of a fence post, and she plucked it out. With one well-aimed swing, she decapitated the chicken. The head landed in the mud with a thud, and the body jerked and struggled under her arm.

Just then, a loud wail floated out on the evening air. I recognised the tone of that cry – the howl of a child who has fallen and is both furious and in pain. The woman sighed. She embedded the cleaver back in the fence post, let herself out of the hens' enclosure and hurried towards the sound. On her way, she dropped the corpse of the chicken onto a tree-stump.

I do not know what I was thinking in those moments. I believe my mind was fractured. As soon as she was out of sight, I tiptoed to the fence. With some effort, I pulled the cleaver free. Then, crossing to the tree stump, I pressed my hand to the dead chicken's side. It was soft and still warm. I lifted it gently and held it to my chest. It was both light and solid and gave me inexpressible comfort. I folded my arms around it. In the distance, I could hear the woman alternately scolding and comforting the child.

'Come now Jerry, wipe your tears,' she said. 'If you're wanting some dinner, I need to go and fetch that old biddy.'

I heard her footsteps draw near and I ran, holding onto the chicken's body, the cleaver still clutched in my fist. I heard a faint cry behind me, but I did not turn or slow.

I ran up the hill and climbed the wall into the churchyard. It was the navy-blue, velvet hour of the evening. A breeze moved through the leaves of the great yew trees. I made my way along the wall of the church and found the gate into the crypt. It was still open, and I slipped inside. It was pitch dark, but I found my way by feeling along the walls. To my inexpressible relief, my bag was there. I gathered it and crept back out of the crypt. I settled on the stone steps, my bag beside me, holding the chicken close to my chest with one arm, the cleaver gripped in my other hand. The chicken's body was beginning to cool and stiffen, but I found I could not let it go. The night deepened outside, and I heard the hoot of owls and the flutter of bats flittering between the trees.

In the darkest hour, I heard them come. Their boots were heavy on the path, and even from a distance, I could hear the commanding boom of Van Helsing's voice.

'You were with me here yesterday, John. Was the body of Miss Lucy in that coffin?'

I heard John answer. He sounded sick and exhausted.

'It was.'

I heard the grate of the key in the lock of the mausoleum and several sets of footsteps passing in. There was a long silence, and then I heard someone speak. I jerked in surprise to hear Quincey's Texan drawl.

'Professor, is this your doing?'

'I swear to you by all that I hold sacred that I have not removed nor touched her,' said Van Helsing.

They continued to talk. But their voices were too low for me to make out what they were saying. I crept to the top of the stairs. I was about to emerge when I heard them come out of the mausoleum, shutting and locking the door behind them.

From where I was standing, I had no view of the mausoleum, but I heard an odd scrabbling noise and shortly thereafter, John's voice asking, 'What are you doing?'

Van Helsing answered brusquely, 'I am closing the tomb, so that the undead may not enter.'

'What is that which you are using?' This time the question came from Art.

'The Host. I brought it from Amsterdam. I have an Indulgence.'

A laugh escaped me then. It was not loud enough to be audible to the men, but my disbelief could not be contained. For a man with his profound religious convictions to commit such a blasphemous act showed the depths of his delusion. He had persuaded a priest to sell him a large quantity of sanctified Communion wafer, and he was using it like a magic spell? It was an act of medieval superstition.

I slipped out of the doorway, although I was still within the shadow of the church. The men spread out, looking around them in the dark churchyard. The night was overcast, but at that moment the moon emerged through a break in the cloud, and there, facing away from me, I saw Art. He stood, his head bent and his shoulders slumped, fidgeting with a cigarette case. I crept a few steps closer. He lifted the case, obviously tempted to take out a cigarette and smoke, but then thinking better of it. As he did so, the gleam of moonlight illuminated the case in his hand. The gold shone like a beacon, and in that instant, I recognised it. Pa's cigarette case, with its intricate embossing. When he had plundered our home, Art had claimed it for his own.

My hand tightened on the cleaver. He stood with his back to me, and if I ran at him, I could embed it between his shoulder blades before he even realised I was there. But I wanted to see his face – witness his fear when I slew him. I turned and circled back around the church. I emerged into the churchyard at the south-east corner.

The men were ranged around, looking in all directions. I took a deep breath and stepped from the shadows onto the path and into a bright shaft of moonlight. I felt a deep, icy calm.

Van Helsing was the first to see me. He hissed and turned to face me, his frown deep and his hands clenching into fists. His eyes roamed over me, and his expression turned to horror. I was wearing the white nightgown in which I had lain in the coffin, but I was still holding the body of the chicken to my breast. The cleaver hung loose in my right hand. I let the chicken fall to the ground, but the blood had stained the bodice of my gown. I must, I thought, appear mad.

The four men – John, Quincey, Van Helsing and Art formed themselves into a line, as if they were the infantry of some holy army. They took a few steps towards me. I looked at each in turn – John, his face taut with tension, terrified by what I might say or do. Quincey, deceptively relaxed, his face expressionless, but his body poised for quick movement. If anyone had the capacity to stop me, it was he. Van Helsing clutched at his little gold crucifix, as if it would protect him against my malevolence. A smile twisted my lips at this sight.

And Art. Facing him now, in the glow of the moonlight, I

was shocked at his appearance. His face was bloated and blotchy. His hair hung lank and greasy over his eyes and his shirtfront was stained. I turned away from the others and fixed my full attention on him. I walked towards him, the cleaver hanging in my hand, concealed in the folds of my skirt.

'Oh Art,' I whispered. He swayed slightly. 'Come to me, Arthur. Leave these others and come to me. My arms are hungry for you. Come, and we can rest together. Come, my husband, come!'

My hand tightened on the handle of the cleaver. Art took a few hesitant steps towards me. Our gazes locked. I looked into his eyes and saw only emptiness. Was he tortured with guilt at having committed a double murder? Or had he discovered that even after everything he had stolen, he still faced ruin? He stared at me, his eyes bloodshot, his hands hanging slackly at his sides. I could not be sure if he believed me to be an undead spirit, or if he knew that he was facing me, the real Lucy, alive and vengeful. His eyes flicked down and registered the cleaver in my hand. He looked up and to my astonishment, he began to walk towards me, his arms at his side, offering me his chest and throat, bare and undefended. *He wants me to do it*, I thought. I swung my arm up, the cleaver in my hand and stepped forward. An end at last.

Van Helsing sprang between us, snarling and waving his silly little crucifix in my face. In momentary shock, I fell back and let the cleaver drop from my hand. As he advanced, I dodged him, and, passing between him and Art, ran towards the mausoleum and the shelter of the church beyond. I could hear the confused shouts of the men behind me.

'She will try to enter the tomb, but the holy Host will prevent her!' Van Helsing said, triumphant.

Such idiocy. I was prevented from entering the tomb, should I have wanted to, by a locked door. I turned to look at them all, hanging back, frozen with terror. Something rose in my breast, an emotion so powerful, it burst from me in a shout of delighted laughter. These four men between them had taken everything from me. And yet I was still here, still standing. They had not won.

The silence stretched as they stared at me. Van Helsing turned to Art in that instant.

'Answer me, oh my friend,' he said urgently, 'Am I to proceed in my work?'

Art slid to the ground then, on his knees, and buried his ravaged face in his hands.

'Do as you will, friend; do as you will. There can be no horror like this ever anymore.'

I stayed to hear no more. The moon passed back behind a cloud and in the cover of sudden darkness, I slipped along the side of the church. I snatched up my bag from the steps of the crypt, and fled out onto the road. I was conscious that I was out alone, wearing a blood-stained nightgown. At least I now had shoes, however.

I followed the road for some half a mile, keeping to the shadows. I came to the Burroughs Pond. I waited beneath a tree until I was certain there was no one to be seen. Then I darted to the edge of the pool. I splashed my face and hands with cold water and did my best to rinse the chicken's blood from the front of my nightgown.

What was happening in the churchyard behind me? How would John explain the fact that my undead body had disappeared and would never return? What had Art meant when he told Van Helsing to do as he would? I did not care. There was nothing to be gained by going back.

I drew a skirt and blouse from my bag and pulled them on over my nightgown. It was cold and dark, but I had shoes on my feet and the moon to guide me. I knew the journey was long and I would have to travel cautiously, staying out of sight. Nevertheless, I felt strong and light. I began to walk south.

At dawn, I reached the edge of Regent's Park. I drank from a water fountain, but conscious that people were beginning to move around, I hurried on, passing down Baker Street. I crossed the Marylebone Road and paused to catch my breath in a doorway. I was standing under a marble portico before some imposing wooden doors, and with a shock, I realised that it was the entrance to Bedford College for Women. I remembered pushing open this door with Pa, that day, two years before, when I had come to sit my entrance examination. I had seen my future that day with such vivid certainty. How completely it had been snatched from me.

I resumed my slow progress. Whenever I saw someone notice me, I dipped my head and kept walking. Now I was in London, there were beggars, drunks and drabs on every corner. I was less conspicuous with my straggling hair and crumpled clothes than I had been on the country roads. By the time I reached Oxford Street, the city was fully awake and carriages and omnibuses rattled to and fro. I crossed the main thoroughfare and kept walking through the leafy roads of Mayfair.

As I came to Shepherd Market, I remembered coming here for the first time, in Art's carriage. A different lifetime. With a shock, I realised that that had been just four weeks ago, at the end of August.

My legs ached, and I was shivering with cold and exhaustion. When I finally reached the door of 17 Clarges Mews, I could barely stand. I rang the bell, then rested my head on the doorframe. With the last of my strength, I slid down the wall until I was sitting on the doorstep. I dropped my head to my knees, and felt tears escape from my weary, closed eyes. A weak ray of sun topped the buildings opposite and touched my face. Day had dawned on this, the 28th day of September. My twentieth birthday, and the day that was to have been my wedding day.

I did not hear the door open, nor her exclamation of

surprise. The first I knew was the clean scent of her gown as Mrs Hammond knelt on the doorstep and put her arms around me.

'Lucy,' she said, 'Lucy, poor angel. What has happened to you?'

28 SEPTEMBER 1894

She believed me. I told her everything, from my first encounter with Quincey to the horrifying scene in the graveyard the night before. She listened without interrupting and when I had finished, she nodded.

'As you know, I have encountered Arthur Holmwood,' she said. 'He is a man of surpassing cruelty. I believe he is capable of anything to gain what he believes is his due.'

'I think he is crumbling now. When I saw him in the church-yard last night, he looked...' I cast around for the right descrip-tor. '...broken.'

'Do not be fooled. Perhaps guilt has momentarily stayed his hand, but he has seen you now. I doubt he believes the Profes-sor's thesis that you are a... vampire. He knows you live now, and I doubt he will let that rest.'

'What are you saying?'

'I want you to be able to stay here, but Holmwood knows me and knows where I live. It was he who sent you to see me that first time, was it not? It may be only a matter of time before it occurs to him to look for you here. Do you have nowhere else you can go?'

'No. You are my only hope.'

'For now, we will do our best to make you strong again,' said Mrs Hammond. 'Today, you shall sleep and eat, and we will furnish you with some more garments. Tomorrow, we will find somewhere where you may be safe.'

We stayed indoors all day. Mrs Hammond, or Anna, as I

came to know her, occupied herself with laundering the few items of clothing I had managed to bring away with me and with altering some of her own clothes to fit me, as I was taller and more slender than she. Once I had rested and recorded the events of the past few days in this journal, I played with little Violet.

That evening, once Violet had gone to bed, Anna and I made halting conversation. She told me her life story. She was the daughter of a shopkeeper from Bath. Aged twelve she had been abruptly orphaned by a fever, which also claimed her younger brother. There was no other local family. She had travelled to London in the hope of finding a cousin of her mother's, but unable to locate her, had ended up in the workhouse.

'I was pretty and shy. And if I am honest, I think I would have ended up selling myself one way or another. I had little schooling and not many skills. I was lucky that I was found by a woman who ran a high-class establishment, or it would have been the street for me.'

'Lucky?' I said.

'Women who walk the street... if someone does not kill them, then it's the pox, or one too many babies. They don't last long. I was more fortunate. A nice room around the corner from here in the Market, decent gentleman callers, in the main.'

'And then?' I prompted softly.

'And then... Charles.'

She said his name with such tenderness. I had never heard my Mother speak it so.

'He visited the house occasionally. All the girls liked him. He was kind and funny and he paid so well. But when he met me...' she blushed and looked down at the skirt she was hemming. 'Well, he said he didn't want anyone else, and he didn't want me to have anyone else either. He was happy to pay to make it so. He'd come and see me every week. And then, after we learned that I was with child, he rented me some rooms of my own. After Violet was born, he bought this house for us.'

She looked around the cosy living room, and I could see tears shining on her lashes.

'We were happy here together. I know perhaps you do not wish to hear it, but we were. He was content when he came to spend time with us.'

'I loved him,' I said quietly, 'and my mother did not make him happy. If there was a place where he could be at ease and beloved, I am glad for it.'

'He loved you so much, Lucy, and was so proud of you. He spoke of you all the time. I used to dream of meeting you.'

We exchanged a smile. She bent her head once more over her sewing, and a coppery strand of her hair slipped free and curled on her pale cheek. There was a quiet grace about her, and sharp intelligence. She would have been a good companion for him.

30 SEPTEMBER 1894

This morning, Anna came into my room, a skirt, jacket and bonnet over one arm.

'Lucy, my dear, I have spoken to a friend who lives in Camden Town who is willing to take you in.'

'Will I be safe there?'

'I believe so. For the time being, it is the best I can do.'

I scrambled out of bed and reached for the clothes she held.

'Anna, you have been so good to me. Thank you. I hope that in some way, I will be able to repay you.'

'You know that is unnecessary,' she said, patting my arm. 'Come downstairs as soon as you are ready. Before you leave this house, there are some changes we need to make. My friends Miriam and Deborah are downstairs. They are excited to meet you.'

After weeks of illness and chaos, it felt strange to lace my stays and button a blouse. I sat at the dressing table to arrange my hair. As I was thus occupied, little Violet crept around the half-open door into my room.

'May I brush it?' she whispered. I handed her the brush, and she stood behind me. She was careful not to tug at any tangles, and she soon had my hair spread across my shoulders in gleaming waves.

'It is mermaid hair,' she said in an awed whisper. She came to stand beside me and put the brush down, I looked at our two faces, so alike, reflected in the glass. I reached out to touch her neat plaits.

'Your hair will look just the same when you are a little older,' I smiled.

She touched the plait herself and then met my eyes again with a pleading look. I understood. Gently loosening the ribbons on her hair, I brushed it out until it too shone on her shoulders. For the sake of neatness, I gathered up a few silky strands in the front and fastened them back with one of the ribbons. She turned this way and that, admiring herself in the mirror.

I swept my own hair up into a twist and buttoned my jacket. I stood, offering Violet my hand.

'Come. Let us go and meet your mamma's friends.'

As we went down the stairs, I could hear lively chatter in the drawing room – female voices raised in rapid, animated conversation, interspersed with laughter. I eased open the door and peeked around it. Anna stood by the fireplace, her cheeks flushed, smiling. I stepped hesitantly into the room and saw the two guests sitting on the settee. With a start, I recognised them: the two young women I had seen in Shepherd Market all those weeks ago. Violet let go of my hand and flew into the arms of the plump, dark-haired one, who whooped with delight and embraced her.

'Why little Vi! How grown up you look!' she said, stroking her hair.

Violet smiled with shy pleasure. She wedged herself between the two women and began examining the bright jewels at the woman's ears and throat.

'Lucy,' said Anna, 'May I introduce you to my friends, Deborah Nicholls and Miriam Kelly.'

The fair-haired woman – Miriam – stood to greet me. She was as tall as I, with brilliant green eyes and a bold, wide mouth.

'A delight to meet you,' she said, and I detected a hint of an Irish accent in her husky voice.

Deborah gave me a wide smile and offered me her hand from the settee.

'Violet will not let me rise, so please do excuse me.'

Blonde Miriam looked me up and down, 'Anna explained to us that you have suffered quite the trial,' she said, 'and we need to fix your hair.'

'My hair?' I frowned in confusion.

'If anyone is asking around the Market for a girl with flaxen hair, you'll be spotted in no time at all.'

'And so?' I touched my topknot self-consciously.

Miriam reached into the pocket of her skirt and produced a paper twist. She opened it carefully. It was full of a greenish powder, which gave off a pleasingly grassy barnyard scent.

'This is henna. It is an herbal preparation beloved of the Ancient Egyptians.'

She beckoned and I followed her upstairs to my bedroom. Anna came up after us with a basin of water, a stack of towels and a small bowl. Miriam tipped the powder into the bowl. I stared at it. I could not see how it would work.

Miriam undertook the task with brisk efficiency. At her instruction, I removed my blouse and sat with the towel draped over my chemise. She mixed the powder into a paste with some warm water and painted it through the length of each strand of my hair, taking care not to get any on the skin of my forehead or neck. Then she twisted the towel around my head and told me to wait for some minutes. When she pronounced that enough time had passed, it took many jugs of water to rinse all the paste from my hair. A strand tumbled across my eyes and I saw with surprise that it had indeed changed colour.

When she was happy that she had rinsed my hair clean, she wrapped it in a clean towel and squeezed the water from it. Then she instructed me to sit by the open window to let it dry. She brought me books, pen, and paper to keep myself occupied while I waited and she, Deborah and Anna took little Violet out for a walk.

I used the time to write to Mina, telling her that I had fled Hampstead and giving her my new address. I did not expect much, as so many of my letters had gone unanswered, but I could not give up hope that somehow, my dear friend might be able to aid me.

I was strict with myself and did not examine the locks as they hung wet down my back. Instead, I waited until they had dried, then walked slowly to the glass and stared at my reflection.

My hair was red – the same glowing russet of the model for Rossetti's *La Ghirlandata*. Pa and I had seen it exhibited. He had thought it garish and vulgar, but I loved it – the model's voluptuous lips, her emerald-green gown and the delicious tumble of her hair. My pale skin suited the bright glow and my eyes looked startlingly blue. I did not think many would attribute the colour to artificial means. They would merely see a tall, slender, redheaded girl. My ordeals of the past few months had made me thin, and there was a new sharpness to my features. I looked older than my age. I suspected that I might be unrecognisable, even to those who had known me comparatively well.

My new hair made me brave, and I decided to slip from the apartment and post my letter to Mina. I fetched a shawl and bonnet and put the letter in my pocket. I hurried down the stairs. As I passed the open door to the parlour, a voice spoke languidly.

'Ophelia.'

I jumped and turned around. A slim young man was sprawled on one of the sofas, a newspaper dangling from his hand.

'I beg your pardon?' I said, trying to keep my voice steady.

'Your profile. *Ophelia*. It was Rossetti's wife in the painting, I believe. Millais nearly killed her. She contracted pneumonia from lying in a bath in a greenhouse to model for that painting.'

I decided that it was best to brazen out the encounter, so I turned and smiled.

'I have been told that I resemble *La Ghirlandata* before today, but I will take it as a compliment that you think I bring to mind Elizabeth Rossetti.'

He sat up then and raised one well-shaped eyebrow.

'You are familiar with the work of the Pre-Raphaelites then?'

I inclined my head. I was about to make my excuses and leave, but he stood and walked toward me, offering his hand. I stiffened instinctively, but as he drew nearer, I saw he was slight in build, and no taller than I was. He took my hand and his grip was cool and light. There was a graceful quality to his movements. I thought it unlikely that he could overpower me or cause me harm.

'I am Philip,' he said. I thought it odd that he gave me his Christian name.

I had not yet thought of a pseudonym. My mind raced.

'I am – er – Miss Jones. P– Polly Jones.'

'Will you sit with me a while, Miss Jones?' he said. 'I have exhausted the amusements offered by *The Times*.'

He gestured at the heap of newspaper pages he had allowed to tumble carelessly to the carpet. He strolled towards the sofa and threw himself down, resting his arms along the back and smiling at me. My heart began to pound in my chest. Who was this man? And why was he sitting in Anna's parlour as if he owned it?

'I… er… I was actually on my way out… to post a letter.'

He checked his watch. 'I think you may have missed the last post. There is no hurry – your letter will not go until tomorrow. Please sit down and let us talk a little.' He smiled lightly. He seemed harmless, but I had been so bruised by my experiences over the last few months that I could not entirely relax my guard. 'I take it back,' he said. 'You are more Burne-Jones than Millais in your looks. And definitely not Rossetti.'

'With respect,' I said, 'I would rather resemble Elizabeth Rossetti, or at least to resemble her when she was still Lizzie Siddal, and was a painter and poet in her own right. I would rather be a maker than a mute doll, known only by the name of the man who depicted me.'

He roared with delighted laughter at this. 'Oh, Polly!' he said. 'You are quite the tonic.'

He was, I realised, not as young as I had at first supposed – perhaps thirty or so. But his skin was smooth, and he looked as if he was not often troubled with shaving. His blue eyes were fringed with extravagant lashes and he wore his fair hair long and curly. Even though I did not know him, I felt safe with him.

He told me how he ran a business importing spices and fabrics from the Far East. Our conversation turned back to art, and we talked of the Summer Show at the Academy. Then Philip idly picked up a book from a side table and it was one that I had read, so we discussed that. Time flew by and I found myself relaxing into my chair. I had not spent time so easily convivial since I had been in Whitby with Mina.

At length, Philip leaned forward, resting his elbows on his knees, and regarded me seriously.

'Now, Polly, I am afraid my curiosity has the better of me. Some of the girls I meet socially take care to be aware of the issues of the day, or have read a little literature or history – enough to make pretty conversation. But their knowledge is cosmetic and shallow. However you – you have had a real education, have you not?'

I saw no reason to lie, even if I did not give any identifying details.

'My father believed in the value of study. I had governesses as a child. As well as their teaching, my Pa supplied an informal education that was both rigorous and eclectic. I attended school for a few – too few – years in my teens before my Pa passed away. Since then, I have taken charge of my education myself. I have...' I swallowed, overcome suddenly with the enormity of my loss. 'I *had* an extensive library at my disposal.'

'You have it no longer?'

'No.' I said shortly. 'My circumstances have changed, rather for the worse.'

Philip saw my sudden disquiet and he frowned slightly.

'It strikes me someone has caused you hurt, Polly,' he said, softly. 'Let me assure you, you will come to no harm at my hands.' He reached into his pocket and drew out a calling card. He held it out to me. 'This is my card. I believe Anna spoke to you of a friend who would offer you lodgings. I am that friend. Please call at my home within the next few days, and we will see you right.' He stood then, bowed and took his leave.

* * *

Some time later, Anna returned with Violet, Miriam and Deborah. Little Milly the maid served us all a warming stew and we sat in warm lamplight, laughing and talking. When Anna excused herself to put little Violet to bed, Deborah turned to me.

'So you met Mr Philip, I hear?'

'I did. I must confess, I was confused by his kindness. I have had some bad experiences with men. They always seem to want something from a young woman, but Philip seems only to want to be kind.' Miriam and Deborah exchanged a glance and burst out laughing. 'What?' I asked, confused. 'Why do you laugh?'

'Philip Graham does not want anything from you, that's true,' said Deborah. 'He is magically protected from your charms.'

'Indeed, there is nothing you could do that would persuade him otherwise,' added Miriam.

My frown of incomprehension seemed to amuse them further, but eventually, Deborah patted my arm and said, 'Philip is an Uranian, my dear.'

'A what?'

'You were, I am sure, aware of the trial of the playwright, Mr Wilde, earlier this year?'

I could not understand her sudden change of topic. But comprehension dawned and I stared at her, open-mouthed.

'Philip is a...' I searched for the word I had read in Pa's books on human sexuality. 'A sodomite?'

'An ugly term. He simply prefers the intimate company of men. He has had a long association with a dear gentleman called Adam Lionel. Philip is a lovely fellow, and kind and generous to a fault. If he has offered you his patronage, you are a lucky girl indeed.'

Miriam leaned over and refilled my wine glass. She and Deborah raised their glasses to me, and as we all drank in the bright light of the fire, I had a sudden vision of my mother. I tried to imagine her expression if she were to learn I was living in Shepherd Market, consorting with prostitutes and homosexuals. I laughed. For as horrified as Mother would be, I had seldom experienced such genuine kindness and generosity as I had found in these rooms.

CHAPTER 25

13 MAY 2024 – KATE

I stepped into Flat 4. A heavy velvet curtain hung just behind the door, and Rita swept it aside. I followed her, expecting to pass into a narrow, dim corridor lined with partitioned rooms, as Rita had described it. Instead, I found myself in a single, enormous room, flooded with morning light. Floor-to-ceiling bookshelves were packed with handsome, leather-bound volumes. I gazed around, open-mouthed.

'But you said...'

'I said Grandpa Cameron partitioned it back in the day, when there were five of us living here. But since I've been on my own, I've had it restored. I got all the books out of storage. The shelves were all still there behind the partitions. I've kept the kitchen and the bathroom, but...' Rita waved an arm. Two beautiful leather sofas faced each other by one window, forming a living area, and in the alcove at the far end was her bed.

'Oh Rita. It's beautiful.'

'It is, isn't it?' For the first time, Rita smiled. 'I don't usually let people in here.'

'I am so grateful that you did.' I walked slowly down one wall of the room, looking at the books. 'They're all properly classified.'

'By subject and then alphabetically,' said Rita, pleased. 'Not my system, I hasten to add. Lucy's. When it belonged to Charles, it was chaos, I believe. But Lucy arranged it and filled gaps in the collection. It was her university. When the library was packed up, everything was placed in numbered boxes, so I was able to put it all back just as it was in her time.'

I found my eyes filling with tears. 'I wish she could have enjoyed it for longer.'

'I do too. I also wish my Nan had used it as Lucy intended – to gain an education and change her own fortunes. She had no interest in it, nor did my father.'

'But you have.'

'I'm eighty-four years old. I've had a lot of time to read.'

'Have you read it all?'

'Not far off. There are some books in other languages, and those were a bit too much for me. But there're all sorts in here. History, philosophy, science... even erotica!' Rita's eyes twinkled, 'It's not the most academic of libraries, but it's endlessly interesting. I like to think I've ended up with much the same education as Lucy.'

'I bet she'd be thrilled. I can't thank you enough for showing it to me, Rita.'

Rita raised a finger. 'Wait a moment. I think you'll like this.'

She bustled off, and with a certainty born of decades of familiarity, reached up and plucked a slim volume off a shelf, handing it to me. I frowned, because the book was instantly familiar. *Pitman's Shorthand Manual* – an older edition than Gran's version, but the same book. I cautiously opened the cover and saw, in the familiar rounded hand: "property of Lucy Westenra".

'She would have used this to write the letter!' I whispered.

'Not just the letter. Not by any means,' said Rita. 'Come. I've got something else to show you.'

She led me over to the alcove where her bed was. On the wall above her bedside table, there was a framed photograph. A dark-haired, much younger version of Rita sat on a bench in the sunlight. Beside her, an arm thrown around Rita's shoulders, her eyes wide and laughing, her smile infectious, was Mum. Noni.

'I'm not a very sociable person,' Rita said softly. 'But she was... well. The only true friend I ever had.'

She placed a hand on my arm, and with the other, indicated another framed picture. This was a small charcoal sketch, about the size of a postcard. A Madonna and child, I thought at first glance. But then I saw the perfect arch of the nose. It was Mum again, in profile, bent over the baby lying in her arms. A baby whose dark eyes gazed back up at her, transfixed, adoring. I let out a small sob.

'She drew that just after you were born,' Rita sad softly. 'She said she'd never loved anyone as much as she loved you.'

'So you stayed friends? After she left here?'

'Of course. Noni was... well. She saved my life.'

I frowned. 'How?'

'You remember I told you about my ex-husband Paul?'

'You said he tried to get you to sign the flat over to him.'

'He more than tried. He threatened, and when I said no, he beat me black and blue. Knocked one of my teeth out and broke my jaw. Noni was coming up the stairs and heard the racket. She burst in here like an avenging angel. All that dark hair crackling around her head like electricity. She ordered him out of here and he was so shocked he went. She got me to the hospital to get me patched up. Then she called the police and made me report him for domestic abuse. When we got back here, she rang a locksmith to change the locks. Packed up Paul's things and put them out on the landing. She saw me through the whole sorry mess... protected me every step of the way. Like I say, she saved my life.'

I stared at her, mute.

'So when you saved me from Alex the other night...'

She laughed. 'Sometimes the universe gives us a chance to pay back, I believe.'

Then, with her strong little hand, she grasped my wrist and guided me over to the large leather sofas. 'Sit.'

I sat. I was still clutching Lucy's shorthand manual. I held it out, so Rita could return it to the shelf.

'Hold on to that. You may need it,' said Rita. 'Now I'm going to make you a cup of tea, because you'll need that too. And possibly some sandwiches. You don't have anything else to do today, do you?'

'No...' I said warily.

Rita bustled off and returned with a pot of tea and a mug, along with a plate full of cheese sandwiches.

'I'm putting these here, but if you want to eat or drink, please put everything aside and wash your hands before you carry on.'

'I'm sorry Rita, but you've lost me, Carry on with what?'

Rita wiped her hands nervously on her skirt. 'I can't believe I'm doing this, Kate. I'm trusting you with a secret I've kept for decades. Only one other person has seen what I'm about to show you.'

Rita walked over to one of the tall windows. They were framed with handsome wood panelling, and she ran a hand down a row of panels to the right of the window. With a practised hand, she found a hidden edge, pressed and then pulled, I gasped as the panel swung open like a small, hinged door. There was an alcove within, about a foot square.

Rita turned to me and said, 'after the library was restored, I sanded and polished all the woodwork myself. I pushed the hidden catch by mistake and found this recess and what was in it.'

She put both hands into the small space and carefully lifted out two battered notebooks, both bound in faded red leather, and a thick pile of typed pages. She carried her precious cargo to me and placed it in my lap.

I carefully opened the topmost notebook. At the top of the first page, in a rounded, childish hand, I read:

Lucy Westenra's journal

'She began to keep a journal when she was fourteen,' Rita smiled. 'That first volume gives quite a picture of the girl she was – wilful, forthright, unafraid. But it's the second journal that's more interesting.'

I carefully opened the second book. On the inside cover in a more mature hand, I read:

Lucy Westenra's Second Journal
   4 April 1894

Beyond these opening words, this page, and all the subsequent pages, were filled with the incomprehensible squiggles of shorthand.

'It took me about ten years, but I transcribed it all. Both journals,' said Rita, pointing to the typed pages. I wasn't as experienced at shorthand as Mina and Lucy were. The whole story is there. If you're happy to stay here, you can read it.'

Speechless, I nodded. I set the journals gently aside and lifted the typed pages. But before I began to read, I looked up at her.

'You said only one other person has ever seen these...'

'You know who.'

'My mum?'

'She was the only person I trusted with the words. She read these when I finished the transcript. She loved the story so much. All those drawings you have on the wall in your flat... well, they'll make a lot more sense when you read what happened to Lucy.'

I rested my hand on the top page. I'd spent months waiting for an echo of my mum in the walls of my flat, but had heard only silence. Now, somehow, touching these pages, I felt something – a whisper. Her breath in my ear. She was here. In this library. I bent my head and began to read.

My name is Lucy Rose Westenra. I was born upon the 28th day of September in the Year of our Lord 1874. I am fourteen years and seven months old and this is my diary...

LUCY WESTENRA'S SECOND JOURNAL

2 OCTOBER 1894

I was settled in Anna's parlour this morning with a book, enjoying the autumnal rays coming through the window. At about ten, I was surprised to hear a tentative tapping at the door. I froze in my seat. Anna was out with Violet and little Milly had gone to collect some shopping. The knock was repeated – still quiet, but insistent. Would Art knock thus? I considered fleeing upstairs, but something made me creep to the window and peer out. As soon as I saw who was standing on the doorstep, I flung the door wide. It took all my will to stifle the cry of joy on my lips as I flew into Mina's arms.

We clung to one another for long moments, and then she withdrew and held me at arm's length.

'Lucy,' she whispered. 'My darling girl. What has happened to you?'

'Everything has happened to me, and more besides. Yet I am still standing, and they have not won.'

I took her hand and drew her into the parlour, shutting and locking the door behind us. She looked around her with some curiosity, but made no comment about the place in which I had found myself. We sat together on the sofa and I explained to her how I had come to be in this house, and told her of Anna's kindness. I gazed at her beloved face. I was overjoyed to see her, but resentment clouded my joy.

'I wrote to you so often,' I said, 'but you never replied.'

'It took some time to nurse Jonathan until he was strong enough to travel,' she said. 'We arrived back in England on the fifteenth of September. On our return, I discovered several letters from you detailing your illness. I was so worried, I said to Jonathan that I wished to leave as soon as possible to come to see you, but then Mr Hawkins fell ill, and he died just two days later. The next day, we received news of your own death.'

'But I was not dead.'

'I did not know that – and your letter telling that extraordinary news arrived just a few days ago. I travelled with all speed to Hillingham and found Beatrice, distraught. She told me you had fled into the night, and that neither she nor Dr Seward knew where you were. I received your most recent letter yesterday, and here I am.'

'But how is it that you are here so very early? Did you travel up from Exeter last night?'

'I was not in Exeter. As soon as your letter arrived, our housekeeper forwarded it to me. I have been in Purfleet, and I came here on the earliest possible train.'

I started as if she had dashed cold water in my face.

'Purfleet?'

'Yes. Jonathan and I are staying at the asylum as guests of Dr Seward, along with Professor Van Helsing, Lord Godalming and Mr Morris.'

I do not remember standing, but I found myself in the middle of the carpet, backing away from her.

'Lucy, calm yourself. Let me explain.'

'I put my trust in you.'

'And you did so rightly. Come and sit down, let us talk calmly.'

'I cannot be calm, Mina, I cannot. In the last month, I have been poisoned and abused. I have been forced to feign death, lying in my own coffin, I have been locked in a tomb with my dead parents, and I have been betrayed by those to whom I entrusted my safety. You... you were my last hope, and I find you are in league with those who would murder and exploit me.'

I was aware that my voice was rising, but I was unable to stop my racing heart. I backed towards the door. If needs be, I would flee into the streets. She would not know the narrow byways of Mayfair. I could lose her if I had to.

'My dearest Lucy. I understand how very grievously you have been misused, and that it is impossible for you to trust anyone. But I want you to know that I have been working ceaselessly on your behalf, and will continue to do so. If you would only sit down and let me explain.'

I gazed into her familiar face. I was so tired of fleeing, of fighting, of being afraid. She saw my indecision and began to speak.

'When Professor Van Helsing came to see me, he witnessed my distress at your death. It was entirely genuine. The letter telling me you had not died had not yet been delivered. The next morning, the Professor was due to return and see Jonathan and me, but before he came to the house, your letter arrived – and everything changed.

'I cannot express my horror at the ordeal you have endured. It opened my eyes to the danger of the situation in which you found yourself and made me see the Professor for what he is – a deluded religious maniac. I endured the meeting, and I waited impatiently for the Professor to board the train to London. As soon as I could, I made an excuse to Jonathan about wishing to pay my respects at your resting place. I caught the train to London the next day. However, when I arrived at Hillingham, the house was deserted, except for Beatrice. I returned home, hoping against hope that you would come to me there. But I found Jonathan in a most agitated state. How I now regret showing Jonathan's journal to the Professor! As a result of the meeting, Jonathan's own curiosity was inflamed. Even though he had sworn he would not, he read the journal of his time in Transylvania – the one he had entrusted to my care. Now he thinks he "remembers" it all, and he believes that what he recorded in that book is true.

'He announced that he was travelling to Whitby to further investigate the wreck of the Dmitry. Then he intended to go to Purfleet to work with the Professor. I could not... would not... let my husband travel alone into this awful situation. I left word in Exeter to notify me immediately if you, or word of you, arrived. Then I travelled to Purfleet to await Jonathan's return from Whitby.'

She paused then and waited for me to respond. Her face was pale and set, and I realised that she too had been altered by what had happened. I could see her pain – torn between her loyalty to me and her fear for her husband's sanity. I walked slowly to a chair and sat down.

'Dr Seward met me at Paddington Station. I recognised him, of course, from your description, but I saw that he was distraught. He told me everything that happened in the church-yard at Hendon, and that you fled into the night.'

'Does he know where I am now?' I said, alarmed.

'You mean, did I tell him of this most recent letter? Of course not.'

'What did you make of Dr Seward?'

'I think...' she hesitated. 'I think he is young. Young in expe-rience, if not in intellect or years. He has made mistakes in trying to protect you, and for those he is most grievously sorry.'

I stared at her, silent. I thought of his drunken assault on my

THE DEATH & LIFE OF LUCY WESTENRA

person, of him leaving me locked alone in the dark tomb. I was not so quick to forgive.

She continued: 'We – Dr Seward, and I – were lucky to have twenty-four hours alone at Purfleet before Jonathan, Professor Van Helsing and the others arrived.'

'And so?'

'Between us, we have built the narrative of all that has happened in this awful year. I had transcribed my journal. Dr Seward records his journal on a phonograph, so I offered to transcribe it. This also meant that between us, we could decide which details could be included or omitted. We used the fake journal you left, along with the innocent letters we have exchanged. We added some fictional letters from you, professing your love for Art. We have built a narrative which justifies Professor Van Helsing and Jonathan's belief in a predatory vampire.'

'Why?' I stared at her in disbelief.

'For you, Lucy. We have curated all the material and built a story in which you have died, then died again, and were thus saved from being "undead."'

'What do you mean – I died again?'

It was Mina's turn to stand. She went over to the window and looked out, twisting a handkerchief between her fingers.

'What happened after I fled the graveyard?'

'The Professor made them all agree that you were an evil being, corrupt and carnal. He asked Art – Lord Godalming – if he should proceed with his plan to desecrate your body, and Art readily agreed.'

'But there was no body in the coffin!'

'Not then. But the following night, when they returned...' She swallowed painfully. 'Even though bodysnatching is a capital crime, there are still some villains who will procure a dead body for a doctor who can pay what they ask. Dr Seward contacted one such scoundrel and he was able to find such a body – a poor young woman who had died in High Barnet. She was nameless and unclaimed, but she was fair-haired and bore a resemblance to you. She had been buried in a pauper's grave that very day. The bodysnatcher disinterred her and brought her corpse to Dr Seward, who placed it in your coffin.'

'And what happened to her?' I knew the answer, but I needed to hear it. I could not be spared the grisly details.

'Lord Godalming insisted on doing the task himself. He hammered a wooden stake through her heart. He believes – they all believe – the body screamed a hideous, blood-curdling screech in relief at this "merciful" act. Then the Professor decapitated her and stuffed her mouth with garlic.'

'And at no point did they realise it was not me? Surely Van Helsing must have known. He saw me just the day before.'

Mina laughed most bitterly. 'She had fair hair and a young face. It is all the same to him. He said to Dr Seward that your appearance was altered because evil had corrupted you. He is so convinced of his version of the truth that he will reject the evidence before his very eyes.'

I felt sick thinking about it.

'God rest her soul. I cannot bear it that this was the fate of her mortal remains. What a travesty. Poor, poor girl.'

'Poor girl indeed,' agreed Mina. 'But the sacrifice of her mortal remains has granted you your freedom. Lucy Westenra is truly gone now. And while the gentlemen are hunting an imaginary vampire all over London, they are not hunting for you.'

'So they seek this – nobleman? The Transylvanian?'

'Yes.'

'And in the midst of this search, they have not questioned why you have come into London today?'

Mina let out a sharp, short laugh, and I was surprised at how bitter it sounded.

'None of them know where I am, nor would they pay any

attention if they did. If they notice I am gone, they will assume I have gone to purchase a bonnet, or some other frippery.'

I frowned. 'What do you mean?'

'After I had undertaken the Sisyphean task of collating the letters, notes, journals and newspaper reports and had created multiple copies, the Professor turned to me and gave me his best and most condescending look. "And now for you, Madam Mina," he said, "you are too precious to us to have such risk. We are men and are able to bear; but you must be our star and our hope, and we shall act all the more free that you are not in the danger, such as we are."'

I stared at her, open-mouthed. 'He dismissed you? What did Jonathan say?'

'He agreed with him! So did Art and Quincey. Dr Seward, at least, had the decency to stare at his shoes in embarrassment.'

'I am not surprised to hear this. The Professor has a low opinion of all women in my experience. He treats us as pretty playthings, or stupid children. But I am disappointed in the younger men. Do they expect that you will wait in your rooms at the asylum, embroidering, while they go forth to commit acts of derring-do?' She nodded. Her face was now dark with fury. I took her hand. 'Do they not know you at all, Mina Harker? You are the bravest, cleverest and most resourceful person I have ever met. They have underestimated you.'

'As they underestimated you,' she gripped my hand in return. 'What will you do now, Lucy?' she said.

'I have very little money. Mrs Hammond – Anna– has taken good care of me, and has found me lodgings in Camden Town with a friend of hers, but I cannot expect her to support me forever. I will need to find myself employment, and soon.'

3 OCTOBER 1894

Philip's card bore an address in Camden Town. It was not an area I had ever visited, but I set off early the next day to walk there. Even though it was early, the streets were bustling. Warehouses lined the Regent's Canal, and there were many workmen already abroad. Once I had crossed over the High Street, I began to climb the hill toward Regent's Park. Here, the streets were quieter and tree-lined and the homes were elegant. I found the address on the card and stood before the house. It was a narrow, terraced townhouse with a neglected air. The front steps were dusty and the window boxes were bare except for a few straggling weeds. I mounted the steps to ring the bell.

I heard it jangle within. What if the household was still asleep, and I was rousing them? This was a mistake. I turned to go back down the steps to the street, but heard the door opening behind me.

I spun around to see a young man, round-faced and dark-haired. He wore a shirt and trousers with his braces loose about his hips. His sleeves were rolled up as if he had been busy with washing.

I frowned, confused. Was he a manservant? He smiled enquiringly at me.

'Can I help you?'

His accent was refined. I revised my opinion. He must be the man of the house. Clearly I had the address wrong, and this was not Philip's home. What is more, I had interrupted this man at his toilet.

'I'm sorry, I...' I stammered.

He leaned forward and peered at me.

'Are you Polly?' he said suddenly. 'Pip described you to me. Face of an angel. Glorious red hair.'

'I... er... yes.'

He bounded forward, holding out his hand. 'I'm Adam,' he

said eagerly, 'Adam Lionel. How splendid to meet you! Do come in. I believe you will be moving in with us in a day or two?'

'Er... yes. I just... I wondered if Philip was here.'

'Pip's already gone off to the warehouse, but Mary and I are just finishing our breakfast. Would you like some tea?'

He swept me into the house on a stream of friendly chatter. How nice it was to meet me. Should he send word to Pip? The warehouse was only ten minutes away. I followed him, struck dumb. If this was Adam Lionel, then according to Miriam and Deborah, he was Philip's lover. Did they live together, openly? And who was Mary? A maidservant?

The black-and-white tiled hallway was cluttered with coats, shoes and hats. A spray of dusty bulrushes in a vase stood on a central table, which was piled with letters and papers. Adam helped me out of my bonnet and shawl and hung them carelessly on a coat hook, before ushering me down the corridor towards the back of the house.

He opened the door, and we passed into a large, stone-floored kitchen. A fire blazed in the range and a fat ginger cat slept in an armchair. There was a long, scrubbed table, much like the one in the kitchen at Hillingham. Here a girl of about twelve sat, her elbows propped either side of a book. She was eating toast as she read, and she did not look up when we entered. She had Philip's fine features and fair hair. She could only be his younger sister.

'Mary, my dear,' said Adam excitedly, 'this is Polly, Pip's new friend. Do come and say good morning.'

Mary reluctantly tore her eyes from the page and stood to greet me.

'What are you reading?' I asked.

'*Middlemarch.*'

'And what do you make of it?'

'Casaubon is a vile old stick-in-the-mud.'

'I always loved the description of him...' I reached into my memory and quoted as best I could: "'... his soul was sensitive without being enthusiastic: it was too languid to thrill out of self-consciousness into passionate delight; it went on fluttering in the swampy ground where it was hatched, thinking of its wings and never flying.'"

"'Thinking of its wings and never flying,'" she breathed, and now she turned her full attention on me. 'Have you read any other volumes by this great writer?'

'Indeed. I have read them all. I am very fond of *Daniel Deronda*, but I think *Middlemarch* is my favourite.'

'George Eliot lived a most unconventional life,' Mary said, guiding me to the table to sit down, 'and yet even the Queen admires her writing.'

'She does. I am told her Majesty has even had an artist paint some scenes from *Adam Bede* for her.'

Mary reached for the teapot and poured us each a cup of strong, stewed tea.

'Well then, there is hope for me yet,' she said cheerfully, and took a large bite from her toast.

'Hope for you?'

'We have an unconventional household, and I am doomed to grow up with my name wreathed in scandal. But when I write a great novel and am welcomed into intellectual society, it will make no difference.'

I laughed delightedly. I turned to look at Adam. He was leaning against the dresser, his arms folded. He rolled his eyes at Mary's pronouncement.

'Wherever you are in intellectual society, Pip and I shall come along,' he said mischievously, 'wearing sparkling gowns and feather headdresses and bring shame upon you.'

She squealed in horror and clasped her hands over her mouth, and Adam guffawed with laughter.

He turned to me then and said, 'Now, shall we take you to the warehouse to see Philip? It is only a short walk away.'

'May I come?' said Mary.

'Have you memorised your French verbs?'

'How can I possibly require French verbs when I am doomed never to visit France?'

'Ah, but should the opportunity arise, how should you get there? Without the verbs, how will you purchase *un billet pour le bateau?*' countered Adam quickly.

Mary stamped her foot and sweeping up her book, left the room.

As Adam and I walked through Camden Town, I risked a sidelong glance at him. He did not look different from many of the gentlemen I had met. A little softer, perhaps, and kinder. Less posturing. But certainly not evil nor degenerate.

The warehouse was one of the smaller ones along the canal. There was a large sliding door on the roadside, and Adam pushed it open, calling as he did so.

'Pip! Pip, old fellow! I have brought you your lovely Polly.'

Philip emerged from behind a wall of tea crates. He wore a heavy canvas apron over his shirtsleeves and carried an arch file bristling with papers. His smile when he saw us was wide and genuine.

'Well, what a delight!' he said, dropping his file on top of a crate and coming over to clasp my hand. Then he reached out and touched Adam lightly on his forearm, and their eyes met in a private smile. It was as intimate as a kiss.

Adam smiled at him 'Now, let me leave you and Polly to talk. Mary and I have much to do. Today, we must wrestle with the geography of mediaeval Baghdad.'

Philip laughed lightly, 'Oh Adam, my dear, if poor Mary is reliant on your sense of direction, she may find herself mapping Timbuctoo instead!'

Philip ushered me into a tiny office, in which every surface was piled high with box files and papers. He cleared a chair for me, sat behind his desk and steepled his fingers.

'Now, dear Polly, I know you will be coming to us in few days, but I am very glad you've come sooner. I need to ask you a favour.'

'A favour?'

'Anna and I have spoken, and she suggests that you might have the capacity to teach. Do you think that is something you might like to do?'

I raised my eyebrows, surprised. 'Why yes. I would like... to teach.' My words sounded weak and ill-thought out in this small room. I needed to say more and before I could stop myself, words tumbled forth. '... To teach girls or young women. I believe that education, and knowledge is the only route to independence. I attended school for a time and gained a place at university, but my mother forbade me from taking it up. Now, I realise this had led directly to the disastrous situation which trapped me and nearly killed me. Had I been able to continue with my education, an altogether different path might have been open to me, giving me freedom. Choice. The world is full of women who are thus trapped. Perhaps, in some small way, I can open the door for a few of them?'

'I see...' Philip said. Then he frowned. 'Well, Polly, I would love to support you in any way I can, so I wonder, would you consider becoming Mary's governess?'

'I beg your pardon?'

'Adam does his best with her, but she is – well, you have met her. She is quick and precocious. She believes she already knows everything. He is able to teach her science and mathematics, but when it comes to literature, she is already more well-read than both of us, and neither of us knows much history or geography. She devises her own curriculum and berates Adam and me for our inability to teach it adequately.'

I burst out laughing and Philip's expression changed from bewildered to hurt.

'Please excuse my merriment,' I said hastily, 'I laugh only

because I recognise myself in Mary. You could have been giving a character sketch of me, just a few years ago. A lively mind, a strong will and a sense that the world would be mine, if only I chose to claim it.'

Philip looked at me intently.

'But something has happened to you, Polly Jones, has it not? Someone has stolen your courage and certainty from you?'

I felt my face grow hot.

'Polly is not my name, as I am sure you have surmised,' I blurted. 'I changed it because I have fled danger and left everything behind. You are right. Someone has stolen from me – my home, my library, all hope of financial independence. I ...'

My courage failed me. I did not want to risk giving him any more information. He held up a hand to appease me.

'You need say no more. Anna has vouched for you, so I trust you absolutely. If you will allow us, we would love to welcome you into our strange little household. We can offer you a wage – not a huge one – but you will be able to save.'

A wage. My own money that I could use as I saw fit. What joy that would be.

'I would love to be Mary's governess,' I said, as firmly and clearly as I could. 'And I would love to join your household.'

We walked back to the house and the news was taken well by all parties. Mary pronounced herself delighted that I would become her teacher, and I saw Adam sag with relief when he realised that he would be freed from the tyranny of the schoolroom.

* * *

I returned to Mayfair, and Anna greeted me with the perfect mixture of delight at my good fortune and sorrow at my departure.

'Come and visit us whenever you can,' she said. Then she

rushed to her room and returned with something behind her back.

'A gift,' she said, and produced a beautiful jade-green bonnet with jet-black feathers. 'I've been trimming this for you, and with good fortune, I finished it this very morning. It will look well on your lovely red hair. It's quite demure enough for a lady governess.'

I thanked her and put on the bonnet. I looked at my reflection in the glass.

'You are right,' I said, squeezing her hand, 'It is very decorous and also very beautiful. Your kindness has been...' I was momentarily overwhelmed, and could only gather her into my arms and hold her. 'Thank you,' I whispered.

4 OCTOBER 1894

I sent word to Mina of the change in my circumstances and address, and this morning I set forth, case in hand, to walk back to Camden Town. Adam showed me to a bedroom at the front of the house. It had polished wooden floors and a floor-to-ceiling window, which opened onto a tiny wrought-iron balcony.

I unpacked the few items I could now call my own, tidied my hair and went downstairs to find Mary. She was, as I had seen her the day before, sitting at the kitchen table immersed in *Middlemarch*.

'Good morning, Mary,' I said, sitting beside her and pouring myself a cup of tea. 'Now. I have not yet had time to prepare a scheme of work for you for the week. I think it would be most valuable for us to spend the day together, so I may ascertain your strengths, and find which areas of your education might benefit from more rigorous application.'

She looked put out. 'I can tell you what I am good at and

what I wish to be taught. I do not need to spend the day completing tedious tests.'

'I will not require you to take tests. And while I am sure you have a view on your strengths, I would like to spend some time with you, so that I may draw my own conclusions.'

I held her gaze. This would be a battle of wills, and I needed to show strength from the start, or she would trample me. She frowned thunderously and prepared to argue, but I cut in swiftly.

'I do not propose we sit at this table and talk. It is a bright, clear day. We can take an omnibus to Green Park and pay a visit to the Royal Academy. An informal lesson on the subject of recent movements in the world of art will round out our day nicely.'

Oh, how she wrestled with herself. For while the prospect of a day out was tempting, she would have to both acquiesce to my demand, and lose a day's reading. I strolled over to the window and looked out, drawing her gaze to the bright blue sky. She relented.

'Very well,' she said. 'Although I would prefer to walk rather than travel by omnibus. We shall see so much more that way.'

I readily agreed, and we gathered our bonnets and cloaks and set out.

There was no need for me to encourage Mary to talk, for she chattered continually. We spoke of books, and while she had read a great many contemporary novels, she knew little of writers from bygone eras and had read little Shakespeare or poetry. Philip had been right – her knowledge of geography and history was patchy and inaccurate. However, when I offered her a few examples of mental arithmetic, her sense of numbers was sound and her speed of calculation impressive. Indeed, she began to offer mathematical problems of her own and soon surpassed my own ability to reckon in my head. We were both examples of the flaws of a self-directed curriculum.

We passed through Fitzrovia and Oxford Circus and made our way down onto Piccadilly. Mary relaxed into my company and took my arm in a friendly gesture as we walked along. She kept up a constant commentary on all that we saw – the displays in shop windows, a lady's pretty picture hat, a handsome hound.

'Oh, look!' she said suddenly, pointing. 'That man must be locked out of his house!'

I looked in the direction she indicated. Among the elegant mansions on that stretch of Piccadilly, there was one dilapidated house, clearly uninhabited. A burly locksmith was bent over, his basket of tools at his feet, engaged in dismantling the lock.

A man stood on the steps, waiting for the workman to complete his task. He was tall and well-dressed, with a top hat and highly polished shoes. He must have caught the motion of Mary's extended arm, because his gaze swung towards us and our eyes met.

It was Art.

I should flee. I should grab Mary's hand and urge her to run until we were swallowed up by the crowds. I should confront him. I should rush at him and claw at his eyes.

I did none of these things. I stood stock-still and kept my eyes trained on him. I saw him frown with confused recognition. He could not possibly know me, I thought. We were on the other side of the road. I was wearing clothes he had never seen before. What was visible of my hair was red, and my face was shaded by my new green bonnet. And most of all, logic would say that I could not possibly be Lucy Westenra, for he himself had killed Lucy, not once but twice. To Art, I was a stranger with a vaguely familiar face.

The last time I had seen him in the churchyard, it had been night. Daylight allowed me to look at him more closely. His clothing had been rumpled at our last encounter, but now he was immaculately and expensively turned out. He looked every inch the Lord. However, although he was far from me, his eyes looked puffy, and there was a softness around his jawline that I had not seen before.

'What are you staring at, Polly?' Mary plucked at my sleeve. 'Do you know that man?'

I could see Art shifting uncomfortably, wondering when the woman across the road would stop watching him.

I do not know what made me do it. I raised my arm slowly, and pointed at him, all the while keeping my eyes steadily on his. It was a gesture of accusation, and I could see he read it as such. He recoiled, and I fancied there was a new sheen of sweat on his forehead. Then, before he could be sure of what he had seen, I dropped my arm, took Mary's elbow, and we melted into the throng of pedestrians.

5 OCTOBER 1894

Mary and I were occupied with a lesson on the French Revolution when the doorbell jangled in the hall. I heard Adam's footsteps in the hallway, so we continued to work. However, moments later, he came in. He looked disconcerted.

'There is a lady to see you, Polly. She says it is most urgent.'

'A lady?'

Adam stood fidgeting in the doorway. He seemed eager to hand over responsibility for this uninvited guest. I stood.

'Mary, my dear, will you continue with the timeline? The dates you will need can be found in this volume – and this.'

Adam looked relieved and when I went into the hallway, he pointed to the closed door of the parlour.

'She is in there,' he whispered.

I opened the door and walked in. Mina was standing on the rug in the middle of the floor with her back to me. Her bonnet dangled by its strings from one hand. She spun around when I entered and I gasped.

Her face was gaunt; the cheeks hollow, and there were deep shadows around her eyes, as if she had not slept for days. Her lips looked thin and bloodless, and there was an angry scattering of pustules across her cheekbones. Most awfully, there was an angry red, blistered weal on her forehead. It was circular in shape. It looked like a burn, or a brand, such as those applied to cattle.

I opened my arms and walked towards her. I hoped that my shock at her appearance had not registered in my face. To my surprise, she put up her hands defensively and backed away. I dropped my arms.

'How are you, Mina?'

Her hand flew unconsciously to her face and touched the ugly blemish.

'I...' she said, but could go no further.

I walked slowly over to a chair by the window and sat down, gesturing to her that she could sit opposite me. She hesitated and looked at the window. The drapes were open, and the street was clearly visible outside. She winced as if the light caused her pain. I stood and drew the drapes closed, sinking the room into a twilight gloom. I saw her shoulders drop, as if some small part of her agony had been relieved. She came to sit beside me, her hands clenched upon her knees, holding herself separate.

'What has happened to you?' my voice was almost a whisper.

'So... so much. There has been...'

She seemed incapable of finishing a sentence. Slowly, I reached out and took hold of her hand, it was icy. I held it firmly. I could feel it tremble under my touch, as if she would jerk it away. Gradually, she relaxed and turned her palm up so we could clasp hands. I willed her strength through my grasp. When the words came, they poured forth in a flood.

'They hunt the Stranger. In Mile End, in Jamaica Lane. In Piccadilly'

'Piccadilly?'

I recalled Art in the steps of the derelict house. So that was why he was there. Mina ignored my interjection.

'It was a game at first, but now it is in deadly earnest. They see the Stranger's malign hand in everything that happens. And now... they believe that I... I am the latest "victim."' She let out an ugly laugh. 'They excluded me, told me I was their beacon, as if I were some patron saint who should sit, like patience on a monument. They left me to go and do their brave doings, and all the while...' again she broke off, and her free hand flew again to her scarred brow. 'How very little they know.'

'Mina my dearest... what happened to your forehead?'

'Van Helsing,' she said bitterly. 'This is one of his little conjuring tricks. I wear the mark of the devil now. He told them all that he was placing a communion wafer on my forehead to bless me, but it burned... it burned so. What did he use? I do not know. Some corrosive. And now I am marked.'

'Oh Mina. How can we make this stop? Does this mad obsession only end when they kill you too?'

'I do not know. But I am certain that someone will die.'

I fell to my knees before her and gathered her in my arms. Her body was stiff, and she held herself apart, but I did not release her.

'Do not return, Mina, my love. I beg you. Stay here. Stay with me. They will never find you. We can shelter here for a time and then leave. We can go away and begin again. Together, we...'

'I cannot,' she said into my hair, 'I cannot leave Jonathan. His mind is so fragile. If I leave them now, they will hound him to madness and beyond.'

She drew away from me so we could look into one another's

eyes. Hers were dark and fathomless. Then she leaned in and kissed me, pressing her lips to mine.

We had never kissed in this way before. It was desperate, searching and intimate. She pressed a hand to the back of my head, keeping our mouths together. My head whirled with the taste of her – sweet and soft, but with an undertone of something dark that was at once foreign and familiar. When we finally broke apart, I slid to the floor, breathless and shaking. She looked down at me for a long moment and then stood.

'I will see this through,' she said. 'I will lead them to the inevitable, awful end of this gruesome story. Goodbye, Lucy, my love. We may never...'

She did not complete the sentence. She gathered her things and swept from the room. Before I could rise from the floor, I heard the front door open and close.

CHAPTER 26

J'd been reading for hours, and I lifted my blurred gaze from the pages. I searched the room, now bathed in late afternoon light. Rita sat by one of the windows, a book in her lap, quietly composed.

'Mum read this?' I croaked. I took a sip of cold tea to soothe my dry throat.

'She did,' Rita stood stiffly and came over to me. 'She was transfixed by the story. She even travelled down to Exeter to see the school that Lucy and Mina attended.'

'The Underhill. I know.' I said. 'Will you just...' I carefully put the pages to one side. 'I'm just going to my flat to get something.'

I took the stairs two at a time and let myself into the flat. I carefully took the nine drawings off the wall, stacking them, and then carried them down to Rita's flat. I spread them out on the coffee table in a grid.

'I think I understand them all now. Or most of them anyway.'

Rita sat beside me and I pointed to each drawing, one by one.

'This one, the doors of Hillingham covered with thorns – that's after Lucy's mother stopped her going to University.'

'That makes sense.'

'Here's The Underhill... I've seen this same view of the school. And this...' I pointed to the hand with the ring, '...that's Lucy wearing the Godalming ruby. And these faces...'

I indicated the portrait sketches '...from her descriptions, this severe-faced woman is Mrs Westenra, this handsome man is Quincey, this is Dr Seward, and this grotesque...' I touched the beetling brows of the frog-faced man...'must be Van Helsing.'

'She didn't draw Holmwood,' Rita observed.

'Perhaps she didn't want to think about him. He was so evil to poor Lucy.' I looked at the rest of the drawings. 'I know Proserpine's Garden was at Ring, Holmwood's estate, and that was where he got the plants he used to poison Lucy.' I looked at the page of flower drawings. 'Mum drew the Deadly Nightshade, and the Monkshood and the Wild Garlic here. And here's a picture of the blood transfusion equipment they used on her... and here's Lucy's tomb.'

'And this?' Rita indicated the last drawing, the two women with their heads together. 'Lucy and Mina, I suppose?'

'Well, yes. Lucy and Mina, but older. Much older. How much further do the journals go?'

'How much have you read?'

'I'm almost finished. Mina's just turned up at Philip's house, distraught, with the burn on her forehead.'

'Well then,' Rita said, handing me the pile of pages. 'You'd better read on.'

LUCY WESTENRA'S SECOND JOURNAL

TELEGRAM, MINA HARKER, PURFLEET, TO POLLY JONES, CAMDEN TOWN, 12 OCTOBER

Leaving for Dover today. Crossing by ferry to France and thence by train to Transylvania. VH, JH, JS, AH and QM all with me.

Love always, Mina.

12 OCTOBER 1894

I stood looking at the yellow slip of paper in my hand. For better or worse, they had followed Van Helsing and Harker's obsession to the place where it had begun. My heart ached for Mina, but at the same time I felt a flutter of relief. Now they were all gone, I was safe. I could move around without looking over my shoulder. I could travel to Mayfair to see Anna and little Violet. I could walk in Regent's Park and breathe freely.

I folded the telegram and slipped it into the pocket of my skirt. It was time for lessons to begin today. To my surprise, there was no sign of Mary. Her book lay open on the table and the back door into the garden stood slightly ajar. I looked out of the kitchen window.

The garden was overgrown and neglected, but a path had been beaten through the long grass and dead nettles to a gate. This, I knew, opened onto the alleyway, which ran behind the houses. Mary stood in the open gateway. She was talking to someone outside. She appeared to hand something over. Then she closed the gate and made her way back up the path. I busied myself in arranging papers and pens for us to begin our work.

'Make sure you wipe your feet, Mary. The garden is very muddy.'

She did as she was bid, and when I looked up, she was regarding me warily. I waited for her to explain but she did not.

I took my seat at the table and said, 'Shall we begin by looking at your penmanship exercises from yesterday?'

'Er...' said Mary, moving crabwise towards the table, 'why should we not begin on something new? You talked of algebra.'

'I am happy for us to attempt algebra, but I would like to see those exercises again.' I fixed her with my firmest stare. 'Where are the exercises, Mary? And the book on penmanship? They appear to be missing.'

She flopped into her seat and regarded me with wide eyes; her face a picture of exaggerated despair.

'I gave them away. There. You have tortured it out of me. And now you can punish me as you will.'

'You gave them away? To whom?'

'A friend.'

'Which friend?'

'Before you came, I had but one friend in the world – little Jenny next door.'

'Jenny?' I frowned, perplexed. I had not seen another child in this street. The inhabitants of the house next door were an elderly couple.

'Jenny is the maid of all work for Mr and Mrs Irving. She has been a kind companion to me.'

'And why have you given her your writing exercises?'

'I have been trying to help Jenny with her reading and writing. It was very difficult in the beginning – I did not know how to teach what I knew. But since you have been here – I have been able to share some of the lessons with her.'

'I see,' I said slowly.

Mary was watching my face with close attention. I did not speak immediately, and she burst into noisy tears.

'I beg of you, Polly, do not tell Mr and Mrs Irving, nor Adam and Philip. I could not bear it if Jenny got into trouble. Punish me instead. I shall write out: "Mary Graham is a wicked, wicked girl," a thousand times over if you will spare her.'

'Oh, Mary. I have no intention of punishing Jenny, nor you. But I do have an idea, and for it to work, we will need to speak to Adam and Philip, and indeed the Irvings.' Her mouth formed a horrified O. I took her hand. 'Trust me, Mary. I think you will like my plan.'

10 NOVEMBER 1894

I have been too busy to update this journal! Philip and Adam have been enthusiastic in their support of my idea, and within days, Jenny was the first extra pupil in our little classroom. After her came Mabel, a costermonger's daughter, a friend of Jenny's. She was a fierce, freckled little urchin, who gobbled up everything I taught her. Soon after Esther joined, then the twins, Carrie and Laura. With Philip and Adam's blessing, I found myself running my own little school for maidservants, laundresses and the children of Camden workers.

Adam and Philip pay me as well as they could afford, but I find I spend much of my small salary on paper, ink and books for my little class. I do not begrudge any of it, but I am conscious that I am not saving money as I had hoped to.

I feel so at home in this ramshackle neighbourhood. I am proud to be giving something to these girls that they would otherwise be denied. I am only sorry that the kitchen table only seats six.

I have to remind myself that this is a temporary respite. I feel so happy and safe because I know Art and the others are far away in the mountains of Roumania. Nevertheless, for these few weeks, I have felt contentment and a sense of purpose I have never before experienced. Just for now, I will allow myself to enjoy it.

25 NOVEMBER 1894

On this chilly, late November evening, the four of us returned from a walk in Regent's Park. The streetlamps had begun to glow, and the acrid scent of leaves burning in gardens filled the air. Although it was not yet six o'clock, the sun had set by the time we turned the corner into our road.

'I shall make us all hot chocolate,' Philip said, 'that will warm us.'

'Who is that?' said Adam, who was walking a little ahead. He pointed, and I saw that a shadowy figure was sitting on our front step. It was too tall to be one of my scholars. I stopped and felt cold seep into my bones. Who could be waiting for us so late on a Saturday? I stayed where I was, keeping Mary with me, and let Adam and Philip walk on ahead. Almost out of habit, I glanced to the left and right, noting a nearby alleyway. If I needed to run, I could dart down there.

'Polly!' called Philip, 'Why! It is your friend, Mrs Harker!'

We bustled her into the house and Adam, Philip and Mary went through to the kitchen to make hot chocolate. Mina stood in front of the fire, her back to me, steam rising from her damp skirts. She untied her bonnet and lifted it off, checking her reflection in the glass above the fireplace. Then she turned to face me.

Her forehead was white and smooth – there was no sign of the blemish I had seen some weeks before. She had lost the haunted, pained look, which had so troubled me at our last meeting, but there was something else in her eyes – deep and unknowable, as if she had seen things of which she would never speak.

'What happened...?' I said cautiously.

'So much, my dear Lucy. He whom they sought – they believe they have slain him. There was a battle in the mountains with the Szgany – fierce mountain gypsies – it was chaos. It was dusk, and impossible to know exactly what happened, but when the fighting ceased, he was gone – if he was ever there.'

'And so... it is over?'

'They believe it is. Van Helsing has returned to Amsterdam. I hope fervently he will never again visit our shores. Dr Seward – John – is in Purfleet, although I think he may have lost his taste for caring for the insane. Art...' she grimaced with disgust. '...I have no idea. Back to Ring, I suppose.'

'And Jonathan? And you?'

Tears started in her eyes, and she turned her head away from me.

'Jonathan is damaged. He saw it through, but he is now so frail. He manages to do a little work each day, but he tires easily and he cannot stand to be out after the sun sets. He jumps at loud noises and fears meeting unfamiliar people. I do not think....' she took a deep, ragged breath, 'I do not think he will ever fully recover. We will live a quiet life now. And I will do all I can to keep him from harm.'

'You have answered for Jonathan, but what of you?'

She took time to reply. 'I am changed, Lucy, as you are. Our innocence has been stolen from us. Or perhaps we volunteered it.' She gave me a weak smile. 'And you? What have you been doing in my absence?'

I told her of my little school, of Adam and Philip's kindness.

'I know I cannot stay here indefinitely,' I said. 'It's not safe, not with Art in England once more. 'But for now, I am happy, and have found a purpose. These few girls will have a better future than they would otherwise have had. It is not a big difference I make, but it is something.'

Mina nodded and sat for a while, looking down at her hands in her lap. Then she reached for the bag she had brought with her. She lifted it onto her knees. It was oddly familiar – a battered canvas satchel, much stained and travel-worn.

'There was one member of our party of whose fate I have not spoken,' Mina said quietly.

At once, I recognised the bag. On our last night together as lovers, Quincey had carried that bag and drawn the blanket from it upon which we had lain. I looked up and met Mina's eyes.

'In the skirmish near the Borgo Pass... when the Szgany fled, Quincey fell.'

I gasped. She grasped my hand.

'He had been stabbed in his side. The wound was too deep to...' she paused and released a ragged breath. 'He died in my arms.'

I tried to think how this revelation made me feel. Quincey seemed like a distant memory – almost a dream. I remembered him with a vague fondness, as if he were an image in a faded photograph. I was saddened to hear of his death, for he was a young and vital man, with a bright future. But my grief was no more personal than that. Mina herself seemed genuinely upset. They must have become close in the months of their quest.

She rested her hand on the old satchel.

'Before we left Purfleet, Quincey confided in me that he was a man alone. An orphan, with no relatives. He had a farm in Texas, but no kin.'

'He told me of his farm once. I believe it was near a town called Happy?'

'Indeed. When we decided that we were going to travel to Transylvania, we all knew that the journey was hazardous and the outcome was unknown. Van Helsing urged us to get our affairs in order. Quincey came to me. He told me he'd made a last Will and Testament. He said: "This was a sad document for me to write, for I learn that when all is said and done, I have no one in the world. No one to love, no one to mourn me." Then he said, "I did love once. You know don't you?" I nodded. "Lucy was the brightest flame. I never met a woman like her before, and there'll never be her like again. It's my life's regret that I missed my chance to tell her how she changed me." He let tears fall, and then he took my hand and said, "So Mizz Harker – Mina– all I have... it all goes to you."'

'What all goes to you?' I asked, confused.

'Quincey bequeathed me his entire estate. A substantial sum of money and the deeds to his ranch in Texas.'

'Oh Mina. I'm so happy for you. This will make things so much easier for Jonathan and you. Perhaps one day, you might travel...'

She cut me off.

'I have no need of it,' she said firmly. 'Mr Hawkins left Jonathan and me more than amply provided for. We have a beautiful home and there is enough money so that even if Jonathan is unable to work, we will be comfortable.'

She lifted the bag and placed it on my lap. I raised the flap and looked inside. It was filled with bristling bundles of banknotes and bags of coins, and a large, folded piece of parchment that I took to be a title deed.

'This is for you. You are the woman he loved, Lucy. I could

not tell him that you lived, but it will be a comfort to him in heaven to know that here on earth, he has provided for you.'

20 MAY 1895

I have again been too busy to write in this journal, and six months have passed since my last entry.

Today, the streets of Camden Town are bright with blossom. After classes were finished, I took my daily walk to St Pancras Church. I carried a book and an apple, and took my customary seat beside the tomb of Mary Wollstonecraft. The sun slanted through the trees and warmed my face. It has been a very satisfying and happy half-year. With the money Quincey left, I was able to purchase a small cottage of my own, a few streets from Adam and Philip's house. There was an empty shop premises next door, and I persuaded the owner, for a nominal rent, to let me use it as a schoolroom. I salvaged tables and chairs and Mary and I spent our weekends sanding and painting them. Adam helped us to install a coal-burning stove to stave off the late winter chill. By March, I was able to open the doors to twenty girls from the local area, aged between five and fifteen.

Anna and Violet come to call every Sunday, and we are slowly building a tentative relationship. I like Anna's quiet, calm energy, and my love for sweet little Violet, my miniature, has grown and grown.

Deborah and Miriam visit often too, and are so impressed with what I have achieved, they committed to a monthly donation to help with the running costs of the school. One afternoon, they came to call, bringing with them a friend of theirs named Janey, a doe-eyed beauty who was one of the Market's most sought-after courtesans. When we spoke about what I was teaching the girls, she admitted that she herself had never learned to read or write. I offered to teach her. She began to come to me several times a week, in the early evening. After a few weeks, she brought a friend, and then another, and soon I was leading a late session of my school for the ladies of the Market. Many of these women are in a position to pay something toward their education, which in turn funds the children who come in the morning, or those other adult women who are less fortunate. I do my best to turn no woman or girl away. My days are fiendishly busy and I fall into bed exhausted each evening, but I have never felt more fulfilled nor free.

Mina writes often and visits when she can. She is a useful source of information and encouragement for my teaching. Jonathan's health remains precarious, and her own life is thus curtailed and small, but she seems happy enough for the moment.

Sitting in St Pancras churchyard this afternoon, I checked my pocket watch. Time to go. I walked back through the bustling streets, thinking of all I needed to do. The ladies would be arriving for a class within the hour. I needed to check the lesson I proposed to teach, and make sure the materials were laid out, ready.

I was engaged in placing cleaned slates on each desk when someone hammered on the schoolroom door. I went to unlatch the door and started in surprise. Anna and Violet, stood outside on the doorstep. Anna's eyes were wild and her normally smooth hair was tumbling free of its pins.

'Anna, my dear,' I said, drawing her in and closing the door behind us. Violet looked up at her mother, wide-eyed and afraid.

'Come on, Violet,' I said brightly, drawing her away with me. 'I have just acquired some lovely new coloured chalks. Would you like to draw with them?' She glanced back at Anna, who gave her an encouraging nod.

'Yes, please,' Violet said.

I set her up at a desk and returned to Anna. I drew up two chairs for us beside the window.

'He came,' she whispered. 'Holmwood – or Lord Godalming – or whatever he calls himself now. He turned up on the doorstep late last night, drunk. Little Milly, the maid, opened the door when he knocked, and he forced the door open, making her tumble to the floor.'

'Oh no.'

'He was out of control – raging. He said he had discovered that Westenra and Co. was still supporting me and my... my "whelp". He swore he would see me cut off, would see us thrown out of our house. I was so afraid he would go upstairs to where Violet was sleeping, that he would hurt us... but then he lurched back out into the night.'

'I am so sorry, Anna. How frightened you must have been.'

'Can he do it? Can he?' her eyes were wide and wet with fear.

'He is the sole owner of the company – that is true. But I am certain that the provisions of my Father's Will protect you. The house is gifted to you, and the payments were to be paid into perpetuity.'

'But how am I to prove that?'

'We need a copy of the ledger of the company – it has notes of the transfer of the house. Then I am sure you can go to Pa's solicitor, Mr Marquand, and he will provide a copy of Pa's Will and help you to protect your interests.'

'A ledger? How are we to get such a thing?'

'Can you not visit the offices of the company?'

'Holmwood told me that he has fired Mr Boyden, the manager, and that the staff at the offices have instructions to bar me from entering.'

'He sounds both desperate and vindictive. Why would he need to claim your small income and your house? It makes no sense.'

'Lucy, I do not know, but I fear for our safety. I do not think...' she paused, 'I do not think he is entirely sane.'

I glanced across at Violet. Her bright blonde head was bent over her drawing.

'I want you to return home and pack a bag. You, Violet and Milly must all come to stay with me for now.' She sagged with relief at this. I sat thinking for a long while, then eventually, I said, 'There is an abridged ledger of the company in the library at Hillingham. It will give you all the proof you need.'

'Hillingham?'

'The house is likely standing empty, or Beatrice may still be there. Either way, I am sure I can gain entry to the house and thence to the library. I will fetch the ledger, and you can take it to Mr Marquand.'

* * *

Once my class was over, I travelled by cab to Hillingham. I alighted across the road from the house and stood looking up at it. The front doors were closed and barred. The garden was now completely overgrown and weeds covered much of the drive. A climbing rose has entwined itself around the closed gates, sealing the entryway like an enchantment in a fairy-tale castle. I waited for the cab to turn around and be on its way, and then I walked slowly round to the side gate. This, at least, was not overgrown and a groove in the gravel suggested it had been recently used. I pushed it open slowly, trying to minimise the sound, and entered the grounds. I was reminded of the last time I had passed through this gate, my feet bleeding, wearing nothing but a filthy nightdress, starving and half-mad with fear. I calmed my ragged breathing, dried my sweating hands on my skirt and walked quickly and quietly around the side of the house.

The kitchen garden was a wasteland – only a few ragged plants remained, and these had been decimated by insects. The kitchen door was shut. I tried the handle. It too was locked. It looked as if Beatrice had indeed fled. I could not blame her.

Was there a way in? I walked back slowly the way I had come, checking windows. All of the downstairs ones were sealed and shuttered, but, to my surprise, when I looked up at my old bedroom window, the shutters were open and the sash unfastened. I gathered my skirts about me, grabbed hold of the wisteria vine and began to climb.

The window was stiff, and I had to hang onto the creeper with one arm as I forced the sash up. It raised with a creaking groan. I pulled myself onto the sill and swung my legs into the room. Dust from the bare floorboards puffed up as my feet touched the ground.

I had expected the room to be cool and dark but instead it was lit by a red glow. I looked over at the fireplace. A log was burning fiercely, emitting a powerful heat. It was immense and oddly shaped, like a human limb. On closer inspection, I could see it was the leg of a table, carved and curlicued. The burning varnish gave off an acrid, chemical smell. The rest of the table lay scattered across the floor, where it had been crudely chopped and dismembered. I recognised it as the beautiful mahogany piece which had stood in the hallway, and upon which my mother had kept extravagant arrangements of lilies, white roses and hyacinths.

It took a minute for my eyes to adjust to the gloom. While most of the furniture was gone, someone had dragged in a heavy wingback armchair from my father's dressing room, and placed it facing the fire. There was a figure in the chair.

'Art.'

My voice was loud in the room, which echoed without the muting effect of carpets and curtains. He did not leap to his feet, nor jerk in surprise.

'You came, Lucy. Somehow I knew you would.'

I crossed the floor and stood before him. He sat slumped in

the chair in his shirtsleeves, his collar open. A whisky bottle and a glass stood on a table beside him. He glanced up at me and then looked away.

'What are you doing here, Art?'

'I might ask the same of you. For you are a ghost.'

'Perhaps I am, but this is my home. Dead or alive, I have every reason to walk these corridors.'

'You look well, for a ghost, Lucy. As you did when I first saw you. So very beautiful.'

'Why are you not at Ring?'

'Disowned,' he gave a harsh laugh. 'The bank foreclosed on the debts. They took the house and what was left of the estate. Our name is in ruins. Mother lives in the gatehouse now, with one serving girl, eking out coal, darning her gloves. She sent me away.'

'So all you have left is the Westenra estate?'

'And not even that.'

'What do you mean?'

'Did you know you have cousins? Second cousins, on your father's side?'

I frowned. 'Cousins?'

'In Finchley. The Fallons. They are Irish.'

I remembered the old woman in the rusty shawl who had attended Pa's funeral with her grandson, of whom Mother had spoken so dismissively.

'Matilda and Gabriel?'

'It seems after a few ales, my old "friend" Bevington would tell anyone who asked how he helped me to blackmail my way into stealing an inheritance. He told the wrong person, who told your cousin Gabriel, and now...'

'The Fallons are suing to overturn Mother's Will.'

'They have brought many witnesses, and the case is so complex. It seems you have more family than you imagined, and they all believe they have a claim. This case will drag on for years...'

'Jarndyce versus Jarndyce,' I said wonderingly.

'What do you mean?'

'The case Mr Dickens wrote of in *Bleak House*. It was a lawsuit concerning a disputed Will. It dragged through the Chancery Court for decades until the estate in question was completely devoured by legal fees.'

He laughed then.

'Well then. You know my fate. Westenra and Co. has been frozen, and all assets have been seized by the court. I have nothing left but debts and more debts.'

'So you threatened Anna Hammond, thinking you could get her to hand over what she had? You will fail.'

He turned his bleary, bloodshot eyes up to my face for the first time.

'Well, this seems perfectly apposite, does it not? The ghost of Lucy Westenra, with flaming red hair, returned as an avenging angel.'

'I have no need to avenge, Art. Look at you. Squatting alone in my old bedroom, burning my furniture. You have ruined yourself without my help.'

He had his coat wrapped tightly around him. He swept it open now, and I saw the dull gleam of metal. A pistol lay in his lap, cocked and primed.

'I could kill you now,' he said. 'No one would miss you.'

'Oh Art,' I said pityingly. 'Many people would miss me. I have left word where I have gone to. If I do not return home, they will come looking for me and they will know, finally who caused my death. It is you that no one will miss. For in your hour of need, you do not have a single friend to turn to, do you?'

He raised the pistol and pointed it, waveringly at me. His hand shook. In a swift movement, I leaned forward and slapped it from his hand. It skittered across the floor.

Tears rolled down his cheeks. He was deathly pale, just like a waxen image, and his red eyes glared with the horrible vindictive look which I knew too well. As I looked, his eyes saw the sinking sun, and the look of hate in them turned to triumph.

He reached over, lifting the bottle and filling his glass. He raised it to me.

'I am glad you are here, Lucy. I am so grateful that I will not do this alone.'

'Do what?'

Art drew a small vial from his pocket and tipped the contents into the glass of whisky. He tossed back the drink and smiled, as if profoundly relieved.

It happened so fast. The scent of almonds reached me, and Art's body arched up out of the chair like a leaping fish. His face darkened in the red light of the flames and black blood bubbled from his lips. Then he slumped, twisted against the arm of the chair. His glittering eyes, now sightless, were still fixed on me, as if they would carry my image burned onto them until the Last Day.

His hand opened then, and something dropped from it to the carpet. I bent to pick it up. It glittered in my hand like a drop of blood – the Godalming Ruby, from my ill-fated engagement ring. I hesitated, then pocketed it. A stone like that would buy a great many books and pencils for my girls.

I turned away from Art's corpse and did not look back. After I left, I would contact the authorities anonymously and say that there was a trespasser in the house, so that he might be found.

* * *

I walked slowly down the corridors of Hillingham. I listened, hoping for the ghosts of sounds – Mother's voice calling, Pa's laugh, music from the parlour, laughter from the kitchen – but the house was silent. I stopped on the landing and drew the key to the library from my pocket.

Beatrice must have dusted it before she left – it was clean and well ordered. I walked over to my desk and lit the lamp, then took my journals from my pocket. I am now writing these words – the last of this part of my story. I will place my journals back in the hidey-hole, and there they will stay.

I will never return to Hillingham. I have learned we cannot go back – only forward. My future lies elsewhere. I will lock the library and leave the key in the door for Beatrice. She will be able to return now. I will pass down the great staircase for the last time, my footsteps echoing on the bare wood.

I will unbolt the heavy front doors and push them wide open. A cool breeze from the Heath will rush in, and the fresh air will carry the scent of pine and honeysuckle to me. A single star will emerge in the wide clear sky, then another and another. Soon, the sky above me will blaze with light and I will turn my face up to it and breathe freedom.

Lucy Westenra. 20 May 1895.

CHAPTER 27

⚜

I raised my eyes from the last page. My cheeks were wet with tears.

'She made it,' I said. 'She survived.'

'She did.'

'And the third death at Hillingham you mentioned? Art?'

'His death ended the court proceedings of course. The Fallons and other relatives sold the house and it was converted into flats, as you know. That's when Beatrice and her husband came back and moved into the library.'

The sun had set, and while I read, Rita had turned on lamps around the room. Rita came over and sat on the sofa beside me.

'I met her, you know,' Rita said. 'Lucy.'

'You did?'

'I didn't realise it at the time. It was about 1950. Nan and I had gone shopping in the West End, and we bumped into a woman in the street. You wouldn't think I would remember something like that – my grandmother meeting an old friend –

but Nan was so upset. She kept crying and touching the woman's hair. I'd never seen her cry before. We went to a tearoom on Dean Street. Lucy – she was called Polly by then, of course – told us that she had run a school for girls and women in Camden for half a century. Nan kept saying, "But are you all right? Are you all right?" And she said yes, she was. She had had a good life so far, and that the school was thriving. She said it was time to hand it on to her deputy – Mary someone – and she was going to go and live in America. She said she planned to start a similar school when she got there.'

'America?'

'Yes, Texas, she said. Of course, it wasn't until I read the journal that I realised she meant she was going to spend her last years at Quincey's ranch. It belonged to her, after all.'

'America. Where Mina went in 1930. And Lucy followed in 1950,' I mused. 'So she would have been seventy-five, seventy-six?'

'Something like that. The same age as my Nan. She didn't look it though. Nothing like it. I was just a girl, but I remember thinking how beautiful she was. Crimson lipstick and flaming red hair – she wore it long. She was very straight-backed and strong.' Rita stroked the soft leather of the journal. 'You know, Kate, that memory is one of the great joys of my life. That I know for certain that she made it. That the school continued. That she gave the gift of knowledge to so many girls. And believe me, there were hundreds of successful London women who credited Miss Polly Jones's school with giving them their start.'

Rita stood stiffly and took the journals and pages over to the secret alcove. She placed them inside and closed the panel. She turned to face me.

'I'm going to ask you to keep Lucy's secret. At least until I die.'

'Of course I will. I only ever wanted to know what happened

to her, to know that Beatrice not posting the letter didn't lead to her death. I wanted to know what Mum knew. And now I do. Thank you, Rita. I can't thank you enough.'

I hugged her impulsively. Rita patted my shoulder and broke away, embarrassed, but I could see she was pleased.

'You can tell that young man of yours, of course. He's Mina's family. He should know what she did.'

'Thank you.'

'In fact...' I could see Rita wrestle with her instincts. 'Bring James here. When he's next in London, let him come and read the story for himself.'

'That's very generous of you.'

'He'll be the first man through the door of this place since 1983. Tell him to wipe his feet.'

I made my way back upstairs to my own flat, carrying the stack of Mum's framed drawings. I imagined her reading the words I had just read, and her hands itching to draw. I imagined her taking the bus to Hendon to draw the tomb, catching a train to Exeter to see The Underhill for herself. One by one, I rehung the sketches on the wall, I was left holding the final image – the two women gazing into one another's eyes. I was sure now that this was Lucy and Mina, older, sharing a deep love and trust. Noni must have used her imagination to picture them together. I hoped her vision had come true. Preparing to hang it, I turned it over, and for the first time, noticed something written on the back in Noni's familiar hand.

The Jones Foundation
    Route 1075
    Happy
    TX 79042
    USA

CHAPTER 28

15 JULY 2025 – KATE

Fourteen months later, I stood in the doorway as James struggled into the spare room in Dad's house with the last of my boxes.

'Why do I have so much stuff?' I said, 'I've only been in London a year and a half.'

'Stuff breeds,' James said. 'It'll expand to fill the space you have available.'

'Your house is pretty big,' I grinned and kissed him.

'Ha ha. We're going to live a minimalist life when we get back.'

'But where will I keep all my souvenirs from the World's Biggest Ball of Yarn Museum? And my Stetson collection?'

'In your self-storage unit on the very edge of town?'

'I'm so excited for this,' I said, tipping my face up to kiss him again.

'Which part?'

'All of it. The road trip. More study. My new job. Living with you.'

'Ah, so I'm last on the list.'

'Last and most important.'

'Smooth talker.' he kissed me deeply. 'Do we have time...?'

'In my father's house, with my Gran on the sofa downstairs? Afraid not. But I promise we can make whoopee in our camper van in at least four different states of America.'

'I'm going to hold you to that.' He released me, and we went downstairs.

* * *

ONCE WE'D EATEN, we showed Dad and Gran our proposed route on a map.

'We've bought a camper van online,' I explained, 'and it's waiting for us in San Francisco.'

'We'll stay there for a bit, and then we plan to go all over California. Then head west.' James pointed to a blue ribbon of highway.

'We're not staying on the highway though,' I said. We're taking all sorts of detours. Vegas, the Grand Canyon...'

'The Big Ball of Yarn Museum...'

'Exactly!'

'I'm envious,' Dad said. 'I think you'll have a wonderful time. Like some kind of seventies' road movie.'

I looked at him, surprised. He smiled at me.

'I've never visited the West Coast. I've only ever been to New York and Boston for conferences. I'd like to see more of it. Your mum went, you know.'

'Did she?' I kept my expression blank and innocent.

'Just before she moved in with me. She called it her last hurrah. She backpacked around for a month or so. She loved it.'

'She always said she wanted to go back, to have more adventures, but...' said Gran.

'She ran out of time,' I said. 'Well, we'll have some of those adventures for her.'

'Are you going all the way across to the East Coast?' Gran asked.

'Unfortunately, we only have six weeks,' James said.

'We plan to fly back from Dallas at the end of August so I can start my PhD and my new job.' I added.

'It's all worked out rather well, hasn't it? It can't have hurt that you did so well in your Master's,' Dad said. 'Although I never imagined you'd end up working in a private school.'

I allowed myself a smile. Even when he was pleased with me, he couldn't resist a dig.

'The Underhill is a very venerable institution,' said James. 'My great-great-grandmother was a pupil, and she taught there.'

* * *

From: kate.balcombe108@gmail.com

To: Rita.Baylis@btinternet.com

19 August 2025

Subject: Re: Texas here we come!

Dearest Rita,

Just a brief note to say we've crossed from New Mexico into Texas and we're staying at a motel just outside Amarillo. It's been a great trip so far.

Texas is flat. I've never seen anything like it. In Lucy's journal, Quincey said he loved to sit on his porch in Happy, watching the sun come up over the plains. He said the air was clear, and he loved to listen to the breeze, bringing him news from all across the world. I can see why he thought that.

James has been in contact with the management at the Jones Foundation. It's still thriving on the ranch. We're going there tomorrow to see what Lucy built. There's quite a campus apparently – a school for girls from troubled backgrounds, and a refuge for women escaping abusive relationships, as well as a writers' retreat for academics. We still don't know if this is where Mina ended up when she came to the States, but I know James is hopeful there'll be some kind of evidence one way or another. We're hoping they might even be buried on the ranch and we can pay our respects. We'll take lots of pictures.

Hoping that you're well and that summer in London is lovely. We miss you. Looking forward to having you with us in Exeter for Christmas.

Heaps of love,

Kate

20 AUGUST 2025 – KATE

THE JONES FOUNDATION consisted of a cluster of modern, low, buildings. There was no sign of the original ranch house. We went through the glass doors in the foyer and James stopped dead. He gripped my hand so tightly, I thought he might bruise it. When I looked up at him, there were tears in his eyes. Ahead of us were tall, wooden doors, and a small gold plaque beside the doors proclaimed, "The Dr Mina Harker Library".

'She made it,' he said.

An earnest intern called Sophie was our guide. She had learned the pamphlets off by heart, and she proudly shared the work of the Foundation. She showed us the accommodation blocks and sporting facilities, and we looked in on sewing classes, English lessons and a science class in a block called the Westenra Laboratory. When we returned to the main foyer, it was clear that Sophie was keen to be on her way. Her sparkling smile remained in place, but she surreptitiously checked her watch.

'I don't suppose,' I said hastily, 'they're here? Dr Harker and Dr Jones? We imagined they might have chosen to...'

Sophie looked dubious. 'They're down by the river. We don't usually let visitors go down there...'

'My fiancé's name is James Harker,' I said, giving my most winning smile. 'He's a direct descendant of Dr Mina Harker's. We'd very much like to pay our respects.'

'Well...' Sophie still looked unsure. She reached for a map of the ranch. She marked a spot by the river with a cross. 'Here.'

'Thank you,' James said, and took the map.

* * *

JAMES DROVE the camper van down the rutted dirt track towards the river. The road meandered round several curves. After hundreds of miles of dead flat countryside, we were surprised to find a small grove of trees.

'The Morris family cemetery must be down here,' I said. 'Mina and Lucy probably chose to be buried here too.'

The road came to a dead end and James parked the van. A footpath wound ahead of us through the trees. We got out and began to walk.

The trees thinned, and I could hear the sound of the river. I stepped out into a clearing. I expected to find a small cemetery, but instead, to my surprise, I saw an old ranch house, solidly constructed of wood – one storey high, but sprawling. A long veranda ran along the front, facing the water. I gasped, just as James emerged beside me.

'The grove of trees, the river.... this is Quincey's house!'

James glanced up at the chimney. A thin stream of smoke escaped from it. 'Well, someone clearly lives here still.'

I took his hand and together, we walked around the side of the house.

There were two rocking chairs on the porch. The two women had their heads angled together, one blonde, one chestnut. They were speaking softly to one another. We approached the steps and the women looked up. I opened my mouth to offer a greeting and my voice died in my throat. Beside me, James let out a ragged gasp.

'Yes?' the blonde woman said, standing. She was slender, and there were fine wrinkles around her bright eyes. She looked as if she might be sixty, or maybe sixty-five. I was about to speak when the woman's eyes widened in shock.

'Noni?' she said.

As she walked towards us, I could see threads of grey in her hair. Her chin was still determined, her lower lip still full. I knew the face as well as I knew my own. I'd gazed at it often enough.

'You're Lucy Westenra,' I whispered, wonderingly. 'You can't be, but you are.' The woman looked wary. She didn't speak. 'You lived at Hillingham in Hampstead.' I saw the tiniest flash of shock and recognition in the woman's eyes, so I persisted. 'My name is Kate Balcombe. I'm Noni's daughter. I live at Hillingham now. I've read your journals.'

The woman gripped the porch railing. She was pale, but she did not deny what I'd said. She glanced back at the other woman who rose and came to join her. There was a stoop to her shoulders, but her hair was still abundant and her eyes were vibrant and alert. She looked from me to James, and her eyes widened in shock. James had tears freely running down his cheeks now.

'Mina?' he whispered.

The woman came down the stairs and reached up a hand to touch his face.

'You're the image of my Jonathan,' she said wonderingly.

'It's not possible,' I said. 'It's just not possible. You would be... you must be...'

'A hundred and fifty years old.' Lucy said. 'But don't tell anyone.'

We sat on the porch of the ranch house and watched the wind ruffling the surface of the wide river. James and Mina huddled together on a swing seat. They talked in low voices without taking their eyes off one another. Lucy and I sat side by side in the rocking chairs.

'How... how?' I said.

'You read my journal. You read about the Stranger in Whitby.'

'The one Professor Van Helsing believed was a vampire?'

'Indeed. It was more complex than that. What the Stranger did. What was taken from us and what was given.'

'Us?'

'Mina encountered the Stranger too. But that's her story to tell.'

'And so...?'

'When we reached our fifties and sixties, it became clear that we weren't ageing as other people did. We corresponded and realised that the same thing had happened to us both. We couldn't understand it at first, so we began our research. There's little information to be had, and much of it is anecdotal, or in folk tales. Our guess is that there are others like us, but for perfectly reasonable motives, they don't make their condition public.'

'And that was your choice too?'

'By the mid-nineteen forties, I realised that if I kept running my school and living among friends, people would begin to ask questions. I was seventy, but looked half that age. My contemporaries were all old, or dying or dead.' A flash of sadness crossed her face, and I thought of Philip, Adam and Mary, Miriam and Deborah, Anna, and Violet. Lucy must have lost them all.

'The early fifties were a time of upheaval, so it made it easier for me to leave without too much fanfare. Mina had already moved to the States and completed her doctorate. I followed. We set up the Foundation to give the gifts of freedom and education to as many girls and women as we could. I led on the academic programmes and Mina built the vocational side of the Foundation and managed the fundraising.

'We ran it until 1980, when it became apparent people were beginning to wonder about our ages again. They seemed less convinced by our talk of lucky genes and a good skin care routine. We "retired" then and went to live in Sacramento. We came back about ten years ago, once there had been a complete staff turnover. They think we're the daughters of the original Dr Jones and Dr Harker. We're patrons – not involved in the day-to-day running, but we keep an eye on things.' She smiled. 'Who knows how long we'll have before we have to move on again?'

'So are you...?'

'Immortal? No. We are ageing, as you can see – just much slower than other people.' Lucy laughed suddenly. 'And no, we don't feed on human blood. We can go out in daylight and we're not afraid of crucifixes or garlic. In fact, Mina makes a lovely pesto, if you'd like to stay for dinner.'

We glanced across at James and Mina. He had taken his iPad out of his bag and was showing Mina the family tree, as she told him an animated story.

'Paprika!' she was saying. 'He came back from Roumania with so many recipes using paprika! But of course, there was no paprika to be had in Exeter in the early 1900s as you can imagine.'

She was both crying and laughing, pointing at the photographs. James's face was aglow with love and excitement.

'We'd love to stay,' I said.

We sat elbow-to-elbow at the small round in the kitchen. Mina put brimming bowls of pasta in front of us. I watched the two women, fascinated. They spoke to one another in easy shorthand, leaving sentences unfinished and nodding in agreement. As Mina passed Lucy a fork, she brushed the back of her hand with one finger, a tiny, intimate gesture. When they shared a joke, they would lock eyes, and I saw them disappear into the glance, as if the room, or the world, were otherwise empty.

When they had eaten, Mina turned to me. 'Lucy tells me you've read her journal.'

'Yes.'

'The journal tells Lucy's story, though. Not mine.'

I resisted the urge to speak. Mina's scrutiny was intimidating – she had the haughty gravitas of the most senior of headmistresses.

'You will have read of my visit to Lucy in Camden, just before we travelled to Transylvania.' I nodded. 'It was the darkest time of my life. Jonathan was so ill. Of course, now I understand that what he had was paranoid schizophrenia. At a different time, he could have been treated. But his delusions were so persuasive, and Van Helsing...' she paused, as if her hatred for the man could still catch her off-guard. '...Van Helsing built them all up to a fever pitch. He whipped them into a kind of collective madness.' Lucy laid a hand over hers and she smiled thinly. 'I was just a girl, of course – not twenty-five years old. I was desperately trying to lead them away from Lucy, but I was so afraid for Jonathan. And in the midst of all of that, the Stranger came.'

'The same Stranger?'

'My own moment of madness. Like Lucy in Whitby, the Stranger found me in the grounds of Dr Seward's asylum. I can't describe the...' she searched for the word '...magnetism. When I was touched, it didn't occur to me to resist. Even though I loved Jonathan, and took my wedding vows seriously, I...' she shook her head and looked down at the table cloth. 'Like I say, a passing madness.'

Lucy cut in, 'We've had plenty of time to discuss it. We don't believe it was a coincidence. The Stranger found Mina deliberately, knowing better than any the loneliness of this life. I was granted a companion on this journey. And we're very grateful.'

Mina reached across and she and Lucy entwined their fingers.

'What adventures we have had. And what adventures we have to come. We've travelled of course, but there's so much of the world yet to see.'

'And so many books to read,' Lucy smiled.

'Could I ask you something?' James said hesitantly. Lucy turned her bright gaze on him and raised her eyebrows. He swallowed nervously. 'When we read your journal... the blood transfusions? You must have had three or four.'

'Indeed. A brutal and primitive procedure at the time.'

'Well yes, exactly. They didn't know about blood types then. Surely it put you at tremendous risk?'

'I suppose so. I used to think that perhaps the way I am...' she waved a hand vaguely '...protected me. But the real reason, which I discovered many decades later, is much more prosaic. My blood type is AB. Quite rare, really, and very lucky. As such, I can receive blood from donors of all blood groups. I was at risk from so much at that time... but Van Helsing's transfusions did me remarkably little harm.'

Mina turned to James.

'Now you know it all. Quite the story. Are you going to the press?'

'No!' James looked truly horrified. 'We would never...' he looked across at me. I jumped in.

'Of course not. We have no interest in causing upheaval for you.'

Mina frowned. She was clearly less trusting than Lucy.

'You could tell the world, but I doubt the world would believe you.' she said calmly. 'But if you do, and the vultures descend on the Jones Foundation, Lucy and I will disappear into the night. It won't be our first time, and we're very good at it.'

'Other than James and me, the only person who knows the story is Rita, Beatrice's granddaughter. She's the one who found the journal and transcribed it from the shorthand.'

Lucy smiled. 'That must have been quite a task. I remember her meeting her as a child. A singularly stubborn little girl, as I recall. Well, we must make sure she knows the last chapter of the story. Perhaps James could take a picture of us together? And I shall write her a letter.'

* * *

MUCH LATER, Lucy and I sat out on the veranda. Mina and James were still at the table inside. Mina had brought out her own family photographs and papers and we could hear her and James laughing with excitement at the treasures.

'I told you that Rita is the only other person who knows your story,' I said, 'but there was one other.'

'Noni. You're the image of her. The same face. The same bright eyes. The zest for life. She came here to find us, just as you have.'

'She did a sketch of you and Mina... I always thought it came from her imagination, but it didn't did it?'

'She was sitting right where you are now,' Lucy smiled. 'Mina doesn't really hold with being scrutinised, but Noni begged to draw us.'

I took out my phone and showed her an image of the drawing. With one soft finger, Lucy lightly touched the curve of Mina's cheek.

'Mina is my one true love, you know,' Lucy said. 'She is a brave and gallant woman. I would dare anything for her sake.'

'Tell me,' I said, 'would you like to go back to Hillingham one day?'

Lucy smiled. 'I go there in my dreams. I curl up in the corner of my library and read until it's too dark to read anymore. Or I climb down the wisteria outside my bedroom and run across the Heath. But I won't return. I vowed I wouldn't, and I won't. We can't go back, you know Kate. Only forward.'

With a quiet click, the last piece of the puzzle dropped into place. I gasped.

'The flowers at the tomb. You send them. You've always sent them.'

'Yes. They're not for me, you understand.'

'Who are they for?'

'The girl – the nameless, desecrated girl who lies in my coffin. Her sacrifice granted me my freedom. She was not remembered in life. She will not be forgotten in death.'

'I almost forgot,' I said. 'I have something for you.'

I reached into my bag, which lay at my feet. I took out a flat cardboard sleeve and handed it to Lucy. She drew out the contents – a bundle of papers, wrapped in a silk scarf. She read the words hastily scrawled in her own handwriting, so many years before:

B,

Please post this. I implore you, do not show this to my mother or to any other.

L.

She opened the package and unfolded the brittle old letter. She frowned down at it, confused for a long moment. Then her brow cleared as the memory resurfaced. She looked up at me.

'Where...?'

'Under a floorboard in Beatrice's room.'

She frowned again, reaching for the recollection.

'I vaguely recall her saying something about not delivering the letter, but I never imagined...' she laughed then. 'I shall give it to Mina. Never has a letter taken so long to reach its intended recipient!'

She refolded the pages carefully.

'In the moment of writing, sending this message was my only hope. But I found other ways to prevail. To claim freedom and find my way to Mina. Time flows on. In the end, it is only love that remains.'

The moon rose high. Resting her hands on the letter, she looked out over the river rolling by, silver and swift, whispering untold stories to the wind.

THE END

AUTHOR'S NOTE

I read Bram Stoker's *Dracula* for the first time unconscionably late in life. I loved it instantly and wanted to rush out into the street and thrust it into people's hands. Did everyone know how good it was? How exciting? How dramatic, modern and fast-moving? It turned out that many people I knew hadn't read it, although pretty much everyone has seen a film, theatre or TV adaptation or some kind of spoof.

I was so determined that people should know how brilliant *Dracula* was, that I wrote and directed a stage adaptation, which was performed at the Bridewell Theatre in London in December 2019.

Three things happened in late 2019 that led me to this current project. The first happened during that production. Two young women took on the roles of Mina Murray/ Harker and Lucy Westenra: Naomi Dunn and Rebecca Thompson. Those two brilliant young women gave their everything to the project. They did research and background work, they infused their performances with wit and intelligence. They were strong, ingenious and resourceful. They bore out my long-held theory that there is nothing so powerful as a clear-eyed, determined young woman. It struck me very likely that the "real" Mina and Lucy would be just as quick-witted and clever as their twenty-first century counterparts. Had Stoker under-estimated them? Could there be more to their stories than he had allowed?

The second spark of inspiration came in the form of Hallie Rubenhold's book *The Five*, which I read around the same time. The book tells the stories of the five women who were murdered by Jack the Ripper. Rubenhold painstakingly traces the misfortunes they endured. What struck me most was how extraordinarily precarious the lives of Victorian women were. Without the protection or care of a man, it was practically impossible for a single woman to support herself and survive.

The final puzzle piece came from the text of *Dracula* itself. Shortly after Lucy Westenra dies, the men gather with Mr Marquand, the Westenra family lawyer, to hear the reading of Lucy's mother's will:

> During lunch he told us that Mrs. Westenra had for some time expected sudden death from her heart, and had put her affairs in absolute order; he informed us that, with the exception of a certain entailed property of Lucy's father's which now, in default of direct issue, went back to a distant branch of the family, the whole estate, real and personal, was left absolutely to Arthur Holmwood. When he had told us so much he went on:--
>
> Frankly we did our best to prevent such a testamentary disposition, and pointed out certain contingencies that might leave her daughter either penniless or not so free as she should be to act regarding a matrimonial alliance. Indeed, we pressed the matter so far that we almost came into collision, for she asked us if we were or were not prepared to carry out her wishes. Of course, we had then no alternative but to accept.

When I reread this extract, the thought came to me: for a woman to be in mortal danger at that time, she need not fear a vampire creeping in at her window. A woman of means who sought freedom – intellectual, financial, even sexual – might find herself in jeopardy from those much closer to home.

Once these three elements dropped into place, the outline of the plot came to me during the course of one forty-five minute drive across North London. The execution has, however, been a little slower.

During the lockdown in 2020, I made a spreadsheet of every plot point of the original novel and wrote a shadow version of every one. I matched dates exactly, and found a new angle on every detail. I went back to Stoker's notes and original sources. I planned the geography of the book, from the location of Hillingham to the churchyard, to the location of Art's estate at Ring and Anna Hammond's house in Clarges Mews. As soon as it was possible, I walked London in Lucy's footsteps.

Also during lockdown, I attended a Society of Authors virtual event with Sarah Waters, an author whose work I admire enormously. She spoke of the editor who reads her work before anyone else – Sally O-J. I took a chance and emailed Sally, who agreed to take a look at my early draft. Without Sally's painstaking, brilliant editorial work, her unfailing enthusiasm and continuous support, I can tell you for certain that this book would not exist. Similarly, the splendid Sara Naidine Cox performed a miracle in proofreading and tidying up the manuscript. I am hugely grateful to her too.

Thanks are also due to dear friends who have sustained me during the long, long, long process of bringing Lucy to publication: Denise, Clare, (whose final, eagle-eyed proofread further improved the text), the North London Writers, from whom I learned so much. And of course, to my beautiful sons, Matt and Ted (Ted says he was pleased to be 'a sponge for my endless yap about the book'), and my magnificent husband Tom, whose love and belief have always kept me going.

BIBLIOGRAPHY

A brief (and by no means exhaustive) list of some of the texts I consulted in the writing of this book:

- Baring-Gould, S. (1865). *The Book of Were-wolves*.
- Chez, K. (2012). 'You Can't Trust Wolves No More Nor Women': Canines, Women, and Deceptive Docility in Bram Stoker's 'Dracula'. *Victorian Review*, [online] 38(1), pp.77–92. Available at: https://www.jstor.org/stable/23646855.
- Demetrakopoulos, S. (1977). Feminism, Sex Role Exchanges, and Other Subliminal Fantasies in Bram Stoker's 'Dracula'. *Frontiers: A Journal of Women Studies*, [online] 2(3), p.104. doi:https://doi.org/10.2307/3346355.
- Eliot, G. (1871). *Middlemarch*. Oxford World's Classics.
- Grand, S. (1894). The New Aspect of the Woman Question. *The North American Review*, [online] 158(448), pp.270–276. Available at: https://www.jstor.org/stable/25103291.
- Jones, W.H. and Kropf, L. (1889). *The Folk-tales of the Magyars*.
- Kuzmanovic, D. (2009). Vampiric Seduction and Vicissitudes of Masculine Identity in Bram Stoker's 'Dracula'. *Victorian Literature and Culture*, [online] 37(2), pp.411–425. Available at: https://www.jstor.org/stable/40347238.
- Miller, E (1999). Back to the Basics: Re-Examining Stoker's Sources for 'Dracula'. *Journal of the Fantastic in the Arts*, [online] 10(2 (38)), pp.187–196. Available at: http://www.jstor.org/stable/43308384.
- Polidori, JW (1988). *The vampyre*. New York: Barron's.
- Routledge, G. (2019). *Routledge's Manual of Etiquette*. Good Press.
- S, B.C. (1894). The Financial Dependence of Woman. *The North American Review*, [online] 158(448), pp.382–384. doi:https://doi.org/10.2307/25103305.
- Schreiner, O. (1889). Life's Gifts. *The Woman's World*, [online] 2, p.408. Available at: https://archive.org/details/WomansWorld1889 [Accessed 22 Mar. 2025].
- Senf, C.A. (1979). 'Dracula': The Unseen Face in the Mirror. *The Journal of Narrative Technique*, [online] 9(3), pp.160–170. doi:https://doi.org/10.2307/30225673.

- Simmons, J.R. (2002). 'If America Goes on Breeding Men Like That': 'Dracula's' Quincey Morris Problematized. *Journal of the Fantastic in the Arts*, [online] 12(4 (48)), pp.425–436. doi:https://doi.org/10.2307/43308548.
- Stevenson, J.A. (1988). A Vampire in the Mirror: The Sexuality of Dracula. *PMLA*, [online] 103(2), pp.139–149. doi:https://doi.org/10.2307/462430.
- Stoker, B. (1894). Dramatic Criticism. *The North American Review*, [online] 158(448), pp.325–331. doi:https://doi.org/10.2307/25103297.
- Swinburne, A.C. (1864). *The Garden of Proserpine*.
- Toth, E. (1975). The Independent Woman and 'Free' Love. *The Massachusetts Review*, [online] 16(4), pp.647–664. Available at: https://www.jstor.org/stable/25088592.

ABOUT THE AUTHOR

Rosie Fiore is the author of eight published novels, including *Wonder Women, After Isabella* and *What She Left*, as well as *The After Wife*, written as Cass Hunter. She is a teacher of creative writing and a Royal Literary Fund Fellow. She lives in North London with her family, and can frequently be found wandering on the Heath or haunting a churchyard.

ALSO BY ROSIE FIORE

- This Year's Black
- Lame Angel
- Babies in Waiting
- Wonder Women
- Holly at Christmas
- After Isabella
- What She Left
- The After Wife (as Cass Hunter)

Printed in Great Britain
by Amazon